THE APPEARANCE OF MYSTERY

GREGG DUNNETT

ONE

THE RAIN BULLETS DOWN, blown near horizontal by the wind, and pushed with such force that it rattles off the deck like ball bearings. The man stands, hunched over in foul-weather gear, his feet forming a triangle against the inner edges of the cockpit. The yacht's self-steering equipment is struggling with the waves, some as big as houses, which are now rolling under the boat from astern.

Once again he fights to reset the steering gear. He lashes the wheel in place, then struggles forward and nearly falls down the companionway steps as the boat lurches sideways into a huge chasm between two waves. Inside the cabin is chaos. Water sloshes knee-deep across the floor, taking with it tins of food, cushions, the tattered remains of the foresail that was ripped earlier. The hull creaks eerily, noises he's never heard it make before. He jams himself down in front of the chart table and stabs on the chart-plotter. It's time to call up the latest forecast run. He can't help but feel his life now hangs upon what it tells him. The boat can't take much more of this. Neither can he. Slowly, sucking its data down from distant satellites, the data loads.

He blinks.

It's bad. Worse than bad, it's like a bad joke. It's worse than anything he's ever *seen*, let alone anything he's ever sailed through. His head goes light. For a moment everything around him – the crazy slewing of every surface, the raging noise of the wind, the rush of water sluicing all around him – is gone. Faded out, while he sees nothing but the forecast screen. *It can't be real.* But it is.

Twenty hours previously he made the decision to change course. The depression forming ahead didn't look dangerous, but it promised an uncomfortable ride. So he diverted south to give it a wide berth. It was a cautious decision that would add days to his voyage, but he was in no rush. And sailing alone, he had no one to answer to but himself. But since then, every new forecast seemed almost designed to mock his caution. First the depression deepened, then it too ducked south, chasing him faster than he could sail. Then it became a storm, then it deepened further, so that some gusts were raging at hurricane strength. He changed course again to escape from its predicted path, and now, finally, it should have been leaving him behind. But the new forecast reveals he's been sailing into a trap.

The storm's forward progress has slowed. So that he's still near to the center, where the winds are at their strongest. Worse, the storm has deepened again. The small Atlantic depression he planned to avoid is now a category four hurricane, and it stretches for hundreds of miles in every direction around him, with no chance of escape.

He sits still now – as still as it's possible to be when wedged on a boat lurching and skewing to crazy angles. There's a sudden whine from the pump as it struggles against its impossible load. The man takes in the chaos around him, and his eyes slide to the radio. But he looks away. He suddenly notices his own face reflected back at him on the inside of the window. The man looking back gives a strange smile. A gambler's smile. He makes one last calculation, then he rolls the dice.

He picks up the radio microphone and presses the button to transmit.

"Pan-pan, pan-pan, pan-pan. All stations." His voice doesn't sound right. It's still like a dream. But he goes on. "This is sailing yacht *Falco*. Yacht *Falco*. That's *Foxtrot, Alpha, Lima, Charlie, Oscar*. Position 32.37732 degrees latitude, -66.455457 longitude." He repeats the position reading twice, then pauses before continuing. Trying to calm himself down. "There's some, err, heavy weather out here. And I'm taking in water faster than I can pump it out."

He stops and listens for a moment, but the radio is silent. He repeats the message, sounding surer now. He waits. Repeats it a third time.

"All stations, all stations. This is a Pan Pan. Sailing yacht *Falco*…" *Jesus, is there even anyone out there?*

He stops. Forces himself to swallow down the sense of anxiety rising up from his gut. He listens again, but the radio is silent.

Again the man inspects his reflection. Why the hell is no one answering? Has he done something wrong? Forgotten something crucial? He goes to press the button to transmit again, but this time he's beaten to it.

"Yacht *Falco*, this is US Coastguard in Miami." The voice is calm. Confident. The sound of someone speaking from where it's safe and dry.

"We have your location as 32.37732 lat, - 66.455457 long. Can you give us some more details of your situation, over?"

The man feels a rush of relief. It's happening. He's doing it.

"Yeah. I'm taking in water faster than the pump will push it out. My steering gear is really struggling. There's waves hitting at all angles, and the forecast…" He stops, not wanting or able to express in words the growing horror of his situation.

"Understood *Falco*." The Coastguard operator doesn't need reminding about the forecast. "How many of you on board please? And are there any injuries?"

"Just me. I'm not hurt."

There's a pause.

"OK. I have you listed as a thirty-two-foot cabin-cruiser? That right? White hull, blue deck-house, *over*?"

"Yeah, that's me."

"And are you the owner of the vessel? Luis Fernandez?"

"Yeah."

"OK Luis. You've issued a *Pan Pan*, meaning you want to alert us you may need emergency assistance, but you don't require it at this point. Is that correct?"

The man hesitates before he presses the button. Is it correct? Should he tell them he's sinking now? His mind conjures up an image of a rescue helicopter, a flash of light and color in the black sky ahead. How long would it take a helicopter to get all the way out here? Might they even not send one at all in this weather?

What would that mean for his plan?

"I don't think so. But the waves out here… They're fucking crazy, I've never seen anything like it. They're coming from everywhere, sometimes they come together and double up. And if I get one of them over me I don't…" He nearly breaks up. "I don't think she's gonna come up through it."

"OK Luis," there's compassion now in the coastguard's voice. "That's understood. I have your position on screen now. I can see you're in some heavy weather. Can you tell me what emergency equipment you have on board in the event you have to abandon ship?"

The words abandon ship stun him into silence for a second. The sudden thought of being out there, in that boiling ocean.

"I think I got a life raft."

"OK. Can you ensure it's ready to operate if needed? Can you do that now for me. Soon as we're done?"

"Sure. I'll try."

"OK Luis. That's good." There's a pause, then: "OK Luis. I'm gonna keep monitoring this channel. Please keep us informed if the situation changes, and every half-hour even if it doesn't, *over*."

No reply.

"Yacht *Falco*. *Falco*. Are you receiving? Please keep us informed. Are you receiving?"

"Yeah. I heard you. Will do."

"Thank you. And good luck. US Coast Guard out."

The man listens as the channel goes quiet. Slowly he replaces the transmitter. Then he drops his head onto his left shoulder, stretching out the muscles in his neck. He holds it for a moment, then does the same on the other side. With the decision made, he feels better. He listens to the wind for a moment, then abruptly joins in with its whistling.

* * *

In his office overlooking the ocean, Lieutenant Oliver Hart sets a repeating countdown timer on his watch for thirty minutes. It's hard to operate the buttons, since his hands are trembling from the call he just took. He can hear the storm battering the outside of the building, and that's just here, nearly five hundred miles from the center of the first major hurricane of the season.

"Jesus fucking Christ," he mutters, as he picks up the phone.

"Hey Gail, you're not gonna like this, but I might have a shout for you. There's a cabin cruiser, out there in the middle of all this. Christ alone knows what he's doing out there."

On the other end of the line, a woman turns to her computer screen.

"Oh heck," she says, when the location pings up. "Oh my lord."

"Yeah." Hart takes a breath. "Just putting you guys on alert right now, but I got a bad feeling about this one. Guy sounded pretty scared."

"Sure Ollie. Thanks."

Hart puts down the phone and calls over his superior, Commander Sarah Withers. He's numbly glad it'll be her decision to send the chopper out if the Pan Pan is upgraded to a Mayday. Or when it's upgraded. Experience tells him it will be. Together they run the forecast simulations in the sector. They both note the yacht's position is right out on the limit of the range of the Sikorsky MH-60T *Jayhawk* helicopters stationed nearby.

"Jesus fucking Christ," Hart mutters again, as the images loop around. Commander Withers doesn't approve of the language, but she doesn't disagree either.

The watch on Hart's wrist suddenly bleats an electronic beeping. Half an hour has gone by.

"I asked him to call in every half-hour." Hart explains, and they both turn to look at the silent radio. For the next four minutes it stays obstinately silent.

"Call him," Withers orders, when five minutes have passed. Hart begins to transmit.

"Yacht *Falco*, Yacht *Falco*, come in please."

Without even knowing she's doing it, Commander Withers takes a lock of hair and twists it tight around her finger. She listens as Hart calls out again and again. But each time, there's no answering call. She thinks about the two pilots on call today for the *Jayhawk*. Both men are known to her personally. Both have young families. Yet there's no way they would refuse to take off, no way they would refuse a mission. It's a matter of pride. The control room has a window overlooking the beach. She turns to it now, seeing rain lashing down the pane. The ocean is a churning mass of dark blues, streaked with white. Ugly dumping waves break far further out than normal. She can overrule them. The final call on whether to launch is hers.

"There's no response ma'am." Hart's voice breaks into her thoughts.

"Keep trying," she orders.

He does so. But his words are met by silence. It's like there's nothing out there. Nothing left alive anyway.

After trying another twenty times Hart's watch beeps again. An hour has passed since the first Pan Pan. Hart looks up.

"Still no response ma'am? We have his last position..." The unspoken implication hangs loud in the control room. If the yacht has gone down, the man's only chance is if the chopper can get to him. And fast.

Commander Withers doesn't respond. For a few moments she doesn't even breathe, resentful for Hart's role in this. He's here simply to relay the order. Her order. Her responsibility. She thinks again about the men who will lift off into the sky in this madness. And without taking her eyes off the blackness of the sky outside, she gives a single nod of her head.

"We launch."

TWO

THE OCEAN IS like a liquid mirror. Not quite still, but nearly. The surface of the water with that thick almost gooey viscosity it gets when there's not a breath of wind. It's actually been stormy recently, so I've had to wait for a day like this, when I can get this far around the coast.

The water reflects the high cliffs above me, but it's also translucent, so you can see how the cliffs don't stop where they meet the sea, but keep plunging down. It's almost like I'm floating, twenty feet up in the air, above a forest of seaweed waving like trees in the underwater currents. The only thing breaking the calm are the dips from my paddle, which fan out behind me like watery footprints. That and the line of my wake, pointing around the headland showing how far I've come.

There's no one else in sight. There wouldn't be. A few years ago this part of the island was made into a marine nature reserve, so the fishermen aren't allowed to come here. You sometimes get people walking the cliff path, but it's a long way, and most of the time the path is too far from the edge to look down at the water. So I'm all alone, but I like it that way.

It's taken me an hour of hard paddling to get here, even in my new canoe, a sixteen-foot sea kayak that was abandoned in the boat yard. Well, sort of abandoned. You have to pay to store boats there, and the guy that owned it stopped paying, so Ben – he owns the boatyard – he said I could have it if I took it away. And there's an alley behind the fish warehouse that no one ever uses. So I spoke to the manager there and he didn't mind. So I cleaned it up and fitted it with some extra gear, like a compass and a solar panel to run a GPS – which I can take off so they can't get stolen – and then some storage tanks for samples. And I built a kind of rack to store it in the alley. And now I use it all the time as a base to run experiments from.

I won't be using the sample tanks today though. If I'm right about what I thought I saw, the last time I came here, then I don't want to capture it. I don't want to disturb it at all. It's way too important for that.

I already programmed my GPS to take me back to the exact spot where I saw it last time. Or where I *think* I saw it. But actually I don't really need the GPS, since I know where I'm going. It's a spot I've explored quite well, on account of the underwater caves. There's caves all around Lornea Island, and these aren't particularly special ones, so not many people even know about them. But they're quite cool because the entrance is underwater most of the time. Anyway, that's how I know where I'm going.

I hug the base of the cliff, not letting myself drift too far out. It means that even if there is anyone on the coastal path they won't see me, so it's like I'm invisible. But it also means I can't see my destination, because of the little rock headlands that cut off the view. So when I round the last one I get a bit of a shock. I'm not alone after all. There's a boat here. A small yacht. Anchored, with its sails down. I'm so surprised I stop paddling. And I almost think about turning around. But then I think. Sometimes people *do* come in here. It's such a beautiful place, and just because I like to think it's my personal area, doesn't mean it actually *is*. They're probably just having lunch and then they'll go. I just hope they haven't dropped their anchor on anything valuable.

I paddle past the yacht, not going too close, and then a few moments later I pass the opening of the cave itself, though only the very top of it is visible above the water. Then I angle back in towards my ledge.

A dozen paddle strokes later and the nose of the kayak crunches up against the wedge of rock where I always pull it out. I found this ledge a while back, and it's really handy. As long as you're here on a falling tide, it's quite safe to leave the kayak here. It's not very big, and it's quite hard to get out of the boat, but I'm well practiced now, and I step confidently out onto the black, slippery rock, my bare toes fighting to grip. Then I loop the kayak's painter around an outcrop of rock and tie it tight. That way it can't slide off and drift away, leaving me stranded here. That wouldn't be fun.

After that I sit down, my feet dangling in the cool water, and eat my sandwiches. Above me the cliffs bend and curve, and they're quite smooth, so it's like I'm sat at the bottom and inside an enormous spoon. But under the water it's a different story. The lower half of the cliffs are made from lots of different sorts of rock, and the weaker parts have eroded away over millions of years. That's what made the caves. But because the sea levels have risen, you can't see them unless you get into the water. Then you can actually swim into the cliff, and resurface. In some places it's like you're actually inside the earth.

I think about this while I set up my camera. How this place has been here, hardly changed for millions of years. And how it'll be just the same in another million years. Long after we're all gone. When all that's left of humanity is billions of crazy fossils. Maybe some other species will discover it all, and make up theories about the age of the humans, only they won't call us that, because they'll have some other name. I think about it while I load the camera into the waterproof case. It's that kind of place. It makes you think these sorts of thoughts. But then I stop thinking and concentrate. Because I don't have that long before the tide comes in. And I've got work to do.

I'm already in my wetsuit, and I guess what I'm really feeling is nervous. Not just about whether I might actually find what I'm hoping to find. But also nervous because the scale of this location does make it an intimidating place to dive. But then I take a few deep breaths to calm down. I spit in my mask and rinse it out. I pull my flippers onto my feet and then fit the mask and snorkel. Then I'm ready. I slide carefully into the water.

It's always the same sensation when you first go in. The chill of the water presses around you, and a few leaks trickle in through the suit. And even though what you can see suddenly expands to include this incredible underwater world, it also contracts because the mask cuts out your periph-eral vision. I have to fight at first, to keep my breathing slow and calm. But when I do, I swim away from the ledge. It's like flying out from a moun-tain top. The rocky bottom drops away. Below me there are giant boulders, some as big as houses. Some reach almost to the surface, so I could easily swim down and touch them, but in other places the floor is way down beneath me, far out of reach.

A trio of large sea bass glide past, barely bothering to change their course to avoid me. Once they grow to this size there's nothing around here that eats them, and they're safe from being fished too, though I don't know if they've worked that out. But I ignore them too. I'm studying the rocks, trying to find the exact spot I was at last time. It was pretty close to the entrance to the cave – where the water shallows and there's more patches of sand. I just need to find the right one. Then I see the boulder I've been looking out for, with one side much redder than the other, and I know I've found it. I surface and take a breath, trying to take a bearing above the water too, from the cliff face.

Then I put my face back into the water and let my eyes adjust to the lower light levels. I dive down and hold on to an outcrop of rock. I study the sand. I'm looking for an irregularity that shows something is burrowed into the sand. Something that shouldn't be here, not this far north. The brown striped octopus, or *Octopus Burryi*, is quite common in the Caribbean and even as far up as the coast of Florida, but no one has ever seen one this far north. Not ever. So *if* I'm right, then this will be quite a moment for Lornea Island.

Although they're called brown striped octopuses, most of them are actually more speckled colored, at least most of the time, like the sandy bottoms they like to live in. But then they can change color too, so they can be hard to identify. I saw this one – or I thought I saw it – the last time I was here. The trouble is I was just leaving at the time. The tide had turned, and I had to get back to the kayak – and then I haven't been able to come back to check, because – like I said – it's been so stormy lately. But I made a really careful note of where it was, and I could see it was in a burrow, which means it *should* still be here.

The big problem is, I might have been mistaken. It could be that I just saw an *Octopus Vulgaris*, in fact it's quite likely given how no one has ever seen a *Burryi* this far north. Which is another reason I'm quite anxious at the moment.

That doesn't mean they're vulgar by the way, *Octopus Vulgaris*, it's just their Latin name. Really it just means they're common. If it was a common octopus, then I've wasted my whole day. But I've seen a lot of *Octopus Vulgaris* and I'm pretty confident I know the difference.

As I wait, my eyes adjust to make more sense of the grainy surface of the sand. Octopuses need oxygen, so they breathe water, just like a fish does. Only instead of slits covering their gills, they expel the water through a squishy tube that sticks out alongside their legs. But it means that even when they're hiding in the sand, keeping still, you can still see the tube if you look carefully, blowing water as they breathe out. And I see it now. It's the size of a dollar coin, and once I've spotted that, I can see the outline of the rest of the octopus around it. I'm already holding my breath, but I feel like I should do it more somehow. I get my camera ready up in front of me and fin slowly toward it.

As I'm overhead I see its eye. Octopuses are pretty smart, and this one knows I'm here. It's probably working out whether it should try to stay hidden, or escape. They like patches of sand near rocks, partly because they eat crabs and things in the rocks, but also because they can escape there easily too. Give them a crevice and you can't ever get them out, or even see them if they go really deep. So I gently pull the camera into position and fire off a couple of shots, because this encounter could be over very quickly. I gently reposition myself to get photographs from every angle, while it's still, and I swim down a few times to get closer-up images too. Then, when I've got all the pictures I can of the octopus hidden in the sand, I swim down and pick up a couple of good-sized rocks. And – I know you shouldn't really do this – I carefully drop the first of the rocks over the octopus, so that it lands with a gentle thud next to where it's hiding. It tries to pretend it didn't happen at first, so then I drop the second stone, watching it sway down through the water. And this one lands too close, because – in a sandy flash – the octopus is suddenly up and out of the burrow, its tentacles trailing behind it. I fire off lots of shots, and I'm super excited because *anyone* can see this isn't an *Octopus Vulgaris*. The eyes are the wrong size and they're slightly too low. And the webbing where the arms meet the body is much deeper. It's definitely an *Octopus Burryi*.

Then something even more wonderful happens. I expect it to disappear in the rocks, but instead it slows and then stops, still out on the sand. I guess it knows it can escape if it needs to, but it doesn't want to use up too much energy, or give up its territory if it doesn't have to. So I let myself drift very slowly closer again, taking photos the whole time. The best ones will be if I can get really close.

The octopus stands up on the tips of four of its tentacles, then slides them down into the sand, while the other four finger the rocks behind it. Then it blows the sand up, so that little clouds color the water. The colors of its body flutter and flicker to match the background, and gradually it sinks into the sand. And then it stops. Watching me, watching it.

I guess the time goes fast after that, because before I know it my camera tells me I've run out of space on the memory card. And then I check my watch, and a whole hour has passed. Which means I have to go or the tide will get too high for my ledge.

I don't want to go though, so I allow myself another five minutes, just watching the octopus, without taking any photographs. And then – and to be honest I'm feeling a bit cold now – I turn to swim back to the kayak. It's not too far, just the other side of the entrance to the cave really. And I'm not really thinking about anything as I swim, apart from what I'm going to do with the photographs, and who I'm going to send them to. And whether anyone will even believe that I took them right here, on Lornea Island. And that's when I get a shock.

Up ahead of me is another diver. It's a man, with a face mask and snorkel, and he's holding a massive spear gun out in front of him. He hasn't seen me, and I freeze at once. The good mood I'm in from seeing the octopus is instantly gone. And after a second I realize it's replaced by anger. I already told you how this section of the coastline has been designated as a marine reserve. That means you're not allowed to fish here. At all, and that definitely includes spear fishing. There's plenty of other places you can go if you want to do that, although I don't really approve of it. I mean, it's not exactly a nice thing to do to an animal is it? To shoot it. And the guns they use, powered by thick elastic bands, are incredibly powerful. When they shoot a fish the spear just punches straight through, like a dart bursting through a stretched-out piece of paper.

This guy looks like an amateur too. When you're spear fishing you're supposed to carry a buoy, so people can see you easily. But this guy doesn't have one. At least his catch-bag is empty, which means he hasn't killed anything yet.

I think what to do. The easiest thing to do would be to go back to the kayak, take the name of the yacht and then report the owner for illegal spear fishing in a nature reserve. But if I do that the chances are nothing will happen. I could take a photograph as proof – but I used up all the space on my card, and I don't want to delete any photos of the octopus. And even so, the guy's got a face mask on, so you wouldn't be able to see who it is, or prove his identity. And even if he did get fined, that's hardly going to stop him shooting some animals *right now*. Then I have a horrible thought. What if he comes across the *Octopus Burryi*? Some people actually eat octopus, even though that's hard to believe, and the one I've been watching was a good size. But if this guy shoots this one, the only *Octopus Burryi* ever seen this far north. Well that would be a disaster. I have to do something. And now.

I decide to confront him. I just have to be careful that I don't startle him. If I do he might accidentally fire the spear gun. And since it would go through me just as easily as a fish, I'll make sure I come up behind him so I can't get hit. So that's what I do. I fin fast to catch him, and swim up right behind him, kind of expecting him to notice me and turn around. But then I get really close, so I can just reach out and touch his shoulder. So that's what I do. Then he goes nuts.

All I mean to do is get his attention, and then point at the surface to tell him I need to speak with him. Instead he totally freaks out. He spins around like I've tried to attack him, and he flails out with his arms and legs. Something hits my mask so that it floods with water. So then I have to surface, and a second later he does too.

"Whoa. *What the fuck?*" The man says. He's got an accent, I notice at once, he's not from the island. Plus he's panting like he's been running or something. "You scared the fucking shit out of me!"

"There's no fishing here. It's a marine protected reserve."

The man pulls the mask from his head, and pants some more. He's got a ring of red around his eyes from wearing the mask. He must have been here quite a while.

"You're not allowed to spearfish here." I tell him again. He's younger than I thought. Early twenties maybe, not much older than I am.

"It's a marine…"

"Yeah, yeah. I heard you the first time." He interrupts me. "And anyway I wasn't fucking spear…" He doesn't finish the sentence.

"Yes you were. I saw you." Then I notice he isn't holding the gun anymore. I refit my mask and put my face into the water, looking for it. But it's not there. He must have dropped it.

"You had a spear gun. I saw it."

"Yeah well I don't now, do I?" Suddenly he starts grinning.

"I saw it. I saw what you were doing."

"Is that all you're worried about? Illegal fishing? *Fuck* man."

"It's nothing to laugh about. There's a $500 fine. If you don't leave right now I'm going to report you to the National Oceanic and Atmospheric Administration. *And* your boat's anchored. You're not allowed to anchor here either."

The man stares at me. He's got very clear dark eyes. His face breaks out into a smile again. A kind of sneering smile.

"OK kiddo. You got me. I thought this'd be a good place to bag a bass or two. But you rumbled me. I'll get outta here right now. OK?" He starts to swim away from me, backwards, towards the anchored yacht.

"What about your spear gun?" I ask. "You can't just leave it here. It's littering." We both refit our masks then and look down into the water. We're over a deep gully here, and the gun is only just visible, much further down than I can swim. The man lifts his head out of the water again.

"You can have it." He grins again, like he really doesn't care about losing it. "I'll buy another one." He laughs again. That's what really annoys me about the fine against fishing here. It should be much higher, because people like him, who are rich enough to have nice yachts, it's just not enough to deter them.

"Sorry buddy." He swims away, and I keep an eye on him as he gets to the yacht, and I return to the kayak. Once I get there I pull out my binoculars and watch him as he pulls up the anchor and motors away. I take a note of the name of the yacht.

It's called the *Mystery*.

THREE

THE MOTOR BURBLES as the boat pushes through the calm water. A slight swell – almost imperceptible here, but enough to push waves into the beaches along the island's east coast – ghosts underneath them. It causes the *Blue Lady* to roll gently as it cuts along, but it's not enough to upset the group of tourists sitting along the bench seat and looking hopefully around them.

"Are we *really* going to see dolphins?"

The voice belongs to a small child. A boy. Blond hair cut in a bowl style, and dressed in red pants and expensive Nike sneakers. Around his neck a pair of binoculars hang, looking absurdly over-sized.

"I'm sure we are," his mother replies. "You just need to be patient." At that moment a young woman steps past, the same young woman who checked their tickets as they climbed aboard, with a faded crew t-shirt and the name of the boat emblazoned on it.

"Excuse me Miss," the mother asks. "What are the chances of us actually seeing something? It's just we've been out here over an hour and..." she looks apologetic. "I know you said it's late in the season, but Charlie was so hoping to see dolphins. He just loves them..." She tails off, then looks around, like maybe they're actually surrounded by them and she just didn't notice.

The young woman breaks her stride and looks down. She takes in the hopeful look on the small boy's face. She crouches down.

"Hey Charlie. My name's Amber. How are you doing?"

Finding the young woman at the same level as him, the boy relaxes a little. "I'm OK."

"Just OK?" Amber's face takes on an indignant expression. "Why? What's up?"

The boy bites his lip, unsure whether this is one of those times when he's supposed to tell the truth, or to not be rude.

"I just really really want to see some dolphins."

"You really *really* want? Wow that's a lot of wanting!"

"It's his birthday," the mom explains. Amber glances up at her and gives a reassuring smile. Then turns back to Charlie.

"So how old are you?"

"I'm five. But later on today I'll be six. Because I was born in the evening."

"Wow! That's awesome, I've got a kid sister just that age."

"It's his birthday treat." The mom cuts in again. "He didn't want a party or anything. He just wanted to see dolphins. I mean whales too of course. But mostly dolphins."

Amber takes a deep breath. "Well," she says, rocking back on her heels. She thinks for a moment, then points at the bridge, where a man in his forties is casually holding the wheel. He's suntanned and looks relaxed and capable.

"You see that man driving? That man is the skipper of this boat. He's called Sam Wheatley, and he just happens to be the best skipper on the whole of Lornea Island. Not just the best whale-watching boat skipper. The best skipper of any boat. And not just the best on Lornea Island either. Probably the best in the whole country. Or even the whole world. So if there are any dolphins around, and I mean any at all, he can catch up with them." Amber smiles again, and this time the boy smiles with her.

"And that's not all. Take a look in the cabin there." She points, and the boy's eyes follow her arm to see a teenage boy sitting at a chart table in the boat's cabin. In front of him are an array of technical looking screens, plus a laptop computer.

"*That*," says Amber. "That is none other than Billy Wheatley. He's Sam's son, and *he* is only the best whale and dolphin *finder* in the whole wide world. So I promise. If there's *anything* around you're going to get to see it. OK."

Charlie's head nods up and down. His eyes wide.

"OK." Amber stands up and turns back to the mom.

"We would normally have seen something by now, but we are right at the end of the season."

The mom smiles, to show she understands, and appreciates the effort.

"OK then." Amber smiles and it looks as though she's about to leave, but she doesn't. She crouches down again.

"Hey Charlie, would you like a soda?"

"Sure! Mom, is that OK?" He looks anxiously up at his mother, who smiles at once, and nods her head.

"Pepsi?"

"Yes please."

Amber moves to the center of the boat where a chest is anchored down. She heaves open the lid, and from the bed of ice she picks out the soda, then takes it back to Charlie.

"So why do you like dolphins so much Charlie?"

"They're really smart! And I like the way they jump out of the water and do tricks..."

"I don't think they'll be doing any tricks Charlie," his mom says. "Even if you are lucky enough to spot some."

"I don't mind that," Charlie replies at once. "I just really want to see one. Do you really think we will?" Charlie's eyes shine up into Amber's, totally trusting that whatever she says next will be the absolute truth.

"Well..." Amber begins. "We did see some yesterday. And the day before, they came right up close to the boat. So I reckon there's a good chance. Whales too, a humpback mom and her little baby."

"A baby whale?" Charlie's eyes go round as coins, like up to now he hadn't thought such a thing could exist. "For real?"

"Course for real." Amber smiles, and the only thing that betrays a hint of anxiety is the way she glances at the flat water around them, before continuing.

"One thing I *definitely* promise you, if there's anything cool around, Billy is gonna find it. There's just no one better." Amber smiles again and stands up. To the mom she continues. "If he wants to come inside and see how the sonar works, you just give me a holler OK?" She pats the mother on the arm and moves away.

FOUR

THE DOOR to the cabin opens and then shuts again. I don't look up.

"Dolphins please," Amber says, her voice bright and cheery. "And if you could rustle up a humpback that'd be cool."

I ignore her and continue what I'm doing, which is reading an article on my laptop. It's in the scientific journal *Marine Biology Association of the United States,* and to be honest it's quite heavy going.

"Little kid, whose birthday it is. I also told him about the humpbacks yesterday, but it's dolphins he really wants."

"Uh huh." I keep reading as she talks. Then I suddenly stop.

"Humpbacks?"

"Yeah, you know the mother and the calf?"

Now I finally turn to look at her. I can't help myself frowning deeply.

"What? You don't remember? Jesus it's like you've left already. Like your brain's checked out and gone down under. You remember, the mother and calf?"

I continue to frown, and maybe I shake my head a little bit too.

"Oh *come on* Billy, don't be weird. They came right up to the boat?"

Now I know what she's on about. "Right up to the boat? They weren't humpbacks. They were *sperm* whales."

Now Amber frowns. Just for a second. "Oh. Yeah. That's what I meant."

"Sperm whales and humpbacks are *completely* different..."

"Yeah I know..."

"Humpback whales are in the *Balaenopteridae* family, part of the suborder Mysticetes. That means they have baleen in their mouths, instead of teeth. Whereas Sperm whales are of the *Physeteridae* family, suborder Odontocetes, which means…"

"Which means toothed whales, I know. I know. Humpbacks eat shrimp. Sperm whales eat fish – or cephalopods – which is squid in actual *English*. I know already. I just got them confused for a second."

I watch her for a moment.

"Krill."

"Huh?"

"Humpbacks. They mostly eat krill, not shrimp."

"Same difference."

"No it's not…"

"I'm kidding Billy. I'm pulling your leg. Lighten up."

I don't reply. I don't know why but I'm in a bit of a funny mood today. So I persevere.

"How could you get a humpback and a sperm whale confused?"

"Because I'm not an *asshole* like you. Will you please stop reading that and find me some dolphins? I've got a kid out there who's six years old today, and who really wants to see some." She goes to close my laptop, but I move it out of the way just in time.

"What are you looking at anyway? You should be out there enjoying this. It's the last trip we're ever going to do on *Blue Lady* 1. And you made this business such a success." She glances at the screen. The title of the article is *Molecular identity of the non-indigenous Cassiopea sp. from Palermo Harbour.* She reads it out loud, pronouncing it all wrong.

"What are they? Casio-whatevers?"

"They're jellyfish," I explain. "An invasive species that probably came into the Mediterranean through the Red Sea Canal…"

"Well that sounds riveting, but it's not exactly relevant to finding something exciting *right now.*" Amber sighs. "Honestly Billy, while you're getting excited in Latin in here, I'm out there chatting to *actual human people* who have paid you to see some whales. So would it kill you to find me some. Please?"

Reluctantly I close the screen on the laptop. Then I stare at her. I still can't believe she hasn't noticed them.

"What is it?" Amber asks, sensing something at last.

I try to keep a straight face, but in the end I can't, and I end up smirking.

"*What?*" Amber punches me on the shoulder, but not too hard.

"OK, OK," I laugh at her. "There's a small pod of spinner dolphins about a mile off. Bearing ninety degrees. I already told Dad."

"Where?" She jumps in front of the screens, then races to look out the window. Already a few of the guests outside are training their binoculars and shouting.

Then I shrug. "Course I could be wrong. They might be humpbacks. The way they're leaping out the water like that. And spinning around. Or maybe they're krill..."

"*Oh fuck off* Wheatley." Amber goes to hit me around the head this time, and I manage to duck out the way, only then I don't see her other hand, and she gets me and messes up my hair.

"So you gonna come out and look? Or stick with your nerdy jellyfish?"

I give her a look. "Amber, they're only *spinner* dolphins."

She stares at me for a moment, then she bursts out laughing. "What are you like, Billy Wheatley?" Then she picks up her megaphone and steps back outside.

FIVE

THE *BLUE LADY* tracks the dolphins, but they seem to be in a hurry to get somewhere, and the motor doesn't have the power to get them close enough for viewing without the binoculars. Then the animals stop, and change direction, so that their path takes them directly towards the boat. The excitement on board rapidly rises as the animals come much closer, leaping and spinning as they do so. But then, as if obeying a call only they can hear, they suddenly dive and disappear. Sam circles the boat, while the tourists wait with cameras poised. But after twenty minutes with the ocean's surface unbroken, it's clear they've slipped away.

And gradually the excitement ebbs away too, replaced by the beginnings of frustration for those hoping to get value for money out of their tickets. But for Sam and Amber it's simply a clear reminder – if one were needed – of why they made the decision to retire the *Blue Lady* at the end of the season, in favor of a faster, larger and better equipped vessel next year. Even so, they're both a little tense, as if both feel a strong desire for the old girl to go out on a high.

After some discussion with Billy, Sam steers the boat further out to sea into deeper water. It may be late in the season, but there are still whales about. They just need to know where to look, and be lucky. After another half hour of steaming as fast as the old motor can take them, Amber picks up the megaphone again.

"So. We've come out a long way now," Amber's amplified voice carries over the whole boat. "To where Billy tells me is the very best chance to have a whale encounter today." Amber does her best to keep her voice optimistic, but everyone can hear the 'but' that's coming.

"And here on the *Blue Lady* we do have an excellent record of viewing whales..." Her voice tails off. And then it comes.

"But these are wild animals and we can't *guarantee* sightings."

"My sister went on a trip from New York," a woman pipes up. "She said she saw whales before they'd even got out the harbor..."

Amber looks around at the sea around them. It's a little too long to be a casual glance, and the ocean remains stubbornly flat, empty.

"What we might be able to do..." she says after a while, still into the loudspeaker but turning now so she can watch Billy, who's still sitting inside the cabin. "Is get Billy to come out here and answer some questions."

The door is partly open, so there's no way Billy can't hear her. But he pretends not to.

"He's actually," Amber gives a smile, settled now on how to entertain the group. "He's off on a very exciting adventure next week. Isn't that right Billy?" She directs the megaphone at the open door, just in case he hadn't been listening. And when Billy continues to ignore the noise, Amber simply carries on talking. "He's been head-hunted. Sort of." Everyone can hear how Amber is enjoying herself now. They give her their full attention.

"Can we have a little show of hands? Who here has seen that show on ABC, *Shark Bites*?"

A few hands go up, one guy shouts back. "Yeah I seen it." Then a couple more hands rise up. Amber turns to answer the man.

"Well... *That* dude, the shark guy, *Steve Rose*. You know how he's actually a serious scientist, as well as a TV celebrity? Well he *heard about* our Billy here, and his incredible ability to find whales. And he's invited him along on a two-month research tour off the coast of Australia." Amber pauses to let that sink in, before she goes on.

"They're going looking for *great white sharks*."

An audible murmur goes up from the boat's seating areas.

"You wanna come out here and talk about that Billy? I'm sure the guys here would love to hear all about it?"

It seems that Amber's won, since, a second later Billy pushes up from his seat. He steps outside, but then he seems surprised to see Amber smiling and holding out the megaphone to him. Instead he moves to the rail, staring at the calm water on the port side of the boat. When he looks up, a few moments later, he sees the eyes of all thirty guests on him.

"I said, Billy," Amber goes on. "That you're off to *Australia*. To chase great whites. You wanna say anything about that?" She holds out the loud-speaker again, but he doesn't take it.

"Erm. I just…" He glances at the water again, frowning. "We're not really chasing… It's more of a survey… A population study…" He stops. He looks at the water again.

"Actually I think there might be some whales now. They might actually breach."

As he speaks the boat's motors slow. From the wheel Sam Wheatley calls out.

"Whereabouts Billy?"

"Just over…" Billy sweeps an arm over the ocean to their left, but it's a vague gesture.

"Somewhere…" At once everyone is looking where Billy is indicating. Suddenly expectant. But there's nothing to see. Behind them the land is just a gray smudge, low over the horizon. Around them the water is blue-black and oily smooth. It's empty.

"I don't see anything," someone shouts, a long moment later.

"It might have just been a shadow on the echo sounder. Or a shoal of fish." Billy replies, but he doesn't look confident. And after another thirty seconds of increasingly awkward silence, the ocean remains undisturbed. Billy shoots a glance towards the cabin and his laptop. Like he'd like to get back there, but now he's not sure how. All the boat's forward motion has now ceased. They're floating still on a near motionless ocean.

"So how do you find them? These whales?" A woman asks. "*When* you find them I mean?"

At once Amber sticks the megaphone in front of Billy, for a third time, and this time Billy reluctantly takes it from her. He turns it on, and speaks in an unenthusiastically- amplified voice.

"Well we have the fish finder, and the sonar, and you sort of recognize the patterns. But sometimes it's not whales it's just something else because the resolution isn't very high. Though you can get better sonar but they kind of have to be designed into the bottom of the boat."

"But you do see them? On most days right? That's what it says on your leaflet."

"Yeah," Billy replies, but again he sounds unconvinced. "It's just it's kinda late in the season now." His voice dies away and there's silence.

The guests fidget, and look around at the empty ocean. Then the woman from earlier calls out again.

"This whale watching trip my sister went on. She said they offered a guarantee. If they didn't see no whales they got a refund on their ticket price."

But if Billy even hears her, he doesn't reply. Instead he hands the loud-speaker back to Amber, then goes back to the rail of the boat and stares at the water again.

"Well, are you just gonna ignore her? What about this guarantee?" A man asks, probably the woman's husband, and his voice verging on mad. He's about to go on when Billy holds up a hand.

"Ooooh." Billy says.

A second later a few bubbles burst on the surface, less than ten feet from the side of the boat. It's enough to draw a few people's attention to that spot of water. And then, suddenly many hundreds of bubbles arrive, fizzing and boiling in a trio of circles. And then, almost in slow motion, the water stretches upwards and then splits apart as the black-and-white flecked bow of an enormous whale launches up and out of the sea. It climbs, higher than the top of the boat, like a missile emerging from the deep. Then it sweeps forward, hanging in the air for a heavy second before crashing back down, landing heavily and sending a curtain of green water showering over the boat.

There's screams all around. Yells of excitement and actual fear. A few of the quicker-witted watchers snap pictures, but most are too shocked.

"Maybe over there," Billy says, moments later and he points a little further away from the boat. This time everyone's ready as, exactly where he says, a second whale explodes upwards. It too hangs for a split second, then ten tons of whale land back into the ocean with another almighty splash.

"I *thought* they were humpbacks," Billy says, but by now no one's listening to him.

SIX

FLYING IS INCREDIBLE. I always knew it would be, but to actually get to do it is amazing. I'm kinda pleased too, that it's my first time on a plane, and I've gone all the way to Australia. I mean, that's nearly half way around the globe. I even had to choose which way around I went. I decided on going west, not because it meant I got to fly over the whole country first, with a stop in Los Angeles, but because then we carried on across the entire Pacific ocean. I wanted to get a sense of just how big it was. Though as it turned out, you couldn't really see much, just lots and lots of blue. Anyway, we've just landed, so now I'm *in* Australia. I'm just waiting for my luggage. Then there'll be someone to pick me up and take me to the research boat. At least I really hope there is. Because if not I don't know what I'm going to do.

I end up waiting ages by the conveyor belt, quite a long time before any suitcases come out, and then even longer when, one by one, they bump onto the belt. And I get a bit worried, because at first I can recognize lots of people who were on my flight who are standing waiting with me, but more and more of them find their bags and load them onto trolleys and disappear, until finally it's just me left, and my backpack still hasn't come. It's just the three same cases going round and round, and there's no one left to take them.

So I don't know what to do then, but then I see a girl with dreadlocks and a backpack that looks a bit like mine, although it's smaller, and I guess

I must look at her funny, because she tells me that backpacks come out on a special conveyor at the end of the baggage hall. When I ask her why she tells me it's something to do with the straps, and then she gets a bit angry because I explain how I tied all the straps down extra carefully and she tells me it's not her problem and walks off. So then I ignore her and go to where she tells me, and then I'm super relieved because my backpack *is* there, just abandoned lying against a wall, and none of the straps have come undone where I tied them. Honestly it doesn't seem like a very good system to me. I don't know what I'd have done if I got all the way here and found all my stuff had been left behind. I was a bit worried too, that it might have got damaged by the baggage handlers, because you hear bad things about baggage handlers, and I do have some quite fragile equipment inside. But actually it looks fine. I heave it over, and check the other side. It's just a bit dirty, but actually I quite like that because it makes it less obvious that it's new, so people won't know I've not done much traveling before.

Then I remember about the people waiting for me on the other side, and how I've been so long that maybe they'll think I didn't come after all. So I struggle into the straps and hoist the backpack on my back. I do have Australian banknotes, for the trolleys, but I decide not to use one, because it *is* a backpack, and the girl with dreadlocks wasn't using a trolley and she looked like she knew what she was doing. So I take a deep breath, and I walk as best as I can through the customs area. I totally expect to be stopped and searched, and probably arrested, because stuff like that *always* happens to me, but there's not even any customs officers there, so I just walk straight through. Then I have to go through some swing doors, and suddenly it's all mayhem. There's a big crowd of people all staring at me, like they think I might be the relatives they're waiting for. And I can't help but know they're all *Australians*. You can sort of tell. They all look a bit more tanned than normal people, and some of them are wearing flip flops – although quite a few people on Lornea Island do that in the summer too. I feel everyone looking at me, which I don't like, but I take a deep breath. I tell myself this is what growing up feels like. You can't have big adventures if you just stay home. Then I step forward, ignoring all the eyes watching me, and start to read the name signs people are holding up. There's quite a few, and I look for the one with my name on it. But soon I've read them all, and there isn't one. So I don't know what to do after that.

I walk up and down past the crowd – they're behind a barrier, except every now and then excited kids duck underneath because their relatives have just arrived and they run up to them and start talking in funny accents. But my backpack is actually pretty heavy, so it makes my shoulders ache. Even so I start to feel myself floating off the ground, like all this is some sort of dream, or maybe the beginnings of a nightmare.

Then I see a woman hurrying into the entrance of the terminal building, and looking around her, like she's late. I think I'd notice her anyway, because of how she's quite young and how pretty she is, but obviously I recognize her, though it's weird to see her in real life. She's dressed in a very relaxed way – in shorts made from jeans, with the material cut off really high up on her legs, which are very long and tanned. Then I'm doubly surprised when she notices me, but instead of continuing to scan the crowd, she breaks into a wide smile. That doesn't happen very much with me and women, especially not very pretty ones, so I'm a bit taken aback. Then she comes towards me, and even more odd – or not odd really, but it feels like it, she mouths my name at me, with a questioning look on her face. I feel myself nodding and walk towards her too, and we meet where there's a bit of a space in the crowd.

"Billy right?" The woman says. She's got a funny Australian accent too. Her blonde hair is tied in a loose pony tail, with strands of it falling out over her eyes. Up close she's *really* pretty.

"That's right."

"I'm Rosie. I'm so sorry I'm late, the bloody plane wouldn't start."

I don't say anything. I ought to – Rosie is the lady I've been emailing about the trip – but she's also the woman I've seen on TV so much, and it's kinda hard to make sense of both of those facts. Up close she smells like fresh flowers.

"You alright? Long flight huh?" She smiles again. Her lips open and her teeth are white and regular, except there's a little gap between the front two. I manage to nod in reply.

"Shall I grab a trolley for that bag? It looks like it's squashing you."

I shake my head and mumble something about being fine.

"OK. We might need a bigger boat though." She smiles again, to show how she's joking. Her cheeks go all round when she does it, and then there's little dimples too. She's actually *beautiful*, like a model, or even not like a model, at least not the ones in magazines, since you hardly ever see them smiling, like they're worried they're going to break their faces or something. Rosie seems quite happy to smile.

"You sure you're OK?"

Hurriedly I nod again, so I don't look odd.

"Yes."

"Alright then. Well let's get outta here."

She leads the way towards the exit. At first I fall into step behind her, and I can't help but watch the way her shorts lift up on the backs of her thighs, not so high that you can see her actual behind, but high enough to show the muscles in her legs. But then she turns to check I'm following her and I look away quickly. And then we walk outside, and I'm hit by a wave of heat. It's like a physical wall or something. We get hot summers in Lornea Island, but it's never like this.

She stops and turns to me.

"Hot huh?" She does that smile again. I force myself to try and smile back, even though my face feels all stiff.

"Come on. The van's got air con." She touches my shoulder and I feel a jolt go through me, like her fingers are electric. "It's just over there." She smiles again, but wonky this time, and it's even more pretty. Then she sets off again, and I follow, really trying to make myself relax. I know we've got a long car journey to where the ship is moored, so at least I'll have time to get to know her a bit before meeting everyone else. That's all I need, a bit of time.

"We had a change of plan by the way," Rosie says from in front of me. "I managed to grab a flight down with a mate of Steve's. So we don't have to do the drive."

Before I can even make sense of this she goes on.

"So we can all fly up together."

I feel myself tense up again.

"All?"

"Yeah. The other students are waiting in the van."

I feel myself tense up again. I'm not the only one on this trip. I'd kinda forgotten that.

"Don't worry Billy." Rosie tells me. "They seem really fun. It's gonna be a good trip."

Then we arrive at a minibus, and I see there's already three people inside, not including the driver. They all look about my age – well actually a little bit older – but I can't really see, because the windows are tinted. Then Rosie lifts the back of the minibus, and we try to stuff my backpack in, and I get a better look at them. But then it's a bit embarrassing because there isn't enough room, so we have to force it in the sliding door instead. The boy who's in there makes a big thing about pulling it in with both hands, and joking about how it takes up three seats all on its own. But actually there's plenty of room, because it's a minibus. Then I climb in and sit down too, next to the boy because it's the only seat I can get to, and Rosie slides the door shut behind me.

The boy holds out his hand. But instead of trying to shake mine, he tries to fist bump me, only it goes wrong because I was too slow working out what he was doing. Then he does something else, which I've seen rappers do on TV, and that doesn't work either. But he doesn't seem to care.

"I'm Jason," he tells me. His voice is loud and I can tell at once he's one of those super confident people. Then he introduces the others and tells me what colleges they're studying at, not letting them speak. I forget what he says, but luckily when I turn around to shake their hands they tell me their names again. On the seat behind me is a girl called Debbie. She has dark brown hair, and she looks quite round. I think she is studying at the University of Miami. And then on the back seat is another girl called Kerry. She's actually pretty too, I notice. Or at least you might think she was, if you hadn't just met Rosie to compare her with. She's studying at Stony Brook. Or it might have been the University of California. One of them is from there. I can't help but notice their bags – they all have backpacks too, but they're all quite a lot smaller than mine.

"So where you studying Billy?" Jason asks me suddenly.

"Erm," I say. And then I feel everyone go quiet, waiting for me to answer. "I'm actually just in high school at the moment."

There's another moment of silence, before Rosie interrupts from where she's just climbed in to the front of the minibus.

"Billy is the youngest ever graduate student we've taken on a trip." She says it in a kind way. "So you'd better all look after him." And that really helps break the ice a bit.

Then everyone starts talking about the subjects they're studying, and the teachers they know. I don't say much, even though I recognize some of the names. I suppose I feel a bit intimidated.

Then the driver starts the motor and drives us out of the airport. And I guess since we're all from America, and haven't been to Australia before, we all go a bit quiet and look out of the windows. It's funny how different the same things can look. I mean, we have freeways at home, just like the one we're on now, but it looks totally different. The road signs look different, and most of the plants and trees that we drive past look crazy different.

It's even more weird when we turn off the freeway and drive down a normal road. At one point we come to an open area, and there's a half dozen *actual* kangaroos. They're just standing in the open, grazing I suppose. Not fenced in or anything like that. We're all quite excited by that, so Rosie tells the driver to pull over so we can watch for a while. But not for long because she says that Steve's mate who's flying us doesn't want to wait too long.

So then we carry on, and eventually we come to an airfield. It's much smaller than the airport we landed at. And we're allowed to drive right into it, and even right up to one of the planes that's parked there. And it's not a big plane, it's tiny, and it's got propellers, one on each side, so it must be quite old too. Then we get out of the minibus and a man in a beige shirt that's hanging open so that we can see his chest, helps us to load our bags into the hold of the plane, just like it was a bus. He swears when he gets to mine. Then we all climb on board and we can just sit wherever we want. The plane is so small I can touch both sides of the cabin at once.

Then I realize the man in the beige shirt is actually the pilot, since he climbs on too, and sits down in the pilot's seat. I find myself hoping he'll do his shirt up, I don't know why, it just feels like he ought to, before he starts flying us. But he doesn't. He starts talking on the radio to the control tower, saying we're all ready to go, and asking for permission to take off. And I can hear the reply, and it's not a proper reply, they start joking about something, I think it's about a sports game or something that must be happening. Then before I really get a chance to prepare myself for my third ever take-off, and my first in a propeller plane, the motors go ridiculously loud, and we start bumping really fast to the end of the runway.

When we get there, I hope we're going to stop, just for a moment so I can collect myself before we take off, but we don't. The motors go even louder, and suddenly we're going straight down the runway. I can see it out of the front window, and when I look out of the side we're going so fast that the green and red of the plants and earth around us start to blur, and to be honest I start to panic a bit. But then we lift off and start going up. But this time it's not smooth and steady like it was in the Boeing 777 and the Dreamliner before that. This time we're going up much steeper. And from the cockpit the man in the beige shirt lets out a whoop, like he's really enjoying himself.

It's like going up a set of stairs. I feel my head go light, like I'm going to pass out, and I panic that the pilot will too. But then we level off, so abruptly I find myself staring at the pilot for signs of whether he looks relaxed or not. We're high up, but nowhere near as high as in a proper plane, more like as high as a hill. It makes me wonder if something really has gone wrong. But then the pilot turns around.

"We're just gonna buzz up the coast for an hour," he tells us. He has to shout over the noise, but he sounds calm enough. Maybe even too calm. Then he goes on.

"We saw a couple of hammerheads on the way down here. I'm gonna see if I can find 'em again for you." Then he turns back to his controls. And then I see Rosie unstrap herself and pull out a camera with a large zoom lens. Then she really carefully makes her way up to the front and sits in the second pilot seat. It's weird. I was so focused on being scared by the take off I'd forgotten about Rosie. But now I'm thinking about her again.

"This is so cool, isn't it?" I'm surprised when the girl in the seat next to me starts talking. She's the one who was sitting on her own on the back seat of the minibus so I didn't get to shake hands with her earlier. But she's holding out her hand now, pale and slim.

"We never met properly. I'm Debbie."

"Hi Debbie." I say. "I'm Billy."

"I know. So you're still in high school?"

"Yeah."

"Rosie was telling us about you. She said you're amazing. You're already doing loads of experiments and stuff?"

"Really? Well I have done some. I wrote a paper on the feeding habits of *Semicassis Granulata*, but I haven't had it published yet. I think I probably need to do a bit more..."

"Semi what?"

I'm surprised by the interruption. "*Semicassis Granulata*. You know, the sea snail? Some people call them scotch bonnet snails but I think it's better to use the Latin names because people sometimes use that name with completely different species of snail. Don't you think?"

"Yeah, I guess..."

"Well anyway, I established how they exclusively feed on *Fucus Serratus*, which no one knew before. At least I don't think they did." I glance at the girl, suddenly wondering if this is really basic to her. But she screws up her face.

"Fuscus..?"

"*Fucus Serratus*. You know? Toothed wrack?"

Her face still looks blank.

"It's a type of seaweed."

I think for a second. Maybe it doesn't grow where she lives. I don't think they have it in the Pacific at all.

"Did you say you were studying at the University of California?"

She brightens at this. "No. I'm from Boston. But I'm studying down in Florida. At the University of Miami. Marine Science." Suddenly she laughs. "Except I'm not studying that much. Not when I heard how *Steve Rose* was offering a month-long research trip. I totally stopped doing any actual work and spent all my time writing the best application I could. I couldn't believe it when I got picked."

I consider this for a few moments.

"My science teacher applied for me," I tell her. "He said it was one way to get rid of me for a month. I think he was joking though."

Debbie waits a moment, then laughs, like she can't quite work out if *I'm* joking. Then she keeps talking.

"I bet you're like me. I bet you've watched every one of Steve's programs. They're just so amazing. I can't believe we're gonna actually meet him."

I go quiet at this. Because she's right about that. I can't really believe I'm going to meet Steve Rose either. *Dr* Steve Rose. Though obviously the Dr is because he's a PhD, not just an ordinary doctor. He's kind of been a hero of mine for quite a long time. Since I started watching *Shark Bites.* That's his TV program. It has one or two series each year, where he does real actual experiments on board the *Shark Hunter*, and films them so ordinary people can see what actual scientists actually do.

"Yeah." I reply.

Suddenly the note of the motor changes and we roll violently onto our side. I grab the side of the seat in alarm, and looking forward all I can see is the turquoise blue of the ocean, coming straight towards us. I think I'm about to scream out in terror, but then I hear the pilot's voice again.

"There you go," He sounds totally calm. "Couple of mature hammerheads. Just like I promised."

He pulls out of the dive, only a few hundred feet above the surface of the water. I can't even spot them at first, even though I see Rosie clicking away with her camera. But then I see them, a pair of silhouettes of the sharks, swimming slowly near the surface below us, their tails flicking left and right in a lazy pattern.

We circle around them for a few minutes, banked right over. And the others are all really excited, but I'm quite pleased when we leave them behind and carry on, because it means the little airplane levels out, which feels a lot safer.

A few moments later I'm still trying to calm myself from all the drama of the plane diving down to see the sharks.

"Have you ever seen *Charlie and the Chocolate Factory*?"

I turn back to Debbie. "Huh?"

"You know. Willy Wonka. That film where the kids get to go round the chocolate factory. That's what this is like. Like we've all won a golden ticket."

She's not pretty, but she does have a nice smile.

SEVEN

THE AIRFIELD where we land is right next to the water. It's the kind of blue you never get on Lornea Island. The kind of blue you see on travel shows and magazine articles. An impossible turquoise so deep it glows. I can't stop staring at it, thinking how beautiful it looks, even though I'm fairly sure we're about to crash into it. I suppose it might even be a nice way to go. It's only at the last possible moment that the tarmac comes into view underneath us, and we bounce down onto it. Then we get out, in this tiny place with just a shed for the actual airport, and we pile into Rosie's really smart 4x4 and she drives us to the dock where *The Shark Hunter* is tied up. I actually noticed it from the plane, you couldn't miss it.

It is weird though, seeing it for real. It's much bigger than the *Blue Lady*, more like a small ship than a boat. The bow and sides are really high, so it has an actual walkway to get on board. And there's a row of neat portholes running down the side, and then at the back there's a platform that's lower to the water. That's where Steve does a lot of the experiments. There's also a steel shark cage lashed there, and a yellow crane for lifting it in and out the water, and next to that a smart gray inflatable boat with a seventy horsepower motor. I know how the ship is packed with loads of other scientific equipment too because I've seen it on *Shark Bites*. I can't believe it's going to be my home for the next month.

I keep looking, expecting to actually see Steve Rose as well, but then Rosie tells us he's ashore doing some last minute jobs. So we have to help get the ship ready to leave. There's a whole pile of supplies on the dock, and we have to carry them all into the galley. And when we're done with that Rosie takes us to see where we're going to sleep. I have to share a cabin with Jason, which I'm a bit surprised about since it didn't occur to me I might have to share. There's an upstairs and a downstairs bunk, and there's a funny moment when he asks which one I want. I say the bottom one, thinking that he'll want it too, but he says he wanted the top one anyway. I guess he isn't thinking about what happens if the sea is rough, but that's OK, because I'd rather he falls out than I do. So I don't mention this, but quickly unpack my clothes. There's nowhere big enough to put my backpack, so I have to leave it on the bunk. Then we get called to the saloon. I hope we're gonna eat, because I'm hungry by now, but actually it's that Steve's come back.

I see him as soon as I walk into the saloon. He's deep in conversation with another man in a black t-shirt. In a way he's smaller than he looks on TV, even though he's also normal sized, and quite big. I don't know if that makes sense. It's just a bit weird seeing him actually standing there. I don't know who the second man is, but he seems to be good friends with Steve, from the way they're laughing together. I get ready to introduce myself, and the others do too, but for a while it's like Steve hasn't noticed us. Or perhaps he thinks it would be rude to stop talking with the man in the black t-shirt. Then Rosie comes in, and Steve notices her right away.

"Babe! You're back. How'd the pickup go?" He comes over to Rosie and puts his arms around her. I'm pretty surprised by that. Then even more surprised when he slides his hands down her back. His hands come to a rest on her bare skin, where her top doesn't quite meet her jeans.

"No problems." She pushes away from him. "You want me to introduce you to everyone?"

"Mmmmm. Sure." He tries to hold onto her, but she wriggles away. "No wait. Let's catch it. Dan, you wanna get set up? We'll do it as a *walk up*. Make it authentic." I guess the man in the black t-shirt is called Dan, since he nods his head and gets to work opening a black plastic case on the floor of the saloon. He pulls out a big TV camera and starts fiddling with it, while Steve turns back to Rosie.

"I missed you babe." It's like he hasn't noticed us students at all.

"I was only gone a day," Rosie rolls her eyes at him. I find myself hoping she's going to push him away again, but instead she leans in and I'm really quite shocked to see that she kisses him. On the lips and everything.

"I missed you too honey." She says when they finish. And it's like she's joking. Or partly joking at least.

I'm still wondering about that when Dan, the man with the black t-shirt, seems to be ready.

"OK guys," he says to us. "I'm gonna need you to climb off the boat, walk down the dock, turn around, line up all together and then walk toward me in a nice straight line, you reckon you can do that?"

I'm not sure what he means, and I guess I'm not the only one, since none of us move.

"Anytime around now would be good." He laughs at this, even though we don't. And then he beckons us to follow him. So we all walk out of the saloon, right past Steve, who doesn't even look at us, and onto the deck of the ship. Then we walk down the gangway, onto the dock and walk away from the boat.

"That'll do," he shouts from behind us. "Now turn around and line up."

We do what he says. And see him leaning into the camera.

"Tallest two in the middle."

We rearrange ourselves. Then wait for what happens next. He's got the camera on his shoulder now, and he's looking into the eyepiece.

"You couldn't manage a smile could you? Come on girls. This is gonna be your TV debut."

I look across at Debbie, in time to see her fix a smile in place. She looks a bit nervous too.

"OK, now walk towards me, keep in line."

We do what he says, and it feels really awkward knowing that he's filming every step. It's almost like I can't walk properly, but it helps to have the others beside me, and to be concentrating on walking in a line. I don't know what's going to happen when we get to the boat, I'm expecting Dan to shout 'cut' or something, but instead, just as we arrive level with the stern of *Shark Hunter*, Steve jumps down from the deck, not using the gangplank, and opens his arms out wide.

"Guys! So nice of you all to join us!"

And suddenly he's amongst us, shaking hands with me and Jason and hugging the girls. And then he gives us hugs too, as Dan comes in closer with the camera.

And then, a few moments later, Dan does shout 'cut'.

"OK mate," Dan says to Steve. "Let's just do it one more time with the *Hunter* in the background."

So then we have to line up again, just like before, but this time we've got Dan and the camera behind us, filming as we're walking towards the ship. And again, just as we draw level with the stern, Steve leaps down and greets us in exactly the same way. *Exactly* the same.

Then we all go back onboard, and I'm not sure if we've really met Steve at all properly yet. I definitely didn't get to say what I wanted to say, which was to thank him for the opportunity. But I don't get long to think about this, because straight away Steve wants us to get going. So he goes up to the bridge, and starts shouting instructions, and then Rosie and Dan show us how to release the mooring ropes, and coil them up properly, and drop them into the lockers out the way. And as we're doing it I notice that Dan's filming this as well. Twenty minutes later both he and Steve seem happy, and the land is sliding away behind in our wake as we steam out to sea. It's late too, the sun is dipping down over what's left of the land. I'm not sure what to do next, but then we all get called into the saloon again.

I'm still hungry, but now I see Rosie has laid the big table for dinner. There's eight places. The four of us students, and then Dan the camera-man, and also Bob, who's the captain of *Shark Hunter*. I've seen him on the TV show. He always seems really grumpy, and he's always worried about the dangerous things that Steve wants to do for his experiments. Then there's places for Rosie and for Steve too. That's all of us on board.

Rosie tells us to sit, so we all do, and then Steve comes in, carrying a crate of beers, that he throws down on the table. He rips open the plastic and throws one to each of us in turn. I don't really want one, since I don't drink very much, but I don't get a chance to say so, and then since I don't know what else to do with it I open it anyway.

"Now are we ever gonna bloody eat?" he calls out. And then Rosie tells him to shut up, but in a playful way, and then she asks Kerry to help her serve up. And then we've all got big plates of sausage risotto in front of us.

Steve does most of the talking while we're eating.

"Sorry about before," he says. "We have to do our little bit of stage management here on the *Hunter*. It's a pain in the ass, but it's all in a good cause. And you will get used to it. After a while you won't even notice Dan. He'll just blend into the background. Won't you mate?"

Dan doesn't reply but holds his beer up in a toast. It's a kind of mocking thank you.

Then Steve starts talking with Jason and Kerry, who are sitting either side of him. He asks them to tell him about themselves and why they wanted to come on the trip, and the rest of us end up listening. And while I think it's going to be awkward, it isn't actually. Unlike before, when he was being filmed, he's actually listening to what they're saying and then he asks sensible questions afterwards. And he's careful to talk to all of us, and when it gets to my turn he tells me I'm the youngest ever crew member of the *Shark Hunter*, but that he specifically wanted me on board because he'd heard of my ability to find whales off Lornea Island. And I get the sense that the other students are quite impressed that I have my own boat and whale watching business. Even if I am still in high school.

And the dinner is nice too. I'm not at all surprised that Rosie is a good cook.

After we've eaten, Steve divides us up into two watches. We have to work six hours on, six hours off, twice a day. When we're on watch we're completely responsible for the safety of the ship and we have to do exactly what our watch leader tells us. When we're off watch we can do whatever we want, as long as we don't fall off the bloody ship – or that's how Steve put it. He suggests that we sleep, because he says how hard he's going to work us. I get put in a watch with Debbie, and I'm a bit disappointed that Captain Bob is our watch leader, because Rosie is the leader of the other watch, with Kerry and Jason. Steve says that he and Dan will kind of float between both watches.

After that Steve says it's time for dessert, and Rosie brings out some chocolate pudding.

"And I hope you can all cook," Steve says, before we can get started. "Because we all take turns with making the meals, and doing the washing up. And all the other chores too. That's how we work aboard this ship. Like a big family."

The chocolate pudding is really delicious.

We're on the first watch, and Captain Bob explains all the things we have to do while the ship is under way. It's funny, he has such a grumpy reputation on TV, but in actual fact he's not grumpy at all. He's just a bit quieter than Steve, but actually he's really nice. In fact he's really interested in hearing about everything that me and Dad have done with *Blue Lady*, and how he's now helping on the build of *Blue Lady II*. And Debbie is nice too, even if she doesn't know much about seaweed.

The place we're going to is called Wellington Island. You've probably heard of it, since it's pretty famous. It's a fur seal colony about two hundred and fifty miles off the coast of Victoria, and it's so well known because every year when the fur seals have their pups, you get lots and lots of sharks, of all different species, coming to prey on them. Steve says it's the largest concentration of sharks on the whole planet. And that's why we're here. We're going to carry out a population survey of the different species of shark to see how many there are, and their ages. Steve has been doing this exact same survey for nearly a decade now, and that means he's gathering really important data on whether shark numbers are increasing or decreasing, so we know if the populations are stable or not. It's also why he needs us students. Our job is to watch out over the water, all the time, to spot the sharks. And then when we see them, to make sure we're accurately recording what size and species we spot. That's why I've been spending so much time watching shark videos on YouTube, so I can tell the difference between a mako and a porbeagle and a bull shark and a tiger shark, just from their dorsal fins. Obviously we don't just have to tell the difference from the surface. We're also going to use aerial and under-water drones. And obviously Steve does a lot of work from in the water, either with the shark cage or without it.

At the same time, Steve is going to record a whole new series of *Shark Bites*, his TV series. So he'll have lots of other experiments for us to do, which will help to show the viewers how real scientists do real science, aboard a proper research ship. Obviously this part isn't quite as important as the actual data gathering role that we're doing. But it will be quite inter-esting to see how TV works as well. And to actually be on TV of course.

The voyage lasts nearly a whole day, or four watches. I had hoped we'd do some experiments as we went, but in the end we mostly sat around playing cards, and doing what Dan calls 'pieces to camera'. They're basi-cally just little interviews, where we sit at the bow of the ship and he asks us questions and films the answers. I only had to do one, but Debbie and Kerry did two each, and Steve did loads of them, so we didn't see too much of him. I expect he's getting the TV work out of the way before we arrive and he's too busy with the science.

Rosie comes up with the idea of a competition to see who can spot the island first, and our watch wins, although we could actually work that out from the chart plotter, which shows our position and how we're getting closer to the island, and even our estimated arrival time. Anyway it's Debbie who spots it first, which still feels exciting. From a distance there isn't much to it, and even as we draw closer, I'm not sure I'd really call it an island now we're here. It's more like a large flat area of rocks that only rises a few meters above the water. It's uninhabited, by humans at least, and there are no trees or bushes. Not really any plants even, it's pretty much just rocks and seals.

As Bob steers us in close we can get our first proper look. There are seals *everywhere*. Every flat surface is covered in them, the adults brown and fat and basking in the sun, while the pups are a much fluffier gray white color. And the water around the island, where a light swell is rolling onto the rocks, is packed too, with seal heads coming up for air or diving down, or just resting there. The noise is amazing, it sounds a bit like a sports stadium full of people, but where everyone is screaming and squabbling with each other. The smell is worse. A mixture of fish, rotting in the hot sun. And seal poop.

"You get used to it," Steve tells us, about the smell. "I promise in a few days you won't even notice it."

We all look dubious about this, but even Rosie says it's true, and I'd trust her.

"At least they look cute," Kerry says. She points at a pair of pups, who are standing up on their tails and flippers, watching us glide by. "Can we go up to them? On the island itself?"

Steve shakes his head. "Uh huh. We can't land. It's protected. Plus it's generally too dangerous to get on and off with the waves. And if you get too close to a pup, the parents will generally try to kill you." His eyebrows flick up as he says this, and Kerry looks disappointed.

"How many seals are there here?" I ask, as we slide by a little rocky outcrop. We're in the calm water now, in the lee of the island.

"We reckon there's a hundred thousand breeding pairs," Steve says. "Give or take."

"Though we're getting closer to an exact figure," Steve goes on, as we all stand watching the amazing scene. "One of our first jobs will be to carry out an aerial survey. We'll get the drone up, fly over the island, then we'll use artificial intelligence to count them. Anyone want to volunteer for that one?"

I feel a burst of excitement. I do an annual seal survey of the colony on Lornea Island. We have about two hundred breeding pairs of grey seals. I've tracked the population for six years now, and it's increasing a little bit every year. I'm about to tell all this to Steve, when Jason pushes in front of me.

"I'll do it. I'm great at drone flying."

"Alright then." Steve gives him a smile I've seen a few times already. He's impressed by Jason. "We'll get you on that soon as we're anchored up."

Then suddenly a light gust of breeze plays over the deck, and with it a change to the smell, it's sweeter, stickier, but still pretty horrible. Steve's nostrils twitch as he tastes it.

"You smell that?" He says, and we all do.

"That's the smell of death. That's why we're here."

I don't know what he means by that, and he doesn't go on, because by then Bob wants hands to help him with dropping the anchor in the right place. He doesn't need us though, just Steve and Rosie, poring over the screens to make sure they're in the same place as previous years. Eventually there's an almighty rattling as the anchor is released, and then a few moments later, silence – for the first time in twenty four hours, as the motor is stopped. Then a few moments later, Steve calls us all to the stern platform of the ship for a briefing.

He points over to the island.

"You see the neck of this little channel here? Where the water meets the rocks, but where it's not so steep? That's the only place where the seals can get in and out of the water. We call it *death alley*. If they want to feed their pups, they've got to eat, and that means passing through this channel. And as the pups learn to swim, that's their only route too. Now the sharks know that, and the seals know that they know. So this is where it *all* happens. That means we stay here, twenty four hours a day, every day, for the next three weeks. We're witnessing and documenting what we see. And I promise you, it's gonna be quite a show."

He stares at the water for a while, as if there's already something happening, but actually there isn't. It really doesn't look that much now. It's a calm area of water, shaped in a vee and which cuts into the island. At the point of the vee the rocks are lower, but along the sides the rocks are steeper like the rest of the island. We're anchored mid way across the mouth of the vee.

"You're gonna see nature at its rawest and at its meanest. You're going to see some daring escapes. And you're gonna see brutal deaths too, because we've got some big bastards swimming around here and they are *hungry*. But we're not here to be sentimental. We're here to get an accurate count. I cannot stress how important that is. The validity of our data depends upon accurate observations. We need accurate species identification. You see a shark – and you'll see plenty – I need to know what species it is, I need to know if it's alone or in a group, and I need to know how old it is." He stops.

"Anyone. How do we tell how old a shark is?"

Kerry's first to answer, which annoys me, since I know too.

"Length. We have to estimate the length."

"That's right. Now apart from swimming up to it and holding out a tape measure, who can tell me how we go about estimating the length of a large, dangerous shark?"

All the hands go up now, because he's talking about Chumley. Steve grins. Everyone knows about Chumley. We've all been wondering where it was hiding.

"That's right. Our old friend Chumley. Our life-size cardboard cut-out of a white shark. Only he's not made of cardboard because he'd go a bit soggy in the water if he was. No, he's made out of finest marine grade hardwood. Chumley goes in the water, anchored front and rear in front of a camera buoy, and then we'll be able to use the measurements marked onto him to get an idea of the size of the sharks as they swim past. It might sound a little rough and ready. But it does the job."

Then Dan interrupts him.

"And it looks good on TV."

Everyone laughs at this.

"We're also going to have underwater and aerial drones, and we'll get you all involved in those. But the core task. The main reason you're here, is to scan the water, keep a close eye on the sonar, spot those sharks early so we can get the monitoring equipment in the right spot."

We all know this. It's all we've been talking about, since we got on board, and now it's actually happening, it's really exciting.

"Any questions?"

There's a pause. I think we're all just itching to get started.

"None. Good. In that case I'm gonna take a swim before we get down to it. Anyone want to join me?"

And with that Steve pulls off his t-shirt. I think he's joking, and I think everyone else does too. Except Dan maybe, who's already got his camera up and pointed at Steve. And the next thing, Steve raises his arms above his head, and then he does this real elegant swan dive right into the water.

He's a bit crazy is Steve.

EIGHT

WE ALL WATCH the water where he dived, which is just a mass of bubbles, and I can't be the only one that's worried we're going to see a flush of red appear in the water, as he's eaten by a shark. But actually nothing happens. The bubbles slow and then stop completely, and Steve doesn't even surface. We all glance at each other, getting more and more concerned but not knowing what to do. But at the same time I sense Dan's camera pointed at us now.

Jason and Kerry are nearest to where he jumped, and they peer over the side of the ship. I see Jason fiddling with his t-shirt, like he's thinking about pulling it off, to dive in too, and try to save Steve I suppose, but he's not sure and to be honest I don't blame him.

Eventually he does rip it off, and Kerry takes her t-shirt off too, but they look down into the water for any clue for where they should jump to find him. Someone – I don't know who – asks whether he might have hit his head on the bottom. But then suddenly there's a roar of laughter from the other side of the ship, and when I turn I see Steve there, treading water and laughing.

"Come on you pussies. You're not afraid of a few fish are you?" Then he climbs out the water, and shakes himself on the deck. He picks up a towel and rubs his head.

. . .

"OK kids. How about we put the cage in? You can take a swim in there? Get used to the water gradually?"

So then we prepare the shark cage. First we unstrap it, from where it's been secured for the voyage, and then we hook it to the top of the crane, and finally we winch it out over the water, then down. It's about the size of an elevator, and it's got floats at the top, so that it hangs suspended just under the surface. There's a hatch at the top, where you climb in and out. Soon we have it hanging down off the back of the boat, bumping up gently against the stern on fenders. Then Steve tells us to get in there. So I have to go and find my swimming shorts.

By the time I'm back Jason is already in there, and Debbie joins him. I watch as she climbs over the bars on the top of the cage, dressed only in a red swimsuit, and then lowers herself into the water through the hatch. She screams out at the temperature, even though it's not cold here. Not compared to Lornea Island at least.

Then Rosie comes out. She's wearing a yellow bikini with red flowers on it. I've not seen her in a bikini before, and even though I'm trying not to look, I can't help but see she has a prominent curved scar across her tummy. It's about the size and shape of a football. And it's pretty obvious what must have caused it.

"Eyes off my woman Billy," Steve says suddenly.

I jerk my head around, panicked that I've been caught staring at Rosie.

"I wasn't..." I begin, but I see that Steve is smiling really broadly, so he must still be kidding me around.

"She gets a bit self conscious about it," he goes on. "But she must feel relaxed with you lot. Sometimes she won't strip off the whole trip."

I frown. I don't understand, and she gives him a sweet smile.

"It's hot," she says. They stare at each other. I can see it means something but I can't tell what.

"Well come on then," Steve says in the end. "Are you gonna tell 'em the story or shall I?"

Rosie's hand goes to the scar, and her fingers follow its raised lip, but she doesn't speak.

"It's a love bite," Steve says. "From a striped tiger. That's how we met, I was working nearby and ended up interviewing her to get details of the shark. She was so bowled over by my considerate and caring approach she moved in with me."

Rosie rolls her eyes.

"What happened?" Kerry asks. "With the actual shark I mean?"

Slowly Rosie pulls her hand away. She starts tying up her hair.

"I was just swimming. Off the beach in Aswell Bay. I wasn't even that far out, and I was heading back to the shore, when I saw this flash of silver or blue, and the next thing it was like I was punched in the stomach. It didn't really hurt, I actually thought it was my friends playing a joke on me, but when I put my hands down I saw they were covered in blood."

She finishes tying her hair and shrugs. "I managed to get out onto the beach, and then I passed out. And when I came to Steve was there. He hasn't left me alone since."

I watch – a bit more carefully this time – as Rosie steps out onto the cage after Debbie. She seems to know where to put her feet better, and she lowers herself into the water with no sound. And then it's my turn. But before I climb off the boat, Steve calls out, and when I turn to look he throws me a diving mask. I only just catch it, which is lucky because it's a good quality one, with real glass. Steve tosses masks to the people in the cage as well, and I fit mine in place. Then I climb over the railings of the ship, and lower myself carefully down onto the roof of the cage. It feels weird, a little bit exposed, as though a shark might jump out of the water and snatch me before I can get inside the bars where it's safe. Then I get to the hatch, where the others are swimming, and jostling around.

"Come on Billy, it's lovely and warm," Rosie says to me. Her hair is slicked back over her forehead, and she's putting her mask on. I sit down on the edge of the hatch and let my feet swing back and forth in the water. Then I take a deep breath and plunge in.

At first I can't help feeling a bit panicky. It's not the sharks so much as the sensation of being surrounded by bars on all sides. Underwater they look magnified, and inside the cage there's a tangle of limbs and the bodies of the other swimmers, so that it feels like being caught in a net. So I fight my way back to the surface and take a breath. From here you can see the side of the ship, and it kind of reminds you how we're in the ocean now, and in an ocean known to be full of very dangerous sharks. Again I have to fight back the panic. But after a few moments I realize we're quite safe inside the cage, and I dive down to look underwater.

You can hold onto the bars, which makes it easy, and I do so, looking through them and out into the blue water. Looking horizontally it's beautiful. Shafts of light are glittering through the water, as the sun's rays are refracted and penetrate the surface. Down below though the blue quickly turns darker, and right below us it's almost black. But as my eyes adjust I can see the bottom is actually in sight, maybe thirty or thirty five meters down. A bed of rocks, long snaking seaweeds waving up at me. I look around, there's loads of shadows, but I can't see anything that's definitely a shark.

When I come back to the surface I see I've missed something. Steve is pulling on diving flippers. At first I assume he's joking again, but then I notice Dan is setting up to film him.

"Anything about?" He asks. And it's Rosie who answers.

"Nothing I can see. But please be careful."

With that Steve looks to Dan, who gives a thumbs up signal. And then Steve fixes his mask in place. He stares at the water below him for a long while, then rolls forward. He hits the water with his hands protecting his face.

Then he surfaces, and swims closer to the cage. We're all still inside it, and Steve's outside, and I can tell I'm not the only one looking past him, and kind of expecting to see a fin arcing through the surface of the water. It feels weird, knowing *I'm* safe, but that I might see him get eaten. And then Steve slips down under the water and out of sight, and I almost panic, because it looks like he's been sucked under, a bit like a fish sometimes just gently pulls on some bait and eats it without making much fuss. But then I remember I can look underwater myself, so I refit my mask, and I sink down.

I've got this real irrational fear that I'm going to see him being torn apart by a pack of sharks – but of course I don't. But what I do see is pretty crazy anyway. He's swimming underneath the ship, checking out the propeller and the rudder. And then he pivots in his own length and he starts swimming straight down.

He's not wearing any kind of scuba gear, just his mask and his over-sized flippers. But he doesn't seem to need air. It's like he can breathe underwater. I have to pull my head up to breathe, several times, while he's underwater, just to keep watching him. And I'm quite good at holding my breath these days. One time I lose him, but then I see he's right the way down at the bottom now. He looks in a few of the darker places, and I can see now that they're caves under the water. A couple of times we see a white flash as he looks up at us, and the light catches his face.

In the end I have to take three breaths before he starts to come back toward the surface, flexing his flippers really casually, as though he's in no hurry. Then when he surfaces he's just very quiet for a few breaths.

"Anything?" Dan asks, after a while.

Steve shakes his head. "Couple of seals. Didn't see anything toothier." Steve replies. "Looks pretty though. Gimme the water housing and I'll get some shots looking up."

So then he goes down again, this time with a video camera locked into a waterproof housing, I get out of the cage and dry myself off.

"Don't try that at home." Rosie interrupts me.

"Sorry?"

"Free-diving in shark infested waters. Steve's a national champion. He won the Aussie free diving championships two years running." She wraps a towel around herself so that her scar is covered.

"And he's a crazy lunatic very probably with a death wish."

She smiles at me, to say how she's joking.

NINE

I GET to help tow Chumley out into position, using the inflatable boat. We anchor it at the mouth of death alley, a couple of meters under the surface of the water at high tide. Then we set up the camera buoy about ten meters in front. It has a solar panel that transmits video footage of the cut-out shark back to the boat. The idea is that when real live sharks swim in front of or behind Chumley, we can measure them against the scale that's marked on it. I've always been quite dubious about how accurate it is, but Steve tells us they've tried lots of different systems, and this is the best anyone's come up with. It's even become the standard, with other scientists copying the technique.

It's quite scary being out there in an inflatable boat though. It has double thickness rubber, but Steve says it still wouldn't survive a proper attack by a big shark. Just as we finished I asked Steve why he didn't have a stronger boat, but he laughed and said it didn't matter because no small boat would survive a proper attack by a big shark. And right after that Dan said we had to go and pretend to anchor Chumley all over again, because he wanted to film it from the air this time.

Back on the ship we stay in our watches and begin monitoring. I spot a few fins, mostly of bull sharks and a couple of makos, and there's a couple of moments of excitement when sharks swim past Chumley, and we get to measure them off. But none of them seem to be eating anything. So even though we start off being super alert to every tiny splash in the water, after a couple of watches where nothing happens we all get a bit bored.

"They're biding their time," Steve explains it to me, a couple of days later. I'm sitting on the observation deck with the rest of my watch and he's kind of sneaked up on us. He seems to do that all the time, just appear out of nowhere. We've not seen too much of him actually, since he's been busy with some TV stuff, and the seal survey.

"The seal pups are still being nursed, fed milk by their mothers, so they don't need to get into the water yet." Steve picks up my binoculars and puts them to his eyes. He looks around for a few moments then drops them again. "The adult seals are cautious, good swimmers, they're hard to catch. So it's not worth the sharks using up energy. But soon the pups will have to go into the water. To learn to swim and to fish. That's when it all kicks off.

No one answers him. And he doesn't really need to say it, because we all know. It's what we're all waiting to see. But I think we're all kind of dreading it too. Hoping it won't happen this year.

"What are you most hoping to see?" Steve turns to me, but then he puts the binoculars back up to his eyes. And I'm not quite sure what he means.

"I think I'm most interested in how the science is actually done," I say. "Seeing it firsthand I mean."

"Uh huh?" He sounds a bit bored by my answer. "I meant what species are you looking forward to seeing? What *excites* you?" He goes on scanning the calm water of death alley.

"Oh," I say. And for a moment I can't think of an answer, so Debbie gets in before me.

"I want to see a great white."

Steve doesn't drop the binoculars, but seems to tighten his grip on them.

"Yeah," he says after a few seconds. "Me too."

Suddenly he starts speaking again. "You know the mechanical shark they built for *Jaws*? The movie? You know they could hardly use it because it broke down so much. They had to come up with all these creative ways to suggest there was this monster shark without actually showing it. And by not actually showing it the movie ended up much more suspenseful than it would otherwise have been?"

No one answers this, but he doesn't seem to mind.

"Turned it from being just another piece of Hollywood trash into a worldwide phenomenon. And it's never been the same since. Nowadays, the whole goddamn world knows what a white shark is. And half the world is terrified to go into the water, case they get eaten by one." He's still scanning the water as he talks.

"You know how many people each year get killed by sharks? All sharks I mean. As opposed to, say, *cows*?"

No one knows which of us he's speaking to, but Debbie answers. "It's about ten isn't it?"

He clicks his tongue in irritation. "Not quite. The average is six. Yet *twenty two* people are killed by cows. Not counting the millions who die from heart disease from all those Big Macs." Then he drops the glasses and smiles, a bit ironically. "And how many sharks do you think are killed by humans?"

I answer this one. "It's about thirty two million."

Steve looks right at me.

"Yeah. It is. Or about that." he says. "Some estimates run even higher. Killed for their fins, for sport, or just caught as by-catch in nets. Either way, we're many orders of magnitude more dangerous to them, than they are to us."

He stops talking and scans the ocean with the binoculars again.

"Everyone loves to hate the great white..." He drops the glasses again.

We're all silent for a while.

"You know what's really ironic though?" He goes on. "Even considering how famous white sharks are, we still know shit all about them. Relatively speaking. Even us scientists. Take this place for example. I've been coming here every year for a decade, and it's always the same. We see the odd bull shark, the odd mako, but no white sharks. Not a sniff. Not until the pups go in the water. But the very moment they do – like to the *hour* – the whites are here. It's like they can tell *exactly* when to turn up. I don't know how they do it. But they do. Every year."

He turns back to Debbie.

"So you'll see your white shark. And when you do..." He hands the binoculars back. "It's gonna be quite a show."

And with that he wanders away.

TEN

FOR THE NEXT two days I work six hours on, six hours off. I record everything that happens in the log book. I spot our first blue shark, and even get
to measure it using Chumley. But apart from that not much happens. I end
up helping Jason with the seal survey, and I help Rosie make dinner when
it's her turn, because she's supposed to do it with Steve but he's too busy.
That's because he's always tinkering with the shark cage, or some of the
other equipment, or filming pieces to camera with Dan. When we're off
watch we play a lot of cards.

"Rock, paper, scissors to see who makes the coffee."

That's Steve again. It's about ten o'clock in the morning, on our fourth
day at the island. It's my watch and so far it's been a quiet morning.

"Come on. Everyone. We'll have two rounds, and then a final. Whoever
wins makes the coffee."

Steve likes this, doing sudden games. I think it's to keep us interested,
because otherwise all this waiting around would be boring. My first round
is with Kerry, and I win that, so then I have to play Rosie in the final. I'm a
bit distracted by her warm eyes on me while I decide whether to go with
scissors or paper. I make a late decision to use scissors, and it means I win
again. Or lose, depending on how you look at it.

"Yee ha! We have a winner!" Steve shouts. "Congratulations Billy, you
get to make six cups of coffee!" So then I have to go inside and busy myself
with the coffee machine. I don't mind. I wouldn't have minded if he'd just
told me to make it. The truth is, even though there isn't much happening,

I'm feeling really happy just to be here. I can't really say it, not to Jason or Kerry at least, because they're doing their best to pretend this is all something really normal to them, but I've never done anything like this and it's awesome. Everyone is really nice, and smart, so that I feel I'm learning, all the time, wherever I am on the ship and whoever I'm talking to. It's like the total opposite of school. I hope this is what college is like, but I kinda doubt it. I think this is just something special.

When I come out again, they're still playing silly games. I-Spy this time. But a kind of silly, ironic version. I hand out the coffee and do my routine scan of Chumley, and around the ship with the binoculars. I check the clipboard to see if anything has been added to the sightings since I went in.

"I spy..." Rosie begins, "with my little eye, something beginning with 'S'."

"Is it *ship*?" Kerry asks.

"Nope."

"Sea?"

"No."

"Seal?"

"*No*," Rosie replies, but from the way she starts giggling, we all know that it was really.

"Is it Billy's scissors?" Kerry starts laughing now. "Billy's invisible..."

"*Shark.*"

There's something immediately different about Steve's voice. He's not playing nor joking, and we all turn to where he's pointing. About fifty yards from the boat there's a slight disturbance in the water. I didn't really have enough time to see it, but I can tell it's where a dorsal fin has just disappeared.

"Did you see what it was?" Someone asks. I don't catch who, I'm too busy getting the binoculars trained on it.

"Uh huh. Just saw the fin go under." Steve replies. He looks at the island. Reaches for his binoculars. "Well, well, well."

"What?" That's Rosie talking. She's looking where Steve is pointing. At the island now. It's a bit hard to see because the sun is in my eyes.

"There. Just at the edge of the water. It's one of the pups, it's going in."

"I got it," she says. I squint, and she moves closer to me. So I can look down the length of her arm.

"*There.*"

Then I see what she's looking at. The seal pups have been rapidly losing their gray-white fur, and instead taking on the blubbery appearance of the adults, but they're still much smaller. I see a couple more flop into the water now. They make more splash than the adults.

"*Shark!*" This time it's Captain Bob. He's standing on the flying bridge, which is the highest part of the ship.

In an instant Steve is up there with him. The whole atmosphere is totally different now.

"Where?"

"Off our port side. A hundred feet out. Coming straight towards us."

Rosie and I go to the other side of the ship. I can see something but it's hard to tell what. It looks like someone is pulling a piece of lead pipe through the water. You can see a little bit of white foam where it breaks the surface. Then it sinks down, and we can't see it again. Steve freezes.

"What was it? Did anyone see?" Someone asks. It takes me a while to realize it's Kerry. She's asking because it's their watch, and she's supposed to note down sightings as they happen. That way nothing gets missed. But no one replies to her.

"Did anyone see? Shall I put it down as another unknown?"

"No," Steve says. Put it down as *Carcharodon carcharias.*"

At once I feel the hairs on the back of my neck stand up. Rosie freezes too, when she hears the name, and when no one else reacts, our eyes lock together.

"What's that?" Kerry asks.

"*Carcharodon carcharias.*" Steve says again. "The most famous fish in the sea." He smiles at me.

"I don't know what that is." Kerry complains. I see Jason frowning too. So I have to tell them.

"It's the Latin name. *Carcharodon carcharias.* It means *Crooked-Tooth Shark.*

"Yeah but what is it?" Kerry asks, frustrated now. So I tell her."

"It's a Great White."

Then the fin comes up again, at a slight angle this time, so we can all see exactly what it is.

"Dan? You filming this?"

"Yes boss."

"Good." Then Steve calls out. "Let's get the drone up, shall we?"

Moments later we're all gathered around the screen while Steve flies the drone low over the silhouette of a large shark, lazily working its tail back and forth. We can see so much more from the air. It cruises by our stern twenty feet away, and even without the drone we can see the shadow of it under the water.

The shark doesn't notice us, nor the drone at all. Or if it does, it doesn't care. It's just cruising towards the vee of death alley. It doesn't seem to be in a hurry.

"Right on time. Just like every year." Steve says. He hands the controller to Jason.

"Keep on it Jason. There's some seals in the water just ahead. See if you can zoom out and get them in the shot too." Jason does what he says, so then we see the shark on the screen, and a little way in front of it, a single adult fur seal swimming back to the island. The shark seems to notice it, and speeds up just a touch. I realize we're all holding our breaths.

"Poor thing doesn't have any idea it's there." Rosie murmurs, but I don't think anyone but me hears her.

The seal swims quite close to the shark, but then it casually banks right, and it moves out of shot. The shark cruises on, again it doesn't look like it cares. But it does seem to be going somewhere. It's moving casually to where the baby seals are, at the head of death alley.

"Oh god," Rosie goes on. "I really do hate this bit."

"Pan the camera up a bit." Steve directs. He's got one eye on what Jason is doing, and another on the scene, and he keeps taking sightings with the binoculars too. He sounds totally calm and focused.

Jason pans up with the camera again, so now we can see three baby seals following each other in a circle. They're playing, a bit like puppies do, chasing each other around and around. They're actually really cute, the seal pups, even now they've lost their baby fur, they still have oversized flippers and really big eyes, and they move in a kind of ungainly way.

"Come on. Get out of the water. Just get out," Kerry says.

Then the first of the pups darts into shallow water and the rest follow, and for a few moments it looks like they're going to be safe, because surely the shark won't be able to follow them. But then it changes direction, and jets out away from the rocks directly towards the shark. The others follow, and suddenly all three are in the frame with the shark again. They turn, and begin playing their game of tag again. We all hold our breath.

Then one of the pups breaks off. I guess it's coming to the surface to breathe. The shark moves its head, just a tiny bit. But then, in a horrible instant, everything happens at once. The seal goes to dive again, but as it does the shark suddenly massively accelerates. The first we see of it is the great tail surging from side to side, and then in a split second it's closed the distance to the seal pup. And it's just *gone*. The greeny-blue of the water in the frame begins to fill with a cloud of red. Then beyond the blood we see the head of the seal caught on one side of the shark's mouth, and its tail emerging from the other side. Then the shark shakes its head, and then there's just a piece of the seal's tail left. Then the shark angles away. Jason keeps the drone camera pointing at the red water, and the very back of the tail sinks down out of view.

There's silence on the boat. Apart from Steve, who whistles.

"OK gang. Make a note of the time and location. I got a look as it came past the stern of the boat. We're ten foot wide and there was a good foot hanging out either side. So that makes it a twelve foot white shark. And I don't think it's going to be the last. Things are going to get busy from now on."

And they do. From that moment on we see an average of one attack per hour. Weirdly they seem to follow our mealtimes, with most happening in the morning and the evening, and then a smaller peak at lunchtime. The white sharks do most of the killing, and the other species come in to scavenge on the bits of seal left over. We're kept really busy recording all the attacks and trying to work out which species it is, and where we can, which individual sharks are attacking. I start to realize the real benefit of Chumley. We have the drone, and also a remote controlled underwater vehicle, but the first has a very limited battery time, and the second is very slow. So it's hard to get them in position in time. But most of the sharks have to swim past Chumley to get into or out of Death Alley, so it gives us two definite chances to confirm the species and check their size. Steve's right, it's a really good system.

But even while we're busy, I can't help but feel a bit confused about what Steve's doing. He's even busier now that the sharks are attacking, but most of the time he isn't helping us with the survey, or doing any science really. Instead he's doing even more of the TV stuff. I kind of got the impression earlier that he had to get the filming out of the way before everything kicked off. But now that it has, I don't really understand why he's still doing it.

This afternoon for example, he had Dan film him going down in the shark cage. There weren't any sharks nearby, they were too busy eating seals, and when I asked Dan about it he told me not to worry because he was going to edit in some footage he'd taken earlier from one of the camera buoys. To make it look more real. That wasn't my point at all. And when I tried to explain, and ask what was the scientific purpose of it he said he didn't have time to go over it.

I asked Rosie about it, and she told me I shouldn't worry, but that if I want she'll get Steve to sit down with me and explain how it all works. But I tell her not to, because he's obviously busy, and I don't want to look naive. We agree that the important thing is I concentrate on doing the jobs I've been given to do. So that's what I do.

I already told you about the clipboards. We keep them on the observation deck, tied on with lanyards and loaded with special waterproof paper and a wax pencil on a piece of string. We use these to record sightings and attacks as we see them happen, with as much detail as we can, so that we don't miss anything when it gets busy. And then, when we have quieter moments, it's my job to compile all the data into Steve's laptop. He has an Excel spreadsheet, where he's recorded the raw data like this for all the sharks they've seen over the last ten years. I'm only updating this year, but I've discovered you can look back at the earlier years. And it's very tempting to compare the data.

The only problem is, you can't compare it very easily. It's the way Steve has laid out his spreadsheet. He's put each year in a separate sheet, so you can't easily see them side by side. But it wouldn't be too much work to put all the years into one sheet and use pivot tables, and then you'd be able to analyze the data easily. You could see how many of each shark was seen each year, and in more detail too – for example you could look at how many male blue sharks were over three meters long. Or how many females had a successful attack at dusk. I think this would be really useful, so I decide to ask Steve if he minds me changing the sheet. I'll tell him how I can save his version first, just in case something goes wrong – even though it won't. But whenever I try to talk to him he's busy doing something with Dan. So in the end I decide to use my initiative and take that as a yes.

And that's when I start to see something odd in the numbers.

ELEVEN

THE SHARKS DON'T ATTACK at night, except when there's a very clear moon. Steve thinks it's because they simply can't see the seals. So it's dark when I knock on the door of Steve's cabin.

"Yeah," he calls out.

I hesitate, because I'm not 100% sure of what I have to tell him. So he calls out again.

"What is it?" He shouts out now.

I open the door, to see him sitting at his desk typing into his computer. It's the only light on in his cabin, and it's casting a glow onto his face. He glances up, sees it's me, then looks back at the keyboard.

"Billy. What can I do you for?" He starts typing again. Using just two fingers.

"Erm..." I begin. "I think I've noticed something odd. A problem maybe."

"Uh huh?" he's still typing. "Are we sinking?"

"No. At least... no. It's..."

"Run out of beer?"

"No."

"We're on fire?"

"No..."

"Good. So it's nothing super urgent?" He hits a couple more keys, then looks up. "Huh?" He peers over the top of his work glasses. "It's just I'm kinda busy here."

"Oh." I say. I wonder if maybe I shouldn't be wasting his time.

"You know, actually doing *proper scientific work*. For once." He smiles suddenly. And I guess I must look confused, because then he goes on.

"Rosie mentioned how you had some questions. About how it all works."

"How what works?"

"How *it* works. The whole thing. This whole deal." He sweeps his arm around the cabin, but I still don't understand.

"Look you wanna come in? I need a break anyway. I'm trying to get this paper finished. It's looking at how reef sharks adapt their attack habits as they grow older. They're like Spielberg's velociraptors. They *learn…*"

I don't understand what he's talking about, and I guess that shows on my face too.

"Jurassic Park? The movie? Tell me you've seen that one?"

"I think my dad's watched it."

"Jesus you kids make me feel old. Well never mind. Get your butt in here. We need to talk."

So I walk into his cabin, and then there's nowhere obvious to sit, except on his bed. And I feel a bit uncomfortable sitting there, because I know that Rosie sleeps in here too.

"You wanna beer?"

I shake my head, but he goes to the little fridge anyway, and gets one for himself.

"So. Billy. Young idealistic Billy. The lovely Rosie tells me you have concerns about whether I'm devoting too little time to pure scientific research, because I'm always playing around making cheap trash TV?" He bursts open the beer and takes a swig.

"Well…" I begin. "No…"

"Because I was too. When I first got into this game." He stops, and looks at me for a long time, so I don't remember what I was going to say. It doesn't matter, since I don't get the chance.

"You sent me a paper. Or your high school science teacher did, on your behalf. On the feeding habits of *Semicassis Granulata*, the scotch bonnet snail. How it feeds exclusively on just one type of seaweed. I read it. I don't think it's quite ready for publication, but it's got promise. And the thing that excited me most, was how no one before had even found a *Granulata* in the Atlantic. They're Pacific snails. At least I thought they were, until you came along, and showed me otherwise. But the problem is…" He stops and rolls his shoulders around, like he's stiff from being hunched up in front of his computer screen too long.

"The problem is nobody gives a damn. About snails I mean. Or seaweed. Or anemones. Or about just about anything that lives in the sea. Unless that is, it eats *us*, or at a pinch, if we eat *it*. The consequence of this is we know almost nothing about ninety-nine percent of what lives in the oceans. And even then, the one percent we do know about... Like our old friend *Carcharodon carcharias,* we don't know much more about them."

He takes another swig of beer.

"And you know why?

I think about this quickly, so I can answer before he tells me.

"Because they're hard to study?"

He glances up. Surprised, then shakes his head. "No. No they're not *that* hard to study Billy. Not with all the technology we have at our disposal. The problem is they're *expensive* to study. No one wants to pay for it. So we have to do what everyone has to do if they want a career in this game. We make a pact. A little deal with the devil."

He stares at me again, and I feel a bit uncomfortable with his wide blue eyes staring into mine.

"This entire trip is funded by our income from six episodes of a television program. Me, you, none of us would be here without it. The science is just an add on. Sure for guys like you – and for me I might add – it's anything but. But it simply wouldn't happen if it wasn't for the TV cash. So if we don't treat the TV side of things seriously, the science disappears."

I try to consider what he's saying. I get it, but it's hard.

"What about universities?" I ask, but he kind of ignores me.

"You know there is nothing inherently special about the shark Billy, but it does capture the public attention in a way that very few other creatures do. And it's my job to use that. Our job. To harness that interest, and to use it to drive forward the sum of knowledge of all the other species that would otherwise be ignored." He takes another big swig from his beer can.

"And that is why, during the daytime, I'm a ridiculous caricature of a scientist, jumping in and out of that ludicrous shark cage and hamming up the danger in order to drive our ratings. And it's also why, at night I stay up till the small hours doing my real work. Do you understand Billy?"

I don't answer at first, because I don't want to sound rude.

"Yeah, I kind of understood that already." I say in the end. "But it isn't why I came to see you."

Steve looks confused by this. He doesn't move for a long while.

"Oh." He says in the end. Then he takes a deep breath. "OK Billy. So why *did* you come to see me?"

Then I take a deep breath too, because what I have to say is really hard.

"Well, this is going to sound a bit odd. But I've noticed a problem in your data."

He frowns.

"What problem Billy?"

"Well it's a bit weird really…"

"Go on." He kind of makes himself smile, even though he maybe doesn't want to. "I like weird."

"OK. It's just I noticed how all your sharks got bigger by ten percent four years ago."

"*What*?"

"Well actually it's 9.8% but that's just an average obviously, and I rounded it up…"

"*What did you say?*"

I pull out the print out I made earlier. The boat has one computer terminal with a printer attached, and Captain Bob let me use it.

"Here. I thought there must be a problem with the formulas in the Excel sheet, but I went through the whole spreadsheet checking them, and they all seem OK, so I can't work out *where* the error is coming from…"

"There is no error Billy."

"…Because it doesn't make sense that you'd get this *uniform growth* in all the sharks. It just wouldn't make…"

"There is no error Billy," Steve cuts in, his voice suddenly hard. I stop talking.

"Of course it makes sense," he says. "You're not thinking."

I look at him now, I mean really look at him. His whole demeanour has changed. It's suddenly like he's earnest and *serious*. It's almost like he's talking to me as if I were a *scientist* too. It makes me feel nervous, but in a good way. But it doesn't help me think of anything sensible to reply.

"Think about it. Were you the same size two years ago as you are today? Or were you maybe a bit smaller?"

I frown. I don't understand what he's getting at.

"I'm not *much* bigger."

"But a bit bigger, yeah?"

I shrug. "Yeah." I don't see how this is relevant.

"They're *growing* Billy. That's why they're bigger."

I stare at him, like he's joking, because it's obviously not *that*. "They can't be. I mean, obviously some are, but not the *entire population of sharks*. The younger ones sure, but adults will already be full size. Adult size."

"Billy, sharks don't have an adult size. I thought you'd know that."

"Well…" Suddenly I can't believe I've been so stupid. "Don't they?"

"No. They don't. Come on Billy, this is basic stuff. Sharks – like most fish – they don't stop growing. The older they are, the bigger they get, allowing for differences in diet and sex. It's the whole reason we can use their size to age them so accurately." He seems to relax now, and he rasps his hand across the stubble on his chin. Meanwhile I feel my face begin to burn hot.

"Well yeah, I mean I know they'll still grow a bit every year, but they still do *most* of their growing when they're..."

"No 'buts' Billy." Steve cuts me off. "That's just the way it is."

I try to assimilate what he's saying into how I understood the problem. It kind of makes sense, but somehow it doesn't quite fit.

"But if it's just that *all* the sharks are growing, why would we only see it in the data four years ago? Wouldn't we see it every year?"

Steve shrugs again. But then he sighs. "OK, that does sound a little odd, when you put it like that. But you also have to remember we're only getting a *very small* sample size here. It's quite possible that the sharks we happened to see before that year were smaller, and the ones we happened to see afterward were larger. Wouldn't that explain it?"

I frown again, trying to keep up. "Well I guess... I guess we could run a statistical analysis to see if..."

"There's not enough data for that!" Steve takes the print-out from me suddenly, and studies it for a moment, all the time still rasping his chin.

"Look I tell you what, I reckon this could just be my clunky old data-base. Sometimes you get a little gremlin in the data. And I'm pretty sure I remember that *was* a good year for shark growth. But let me have a look at it? I'll figure out what's going on here." He doesn't give the paper back, instead he puts it down on top of his own papers, by the side of his laptop. Then he smiles at me.

"And while we're here chatting, how about we give you a turn flying the drone tomorrow? I've noticed how Jason's kinda taken over. I'm sure you'd like a bit of drone flying huh?"

I think about this. It's true, Jason has been hogging the drone, even though I'm a good drone pilot too. But I don't really mind, I have a drone at home anyway.

"Or if you prefer," Steve says suddenly. "That offer of a swim still stands." He grins. "I'm not kidding either. I'll take you out for a dive, any time you like. I promise you, getting in the water with those creatures, unprotected. It's like nothing else. And it's safe enough, while they're concentrating on the seal pups." He raises his eyebrows, actually waiting for an answer.

"Erm. I'll think about it," I say.

"Do that. But don't think too long." He points at me, and then he turns his hand over like he's squeezing something. "Sometimes you've gotta stop thinking and just grab life by the balls." He grins again. "You know what I mean?"

I nod.

"OK. Well I better get back to this paper. The science isn't gonna do itself." He waits until I take the hint and get up to leave.

And – still not really understanding what just happened – that's what I do, closing his cabin door behind me.

TWELVE

It's late by then, but I don't feel like sleeping, so I take a walk around the ship's deck. I can't go far, since it's not that big, but it's a nice starry night, and much cooler than in the day. I end up doing two laps before I have an idea of what I need to do. Even though it feels kind of crazy.

After that I go and check the store room. I figure I might as well get what I need when most of the crew are asleep. The store room isn't really a room, more a kind of large closet, but it still has almost everything you could need for measuring and weighing and experimenting, plus a good set of tools for fixing things that go wrong. But even after a long search I can't find what I'm looking for, which is kind of odd.

So then I go and ask Captain Bob, who's still up in the bridge, and he tells me there's a box of odds and ends under the companionway steps, and I'll probably find one in there. So I go and pull that out and search through it. And it's full of bits of old radios, and slightly rusty tools, and a compass that's had paint spilled on it, so you can't read the bearing very easily. But I still can't find what I'm looking for. So eventually I head back to my bunk, and go to sleep. I figure I'll work it out in the morning.

And when I wake up, I have an idea.

"Debbie," I ask, when we're both quite slow finishing breakfast. There's just the two of us there. "How tall are you?"

"What?"

"It's just obviously I couldn't help notice you were quite short, so I thought you might know your height. You know, *accurately*."

"*What?* What the hell is that to you?"

"Oh I don't mean it in a rude way. I mean I'm really short too, but I don't know how short, or at least, not *exactly*, because I keep growing. So I wondered if you did. Know, I mean?"

Debbie stares at me in a way that's not very polite, frankly.

"Do you know?" I try again.

"Yes!"

"Well, would you mind telling me?"

She gets up from the saloon table and picks up her breakfast things to take them back into the galley. I think she's not going to reply at all.

"You'll have to tell me why."

"Oh. OK, sure." I get my own bowl and follow her to the sink. "Well it's a bit weird," I say. "But I need to check something with a tape measure, only I can't find one anywhere on the whole boat. Don't you think that's odd?"

Debbie screws her face up, confused. "Why would that be odd?"

"I don't know. Just, we've got pretty much every piece of equipment you could imagine on board. And yet we don't have a tape measure. I thought it was odd."

"Well. Maybe there was one, and it fell overboard."

"Yeah," I say. "Maybe."

She turns away.

"So… Do you know?"

"Yes. Of course I know. But you haven't told me what you want to measure yet."

So then I tell her. About the data, and how all the sharks got ten percent bigger four years ago. Well nine point eight percent bigger.

"So I just want to make a tape measure so I can double check that there isn't a mistake with Chumley. Like the measurements we're reading from him aren't wrong."

Debbie stares at me now, like I've grown a jellyfish on my face.

"How could it be wrong?"

"It probably isn't. But it's the only answer I can think of. And I need a tape measure to check it. And I don't have one."

Debbie turns to go.

"So do you know? How tall you are?"

She stops. "I'm five foot. OK?"

"Five foot exactly?"

"Yes."

"Like properly exactly? I mean could you tell me in centimeters?"

"No! I don't know. I've never had to be a *tape measure* before." With that she stalks off. Which isn't much good to me.

I ask Jason too, because he's quite tall, and maybe he might know, but he just says he's about six foot one. But then I have a better idea anyway. We're not really allowed to access the internet on board, because our connection is by a satellite phone, and it's really expensive, but I look anyway, to see if I can just print off a measuring stick. Only I find you can't, or at least not easily, because the size you see an image that's on a computer screen depends upon lots of factors, like the size of your monitor, so it's not accurate enough.

But then I stop being a complete idiot and realize I can use the monitor itself. I type the brand and the model name into google along with the word 'dimensions' and it tells me exactly how wide and high it is. Both the actual screen, and the screen and the frame around it. So now I have four reliable measurements. I mark those off on a piece of paper, and then I fold it in half at each point, so that I get eight measurements, and from that I make a scale. Then I grab some thin white rope from the storeroom, and I mark that off with measurements all the way up to twenty meters. My very own tape measure.

Next I go to speak with Rosie.

"You want to do what?" She says.

"I want to take the RIB and check the measurements on Chumley."

"Why?"

"I just think we should check it."

"Why?"

I shrug. I don't tell Rosie about the problem in the data, and I don't think I ought to yet. I should let Steve see if he can figure it out first. I mean, it could be really embarrassing for him if it turns out that some of the data he's published is inaccurate. Besides, it's more likely that I'm wrong anyway.

"And how are you going to do it?"

"Well if we just take the boat over to the buoy, and pull it up, I can quickly measure it, and then we'll get it back in position and..."

"Aren't you busy enough? Haven't we given you enough to do?" Rosie breaks into a smile now. She means it to be incredulous I know, and it's not her fault it makes her look so pretty, but it still distracts me.

"Yeah I just... I like to be thorough."

She laughs, and I think she's going to say no. But then she shrugs.

"OK. Well I don't think anyone's using the boat right now. So if it'll make you happy."

So then I go off and get us life jackets, and roll up my rope tape measure ready to use, while Rosie connects the hoist for the rigid inflatable boat or RIB. It's stored on the back of the ship, so there's no chance of the sharks mouthing it to find out what it is, and puncturing it. But it makes it a bit of a hassle to launch.

But when I come back there's a problem. It's Steve – and Dan obviously – it turns out they need to use the boat after all to get over to the island. Steve wants to do some filming close up to the seal colony. Normally Steve would tell us this at breakfast, while he explains the plan for the day, but apparently he didn't this time. It's obviously annoying because it means Rosie and I can't use the boat now after all, and I think Steve senses my disappointment since he comes over to talk with me about it.

"Hey Billy, how's it going?" He looks a bit tired, and it occurs to me that maybe he was up late going over the data, trying to find the error. But he doesn't say anything about it.

"Did Jason get you set up on the drone yet?"

I shake my head.

"Well maybe I'll have a word."

I'm about to tell him that I don't mind, that I've flown my own drone a lot, when he goes on.

"Say, you've got your buoyancy aid on, why don't you come along?"

I'm a bit surprised by this. Since there isn't room for us in the boat when Steve and Dan are filming.

"We're gonna take a little walk through the colony, see what we can see."

"Through the colony? Actually on the island? I thought you said we weren't allowed…"

"We're not allowed. I never said we didn't though. Come along. And I'll grab Jason now to hand over the drone. Bring it along, it's always good to get some extra footage."

I can't help but feel a bit excited. "Really?"

"Sure. It'll be fun."

So then I get in the inflatable boat after all, but not to do what I wanted to do.

THIRTEEN

ROSIE DRIVES THE RIB, while Dan films her closing on the island, and Steve tells me what he's doing.

"We want to grab some shots of the pups close up," he shouts, over the roar of the motor. "While a few still have their baby coats on. It's too dangerous to go when they're all young, since fur seals are so bloody territorial, but now the numbers have thinned out we should be OK. You need to keep your eyes open though, when we're in the colony. You got that?"

I nod. "What do you want me to film?"

"What's that?"

I ask again, shouting this time so he can hear me.

"Oh right, with the drone. Whatever really. Dan'll grab most of what we need, but any aerial footage you can get will work too. Just keep the drone up high, so you're not getting Dan in the shot."

I think about this. I reason that I'll need to keep it flying quite low, and pointing away.

"OK, we're coming into the landing area now." Steve's voice cuts into my thoughts. "Get ready to jump, and don't fall in."

Rosie uses the motor to hold the front of the boat close to the rocks. There's hardly any swell in the neck of Death Alley, but even so the water is sucking and frothing as it rises and falls around the rocks, and it's not easy to step out. Steve goes first, and he's able to wedge his big boots into a couple of cracks in the rock and hold out his hand for me to follow, the drone case on my shoulder. Then Dan follows him, and Rosie backs the boat back out into the water.

"Take the RIB back to the Hunter," Steve shouts to her. "We're gonna be quite a while."

Then we walk a few steps inland. It's so cool. I've been monitoring the seal colony on Lornea Island for years, but they're only common grey seals, and I've never actually gone into the colony, I've always watched through binoculars. Now I'm actually walking through one of the biggest colonies of fur seals, in the whole world. And now there's hundreds and *hundreds* of seals, all around me. The noise is incredible. And the smell is back – Steve was right, we got so used to it from the ship that we didn't notice, but now we're up close it's stronger than ever, a little bit of drying seaweed, but mostly fish guts and seal poop. The rocks are mostly flat, but we have to pick our steps carefully, avoiding walking in front of any of the adults. The seals turn around to watch us as we step past. They don't look totally happy that we're here, but they're kinda lazy too, so while they're bending around to keep their eyes on us as we pass, they're not doing anything more than that.

When we reach one of the higher parts of the rock we stop, and Steve talks with Dan. He tells him to get set up with the tripod, and then he beckons me over to where a seal pup is lying on its own, and watching us. It's probably four weeks old, one of the later ones to be born, and it's still covered in a gray fluffy fur, so that it looks more like a cuddly toy than an actual wild animal.

"Beautiful aren't they?" Steve grins at me. Very carefully he reaches out a hand and, keeping his eyes fixed onto the huge, soft eyes of the seal, he lets it sniff at his fingers.

"Alright buddy. We're not here to hurt you." Steve's voice is soft and soothing. "We're just gonna use you for a few moments. Tell your story." The seal heaves itself forward a little bit, to move away, so Steve pulls his hand back.

Quietly he stands up and turns to Dan. "OK. Let's do it."

Then he squats down again, and Dan drops to one knee to get the camera at the same level.

"Rolling," he says.

"We're here in the largest fur-seal colony in the world..." he begins, in his TV whisper. I sort of tune out and concentrate on getting the drone out of its case, as quietly as I can. I'm a bit worried about the noise when I fire it up, but I'm quite a long way away from Steve now, and he's using the microphone anyway, what with all the noise of the seals around us. So then I take off, and fly low above the colony, using the screen in the controller to see where I am.

"And now we've come across this little fella," I hear Steve continue. "At four weeks old he's already graduated from his mother's milk to fish and squid. Hence why he's all alone here, waiting for his mother to come back and feed him. In itself that isn't unusual, but what he doesn't know, is that when she went into the water earlier today, she had an encounter with one of the many prowling great whites in these waters." Steve twists to face the camera.

"This little pup's mother isn't coming back, which means he faces a slow death by starvation." He stares seriously into the lens.

"OK, got that," Dan calls out, after a few long seconds. Then Steve gets up at once and stretches his legs.

"OK. Get a close up of its eyes will you? Make it look tragic. Then we'll go again." He turns to me.

"So Billy, obviously we don't know if the mother is coming back or not, but we'll cut this in with footage of an adult being attacked in the water. Make it look like that's this pup's mother. So that we're telling a story that's not *literally* true, but that speaks a truth about the lives these animals live."

I nod. I wasn't really paying attention, it's a different drone to the one I'm used to and it takes a lot of concentration to fly so that I don't get into Dan's shot. And the images on the little screen of the controller are amazing, especially the way I can go anywhere I like. But I start to notice that there's not just seals and seal pups and seaweed and rocks on the island, there's a surprising amount of trash too. Plastic and fishing buoys.

Steve crouches down again.

"But as bleak as things look right now for this pup, it's not quite all over yet. Because we've witnessed an incredible behavior among these animals that makes them seem almost human." He stands up and walks a few paces away from the seal, to where another adult is lying. "Once the neighboring parents realize it's been left alone, there's a good chance they might actually adopt him as if he were their own pup."

Steve turns to the camera, still crouched right down by the seals. "At first glance it seems to make no evolutionary sense – why risk your life looking after the genetic offspring of other individuals? But when you consider the wider picture, things come into a different focus. If there's a real possibility of being eaten alive, every time you go out for lunch, it starts to make sense to have a back-up plan for your kids. So you look after your neighbor's pup if the worst happens to them, and hopefully they'll do the same for you..."

"Hey look at that!" I interrupt him. I don't mean to, but there's something I've seen on the screen.

"Billy! What the fuck?" Steve stands up. "What is it?"

I'm closer to Dan, so I turn the controller to show him the screen. The drone's still in the air, hovering over another part of the colony.

"There. That seal's stuck." It's hard to point because both my hands are busy flying the drone, so I fly lower. I descend right over the large male seal, its tail and side flipper completely tangled in the fishing net.

"Shit, is it dead?" Steve asks. But then the seal looks up at the drone, like it's annoyed by the buzzing presence.

"OK. Not dead, but definitely fucked."

"Should we release it?" I ask, and we both look over at where the drone is actually flying. It's probably a half mile away from us, right on the other side of the island. Steve shakes his head.

"Too far away, we can't get there. Too dangerous to cross the whole colony. Even if we could, it's definitely too dangerous to approach an adult male."

I don't reply. But I guess I must have that look on my face.

"It won't be able to swim with that net round it," I say in the end. I pull the drone back, so we can see how it's caught from another angle. "You could probably just cut that line there, and the rest would fall off."

There's silence for a minute. Then Steve swears loudly. "Shit Billy. Alright. All-fucking-right. Dan, you fancy taking a walk?"

Dan's already joined us, but he shakes his head. "Can't get the main camera all that way across these rocks. Besides, don't you want to wait until this one's mom comes back? Finish the adoption narrative?"

Steve looks at the pup he was filming, and the neighbor which has moved away from the noisy humans. He clicks his tongue in irritation.

"You got the handheld camera?"

"In the bag."

Steve nods. Then he makes a decision. "OK. Dan you stay here and get some footage of the pup. Billy, land the drone and grab the hand held cam. We'll *try* and get over there, but I'm not promising. I can't take any risks with you."

So that's what we do. I bring the drone back and land it and pack it away, while Dan gets the handheld camera ready. It's just like a little handy cam, but apparently it's a very expensive one, and Dan makes a big point about how I have to have the carry strap around my neck at all times, in case I drop it. And even then he doesn't look happy. Then me and Steve set off. Without the drone up it's actually very hard to see exactly where to go, and we can't just walk in a straight line, because of the rocks and all the seals lying in the way.

"Stay close Billy," Steve says, when I drop behind a bit. It's amazing as you walk between the seals just how different they are. From a distance they all look black, but closer up there's all sorts of different patterns and colors. It's like when you see a crowd from a long way away, all the people look kind of the same, but if you walk through them you realize they're all individuals. All different.

"Jesus will you keep up? I'm gonna have to tie a rope to you." Steve hisses at me. So I have to catch him up again.

It takes us about twenty minutes to get across the island, and then another ten to find the seal with the fishing net wrapped around it. But then we do, hidden in a little dip. The net of the rope has cut into its skin, so that it's weeping blood. And it seems angry about it. It's making a horrible bellowing sound, and lurching around, every time we try to get close to it. Steve shakes his head.

"This don't look good," he mutters, and I don't think he's talking to me. I start filming anyway, not sure what else to do, but Steve doesn't even seem to notice. He keeps walking around the seal, looking at it from all angles but never getting close. In the end he stops and pulls the diving knife he carries around his leg from the holster. Then he seems to remember I'm here.

"Stay back Billy," he says. He doesn't have his TV voice on now.

He starts whistling tunelessly as he edges towards the back of the seal. The fishing net – blue nylon rope – is bunched up in a big ball on the rocks, and there's only a couple of lines from it that are wrapped around the seal, but they're wrapped around pretty tight.

"Poor bastard must have dragged the whole lot out the water." Steve moves so that he's by the net, and he takes hold of the line to the seal. Gently he lifts it up. At once the animal goes into a huge convulsion, its massive body trying to writhe, but it's constricted from doing so. It lumps back down. If either of us get trapped underneath it would be like being hit by a truck.

"Easy boy, easy." Now we're up close it's clear this is one of the bigger seals we've seen. Easily two meters long and probably 600 pounds. 250 kilos. As Steve edges closer it occurs to me it could easily knock him out, and then I wouldn't know what I'd do. I bite my lip but keep pointing the camera.

Steve moves closer, keeping a close eye on the animal's tail flukes, which are the most likely part to hit him. Then he slides the blade of his knife up the rope, until he's almost touching the animal's side. Then, watching its eyes, he slides the blade under one part of the rope, where it's wrapped around the skin. Then he turns it outward, against the rope, and gently begins cutting. It's lucky the knife is so sharp, and the tough rope just melts from the blade. But there's lots more places where the seal is caught, and some where the rope is deeply embedded into the skin.

A couple of times the seal lurches, still trying to get away, even though Steve is trying to release it. But Steve's able to see it preparing to move by leaning its weight forward, and each time he steps back, and waits for it to subside. And slowly he's able to strip off the main part of the net, until only one section remains, where it's cut into the skin. But he cuts it so he has a free end, and then he nods to me.

"Move back a bit. I'm gonna rip it out."

I don't answer, but I just nod.

And then before I'm really ready, Steve pulls the rope. Instantly the animal convulses with pain, and lets out a roar, and then it pulsates forwards as it turns on Steve, but he's faster. He scrambles away until he's close to me. Then finally the seal quietens down, perhaps understanding that it's free at last. It twists its head and licks at the wound like a dog. Steve scrambles closer to me, then crouches down again. He's breathless as he speaks, and at first I don't realize what he's doing. But luckily I work it out quick enough.

"Even right the way out here, we can't escape from the issue of plastic debris in the waters. This alpha male would have paid the price with its life, had it not been for one of our student helpers, young Billy Wheatley, who spotted it with the drone. It was a long way away and I didn't think we stood any chance of saving it, but he insisted, and as a result..." He beckons to me, and after a moment I realize he means to take the camera. I let him and he turns it around, so now the lens is pointing to me.

"It's got a fighting chance to see another day. Thank you Billy." He keeps filming me a bit longer, then cuts the recording with his thumb.

"Good job Billy. Now let's get the hell out of here."

It's getting dark by the time we get back to the Shark Hunter, so there's no point me asking again to go and measure Chumley, and because it's been a pretty full on and amazing day, I'm relieved to get back to my bunk.

But the next morning it all goes off.

FOURTEEN

It begins as I'm having breakfast. There's a shout from Debbie on the observation deck, because it's her job to check all the equipment, and when she gets to check the feed from the video buoys she notices the problem.

"What's happened to Chumley?" She calls out.

And then, because it's Rosie's watch, she goes over to the screen to see what the issue is, and then I look as well.

The screen's working, and obviously the camera suspended under the camera buoy is working too, because we can see the water. And that looks like it always does in the morning, with the shafts of sunlight shooting through it. But there's no big wooden shark.

"Where the hell is Chumley?" Rosie asks.

We look out to where it should be moored, tethered at the front and the back between two orange buoys. We see at once that they're still in place, and they don't look like they've moved, like the anchors on them have dragged or anything like that. So then we decide to go over in the RIB and see what's happened. And that's actually easier than it would normally be, because Steve decided not to lift the RIB back onto the back of the ship last night when we got back from the island, because it was too late. So then Rosie drives the RIB over there and Debbie and me pull the first of the orange buoys on board the RIB to see what's happened. It's quite heavy, which means the anchor is still in place, but as we get the rope on board we see that the point where Chumley used to be tethered, he isn't.

Instead the loose end of the rope is frayed and hanging loose in the current.

"It must have been bitten through," Rosie says, as she sees it.

"By what?" I ask.

No one answers that.

"But where's Chumley?" Debbie asks.

"It must be tied to the other buoy." Rosie replies. So then we throw the first orange buoy back in the water, and motor over to the second. But when we pull that up we see exactly the same problem. The rope which should be tethered to the front of Chumley is loose, its end twisting in the current.

"It looks cut," I say, the moment we get it on the RIB. I grab it and inspect it. You can see the marks of a serrated edge.

"Bloody hell," Rosie says when she sees too. "To take both ends out – that's almost deliberate. They must have taken against him."

"Who? What?" I ask. I don't know what she means.

"I can see how one side of the tether might have been taken out. That could have been an accident, one of the sharks mouthing a little to see what it was, but both sides. It must have been a deliberate attack."

"Well where is it now?" I grab a scuba mask from the locker under Rosie's seat, press it to my face and use it to peer down into the water. Through the blue clear water I can see the rocks, twenty meters down. The rope of the buoy arcs down to the concrete filled tire of its anchor. I pull my head back out the water, my hair wet now and plastered over my forehead. "I can't see it down there."

"It's got neutral buoyancy, so if it broke free it would have drifted away," Rosie replies. She looks around. "It could be anywhere."

There's a silence on the little boat, then she slaps the inflated tube with her palm.

"*Fuck it!* That's a really big loss. That means we've lost the consistency of having the same measuring system this year." I'm surprised by how mad she suddenly is. I've never seen Rosie angry before this.

We leave the orange buoys in place, but we un-clip the tether lines from the anchor lines, so that we can have a better look at the damaged ends back on the *Hunter*. Half an hour later we're all gathered around them, on the saloon table, and drinking coffee. We've also got Rosie's laptop open and replaying the feed from the camera buoy from last night. Of course it's dark, but we want to see if there's anything we can see, like the flash of a white shark's belly, from when it happened. We watch the whole night on 16X speed, but you can't see anything, the screen is just black the whole time. Until the morning, and then as the water lightens you can see how Chumley is just gone.

"It looks cut to me," I say, looking again at the end of the line. The rope is quite thick, like the stuff that climbers use, and the edges have funny marks on it. Steve inspects it too.

"Wait here," he says a moment later. Then when he comes back he's carrying the jaw from the shark he keeps in his cabin.

"You can identify a shark by its teeth. A mako has long pointed teeth, for catching prey at speed. A nurse shark has rounded teeth for crushing shellfish. But a white shark, like this guy here, see how the teeth are triangular and heavily serrated?" We lean in to see what he's showing us.

"These are teeth designed to saw through meat and bones. To tear away mouthfuls of flesh." He puts the rope inside the mouth and pushes the jaw together so that it clamps down. "And you've got to remember there would be thousands of pounds of pressure." He pushes down harder, and at the same time tugs on the end of the rope, so that it comes away. It kind of looks like the jaw has cut through the rope, even though it hasn't.

"I think from the marks on the rope we can identify this as the work of a white shark." Steve says. And then everyone starts asking him if he's ever heard of this sort of thing happening before – because for all the reputation of Great Whites as attacking humans and boats and things, us scientists know it's not usually true. They much prefer seals. And Steve goes on about how it's possible that one of the white sharks here saw Chumley as a threat, or just got pissed off with seeing it. And how next year they'll need to tether it with steel wire instead of rope. And how they probably were just lucky that this didn't happen before.

And I can't help but notice how well he's taking the loss.

FIFTEEN

I SPEND the morning with the binoculars. I'm supposed to be looking out for sharks, for the population survey, and I am doing it, but at the same time I'm also searching for Chumley. It's occurred to me that it might have washed up in one of the gullies or inlets that make up the rocky shore of the island. But after I've scanned the whole coastline – or at least the part that's visible from the ship – I can't see anything. So then, when I get my half hour for lunch, I go back to the saloon.

Since you don't have to work the entire time you're on the boat, and since we don't have easy access to the internet, Captain Bob has a little library. It's not really a library, it's just a wooden chest with paperback novels and copies of marine biology journals, and a few old magazines like *Surfer* and *National Geographic*. And there's one article I'm looking for in particular. It's one written by Steve a couple of years ago, and it's about here – about Wellington Island and the fur seal colony and how he does this population survey each year of the sharks. I know about it because everyone was looking at it earlier in the voyage, but actually I first saw it two years ago because I subscribe to *National Geographic*. Back then I thought it was super cool. And certainly I never realized how significant it might be.

It doesn't take me long to find, and when I get it I study the pictures. The one I'm looking for shows Steve, with his top off, fixing the tether lines to Chumley on the deck of *Shark Hunter*. You can see Rosie at the other end, and she looks really pretty in a bikini top and white shorts. I remember noticing that when I first saw this article, though back then I never imagined I might get to meet her one day. Anyway, that's not what I'm looking at now. I examine the photo again. They're both standing on the observation deck of the ship, and Chumley is leaning up against the railings. I think for a moment, then pick up my measuring rope from my bunk, and take it, and the magazine, outside. I prop up the magazine sort of where I think the photograph must have been taken from. Then I go and lay my measuring rope in a straight line where Chumley is in the photograph. Then I go back to the magazine, and I check again, and I have to make some adjustments, but in the end I get the measuring rope on the actual ship, exactly where Chumley's measuring marks are on the photograph of the ship. I check to see if they match up.

It's not perfectly exact you understand. I can't tell to the centimeter that it's off. Which is kind of how much I was expecting it to be. But it is off. By nearly half a meter. Ten meters on Chumley is marked off at nine and a half meters on my rope. You can tell because the upright posts that make up the railings are installed at half meter intervals. I check it again, making sure I haven't accidentally run my rope past another of the railing posts. But there doesn't seem to be any doubt. The measurements on Chumley are wrong.

"What are you doing?" Rosie's voice interrupts me. I close the magazine in a hurry and kick my measuring rope out of place. Then I turn to look at her. Her forehead is a little bit wrinkled where she's screwing up her face, and she's still in a bit of a bad mood, like everyone is, because we all know the data we're going to collect this year isn't going to be that good. She doesn't look suspicious at all though. Just curious about what I'm doing. I'm so tempted to tell her, but I know it's Steve I need to speak to, not Rosie.

"Nothing," I say.

Of course he's filming all afternoon with Dan, out in the RIB and then in his shark cage, and over dinner they're busy editing and going over what they've shot, so it's late by the time I knock on his door. Even so, I get the feeling he's been expecting me.

"Billy," he smiles this time and doesn't make any sarcastic comments. "Come in. Sit down."

I do what he says, sitting on the bed again. He shuts the lid on his laptop, then steps out from behind his desk. He pulls the chair out from under the desk and spins it around with one hand, so it has its back towards me. Then he sits on it, backwards, like he's trying to be cool.

"So what can I do for you?"

"It's about Chumley." I say. And then I wait. He waits too, but has to break the silence eventually.

"What about Chumley?"

I pause again, just to make the point.

"He's not as long as you said he was."

Then there's a really long pause before Steve speaks again, and he tries out a weird mix of expressions on his face.

"What makes you say that?" He says in the end.

Then I just hand him the copy of *National Geographic*, folded from where I've been holding it, open on the page with his article. He unfolds it and looks at it for a while, then looks back up at me.

"I measured it. I couldn't find a tape measure so I had to make a measuring rope, and then Chumley went missing, so I couldn't measure the actual Chumley, but in this photograph you can see how long it is against the railings of the ship, so I could put my rope against the railings and work it out. And... and the scale's wrong."

Steve goes back to studying the photograph. Then he tosses the magazine onto the bed beside me, and looks to one side. After a while he turns to look at me again. But neither of us speak. Not for a long time, I just feel his big brown eyes gaze into me. And I just stare back.

Eventually he sighs.

"You ever see *Killer Shark* on NBX?" He says suddenly.

The question surprises me. "That other TV shark show?"

"One of them Billy. One of them."

I don't reply because I want to work out why he's asking this.

"Well? You ever see it?"

In the end I shrug. "Sometimes."

"You like it?"

I shrug again. "Not much. It's a bit..." I can't think of the word.

"Hyperbolic? Overblown?" Steve suggests. "Shite?"

"It's just it... Well they're not actual scientists are they? It's just... sort of an entertainment show."

Steve nods. "Yeah. Russell Owens, the guy that hosts it, he's a total fucking asshole. I met him about seven years ago. We were both holed up in some harbor in a storm. The Caribbean I think. We had a few beers together, we got talking. He seemed real interested in what we did, and I thought we were just chatting. But then a few months later I heard how he'd refitted his boat – daddy's money of course – and talked his way onto the network. Then he started grabbing a big chunk of our ratings."

I frown again. I don't get why this is relevant.

"He took *my* formula, combining the thrill you get from interacting with sharks with real front-line research into how they live…" He locks his jaw for a moment. "And he never bothered with the second part. He just makes out sharks are deadly killers out to get anyone who goes in the water. And that's that." Steve pauses a moment, and shakes his head.

"And the network chiefs, they… here's the thing Billy. They don't really give a shit. That's the hard cold truth of it. There's only one thing they're interested in, and that's *ratings*. A couple of years after Russell came along they wanted to cancel my show. And it was only when I convinced them…"

He looks aside again. Like he wants a way out of telling me this. But he knows there isn't one.

"Which of these sounds more dangerous Billy? A ten meter great white – or a nine meter great white?"

"Well it sort of depends whether they're in a cruising mode or an attack mode…"

"Yeah, OK." He holds up a hand. "You might know that, but what's a regular viewer gonna think?"

I don't answer. I don't really know.

"Bigger is *badder* Billy. The bigger the shark, the bigger the mouth. The bigger the mouth the bigger the *teeth*. It's a no brainer."

"What's a no brainer?"

"The TV guys were gonna replace my show with Russell's. So I went to meet with them. I gave them the full bullshit about how it was important to educate people about sharks and other marine life – because we all have to live on this planet – but I wasn't getting anywhere. You could see it in their eyes. Until I said one thing." He holds up one finger.

"What one thing?"

"I didn't even mean to say it. It just slipped out. I told 'em that with our scientific background we were better placed to track down and film the larger specimens. And they just *jumped* on it."

"What do you mean?"

"They thought I meant *Jaws*. They thought I was telling them I was gonna find the actual Jaws, from the movie. You know, thirty five feet long, made of fiberglass a remote control mouth. That's what they really want. That's all they want. And somehow they got the idea that since we were rooted in science, we could get them the bigger sharks. More *dangerous* sharks. The sharks that people want to watch." He puffs out his cheeks, and then exhales slowly.

"But that's nonsense."

"Yeah it's nonsense. It's total fucking bullshit."

"So what did you do?"

"You know what I did. You just told me what I did. I started finding bigger sharks."

"But how?" I can feel my face is all screwed up from frowning.

It takes him a while to answer. "By then we were already using Chumley. We wanted to bring some kind of rigor to the job of estimating the sizes of sharks. And other people were already doing the same... with their own Chumleys." He tails off. "So I changed the scale."

"You changed the scale?"

Steve nods.

"You faked it?"

He hesitates, but then nods again."

"Oh my God," I say. "You did it four years ago?"

"Yeah."

"And that's why the sharks grew by ten percent that year?"

"Uh huh."

"Or nine point eight percent?"

"If you say so."

"So they didn't *really* grow by that much?"

"No Billy. They didn't."

I'm stunned. After a while I can feel my mouth hanging open, and I quickly close it. I mean I kind of knew this already, but to hear him admitting it is amazing. Shocking.

"But you've written articles. *Papers*. On the population sizes of white sharks. And other species. And it's all based on the data measured by Chumley. The data will be inaccurate."

"Only a little. Not enough to make a real difference."

"But it's still wrong!"

Steve rubs his face. I hear the bristles of his stubble rasp under his fingers.

"I meant to correct it. At first I mean. But then I realized I couldn't. I always had students like you helping to gather the data, and they might notice if the papers we published then used different data. So I had to keep it the way they recorded it. And it... worked!" He shrugs. "I gained a reputation for being able to track down the bigger sharks. I could take it to the TV guys, it *worked* Billy..."

"But."

"No. No buts. It *worked*. The TV guys – they all play fucking golf together – they loved it. I got bigger sharks, they got bragging rights. They put *Shark Bites* in the prime time slots, and we won the war of the ratings against Russell *Fucking* Owens."

I'm silent for a long while.

"But the data is wrong." I say in the end. But Steve snaps right back.

"And if I didn't do it, there wouldn't have been any data at all."

We both stare at each other for a moment, both breathing hard.

"But... I say again."

"No Billy. That's just the way this is."

I don't speak for a while. I'm trying to make sense of this.

"Welcome to the murky muddy world of how science really *fucking* works. I'm sorry it's such a..."

"Does Rosie know?" I interrupt him.

"Huh? *What?*"

"Does Rosie know what you're doing?"

"No. *God no.* No one knows. Rosie? Why the hell would she..." He shakes his head. "Look, *I* repainted Chumley. Alone. I figured if anyone did notice the scale was off, I could just say it was a mistake I'd made. But no one noticed. Least not until you came along."

I think about this. Somehow I'm pleased that Rosie doesn't know.

"And she's not gonna know either," Steve suddenly interrupts me. I look up.

"No one's gonna know."

"Did you cut Chumley loose?"

He looks away, rubbing his chin again.

"Yeah. Rosie told me you wanted to measure it. So I sneaked over last night. I towed it around the other side of the island. Anchored it up there."

I don't reply. I pick up the copy of *National Geographic*. I flick through the few pages of Steve's article.

"It's half a meter Billy. No harm no foul."

"It's not though is it?" I say. "Not if we're *aging* sharks from their length. It doesn't just mean they're a bit smaller than we think, it also means the population is *younger*, and that might have important consequences for the health of the population."

Steve raises his eyebrows at this, but he doesn't reply. Then suddenly he jumps up and walks to the back of his cabin. He opens a cabinet and pulls out a bottle of whisky, and two glasses. Without asking me he pours two drinks and hands one to me.

"I don't like whisky."

"Try it. One day you will."

I take a sniff, it nearly burns the inside of my nose out. I put the glass back down. Steve smiles.

"You know Billy, one lesson I've learned in life is this. There's always something good that comes out of a crisis." He pauses to take a sip of his own drink. "And you know what's good about this crisis?"

I frown up at him, but don't answer.

"You're what, seventeen years old?"

"Sixteen."

"Sixteen? Shit. I didn't know we took kids that age."

I hesitate. Then I tell him. "Actually I'm not sixteen for another month, I just put that I was on my application form, because you had to be sixteen to apply."

Steve considers this for a moment, then he raises his glass in a kind of toast. "Well there you go. Everyone's gotta bend a rule here and there." He shakes his head and seems to relax. "You know Billy, this is the start for you. The beginning. Of your whole *career*, and I can help. You know this... *celebrity* thing, it's bullshit, but it does mean I know folks. In every Marine Bio school in the country. In the whole world come to that. And it's a *very* cliquey world. So your little piece of detective work here has gained you a very powerful ally. It's gonna open a lot of doors." He raises his glass again. "Can we at least toast to that?"

I don't move. And after a few seconds Steve picks up my glass and holds it out for me.

"Come on Billy. This is a fourteen-year-old single malt. I had it shipped in from Scotland and it costs a fortune." He holds it closer, and eventually I take the glass from him. The liquid inside it is golden and so thick it clings to the sides of the glass. I sniff it, and a cough catches in my throat. Steve smiles. Then – I guess I'm curious now – I bring it to my lips and take a sip, and a dribble of fire fills my mouth.

"Atta boy! To your career Billy! To taking a few risks. To grabbing life by the goddamn *balls* and squeezing it tight."

He clinks his glass against mine, and takes a large sip from his glass. I put mine back to my mouth, and pour a proper sized sip in this time. I let it fill into my mouth, and then throw it back, feeling it burn down my throat.

I can still taste the whisky the next morning, when my alarm wakes me for my shift. I swing out of my bunk, making sure not to wake Jason, who has one leg draped over the edge of his bed and is snoring gently. Then I dress as quietly as I can, and slip out into the saloon. Debbie is on the same shift, and she pushes a cup of coffee towards me. Then she says something but I don't hear it, because I'm still thinking about last night.

"I said good morning," she says again.

"What? Oh yeah. Morning."

We don't say anything after that, but both sit and drink our coffee. Normally I'd have a bowl of cereal too, but I don't feel hungry this morning. So when we've finished our coffees we head out onto the observation deck to begin work. The sun hasn't risen yet, but there's already light in the sky. We start monitoring the sharks at sunrise, and go all the way through to sunset. It doesn't matter if we miss some that appear before sunrise, what's important is we follow the exact same methods as previous years, so that the data is comparable. That's why the loss of Chumley is such a blow.

"Shark," Debbie calls out. I look up from the screens and follow her outstretched hand. About twenty five meters away there's a disturbance in the water. It's hard to see anything about it from here, and it's not by any of the camera buoys. But we have the drone ready to fly so I grab the controller, and it buzzes up off the deck. I fly it over the disturbed area. This early in the day, the water's still a bit dark to see clearly, but there's something black floating in the water.

"What's that?" Debbie asks, and I bring the drone lower.

"It's the back half of a seal," she says. We've seen lots of them now, but they still make you feel a bit queasy.

"Go up again, see if we can see what did it." So then I fly a bit higher again, until we see the shadow of a shark turning slow circles around the half-seal. We're all experienced now in seeing what type of shark it is from the outline, and without even checking with me, Debbie writes it down as a male white shark.

"Look, it's still got the other half in its mouth." She notes down the time and nature of the attack on the clipboard, and I bring the drone back.

"Say Billy, did you ever find your tape measure?" She asks, as I plug the drone in to recharge. I shake my head.

"You wanted to check the measurements on Chumley didn't you? Guess there's no point now anyway, what with it getting lost and everything."

I think about this for a moment, it's just occurred to me how I could use the drone to try and find it. But... But what exactly would be the point? I know now that Steve put the wrong measurements on it. The question is what I should do about it.

"I don't get why we need it anyway," Debbie's voice interrupts me. "We should use the drone to measure them. Fly the drone at a known height over every shark that comes in there, and take a picture. We could work out the exact length of all the sharks super easy." She shrugs. I'm quiet for a bit, then I look up at her.

"That's actually a really good idea."

"I know it is. You're not the only smart one Billy."

"No, I mean it's a *really* good idea." I say.

She rolls her eyes. "I said I know. I'm actually gonna tell Steve about it, see what he thinks."

Something about this makes my face drop.

"What?" Debbie asks. "I thought you liked the idea?"

I try to make myself look positive again. "I do."

"Well? What is it then?"

I hesitate. I know I shouldn't say anything. But in the end I can't help myself.

"There's no point."

"What? Billy, are you alright? You're acting super weird this morning," Debbie says. "Even for you."

And then I don't say anything for a while, because I haven't decided if I should say anything to anyone or keep it quiet. And then I know what I'm going to do. I can't not.

"He'll just lie about it anyway."

"*What*? What does *that* mean."

And then I tell her. This early it's just the two of us on the observation deck, so I tell her everything. How I found the inconsistency in the data, and then how I wanted the tape measure as a mistake on Chumley was the only way I could think of to explain the problem. And then how Steve discovered what I was doing and made it look like Chumley was attacked, just to stop me measuring it.

"No way, I don't believe you." Debbie says when I'm finished. And for a while I wonder if it's better, even now, that she believes him and not me. But then I pull out my phone and open up my voice recorder app, and scroll through my recordings until I find the one I made last night, taping Steve as he admitted what he'd done.

"I wasn't sure if he'd admit it or not, so I taped him." I press play, and we both listen to the part where Steve admits to getting up in the middle of the night to hide Chumley. I stop it before he tries to bribe me.

. . .

Debbie's mouth is literally hanging open. Opening and closing like a fish just pulled from the water. "Oh my God. Jesus Billy! What the *actual fuck*?" Debbie says when I stop. "Oh my God!?"

I look at her, I don't say anything.

"What are you gonna do?"

I don't know the answer to this. It's all I've been thinking about since I worked out what's been happening.

"I mean like, if you tell anyone, it's gonna totally *waste* his career. But if you don't, it's like you've uncovered this massive scientific fraud. And you didn't do anything."

She actually smiles as she says this. And I know why. It's because she knows what a massive thing this is, and it's a kind of relief that this is my problem not hers.

"So what are you going to actually do?"

"I don't know."

I spend the whole day thinking about it. On the one hand it's not like he's a *murderer* or anything. On the other hand what he's doing is wrong, and it's totally against the ethos of scientific endeavor. I mean, look at it this way – what if all scientists behaved like Steve? I have this book that Dad gave me for Christmas one year. It's called *On the Shoulders of Giants*. It's all about how all the great scientific advances are built upon other work that other people have done. So that all scientists don't have to start right at the beginning with finding out the boiling point of water, or giving all the fish names. So if Steve's work is based on a lie – even if he thinks it's only a little one, then it still matters. Because we don't know what might be built upon his research. And his little lie will get amplified every time someone builds upon it. And it could bring everything tumbling down.

And it's not as if it's *that* little a lie anyway. Given how we only know the age of sharks from their size, his lie doesn't just affect the shark's size, it also affects the sharks' ages, and from that the whole health of the population. We – all the scientists working in this field – think that the average age of white sharks is actually older than it really is, all as a result of Steve's lying. I don't think I can just ignore that. Even if I wanted to. I don't think anyone could.

The truth is, there's never been any decision to make. All the thinking I've been doing, I realize, it's just because I don't like the conclusion. But there's no decision about what I ought to do, and therefore no decision about what I'm going to do. It's just it makes me sad.

Once I've made the decision I figure I just have to get it over with as quickly as possible. I wait until the day is over, and everyone's gone to their bunks, then I go into the work area and I download my audio clip onto the computer and I compress it down, so it doesn't take as much data to send. Then I write an explanation of what Steve's been doing, and add in the photographs I took of the railing of the ship, with a photo I took of the article in the National Geographic with Chumley. Then I attach two data files, the raw Excel sheet with all the recordings of the shark sizes over the last four years, and a second where I've calculated what the actual sizes should be, in case they want to correct their articles. Then I send it to the *Journal of Marine Biology*, which is where most of Steve's papers on shark population have been published. They're the experts in things like this. They'll know what the right thing to do is.

Then I do nothing. The next day it's like nothing happened at all. Steve doesn't say anything, but he's friendly and a bit more attentive than normal, even though he's still doing lots of filming. I work my shift, trying to avoid talking too much to Debbie, and then afterward I hang around on the observation deck, and then it's my turn to cook dinner. And then I go to bed early. But the day after that things go crazy.

SIXTEEN

I'M ALMOST FINISHED with my morning watch when Captain Bob comes to find me. His face is a weird kind of white color, even through his tan.

"Billy, you need to come with me," he says. "I don't know what you've done, but Steve is saying he wants to throw you overboard."

We'd had a busy morning – busier because we still don't have Chumley to help us estimate the sizes of the sharks – and I'd almost forgotten what had happened, so I feel my lips curl up in a bemused smile.

"I'm not kidding, and I don't think he is neither. He's raging mad. What'd you do?"

I don't get the chance to tell him, since then Steve comes around the corner.

"Where the fuck is that *fucking* kid?" He sees me as he speaks, and then lunges towards me. Bob is quick to move his body across mine.

"Whoa there Steve, think what you're doing."

"Let me at the little *fuck*."

I try to shrink back out of the way, but there's nowhere to go on the ship, and I'm not going to go in the water, we've just seen the biggest female white shark we've yet seen, and her hunt wasn't successful this time.

"*Steve!*" Bob says. "You need to calm down. What the hell is this all about?"

Steve doesn't reply. He just stands there, too close and with his chest heaving up and down. "Ask the fucking kid."

Then he turns and stalks away. He slams the door frame with his palm as he walks through it, and then he's gone.

So then everyone is looking at me, standing right at the back of *Shark Hunter*, with Bob still standing in front of me.

"What did you do Billy?" Rosie asks, her face white with shock. I feel myself thinking it's unfair the way she says it. As if she's blaming it on me. I look at the others, they all look totally confused, except Debbie. She looks scared.

"Steve was lying about the sizes of the sharks. Exaggerating how big they were." I say.

There's a silence. Then Rosie starts shaking her head.

"What?" Her forehead creases in a frown. "What are you talking about?"

I don't reply, and she goes on.

"How could he? When we were making the observations? And anyway *why* would he? What would be the point?"

"He says it was to make the TV series more exciting. People like bigger sharks."

Rosie starts to answer this, but then she stops. She screws up her face.

"But *how* could he? The observations, we made them."

So I explain. About how he changed the markings on Chumley. There's silence again when I've finished. Like everyone is stunned.

"So what did you *do*?" Rosie says after a while. So then I go on to explain how I sent an email to the editor of the *Journal of Marine Biology*. How it was the only responsible thing to do.

"Jesus Christ," Rosie says to that. "You've fucking ruined him."

After that Captain Bob takes over. He takes me to his cabin and he locks the door. He tells me how I have to keep out of Steve's way, and he'll try to calm him down. And then he's gone for a long time, but after a while I can hear shouting from somewhere else on the boat. Eventually Captain Bob comes back.

"We need to get you off the boat Billy," he says. "You're not in danger, Steve isn't going to throw you overboard anymore, but..." He hesitates just long enough to sigh, "he's refusing to let me take you back to the mainland. So I've put out a call on the radio to see if there's any other boats nearby that'll take you. And you're in luck, there's a Swedish couple on a yacht that's only a couple of hours away. They're on a passage to Port

George, you can get a bus from there to Melbourne and the airport. You'll have to figure the rest out yourself."

"What about the study? I'm supposed to be here for three more weeks, doing the shark population survey?"

"I think we can safely say that's over. For you at least. I don't know if we're gonna stay to complete the work. I don't know anything right now, except I need you off my ship to avoid a murder."

"But..." I think about this. "Who's going to go with me?"

"No one's going to go with you."

"But..." I stop. Suddenly I've run out of questions.

"You better go and pack your stuff ready for when they get here. I just hope it's soon enough before Steve changes his mind again."

Captain Bob escorts me from his cabin to the front of the ship where my bunk is. On the way we pass Rosie in the corridor. Her eyes are red, like she's been crying. I open my mouth to speak to her, but I don't know what to say, and anyway she turns away, like she won't listen.

When we get to my bunk Bob turns, to leave me there alone.

"Aren't you going to wait with me?" I ask. "In case Steve tries to throw me overboard?"

He thinks about it for a moment.

"Just pack your stuff Billy."

So I do what he says. Shoving all my clothes into my backpack, and powering down my computer, which is charging on my bunk. When I look up I see Jason standing in the doorway.

"I guess you can have the bottom bunk now," I say to him. It's kind of a joke, but he doesn't laugh. Instead he shakes his head.

"Dick move, Billy." He says. "Fucking dick move."

SEVENTEEN

I WAIT BACK in Captain's Bob's cabin while he logs onto the internet and looks for a ticket back from Australia to the United States. I don't have any money, so I'm worried about how I'm going to buy it, but he says I shouldn't worry, and he'll sort it out. And when that's done he goes out, so I just sit there, watching out of his little window. After an hour I see the sail of a yacht on the horizon, and slowly it comes closer. Finally the sails come down, and I see a woman on the deck, staring over at us. Then Captain Bob comes back to the cabin, unlocks the door, and leads me out onto the deck.

I'm surprised because everyone's there. It's like I'm the entertainment. Even Steve, and I get the sense that everyone is kind of on his side, which seems pretty unfair, given how I didn't do anything wrong.

It's Steve himself who insists on driving the RIB to take me over to the Swedish yacht. I can see how Rosie and Captain Bob don't like the idea, but he waves them away. So a little bit nervously I step into the boat and Jason lowers my giant backpack behind me. Without a word Steve fires the motor and flicks the painter clear. He puts loads of power down, pushing a huge vee into the water and making the bow rear right up, so I have to hold on really tight. Then we plane super fast toward the yacht and he doesn't even look at me. It's far too noisy to talk. Then, just before we're going to smash into the side of the yacht he throws the throttle into reverse, so we stop in our own length. It's really reckless driving.

On the yacht there's a man and a woman, both in their sixties. You can see on their faces how curious they are, about what's going on, but they don't say anything, except how we should pass my bag up. I'm nervous as I stand in the RIB, to pass it up, because Steve could easily fire the motor again, and I'd lose my footing. But he doesn't. And then it's my turn to climb up after my bag. Still Steve hasn't said a word, and I look at him now, thinking he must want to say something, and this time he meets my eye. His jaw is set hard, and his eyes don't waver as he stares at me. But still he says nothing. I turn back to the yacht, and climb aboard. By the time I've finished shaking the hands of the Swedish man and his wife, Steve's spun the RIB around and is already speeding back to the *Shark Hunter*.

The Swedish couple are called Eric and Agnes and they're really nice, especially Agnes. She tells me how Eric used to work in insurance, and she was a teacher in a primary school in Gothenburg, but now they're retired and sailing around the world. I was a bit confused at first, since I thought Gothenburg wasn't a real place, but where Batman lived. But then we worked out it wasn't Gothenburg but Gotham City, and she thought that was really funny. Then she told me lots of stories about their trip, about how they were really worried about pirates in the Malacca straights, and how they nearly got shipwrecked in a storm off the coast of Kerala in India. Eventually she asked me about what happened to me on *Shark Hunter*, and I told her the whole story. Then she frowned a lot, and didn't say much for a while.

Eventually she asked if I was tired, and said I could lie down in the bunk in the forepeak. Because they don't have guests on the boat much they use that cabin for storage, but she makes me a bed in among the spare sails and supplies. Then, when I wake up, we're really close to land, and I help out on deck getting the fenders ready.

Agnes takes me in a taxi to the bus station, and she waits until the bus to Melbourne comes up. A local lady explains to us how I have to get a second bus to the airport, and it's pretty easy to just follow her instructions. Then at the airport I just have to go to the Qantas desk, and there's a ticket waiting for me. Actually it's two tickets, the first to Los Angeles, and then another one to Boston.

It takes thirty eight hours in total before I get back to Boston, and from there I have to get another bus down to the ferry terminal, and then wait another four hours before the boat leaves back to Lornea Island. And then I have to get another two buses on the island, the first to Newlea, the capital of Lornea Island, and that feels weird, because normally it feels like quite a big place, but after all the travel it suddenly feels really small. Then I catch the local bus that stops at the end of my road in Littlelea. Finally, almost three days since I waved goodbye to Agnes, I'm outside my front door, and fitting my key into the lock.

EIGHTEEN

IT'S REALLY hard to stop myself calling out to Dad, even though I know he's not here. But I don't, and instead I just pause and listen. The whole house is cold and quiet. Dad knows what happened now. He actually offered to come back with me, but I told him not to, because it's important he stays to work on the new *Blue Lady II*. She's still on the mainland, in a boatyard there, and Dad's saving money by working on the fitting out himself. It's only a few weeks before he's back, and I told him I'd be OK, and I had lots of school work to catch up on anyway. But I don't do that straight away. Instead I dump my backpack in the kitchen and go upstairs for a bath. Until I remember that there's no hot water. There's no food in the refrigerator either, so I heat up some beans from the cupboard. Then I wait for an hour and have another go at a bath, but the water still isn't hot, so I only sit in it for a little while before I get cold and have to get out. Then I just give up and go to bed.

It's weird waking up the next morning. Obviously I know where I am, but it still feels wrong. Too quiet I suppose. And still. I guess I'm just disorientated after all the traveling, and before that being on the ship with lots of people everywhere and Jason sleeping in the bunk over my head. Here I might be at home, but I'm completely alone.

I don't get up for ages. There doesn't seem to be any point. I'm signed off school – Dad said I should phone them and explain what's happened, and see if they'll let me back early. But I don't do that. Instead I search the house for food again, and in the end I give up and catch the bus into

Silverlea. There I go to the store and I buy as much food as I can get in my backpack. Then I bring it home and decide to watch TV, but I see that *Shark Bites* is on, just an old one on repeat. And then I can't *not* watch it, because I know all the people on it now, except it's a different group of students. I see how well Rosie gets on with them, and that makes me feel rotten. So I go back upstairs and run a bath again. And this time the water is actually *really* hot, because I forgot to turn the water heater off, which would make Dad mad if he was here. But he isn't, so I have a really full bath, and when I eventually get cold, I just let some of the water out the plug and turn the faucet on again to top it up. But then I end up all wrinkled. So I have to get out. And even though it's still early I go to bed and sleep again.

On the third day I decide to do something more useful than eating and sleeping and having baths. So I call Amber. I figure she'll want to know what happened, and she'll probably be quite pleased that I'm back, because I can help her with the job of sorting out the old *Blue Lady* and putting her up for sale. I dial her number.

"*Billy!*" It's nice to hear her voice. "How you doing? I mean..." She stops and changes to a really bad Australian accent. "*G'day mate. How's it hanging down under?*"

"I'm not there. I'm back."

"What? Oh." Amber switches back to her normal voice. "Why? What happened? You didn't do something terrible did you?"

"*No.* I didn't do anything. Well I didn't do anything terrible." So then I tell her what happened, and about what Steve was doing. And because it's Amber I give her the longer version, because I know she'll want to know everything. But then half way through my explanation she stops me and asks if I can hurry up a bit.

"Why?"

"Nothing, it's just you've caught me right in the middle of something."

"Oh." I say. "What?"

"Nothing. I'm just... I'm just with someone, that's all."

So then obviously I have to ask who.

"*Billy!*" Amber says.

"What? Who are you with?"

She doesn't answer that. "Look, I'll call you later," she says instead. Then she adds: "I'm sorry it didn't go well with the shark guy. I'll call you later." And with that she calls off. So then I don't know what to do. After a while I make myself a really large sandwich, and then I feel a bit sick so I have another bath.

I wait that evening for Amber to call, and even though I check my phone to make sure it's not stopped working, she doesn't call. I mess around on the internet for a bit, and then I go to bed.

The next morning when I wake up I'm determined to do something more useful, and I decide to ride my bike down to Holport where the *Blue Lady* is moored. I can make sure nothing's happened to her while I was away, and see if Amber's made any progress with cleaning her up for selling. So that's what I do.

It's nice to get out of the house, and it's nice to remember that Lornea Island is actually a really nice place, even if it's not as hot and the colors aren't as bright as Australia. Actually the colors here *are* pretty spectacular. We've got all the fall colors here with the leaves turning into thousands of different shades of orange in the trees. And when I ride down the hill into Holport it looks small and familiar and homey, because I've been here hundreds of times before. I punch in the combination at the gate on the pontoon, and then push my bike as I walk out, because the security guards don't like it if I cycle.

Blue Lady is in the last berth, right at the end of the pontoon, because that's the cheapest one you can get without having to get a mooring. When I get there she looks fine, pretty much exactly as when I last saw her, but I hoist my bike onto her little stern platform anyway and pull out my keys to open the cabin.

She feels small after spending so much time on *Shark Hunter*. And she smells a bit musty inside, but everything is in order, and Amber's done a good job tidying. I begin to feel a bit foolish for coming all the way out here for nothing. But then I notice something a bit strange – we've got a new neighbor. For ages the berth next to ours belonged to an old guy who kept his fishing boat there. But then he died from a stroke, and his family sold the boat, so there was a space next to us. But now there's a yacht parked there. I didn't register it as I wheeled my bike past – probably because I was checking how *Blue Lady* looked. But now I look at it, and I see it's a bit familiar. I have to think hard to work out why. But then I realize. Ages ago – when I was photographing the octopus – it was the boat that belonged to the guy who was spear fishing in the marine reserve. At least, I think it is. It certainly looks like it. Because I want to make sure, I walk out of the cabin for a better look.

And that's when I see that someone's actually living on board. You can always tell – boats that are empty have covers over everything, and they're all boarded up and dark. But this one has washing strung out on the guard rail, and a large red towel hung over the boom. And now I listen I can hear music too, coming from the yacht's cabin. I look at the name on the front, and sure enough the name painted there is *Mystery*. That looks a bit shabby too. Like the rest of the yacht. I frown. I feel quite bad about this. Like this is all I need.

I'm still feeling annoyed as I make myself a cup of coffee and turn on my laptop – not for any particular reason. I can get the internet on board *Blue Lady* because I tether my cell phone to my laptop. I couldn't do that in Australia, because we didn't have a cell phone signal out by Wellington Island, and even if there had been, it would have cost a fortune. But then I don't know what to look at online. So I shut it down again and drink my coffee. I did think I might end up sleeping on board *Blue Lady* tonight, because we have a little bedroom set up, and there's always some dried packet food in the galley. But I'm not sure I want to now, knowing that the other boat is right next door, with that man living on it. So that means I now have to cycle back quite soon before it gets dark. And it's mostly uphill on the way back. So even though I'm feeling a bit sorry for myself now because everything keeps going wrong, I still wash up my coffee cup, and make everything tidy, ready to leave. Then I hoist my bike back onto the pontoon and leave it there while I lock the cabin door. Then I climb off the *Blue Lady* and start to wheel my bike back up the pontoon. But then just as I'm passing the new yacht I get unlucky again. Because a man bursts suddenly out of the cabin.

He can't not see me, and I can't not see him. And that interrupts what he's doing, which seems to be laughing and being chased. And because I interrupt him doing that he looks a bit surprised and even a bit embarrassed. But only for a moment, before the person who was chasing him comes out of the cabin too. And then I'm the one who's surprised. Really surprised.

"Amber?" I say. And she stops laughing too.

NINETEEN

"BILLY! WHAT ARE YOU DOING HERE?" Amber stops. Her face, which was full of smiles as she climbed out of the yacht's cabin is suddenly white. It's like I'm her mom and I've caught her doing something bad.

"What do you mean? I told you I was back."

"Yeah but... You didn't say you were coming *here*."

"I wanted to check the boat." I think for a second. "What are *you* doing here?" That seems to me to be the more pertinent question. She looks suddenly embarrassed. And then the man answers before Amber anyway.

"You're Billy? *The* Billy?" His accent takes me right back to when I saw him before, spear fishing in the reserve, but this time he's not angry and his smile is different.

"You work with Amber? On the *Blue Lady*?" His whole face seems to smile with him, and I can see – even though it annoys me a bit – that he's very handsome. "Amber has told me everything about you." He glances across to her, and smiles again. I sense he's both comforting her and teasing her at the same time. "I mean *everything*. Amber never shuts up about you."

She pushes him now, from behind. "Shut up Carlos." But he just laughs. "I mean every *little* thing. The way he says it, it rhymes with beetle. He grins again, until she pushes him harder.

"Seriously. *Shut up*." Amber looks miserable, and she won't meet my eye. There's a moment of awkward silence, but then he seems to smile his way through it.

"No I really mean it. She told me how you have the boat together, and how you run a business. And how you find whales, even when no one else can find them. That's super cool man. Super cool."

He reaches over from the cockpit of the yacht to shake my hand. And he fixes me with his eyes until I do so. Dark eyes that seem to compel me to do what he wants. I move across and shake his hand.

"I'm Carlos," the man says. He rolls the 'r' in his name so that it burrs. *Carrrrrrrlos.*

I look again at Amber, but she's got her head hung down now.

"Say, we were just gonna have a beer." Carlos says. "Why don't you jump up and have one too? If you're not doing anything I mean..?"

I look at my bike. If I don't go soon it's going to get dark. And though I have lights the roads aren't safe for cycling after dark. "No, I have to..." I stop, as an idea hits me. "Say, Amber have you got your car here? Could I maybe get a lift? When you go home?" If I can get a lift I won't have to cycle up the hill. But Amber doesn't answer. She looks embarrassed instead.

"What?" I ask, since I don't understand the way they're looking at each other.

"Hey, nothing man," Carlos waves a hand to dismiss any problem. He turns to Amber. "We can run him home later on, can't we babe?"

Babe? – He says the word so casually I almost miss it. But obviously I don't, because no one has ever called Amber babe before, without her hitting them. I stare at him, and then at Amber. She pushes him on the shoulder again and looks like she wishes she was a hundred miles away. In the end she turns to look at me and rolls her eyes.

"What?"

I don't reply.

"Oh for fuck's sake. I'll run you back Billy. Just stop looking at me like that."

So then I don't have any other choice, even though I think I'd rather not have a beer. I put my bike back onto *Blue Lady* and when I've locked it safely I climb onto the yacht. I seem to spend half of my time on yachts these days. Both Amber and Carlos have already gone below, but I can hear them talking, and the yellow glow from the lights looks quite welcoming.

"Come on down Billy, it's cold out there." Carlos calls to me, his voice friendly now. I climb into the cockpit and look down into the cabin. It looks cozy down there, but it's a lot less tidy than Eric and Agnes' yacht that I sailed on in Australia. There's a funny smell too, though I'm not sure what.

"Come on, get down here," Carlos says again, clearing some space on one of the bench seats. So I climb down the ladder and sit down next to Carlos. Amber is half sitting, half-lying on the other side, and she sits up too.

"Have a beer," Carlos says. He reaches into a cupboard behind his seat and pulls out a bottle. It's funny, I never really drank beer before Australia, now I quite like the taste.

"So..." Carlos says. "Amber was telling me you were over in Oz, but had to come back?" He waits.

"Yeah," I say in the end. "I never really explained the whole story though."

"Something about the wrong size sharks?"

"Yeah."

Carlos raises his eyebrows, and stays quiet. And then I start to explain what happened. It's a bit weird, even though I've never met Carlos before – apart from when he was spear fishing – he seems a lot more interested than Amber does, and he asks really sensible questions, and he seems to know quite a lot about sharks too. I'm kind of surprised by that, given what happened when I first met him. And by mistake I sort of tell him that, which makes him confused.

"How do you mean?" he says, his accent suddenly stronger. "Have we met..?"

"Well not met exactly. But in the nature reserve..."

"Huh?" He leans forward, suddenly he seems quite agitated.

"You were spear fishing in the reserve. And I stopped you."

He frowns deeper, and then slowly it must dawn on him. "That was *you*? You were that kid!" He bursts out laughing. "Oh man! You were that kid!" And Amber doesn't know what he's talking about, so he explains it for her, even though she's being so weirdly sulky.

"I tried to do some fishing. When I first arrived. I didn't even know I was inside a nature reserve. Billy here put me right. He scared the shit out of me in the process though." He laughs again, as if this is the funniest thing ever, and both me and Amber look at him as if this is all getting a bit weird.

"So anyway," Carlos continues once he's calmed down. "You were telling me how this guy had the wrong measurements on the sharks, and you figured it out."

"Yeah," I continue my story, explaining about Chumley and how Steve needed bigger sharks for his ratings. Carlos listens intently, and it's obvious he's paying more attention than Amber did the other day, but then he suddenly hunches forward and leans over the table. From the mess everywhere he pulls out a metal box and pops off the lid.

"Go on," he says, since I hesitate a bit. Inside I see something strange. There's a packet of tobacco in there and rolling papers, plus a bag of some dried green plant.

"So how did you get off the ship? This *Shark Hunter*?"

"Err..." I try to keep talking, but now I'm watching him as he pulls out three papers, deftly licks one of them and joins it to the other two. I guess I must go quiet after that because he looks up again and smiles.

"Do you smoke, Billy?" he asks.

"Err..." I say again, and then Amber opens her mouth. It's the first thing I've heard her say. "Hey... Maybe you shouldn't..."

"It's alright," Carlos cuts her off with another grin, which he turns back onto me. "Billy doesn't mind, do you Bill?"

I don't get the opportunity to answer this, and I don't know what I'd say even if I did. Instead I watch his fingers as they work. I guess he's concentrating, because he doesn't seem to notice that we've all gone quiet. I don't think Amber likes the silence, because she's the next one to speak.

"Is your Dad back?"

I'm surprised by the question. I thought she already knew.

"No. He's still on the mainland. He's working on the new boat."

"When's he back?"

"Few weeks."

The silence comes back. Really I want to ask *her* questions, like what the hell she's doing on this boat, and why this guy called her babe and she didn't punch him in the face. And if she's just going to sit there while he takes *drugs*. The thing is, I can't. I can't ask her any of that.

Carlos pulls out the bag of marijuana – I know what it is – and he opens it. He pulls out a pinch of the dried plant and tears little pieces off, then he sprinkles them along the length of the papers he has laid out in front of him. I can smell it, it's really strong. I realize now, that's what I smelt when I first stepped into the cabin, I just didn't recognize it.

"You ever been to Europe Billy?" Carlos looks up suddenly and smiles at me. I have to look away from his hands really fast.

"No."

He goes back to his work, and then because I can't just leave a long silence I ask him:

"Is that where you're from?"

"Yeah." He leans back and picks up the joint with both hands, then he rolls it into a tube and licks the glued edge. He twists it, and moments later he's tapping a perfect little cylinder on the top of the table.

"Yeah, my dad comes from Genoa. It's a city in Italy, on the west coast. He has a factory there where they make metal things, you know – parts for motors. But my mother comes from Barcelona. So I am fifty percent Italian and fifty percent Spanish." He chuckles. "And maybe ten percent crazy no?" He looks up at Amber and smiles. So then I have to ask something else.

"What does she do?"

"What? Who?"

"Your mom?"

"Oh!" He looks pleased with the question. "She is an artist."

He glances at Amber again.

"Like Amber, only not so good."

I feel a bit awkward hearing that, since Amber isn't an artist. She is studying design, but it's hardly the same thing.

"Yes. It's true. She makes pottery and glassware, and also some paintings. She sells to the tourists that come every year. She has a little studio off Las Ramblas. It's very cool." Then he seems to have an idea. "Hey I can show you? If you like. If you come with me, next year?"

For a moment I think the offer is aimed at me, but then I see from how Carlos twists around in his seat and looks at Amber that he means her. He gives her a really broad smile now and I watch as her face changes from looking annoyed to biting the corner of her lower lip. It's a gesture I've seen lots before. She only does it when she likes the sound of something. But she doesn't reply.

"Do you know Las Ramblas Billy?"

I frown. Annoyed that I don't know what he's talking about.

"It's a street in Barcelona. A very famous street. You can see everything there. Arts, fabulous architecture. Entertainment, shopping. You'd love it."

"Oh," I say, dubious about this. I don't even *like* any of those things. But I don't answer. I'm more interested to know what he meant by if Amber comes with him next year.

"What are you…" I start. I'm trying to think of a polite way to ask what he's doing here, and when he's going to leave, but I'm distracted by him tearing a corner off a magazine cover and rolling it into a tiny tube, and then inserting it into one end of the joint. I didn't know they did that.

"What are you… like how did you get here?" I ask in the end. It's not quite what I meant to ask.

"I sailed here."

"What do you mean?"

He shrugs. "I sailed here."

"You *sailed* here?"

"That's it."

"What, like all the way here?"

"No Billy," Amber cuts in and I hear the sarcasm in her voice. "He sailed half-way here, and he's still out in the middle of the Atlantic."

I glower at her but Carlos seems to find this an awesome joke. But then he goes on like he hasn't heard her at all. "Yeah. I came out the trade route. Out of the Mediterranean and down to the Canary Islands. Then across with the north east trade winds." He looks up and smiles. I can't help but look around. It's quite a small boat to cross a whole actual ocean. And he's not very old either, I mean older than me but not by that much. As I look he balances the joint on his lower lip, so that it hangs down, and then picks up a closed Zippo lighter. He flicks his arm, faster than my eye can follow, and suddenly it's open and there's a flame standing upright, bright and steady. He puts it to the end of the joint and it crackles and glows orange and white. He snaps the lighter off.

"Did you come straight here?" I ask. I'm sort of mesmerized by the drugs, but I'm also interested now. I mean Lornea Island is very nice and everything, but it's a long way to come from *Europe*.

"No. I crossed to the Caribbean. Hung around there for a while. Then I've been working my way up north. I planned to cross back on the northern route before it got too late in the year, but the weather set in early. So now I'm kinda stuck here until the spring." He shrugs, and then takes a deep draw on the joint.

"Stuck here till the spring?" I repeat.

"Yeah. I have to wait until the weather gets better. Don't want to get caught in a hurricane."

His eyes go wide as he's saying this. Like a hurricane is some sort of bogeyman.

"So you're staying here until the spring? Aren't you going to go home, and wait there?"

Carlos laughs. Then waves an arm around the boat's cramped interior. "I am home. This is where I live, man."

I look around the boat again. This time I notice details. The rug he has on the floor, the line of jars – peanut butter, chocolate spread – in the galley. He's got a Samsung phone, just like mine.

"And what a place to get stuck huh?" His voice cuts across me. "*Lornea Island*. I swear I never even heard of it until I saw it on the chart."

The way he says it, it sounds like he doesn't like it very much.

"There is one good thing though, about getting stuck." He looks across to Amber and raises his eyebrows. She sees and rolls her eyes a bit. But though she's trying not to show it, I can tell she wants him to go on. "Because otherwise I wouldn't have met Amber here." He smiles again and then offers the joint across to me, holding the lit end upwards. I totally wasn't expecting that.

"Erm. I don't…" I say, or something like that.

"Go on."

"No I…" I sense that Carlos finds it funny how uncomfortable I suddenly am.

"You sure?" He's still leaning across the cabin holding the joint out to me. "It's really good stuff. I got it from this guy in a bar in town here. It's OK for a place like this."

"No thank you. I don't do… drugs." I say, in the end. I wince a bit at how it must sound. But I'm not gonna start taking drugs just so I don't sound uncool.

"Hey don't worry man." He pulls the joint back, takes another draw on it, and then exhales a big cloud of blue smoke. "Best way to be."

Then he surprises me again by holding out the joint to Amber. I mean it's not *that* big a surprise, or at least not that he offers it. The surprise is that she takes it. She actually hesitates for a few seconds, then gives a bit of a sigh and takes it from his fingers. I really have to bite my lip to stop myself calling out to her.

"It's alright Billy," she tells me in an irritated voice. "It's only a bit of dope."

I don't reply – I don't think I can. Instead I try not to watch, but I can't help seeing how she puts the joint in her mouth and sucks some in. Carefully, trying to look natural.

"So what did you think of Australia?" Carlos asks suddenly.

"Huh?"

"Down under. What did you think?"

I don't know what he means. I've just explained to him how everything went totally wrong.

"Apart from the shark thing I mean."

It's really hard to concentrate, since I'm still watching Amber handle the joint.

"What did you think of the people?"

"Sorry?"

"I'm thinking of sailing there. Next year. Just… keep going, after I cross back to Europe. Just keep going." He shrugs. "It's amazing, people think it's such a big deal to cross an ocean but it's not so hard…" He talks some more but I stop listening now. I can tell some people would think he's charming, but I think I've decided now. On balance there's just something about Carlos that I don't like. And now he's just annoying me.

"When did you say you were going home Amber?" I ask suddenly, and she jerks her head around to scowl at me, like I'm the one being rude.

"What?"

"You said you'd give me a lift. Once we'd had a beer. Well I've finished my beer, and it's probably best if you don't smoke too much drugs before you drive. So I'm asking if you're going home soon?"

I catch her, glancing at Carlos, and I see him smirk. I don't know exactly what it means, but he doesn't try to hide it, and I decide I don't really care what he thinks. He's the kind of guy who goes spear fishing in a marine reserve. And smokes drugs.

"I wasn't going…" Amber starts to say, but then she stops herself before I know what she meant to say. Then she takes a really deep breath, and she even smiles a little bit. "Fuck's sake, Billy," she says in a voice a little more like she normally sounds. "Come on, I'll give you a lift home."

She looks at Carlos again, shakes her head and passes him back the joint. For a moment I see something pass between them. And then she gets up.

TWENTY

IT TAKES ages to actually leave. First Carlos seems to think he's going to come with us, even though I don't want him to, and there's no point because then Amber would have to come back here and drop him off, before going home – and also because there's no room for him and my bike. And then it takes ages to get the seat down in Amber's car, which is only small, and fit my bike in, because we don't have the tool to take my wheels off. But finally we fit it in, and me and Amber get in the car.

"So," I ask as she starts the motor. "What are you playing at?" I try to keep the anger out of my voice.

"I'm giving you a lift home?" She replies, not looking over.

"I don't mean that. I mean hanging out with that... that..."

"With *Carlos*? Is that what you mean?" Now she looks.

"Yeah."

"What's wrong with him?"

The list is so long I don't know how to answer. I start with the obvious. "Smoking *drugs*?"

"Oh grow up Billy. It's just a bit of dope. I've been smoking it for years."

"*What*? When?"

"When you're not looking. I do have other friends you know."

I shake my head at this. For a start it's not actually true.

"You know, in my class. At college." Amber graduated last year so we're not together at Newlea High School any more.

"You smoke drugs at college?"

"Not *at* college Billy."

"Well where then? You can't do it at home. Your mom would kill you, especially with your sister…"

"Oh for God's sake Billy, does it matter?" This silences me. And we sit like that for a long while, pulling up the hill out of Holport. At least I don't have to cycle up it.

"Babe?" I say, when we've driven a few miles. "So is he like…" I don't want to say it. "Is he like your..?"

"I'm dating him Billy. If that's what you're asking"

Dating? Amber?

She carries on. Unusually for her she's going quite slowly. I wonder if it's because she's worried about being affected by the drugs.

"Where did you… How did you…?" I don't seem to be able to finish any of my questions. I could be affected too. I could definitely smell the smoke so some must have got inside me.

"When I was sorting out the *Blue Lady*. Carlos was in the berth next door. We got chatting."

"What about?"

"Just *chatting* Billy. The way people do. Some people."

I ignore this. "Does your mom know?"

"Course she does." Then she sighs at me. "It's cool Billy. Honestly. We're just… having a bit of fun."

I can't help wondering what exactly that means. I've already seen it involves drugs.

"Has she met him?"

"Who?"

"Your mom?"

"What? *No!* Jesus can you just drop it? We've only known each other a few weeks. We're not exactly at the meeting each other's parents stage."

"But he said he was going to show you his mom's studio? In Barcelona?"

"He was just… It's just a thing." She leaves that hanging for a while, but then explains. "He said when he sails back next year I should come with him. You know, for the adventure. I always wanted to see Europe."

I consider this for a while. "But what about your college course?"

"I don't know."

"How long will it take? How much would you miss?"

"I don't *know* Billy. It's just… talk at the moment. You know, we're feeling each other out."

The expression brings a horrible image to my mind and I turn to look at her. I know she sees it too and keeps her eyes on the road. "I didn't mean *that*."

There's a silence between us, and I watch the trees go past in the dark, out of the window.

"I am eighteen," she makes me look at her again. "It's not exactly unheard of for eighteen year olds to be dating."

"I know."

"And the only reason I *don't* date much is because the guys on Lornea Island are so fucking weird." She glances across at me, then snorts a little laugh. "And because I spend all my time with you."

I'm about to protest that she doesn't have to spend time with me, it's just that we both help Dad run the whale watching business, when she carries on.

"I thought you'd be happy for me."

"I am." I say. "Happy for you." Even though I can tell I'm not really.

"I can't exactly date you, can I!" Amber jokes. But neither of us laugh.

Finally, as we get to my house Amber asks me what I'm going to do. I think she means right now at first, but then I see she's talking about more generally.

"I suppose I'm going to call the school, tell them I'm back early," I say. "Go back to class."

"Yeah. You should," Amber says, and then we're both silent for a few seconds, before she pushes open the door.

We have to wrestle to free my bike. Then I don't ask her, but I kind of expect she's going to come in – I don't know why, it's just that she normally does. She knows the inside of our refrigerator better than I do, and she always finishes off the Diet Coke. But then she goes back to the driver's door.

"Aren't you gonna come in?" I say.

"What for?"

I don't know what to say to that, so I just shrug. "I suppose you have to get home?"

"Yeah," Amber says. And then she won't meet my eye. She kind of shuffles the keys in her hand.

"Yeah, something like that."

TWENTY-ONE

I HAVE a good think as I sit in the bath. After a while I start to wonder if I've been a bit harsh. After all, Amber is eighteen, and it's true that most of the guys on Lornea Island aren't exactly the sort of people she should date. And maybe I overreacted about the drugs too. I mean, it's only marijuana, not heroin. Lots of guys at school smoke it, or they say they do – they're probably lying. But I'm sure I read how half the states in the country have legalized it now for medical use. I'm not sure what it's for, but Amber can be quite a stressed person, so maybe it could help with that.

In a way I change my mind about Carlos too. He says he didn't know you're not allowed to fish in the marine reserve, but it *was* only reclassified recently, and he wouldn't have got to hear about it over in Europe. And it's not as if there's signs up or anything. If he just sailed up there, he might have just thought it was a nice place to drop the anchor and do some fishing. There's something else too, it takes me a while to work out what, but in the end I realize I do know after all. I feel a bit guilty over how I told the Journal of Marine Biology about Steve. I know it was the right thing to do, but maybe I should have told him first. Maybe to warn him or something. I don't know.

In the end I make a decision. Actually two decisions. The first is, instead of phoning the school tomorrow like I said I was going to, and asking if I can come back early, I'm just going to go in, like normal. Now I think about it, I don't know why I didn't work this out before. I had to spend ages persuading them I could go off on the trip in the first place, because of all the school I'd be missing, so they're hardly going to complain now I'm coming back earlier than planned.

The second thing is that I'm going to apologize to Amber. It's not that I really *need* to, but she is my best friend, so I'm going to cut her a bit of slack.

After that I feel a bit better, and I practice holding my breath underwater for a while. I've been doing this for ages now. Dad got me into it, he used to do it for his surfing, sometimes when the waves are big he gets held under for a long time. I don't like surfing that much, but it's good practice for snorkelling and free diving. I can do over a minute easily now, and my best time is one minute fifty nine seconds.

Actually I think there's another reason I'm a little bit funny about Amber. It's definitely not true now, but a few years ago, when we first met, I used to have a bit of a crush on her. Not that much, but she can look quite pretty from some angles, when she's in a good mood, which isn't very often. We did this thing where we opened a detective agency together. We were really immature back then, her more than me obviously, because I'm very mature for my age. But I definitely don't now, have a crush I mean. I think of her more as a sister. And that's why I'm being a bit protective of her now. Or over-protective maybe. Whichever, I definitely think I should say sorry.

So then I get out of the bath and fix myself some dinner, and get an early night so I'm fresh for school the next day.

* * *

I catch the bus which gets me into Newlea at 08:33. Then I realize I've been a bit dumb, because even though school starts at 08:45, the first class that it's actually worth me going to isn't until 10.30. I'm not going to go back just to sit through registration. So instead I head over to Amber's house. It's only a few blocks away, and I know she doesn't start college until 11:30.

I feel a bit nervous as I walk up to Amber's front door. I'm not exactly the best at saying sorry. But even so I'm determined to do it. I glance at my watch: 08:45. I just hope she's up already. She's not exactly the earliest of risers.

I knock on the door anyway. Then it's Gracie who answers.

"Hi Billy," she says.

I like Gracie. She's Amber's baby sister, only she's not a baby anymore, she's six. But she's really funny. She comes out with us on the *Blue Lady* sometimes, and I'm teaching her about all the birds and the different types of whales.

"Why aren't you in Auster-rail-eria?" She demands, cocking her head on one side.

I try to give her a relaxed smile. "It's a bit of a long story. Is Amber up yet?"

"I don't know. I like stories. Can you tell me it?"

"Sure. Sometime, but not now. Because I really need to see Amber. Can you see if she's up yet?"

Gracie looks at me funny, then shrugs. "Not really."

I'm confused by this. It's not like Gracie to be awkward. "Why not?"

"Because she's not here."

"Not here? Where is she then?"

Gracie shrugs her shoulders. "Don't know. Maybe she's at college?" She adds a little hopefully, but that can't be right because Amber doesn't have any classes that start this early. There's no point telling this to Gracie though, because she can't tell the time yet.

"Have you had breakfast yet?" I ask instead.

"Yep."

"Did Amber go out before or after you had breakfast?"

Gracie tips her head on one side again, but doesn't answer.

"Before or after you had breakfast?" I say again, in case she didn't get it the first time, but then she giggles.

"I'm just trying to work out if..." But I don't get to finish what I'm saying because at that moment Amber's mom comes to the door, I guess to see who it is.

"Oh hi Billy, you're back are you?" For a second I think I'm going to have to go over the whole Australia thing again, but instead she just looks at me expectantly. So I ask her if Amber left for college already. But Mrs. Atherton frowns at that.

"No... Well I don't think so. But she stayed with a friend last night, so I don't know. A girl called Jane that she knows from her course."

"Jane?" I think. Amber didn't mention anything about a Jane yesterday, and I've never heard her talking about one before.

"That's right." Amber's mom gives me a breezy smile, kind of like she wants to get rid of me from her doorstep. I think some more. Amber did say she'd made some friends on her course. Even if it was in the context of them smoking drugs together.

"Erm, do you know where Jane lives?" I ask. "It's just I need to speak with Amber this morning. If I can."

Amber's mom lets out a long sigh, she does that a lot when she's talking to me. It's why I don't much like talking to her.

"I don't have the address. Why don't you phone her?"

"Yeah OK, I'll do that." I start to turn around, a bit disappointed, when Mrs. Atherton goes on.

" I know it's somewhere in Newlea though. She has been there a lot recently. She was studying there yesterday afternoon and it got late so she just stayed over," she gives me her *you-know-teenagers* look, which is a bit ironic because I'm a teenager too.

"Hey, there's no problem is there?" She says now. I guess she notices my face. And I decide I won't drop Amber in it. Obviously she hasn't told her mom about Carlos after all.

"No." I say. "There's no problem. It's nothing urgent." I turn to go, until Gracie distracts me.

"Bye Billy!" she says. So I turn around and wave.

"Bye Gracie. Have a nice day!"

And then I walk back down the drive and back towards the school.

TWENTY-TWO

I walk towards the school. I can feel my face tight, my brows knitted together. I guess I'm just angry that Amber lied to her mom, about being at this Jane person's house, if she even exists. And that she lied to me, about whether her mom knew about Carlos. I guess she figured that if I thought her mom knew about him – and didn't mind – then I'd be more likely to not mind either. Well if so, that plan's backfired.

I see the school up ahead of me. And something makes me slow down. I'm not in the mood for school now. I pause for a moment and think. I suppose it's *possible* that Amber dropped me off last night, and then went to this Jane person's house instead of going home. My hand finds my phone, automatically, inside my pocket. I could call her. Though I don't know exactly how I'm going to ask. It might look like I'm snooping. And I'm definitely not snooping. I'm just concerned with who she's hanging out with. I'm just looking out for her.

So I let go of my phone and think a bit more. There is another way I could find out where she stayed the night. If I'm quick.

I turn around and break into a jog. It's only a couple of blocks to the bus station, and there's buses to Holport that go every half an hour, which means there's one in five minutes. I'm out of breath when I get there, and it's just pulling out of the station so I have to run out in front of it and wave my arms. The driver gives me a mad look, but he pulls up and the door hisses open. I show him my pass and swing into the first empty seat, feeling my heart beat hard in my chest. It's about a half hour on the bus, but I don't really get the time to think whether this is a good idea or not, because it's going to be touch and go whether I get there before she leaves for college. If she's been there at all, that is.

The bus takes an age. I have to work really hard not to curse when people get on and take ages to pay. Why can't they just get a pass like I've got? Or at least have the right change ready. But finally we pull into Holport and I hammer the button to make the bus stop, then jump off as soon as the doors open. It's quicker for me to run down to the harbor rather than wait while the bus goes around the whole town. I race through the alley that leads to the fishing harbor, and then along the dockside until I get to the main marina where *Blue Lady* is moored. And looking out I see the mast from Carlos' boat *Mystery* alongside her. Then I stop. I have to put my hands on my knees to catch my breath. Then I check the time. If Amber *is* here, she could be leaving right about now to drive to college. I have to make sure she doesn't see me before I see her.

I scan all the normal spaces where she parks her car, and then I see it. She's got it parked right against the window of the chandler, which they hate, because it blocks people from seeing into their display window. I trot up behind it, and glance in the rear window. The seats are still down, from where I had my bike in there last night. Otherwise it just looks like Amber's car. I check the doors, and they're locked. Then, feeling a bit stupid, I go to the front and feel the hood. To see if it's hot, which would mean it's been used recently. The hood's cold. So much for *Jane*.

I look around. I feel a bit stupid and frustrated now. Like I don't know what to do next. I think I expected to see Amber getting into her car, ready to go off to college. And maybe I hoped she'd see me and realize she'd been busted, and maybe apologize for not telling me the truth. But all there is here is Amber's car. I look again out into the basin at where the *Mystery* is moored. I can't see much from here, since she's moored right at the end of the pontoon. But I could go out there. I could even pretend I was just checking something on *Blue Lady* – that would give me the perfect excuse, and then I could casually glance into the cabin windows of *Mystery* and see if Amber's there, and she'd know she's been busted. I pat my pockets again, feeling better just to have a plan, but then I realize something awkward. I don't have the keys to the boat. I was meant to be going to school today, not coming down here to Holport, so I left them at home. That means I can't pretend to be grabbing something from *Blue Lady*, because I won't be able to get in. But at the same time, I really want to check in the windows of *Mystery* now. To see if Amber's there, and what she's actually doing.

Which just leaves one thing. My kayak. I can paddle out to the *Mystery* on the other side of the pontoon – where they won't be able to see me – then paddle around the top and go right up alongside them. Then I can look right into the windows and see exactly what Amber is doing.

I run around to the alley where it's stored, and unstrap it, from where it's hung off the ground. I lower it down, right onto my trolley-wheels, and then pull it down to the launch ramp.

I don't take my shoes and socks off. The water inside the harbor is always flat, and I figured out a way to launch without even getting my feet wet. As the kayak slides out into the water, and floats off the wheels, I pull them out and collapse them, then stash them in the front of the boat. Then I pull it alongside the ramp and jump in, and then paddle quietly out. I have to duck under the walkway to the pontoon, and then paddle out past the sterns of the boats on the opposite side to where *Mystery* and *Blue Lady* are berthed.

When I get to the end of the pontoon I slow down. From here they *could* see me, if they were looking out for someone. So I stay real close to the tied-up boats to make use of the shelter they provide. I work my way towards *Blue Lady*. Once I'm in her shelter I speed up again, until I get to her bow. Here I stop and peer round. It's a bit difficult to peer round actually, because there's three feet of kayak that sticks out in front of where my eyes are. But I figure that, in the unlikely event they see anything, they'll think it's just any old kayak, they won't know it's me. And when I can see, the *Mystery* looks all tied up and empty. No one on deck.

Trying to keep my paddle splashes to a minimum I slip forward, out of the shelter of *Blue Lady* and across the gap between the two boats, until I'm under the overhanging bow of *Mystery*. I go straight around to the far side, away from where she's tied up against the floating dock. It's dangerous here. I make sure the hull of the kayak doesn't touch the side of the yacht, or worse, bash into it, because that would make a lot of noise inside the yacht. I can touch it with my hands though, just as long as I'm gentle. So I ship my paddle and pull myself carefully along the length of the yacht, towards the middle, where the windows are. Here I realize I've misjudged things a bit. I can't actually see into the window after all because I'm too low down in the kayak. The only thing I can do is stand up. And I don't know if you've ever stood up in a kayak, but they're not designed for it. They're stable enough when you're sitting down, but as soon as you move your weight high up, they become really unstable. It's OK, because I'm quite good at balancing, plus I've got the side of the yacht to hold onto. But I've got to be careful.

Very carefully I get to my feet, and pull myself level with the window. It's then I notice something weird. As I pull myself along the side of the yacht's cabin, the paint starts rubbing off in my hand. I feel a stab of concern that Carlos could accuse me of damaging it, even though it's his fault for not painting it properly. I try to ignore the little bit of blue where I've rubbed the white paint off and get to the window. Then there's a kind of drape, fixed inside with Velcro. It's half drawn, which is annoying, because I have to move even more, and I'm already a bit off-balance. And as I pull myself forward even more I hear a noise. I recognize it. And now I hear it I don't know why I didn't notice it before. I guess I was concentrating too much. But even so it makes me feel like a plug has been pulled underneath me, and all my emotions are draining out. And when I finally look into the window, I already know what I'm going to see.

It's still a shock though. The kind of shock where it takes me about five seconds for my eyes to make sense of what I'm actually seeing. It's all limbs, and movement. And Amber's hair – dyed black these days – splayed out on the floor behind her. Her mouth open, gasping. They're naked, having sex. Right there on the floor of the cabin. In a way it's lucky that Carlos is on top of her, because that means I don't get to see any of Ambers 'bits' – I'm not a pervert, I don't *want* to look. But it's such a shock I can't look away at once. It's like my eyes are drawn to it. To Carlos' butt – tanned just like the back of his legs, I guess he must have done naked sunbathing while he crossed the ocean – rising and falling. And the thought of what's actually happening. I'm just about to recover enough to pull my head away when Amber turns her head. I don't know if she's heard something, or noticed something, or if head moving is just a thing girls do when they're having sex, but either way, I can't let her see me. I just *can't*. I whip my head back, and then, forgetting I'm standing in my kayak, I go to step away too, and it's too much. Even for my good balance, and the fact that I'm holding onto the side of the yacht, because then I'm not holding onto the side of the yacht anymore.

As I fall, I feel the kayak's hard plastic shell thump into the yacht's hull. I feel the bump even through my falling feet.

And then I'm in the water. It closes over my head.

TWENTY-THREE

"WHAT ARE YOU DOING?" The large man asked, while trying to fit the seat-belt over his ample stomach. His companion, younger, fitter and dressed in a significantly shinier suit, continued what he was doing, which was leaning over the car's touch-screen and programming the GPS.

"I'm putting the address in."

"You don't know where Jimmy the Fish lives?"

"Sure I know where Jimmy the Fish lives. I just wanna get the traffic information."

The bigger man paused for a moment.

"It's just a couple blocks."

"Yeah... you say that..." The younger man's voice faded out as he continued to press at the touch screen.

"And?"

The younger man ignored him, concentrating on the screen.

"And what?" The big man pressed. "If it's just a couple of blocks..." Now his voice faded out too, but in his case it was out of frustration, sensing too late how he had fallen into a familiar trap.

The large man balled his hands into fists and forced himself to stay calm. His name was Tommy Battaglia, but many people knew him as Tommy *the Teeth*, at least behind his back. The reason for this was obvious every time he opened his mouth. As he passed through puberty he'd developed significantly more teeth than was normal. Had he gone to a dentist he might have learned the problem was relatively common – and the fix was too – but by then he was already living on his wits on the streets, stealing cars for the Old Man. There wasn't much time for dentists. Besides, the intimidating look the extra teeth gave him came in useful as he graduated to holding up goods trucks running protection rackets. Now, over three decades later, his mouth was just a mess of overcrowded, over-sized and filthy teeth at awkward angles to each other. And his breath always stank.

"Jesus Tommy, will you chill?" The younger man said, well aware that Tommy had already dropped it, but still hoping to provoke a further reaction. The younger man was called Paulie, and there was nothing wrong with his teeth. Indeed on being told he had to work with Tommy he'd been to see his dentist for additional whitening treatment, so that his set of perfectly straight teeth shone white in what he proudly regarded as an above-averagely-attractive face.

"There could've been a crash," he went on. "Or they could be fixing the street. Or…" He ran out of possibilities and fell silent, annoyed that he couldn't think of anything further to irritate his companion. When he found out he was being sent to work with *Tommy the Teeth* he was angry. The move came in the reorganization that followed the Old Man's death. It was a surprise passing, at least some aspects of it. The death of someone who had been known as 'the Old Man' for as long as anyone could remember couldn't be considered surprising. But the manner of his passing – peacefully, in his own bed – was not how anyone would have guessed it would happen. Furthermore what came next was a series of shocks that had totally restricted the whole organization. Rather than power shifting down the family, the Old Man had given instructions that his replacement should be the son of his most faithful advisor, Angelo Costello. For Paulie this was a welcome surprise, and an opportunity. Paulie had been nothing to the Old Man, just another lowly foot soldier whose face he couldn't have picked out in a line up. But Angelo was Paulie's family. Technically they were only second cousins, but as kids they'd known each other. Sure, they'd lost touch since then, when Angelo was sent off to private schools and then onto whichever Ivy League college it was he went to. But they'd *played* together when they were just little kids. They were family.

So it was disappointing that, instead of getting the position of some authority Paulie felt he warranted, he'd been paired up with Tommy *the Teeth*. He took it out on him by taking every opportunity he could to piss him off.

"And if so," he went on now, suddenly remembering the basics of how the GPS worked, "the computer – which is fed data about traffic flows from all round the city – would take that information and direct us a quicker way. And *then* I wouldn't have to sit here staring at your ugly fucking face." He clicked the button marked 'go' and the screen changed to a map, showing their route in red ahead of them.

"There. That was painless wasn't it?" Paulie said.

"Just drive the fucking car," Tommy said. Then added under his sour breath. "Fucking jerk."

Paulie pressed the start button on the Toyota, whistling to himself. They'd argued over start buttons too. Tommy had whined about how every car had them these days. When Paulie had asked him what was so bad about push starts, Tommy had replied how they were harder to hot-wire. Paulie grinned to himself at the thought. It was true, push-button starts *were* harder to hot-wire – but then who the fuck cared about jacking cars these days? Tommy, in the twilight of his life, was harking back to his younger days. Back when he was the future. Well that was ancient fucking history now, Paulie thought, with a buzz of excitement. *He* was the future now.

"What's got you so fucking pissed anyways?" Paulie asked, tiring of his whistling before it had time to irritate Tommy.

"I ain't pissed."

"Yeah you are. You're like a bear that's been kicked in the balls."

Tommy turned, grinding his mismatched teeth.

"It's this fucking bitcoin *bullshit*," he said suddenly.

Paulie glanced across. He hadn't been expecting an answer.

"What about it?"

"What about it? I don't trust it."

Paulie hesitated while he negotiated a junction.

"OK." He shrugged. "Then sell it."

"I don't trust selling it. And it's a fucking hassle. Scrabbling around on my goddamn cellphone. I don't see why we can't just get paid in the old way." Tommy shook his head.

"What? Cash?" Paulie allowed himself a laugh. "You want an envelope stuffed full of hundred dollar bills at the end of every week?"

"It worked fine." Tommy growled with enough menace to remind Paulie there was a point beyond which it wasn't wise to push him.

"Maybe." Paulie drove on for a while, wondering whether they were there yet or not. He decided to keep going. "But it wasn't exactly conducive to modern life. When was the last time you took a vacation Tommy?"

Tommy looked across, his face dark.

"I don't do vacations."

"Yeah I know. But say you did. And say you wanted to buy a flight. How you gonna do that with your pile of cash?"

Tommy glowered. "Go to a travel agent."

Paulie shook his head. "They're *gone* Tommy. They don't exist. They all got changed into *vegan* coffee shops. Or maybe you didn't notice?"

Both men were silent for a moment.

"Airline desk then. At the airport," Tommy said.

"Oh yeah. *Very* convenient. So you go all the way down to the airport, at great fucking expense and inconvenience. And what do you find, huh? There's a long fucking line, or worse, the desk's closed?"

Tommy didn't answer. Instead he tried to adjust the seat, which got stuck.

"Why'd you drive this fucking Jap car?" he asked.

Paulie ignored him. "And if it is open, the ticket's five times the price. Oh yeah, and the moment you pay with cash you bet your life you've got an alarm ringing under the desk. Bend over big boy, you're gonna get a glove up your ass." He grinned, catching sight of himself in the rear view mirror and enjoying the sight. He ran a hand over his hair, shaved high up the sides and the top combed back and held in place with gel.

"At the very least," he said, forgetting for a moment whether he was still trying to wind Tommy up, or in a rare moment where he actually enjoyed talking to the guy. "You're gonna be drawing attention to yourself. You don't get none of that with bitcoin."

"Yeah. I get it. I just don't fucking trust it."

Paulie smiled. The truth was, *he'd* been surprised, and just as ready to join the general outrage when one of Angelo's first changes had been to make all payments within the organization via a crypto currency. He hadn't known what the fuck Bitcoin was. But since then its value had nearly doubled, effectively doubling his, and everyone's income. Suddenly the new boss had seemed like a fucking genius, and everyone was wishing the Old Man had brought it in, or died sooner so they could have got into Bitcoin when it was tripling its value every few months.

They were there. Paulie turned the car into a residential street, and drove along it, looking up through the windshield for the apartment where Jimmy the Fish lived. He stopped right outside, just as a young couple exited from the communal doorway. Paulie waited until they had walked past the car. He watched them until they were twenty yards away down the street and hadn't looked back.

"I'll look over it for you. If you want," he said suddenly. "Show you how it works." He wouldn't admit to himself why he was suddenly being nicer to the guy, but on some level he did know. Whether or not he liked spending time with Tommy – and the answer was he didn't – there were times when it felt good to have someone with his years of experience backing you up. You simply didn't get to his age in this life if you weren't careful. And lucky. He might look like the monster from a horror movie, and have bad breath to match. But he knew the business. He knew the fucking trade.

Tommy looked uncomfortable. He didn't say anything but suddenly he reached into his jacket and pulled out his gun, a 9mm Sig Sauer P938, that Paulie knew would have been meticulously sourced with all identifying features removed. Paulie didn't react at all. Instead he just watched as Tommy released the magazine, ensured it was full of rounds, all loaded correctly, then slid it back into position. Then he pulled back the slider, checked the chamber was clear and loaded a round ready to fire. Every movement was automatic, beautifully practiced.

"I mean it," Paulie went on. "I know we don't always... exactly see eye-to-eye. But there's a reason Angelo put us together. I can teach you shit like this and..." Paulie hesitated. He wasn't going to spell it out for the guy. "You know, you've been doing this a while. You pick stuff up." He shrugged. "That helps me too."

Tommy reached into his jacket again, and this time pulled out a silencer. He held it up and sighted down it, checking it was clear. Finally he grunted.

"Yeah sure."

Paulie nodded. "Obviously I'll take a commission. I ain't gonna do it for free."

* * *

The two men got out of the car and walked to the intercom. Paulie pressed the buzzer for Jimmy's apartment and waited.

Moments later an electronic voice responded, "Who is it?"

"It's me," Paulie replied. "Paulie. Let me in will you..."

He was met with a short silence.

"I wasn't expecting you…"

"Just buzz the fucking door Jimmy," Paulie slammed his finger back on the intercom, glanced at Tommy and shook his head, like he couldn't believe the way the fucker was reacting. A few seconds later the buzzer sounded, and Tommy, who already had his hand on the outer door, pushed it open. They went inside.

There was no elevator. Tommy glanced up the stairwell before they began climbing, listening for any sound that wasn't right. They moved quietly, their eyes darting this way and that, checking everything. They made their way along the passageway until they were standing outside Jimmy's apartment. Here Paulie tapped on the door with the back of his hand. Straight away it opened, and a skinny man, wearing just jeans and a vest looked out. He clocked Paulie, but then Tommy too, and his nose started twitching, like a rabbit sniffing a fox.

"We come in for a moment?"

"You didn't say you had Tommy with you." Jimmy sniffed.

"You didn't fucking ask."

Paulie grinned at his own response and went to push past the skinny man, but he stepped back from the door at that moment, so that Paulie almost stumbled into the room. Tommy stayed by the door, closing it behind him. The apartment opened right into the living room. The TV was on, the sofa drawn close-up to it, and looking worn out. The remains of a pizza sat in a cardboard take-out box on one arm, and around the floor, and the rest of the sparse furniture, were scattered beer cans and dirty plates. But the most striking feature of the room was the wall given over to a giant fish tank. It divided the room from the kitchen, and reached from the counter top all the way to the ceiling. And was filled with tens of thousands of tiny tropical fish, and aquatic plants, and beautiful features. Everything about it was lovingly maintained, the water sparkling clean.

Jimmy rubbed his face.

"You wanna sit down?"

Paulie took his gaze off the fish tank and eyed the sofa. "Not particularly." He turned to glance at his partner. "Tommy, you feeling tired at all? Wanna put your feet up?"

Tommy, who hadn't moved from the doorway now responded with the barest of movements of his head.

"No, we're good," Paulie interpreted.

"OK." Jimmy replied. He was struggling to lift his eyes from the floor. "Well what's the problem? I wasn't expecting no one to come. I still got plenty of product."

"Oh we know that."

"And I don't owe nothing. I'm up to date on payments. So I don't get what this is about."

"What you watching?" Paulie ignored him, instead turning to the TV. "Is that *Breaking Bad?*"

Jimmy didn't reply, until Paulie turned and asked him a second time.

"Yeah."

"Oh man, I love this show." Paulie looked back at the screen, genuinely animated now. "This is series three right? The one with the chicken shop guy? The guy who runs the whole fucking drugs scene in New Mexico. I just love that. The idea you can run a whole organization from a chicken shop." Paulie smiled, and turned back to Jimmy.

"I mean I worked in a chicken shop. KFC, just for a few months you understand. But it's a busy fucking job. You ain't got time to be shifting product on the side, believe me." He turned back to the screen, where two sinister looking men were having a meeting in the booth of a fast food restaurant.

"I told Tommy here he has to watch this, but he's more into wildlife shows. Ain't that right Tommy?"

Tommy didn't move at all, but Paulie goes on.

"Oh yeah, he loves something called *Blue Planet*. Guess maybe you'd like that too?" He gestured to the fish tank again, but Jimmy didn't answer, his eyes were full of a cautious fear.

"But the problem we both have, we don't have much *time* for TV, because we're always working." Paulie snapped back around until he was facing Jimmy directly. "Unlike you, or so it seems. You've got all the time in the world. Time to be watching *Breaking Bad* at..." he glanced at his watch, a heavy metal Rolex. "Three twenty on a Thursday afternoon." Paulie shook his head. "I ain't sure Angelo's gonna like that. He likes his guys to work hard, you know? He likes to get value."

"I was just... I have people coming around. Customers."

"Oh yeah." Paulie gave the appearance of suddenly understanding. "Oh I get it. This *is* work for you guys. Sitting around, watching Netflix. Every now and then the doorbell goes and you do a little deal. You *are* working. Yeah you're really putting the hours in. I'll be sure to report that back."

Jimmy pulled his face into a unconvincing smile of thanks, then it dropped away.

"In fact, now I come to mention it," Paulie went on, spying the TV remote and picking it up. "One of those *customers* who came around –

keeping you so fucking busy – it turns out he wasn't no customer after all. Least, not in the normal sense of the word." Paulie seemed to have lost all interest in Jimmy directly. He paused the show, then clicked *back*, to check which episode was showing.

"Series three. Didn't I say?" He turned to glance at Tommy, who drew back his lips into a kind of crooked half-smile to acknowledge Paulie's accuracy.

"No," Paulie turned back to Jimmy again. "He was actually a guy doing a favor for Angelo. You ever hear of mystery shopping?"

"Huh?" Jimmy replied. For a moment he'd been distracted by the sight of Tommy's teeth up close. But now he was back, worried by what Paulie was saying.

"*Mystery* shopping. Say you own a chain of stores, and you wanna improve customer service. So you roll out all these rules saying how staff have to be respectful to their customers, and serve them inside thirty seconds, or whatever the hell you wanna do. But how do you make sure it's happening? How do you know your staff are doing what you tell them?"

"I dunno," Jimmy said after a while.

"*Mystery shopping.*" Paulie smiled, almost warmly. "You send someone in who *pretends* to be a customer. You get them to report on how they got treated. All the big stores do it. I guess Angelo learned about it when he was studying the MBA the Old Man sent him on. Anyway. That's what he's been doing. With you."

Jimmy did a good job of keeping his face from tightening up, but his eyes betrayed his fear. Paulie scrutinized it, enjoying the fear now on clear display. Then he carried breezily on.

"So this guy – or it might have been a girl – I don't even know myself. Maybe they bought from you all the time, or maybe it was just the once. Who the fuck knows?" He shrugged. "What's important is, they *did* buy from you. And they took their little baggie of coke right back to Angelo. And he had it *tested*." Paulie stopped and stared at Jimmy. Jimmy swallowed.

"And do you know what?"

Jimmy breathed several shallow breaths before answering. "Look I can explai…"

"Turns out someone had cut the product."

The change in Paulie's tone seemed to lower the temperature in the room, and an ominous silence descended. Jimmy didn't answer. Instead he glanced over at the door, the only escape route in the room. But Tommy was still blocking it, and he was no longer smiling. His eyes were black and his heavy frame gave no chance for Jimmy to get by.

"See," Paulie continued. "Angelo provides the product to you at a very specific level of purity. He likes to do it that way because it gives his customers a product they know. A brand identity, if you like. You know how important brands are Jimmy?"

Jimmy didn't reply.

"They're *very* important. That's why Angelo's so fucking hot on them, because he's a real smart guy." For a second Paulie considered why, if Angelo was so smart, he didn't appreciate him – Paulie – more, but he shook his head to dispel the thought. Forced himself to concentrate.

"So when our mystery shopper turned up with product cut with *boric acid*, and…" He pretended to think for a while. "what was the other thing Tommy?"

"Powdered milk."

"Yeah, *powdered milk*." He winced. "Well, it really upset Angelo because it damaged the brand. His brand. He took it personally."

Paulie sent a sideways glance in Tommy's direction, just for a split second, but in response, the big man reached into his jacket. He pulled out his gun, then reached in a second time and withdrew the silencer. He casually screwed the two together, then let his hands fall by his lap, the weapon hanging casually from his large hands.

Jimmy, who had watched the entire performance, turned back to Paulie. "It was just the one time. I swear it. I was short of the money I owed to Angelo and I needed to make it up. That's the only reason I did it."

Paulie put a finger to his lips, like he was a judge, hearing Jimmy's case.

"I swear to you. I swear it Paulie. It was just the one time. You know loads of guys cut it all the time, but I don't. I know Angelo don't like it. I swear I respect that."

"You respect that? You respect Angelo?"

"Yeah. Fuck yeah. I love the guy. I understand. I fucked up. It won't happen again. And I'll make it up. Whatever it takes. I swear to God I will. On my mother's life."

Paulie didn't answer, and for a few moments there was silence. Apart from a whining sound escaping from Jimmy's lips.

In the end Paulie shook his head. "You know Jimmy I believe you. It *was* just the one time, or our mystery shopper would have picked it up. And you've never been behind on the money. Which reflects well..." He sniffed.

"But you know how things are Jimmy. With the Old Man gone, and Angelo in charge, he has to make sure nobody thinks of the transition period as an *opportunity*. To take advantage. He has to build his reputation."

"Yeah but you can talk to him. Paulie. You've got his ear, he *listens* to you. And you *know* me, from the old days. It ain't *ever* gonna happen again, I swear to you..."

"Oh I know that," Paulie cut in, his voice suddenly quiet. "I know that for a fact."

Jimmy opened his mouth to protest further, but something stopped him.

"That's why we're here," Paulie went on. "Having this little chat. We're here to make sure nothing like this happens again. Ever."

Paulie turned to glance at Tommy, who now lifted the pistol so that it was pointed at Jimmy. His arm was steady, his eyes still dead.

"Paulie, *what the fuck*? Cutting ain't *nothing*. I'm a good earner. You *know* that! It don't make no fucking sense to *shoot me* for this."

Paulie stepped away from Jimmy before he replied. "Like I said Jimmy. We're not making the decisions. We're just here to pass on a message from Angelo."

With that Paulie took two steps back until Jimmy was left alone on the far side of the room. He turned his head to Tommy and his raised gun. He seemed transfixed by the sight of it, unable to move.

"Tommy? Don't do this. Everyone cut with the Old Man, you know that! It wasn't..."

He was silenced by two muffled clicks that came in quick succession. The gun bucked, even under Tommy's expert grip. But Jimmy never heard the shots. Not properly at least. Instead his shocked and terrified brain tunneled in on the fact that the bullets hadn't hit him, but had instead slammed into the thick clear glass of the huge fish tank behind him. He turned, in time to see a crazy network of cracks spreading out across the front until they reached the sides and corners. For a moment little else happened, inertia keeping the water in place, but then the wall bulged and finally the weakened glass gave way, collapsing outward.

Within a second thousands of gallons of water, shattered glass and tropical fish surged out in a huge wave. It was close enough to engulf Jimmy, knocking him to the ground and surging across the room's filthy carpet. Tommy was far enough away that he didn't have to move, but Paulie had to leap clear, laughing as he did so.

Then Tommy casually unscrewed the silencer and put the gun away, while on the floor around him, ten thousand tiny fish flapped and wriggled on the carpet. As Paulie turned away he stepped on a dozen of them.

"Oh," he said, looking down in distaste. "And you might want to think about getting another nickname."

TWENTY-FOUR

ONE WEEK later the silver Toyota pulled up outside another apartment, this time the cheap brown-brick block where Tommy lived. Paulie leaned forwards and looked up through the windshield at the second floor, then he leaned on the horn for a long blast.

Inside Tommy went to the window of his bathroom. He was naked except for a towel wrapped around his waist. As he did so his phone, balanced on the windowsill rang out.

"Yeah?"

"Where the fuck are you? I told you Angelo wants to see us."

Tommy pulled back the blind in the bathroom and looked down, just as Paulie hit the horn again. This time the sound blared up from the street. A moment later it also sounded through the ear piece of the cell phone, routed half way across the country and bounced up and down into space.

"Alright, alright. I'm coming. What does he want?"

"How the fuck should I know? Just get a move on."

Two minutes later, Tommy came out of the door of the apartment building and crossed the street, tucking his shirt in as he walked. Paulie watched the way he lumbered and shuffled with obvious disgust.

"I got neighbors you know." Tommy said as he clambered into the car.

"Yeah. You got an appointment to see Angelo too. Which of those is more important?"

Tommy answered by pulling hard at his seatbelt, then swearing as the mechanism locked.

"Fucking Jap car," he said.

Paulie kept to the speed limit, and soon they pulled up outside a pair of iron gates that protected a large house that overlooked the water. The gates offered the only way past a ten foot high wall, and security cameras were mounted on each post, and at regular intervals along the length of the wall. The cameras on the posts looked like a pair of vultures. For a moment the two men waited as they swung to inspect them, their motors humming. Then the gates swung open. Paulie drove in, through a well-kept garden, and up towards a heavy stone house. He parked in a bay between a Cadillac and a Porsche. They both got out.

A thick-set man in a dark suit already had the front door open for them. He checked around the grounds, then lifted a hand-held radio to his mouth and spoke quietly into it. As Tommy and Paulie came up to the door the man nodded at them, and ushered them inside. They stepped into a wide hallway decorated in a traditional style. A blue-painted vase – it looked Chinese, or at least expensive – sat on a massive oak dresser that was stained near black. Inside the glass doors was a display of antique pistols.

"Hey Barney," Paulie said, unbuckling his own gun with no hesitation, "What's happening?" He put the gun on the table while the man took the weapon carefully, checking the chamber was empty, before slipping it into a drawer. Then he turned to Tommy.

A little reluctantly Tommy reached for his own gun. Giving up your weapon before going in to see the boss was a new rule of Angelo's. It still felt weird, disrespectful somehow, like it implied how you might be tempted to use it otherwise. In the Old Man's days you simply had respect. If there was any doubt that you might not have respect, well in that case you would never get this close before someone put a bullet in your head. As he had done a thousand times in recent months, the realization that times changed passed through his mind. He released his gun from the holster, pulled the slider back to show it wasn't loaded, and handed it handle-first to Barney. As he did so a look passed between the two older men, both were survivors from the old regime.

"I'll take care of it," Barney said quietly, and Tommy nodded.

"You know what this is about?" Paulie asked brightly, as Barney led them down a corridor, and up some stairs.

"Nope," Barney said without turning around. At the top of the stairs was a large landing, with some chairs arranged, not dissimilar to a doctor's waiting room. There was even a low table with magazines.

"Wait here. He won't be long." Barney turned away and walked back downstairs, leaving Tommy and Paulie alone. Paulie sat down, but Tommy went to the window and glanced outside at the harbor. Then he looked around the landing, taking in the differences that Angelo had made since the Old Man's death. Some of the paintings were missing, he saw. The Old Man had developed an interest in art in his later years. Classical stuff, always Italian painters, and probably not as valuable as it was intended to look. But even so, Tommy had appreciated them, especially the couple of times the Old Man had taken the time to explain them to him.

"The paintings are gone," Tommy said.

Paulie glanced up from a magazine called *Jet Ski Rider*. "What? Oh yeah." He shrugged. "Angelo probably sold 'em. Good thing too. It used to be so fucking dreary in here."

Tommy frowned, but didn't get the chance to say anything more, because at that moment a door opened and another man, dressed impeccably in a dark blue suit and silk waistcoat walked out. He looked at Tommy first, and there was something in his eyes, a silent respect, but it was Paulie he spoke to.

"Angelo's ready for you now. Please come through." The man's voice was very quiet and very calm. He didn't wait for an answer, but led the way into a huge office, half paneled with oak, and with one wall given over completely to books. The largest piece of furniture inside was an enormous desk, not dark like the rest of the room but painted matt white. A young man with blond hair sat behind it, frowning into an Apple laptop. An iPad sat beside it, balanced on a frame. He was dressed expensively but casually – a white cotton shirt with the sleeves rolled up showed off his tan. Tommy noticed he wore nothing on his feet.

Angelo glanced up as the three men walked in. He offered a brief smile but continued working, and only after a few moments more did he push the computer away and get up. He walked first to Paulie, and embraced him warmly. Then he nodded at Tommy, but didn't touch him.

"Sit, please. Take a seat," he said, indicating the chairs in front of the desk. Tommy and Paulie did so, while the man with the blue suit took his own seat too, over by the wall.

"Thanks for coming by. I appreciate it." Angelo spoke with a nasal tone that made him sound whiny, but his eyes were sharp and alert.

"No problem," Paulie answered. He considered adding a casual 'cuz' to the end, but his nerves failed him. He settled for a breezy reply instead. "What's up?"

Angelo didn't answer at once. He went back behind his desk and sat down. He leaned forward. Then sat back. He seemed about to speak, but then looked away. Everyone waited.

"I got a little job for you," Angelo said in the end.

"Sure." Paulie felt his chest inflate. This was the first time he'd actually been in to see Angelo since he took over. Mostly the orders flowed down through the ranks. So whatever this was, it sure wasn't 'a little job'. It was something bigger. It was an opportunity.

The room fell silent again. And for a moment they all watched Angelo as he stroked his chin.

"It's a little different. It's gonna take a bit of explaining."

"No problem." Paulie glowed inwardly.

Another silence filled the room.

"The Old Man, before he... passed. He was having a few issues. Down at the port." Angelo said at last. "I'm sure you know about it." He stopped for a moment, as if realizing that maybe this was something they wouldn't have known.

"Nothing serious," he went on. "Just the cost of bringing product in was creeping up. You know? Guys getting too greedy, you know what I mean."

"Sure," Paulie said enthusiastically. The truth was though, he had no idea. He'd always been way too low-level to be party to any information like this. The fact that he was hearing it now was giving him a huge sense of excitement.

"To tell you the truth, I wonder if it didn't contribute in some way to... you know..." Angelo didn't finish the sentence.

"To his heart attack?" Paulie finished it for him, and immediately wished he hadn't, as Angelo looked up sharply.

"Yeah." Angelo dropped his head again. Everyone did when the subject of the Old Man's passing was raised. It was an unspoken mark of respect, that Paulie dimly realized he'd just violated in some way. He cursed himself, told himself to be more careful.

"Anyway," Angelo went on. "After he died, I wanted to take a look at it. See if we could sort it out." As Angelo started talking again it looked like he didn't really care about respecting the Old Man. But why would he, all this was his now...

"So I asked Paulo, he handles things down with the Colombians, I asked him if there were any alternatives to our regular routes. You know we generally have it come in on containers?" Angelo said this casually, as if it was common knowledge, but Paulie felt a buzz of thrill again. He didn't know. He knew that high up in the organization this was what got discussed, but he'd never been present before when it was. He forced his face to stay neutral. He glanced at Tommy, and was disappointed to see he was almost looking bored.

"So we had another look at flying it in," Angelo was continuing. "I went down there, to meet with him. We looked at small aircraft, coming in to airfields. No customs to pay off. Or even dropping it from the air..." With his hand he mimed an aircraft flying over his desk, but then winced. "I didn't like it. You have to file and record flight plans. Planes are tracked. It's... messy." Angelo shook his head. "But then Paulo had this idea. We were sitting in this restaurant in Caracas. Overlooking the harbor, and we were watching these sailboats, and then Paulo turned to me and he says 'why can't we just sail it in?'" Angelo looked suddenly at Paulie.

Paulie didn't know what to say, so he decided to stay quiet. After a worrying silence, Angelo continued.

"So we looked into it. Now me, I don't much like sailboats." Angelo glanced out the window as he said this, where Paulie knew he had a large motor cruiser moored on a dock outside the house. He knew because he'd heard about the parties. Word was Angelo threw the most amazing parties, for his closest friends. They were little short of orgies, limitless amounts of coke and girls imported from Eastern Europe and South America.

"But Paulo, he knows a bit about them. He said how a load of retired folks travel around in them. How they go where the hell they like. Without having to tell no one *where* they were going. And how the whole customs thing is kind of voluntary – you come into a harbor, and if there is any customs guy, he don't know where the fuck you've come from. You tell them if you've come from the next town down the coast, or across the whole fucking sea." He paused again, as if reliving the original conversation.

"But we couldn't ask these guys. These old timers. I mean they're pretty unlikely smugglers," Angelo laughed suddenly. "And they're rich enough anyway. They don't need the money. So I left Paulo with a challenge. Find me someone who could do a test run. Just a token amount. See what the costs were. See how it works."

There was a soft electronic ping as an email hit Angelo's computer. His eyes moved to it without moving his head. He read the first few lines, then went back to his story.

"Then two weeks later Paulo calls me up, tells me he's found the perfect fucking guy. An Italian, he's sailed his boat all the way across from Europe, and now he's heading here, to the States, before going back home again. He's alone. And best of all, he's *totally* up for it. So we check him out. Paulo takes him out for dinner and while they're doing that we get on the boat, and sweep it. It's clean. *He's* clean. It all checks out. So we have to make a decision. I figure we give it a go, and we load him up. Ten keys." Angelo snorted loudly, like it was a reflex action to the mention of cocaine.

"Then I think, *fuck it.* Let's really do this. So we put a bit more on board. *Eighty keys.*" He paused, to let the implications of such a large amount sink in. "We bury a tracker in there, make sure he sees it. Make sure he knows we're gonna be on top of him the whole fricking time. We agree how he's gonna come in this little harbor north of Florida. We're gonna move the product the rest of the way by truck."

Angelo smiled wistfully. "Eighty keys. If we can get that in without paying off the guys at the dock. That's..." He stopped suddenly, as if realizing revealing his profit margins was going too far. "That's a sweet fricking deal. That's what it is. So anyway. Paulo waves the guy off at the port, and the both of us watch this tracker as the guy sails north." With this Angelo turned the iPad around, and pulled up an app. It showed a map of Central America and the southern United States. Marked out on it, was a dotted line, showing the route taken.

"He goes up through the Caribbean. Shoots east of Cuba, and everything's looking good. But then he changes direction. On the computer. I'm like – what the fuck? And I call up Paulo. I ask him – what the fuck? And he tells me the guy's *phoned him* – from the sailboat – to say he's skirting round the back of some bad weather."

Those words are left hanging for a few seconds, as Angelo seems to become more present again. He looks at the two men in front of him, then chooses Paulie and lets his eyes rest there. "And look, you can toggle on the weather. On the map here." He does so now, spinning the iPad around so he can see it better himself. Suddenly the screen changes, to show the weather systems overlaying the route. "And it's not bad fricking weather the asshole's sailed into. It's a goddamn hurricane."

There was another silence. Paulie wondered if he was expected to do or say something, maybe even give a snort of laughter at this unknown man's stupidity, but he knew nothing at all about boats, so wasn't sure if this was appropriate or not. In the end he settled for scratching awkwardly at his nose. It seemed to do the trick since Angelo continued.

"At first the guy ain't concerned. He reckons he can get around it, or below it. Or it'll somehow miss him – or whatever. But all the time I'm comparing where this little boat is and where the weather guys say this storm is. And I can see he's not gonna get around it. The whole fucking lot is gonna land on top of him. But what can we do? We can't get out there. We just have to wait. Then the guy phones again, says he's damaged the boat. The steering or some shit. So he has this idea he's gonna call the Coastguard to get some help. Obviously Paulo tells him *that* ain't happening. Not with eighty keys of finest Columbian on board. But when he does the guy panics, says he'll throw it over the side. So the whole thing's going to *fuck*." Angelo's voice hardens suddenly. "And I'm thinking, how we gonna get eighty keys out of the ocean? And clearly we ain't."

He was silent for a moment, thinking. Then Angelo shook his head again. "The next thing, there's *another* call from the guy. He tells Paulo he's gonna have to issue a mayday, the boat's fricking *sinking*. He's right in the middle of the hurricane and his boat's going under." Angelo held up both his hands in surrender. Then he sat back in his chair. "And that's the last we hear from him. We found out afterward he did issue a..." Angelo searched the air for the word. "Not a *mayday*, something else..." He turned to the man in the blue suit. "What'd they call it?"

"A Pan Pan," the man said.

"Yeah. Fucking Pan Pan. The Miami coast guard picked it up, and when they didn't hear anything else, they sent out a helicopter to look for him. But by the time it got there, the yacht was already sunk. Gone. About four hundred miles out."

The story seemed to be finished, and though Paulie was beyond thrilled that Angelo had shared it with him, he had no idea why he had. Even so, he had to say something.

"Fuck," he said.

"Nah," Angelo replied, unexpectedly. He waved the comment away with his hand. "It's only eighty keys. Not a big fucking deal. Just a shame because it would have been nice to bring that in..."

He paused again.

"But shit happens. Shit fricking happens."

There was another silence as they all considered the wisdom in this.

"But then I had a think about it," Angelo went on, leaning forward suddenly. "And I wondered something. Why would a guy, who's on a *sinking* sailboat – in a goddamn hurricane – why would that guy bother to make a call?"

"What?" Paulie frowned.

"Why would he call Paulo? I mean what does he think we're gonna do? He issues the *Pan Pan*, which is this call you make when you want to alert the helicopter, but you don't know for sure if you need it – you know, you wanna put them on standby. Then he calls *Paulo*. He tells *us* he's sinking. But he doesn't make the Mayday call. It's never registered. Doesn't that strike you as odd?"

Paulie considered. With zero experience in shipping in the product, and even less in sailing, he had no real idea, but at the same time he sensed how this meeting was some kind of test. If he could only think of the right thing to say.

"Guys like that. They know they've gotta show respect," he replied, giving it his best shot.

Angelo's brow furrowed just enough to make Paulie know he'd got it wrong. "I fricking wouldn't," he said dismissively. "What? I'm about to drown and I got time to make one call? I make the mayday call. Every fricking time."

There was another silence, and eventually Paulie shrugged. "Sure," he said, feeling an ache in his guts. He shifted awkwardly in his chair. "Yeah, me too."

There was another long silence, during which another email came in. Again Angelo glanced at it, gave it a few seconds of attention, then looked up again.

"And then I got a call." He smiled now, just a subtle twisting of his pale lips.

Paulie was totally lost now. He tried to keep the anxiety off his face.

"Just a call. From one of my guys – you don't know the guy." Angelo dismissed that idea out of hand. "My guy wanted to let me know about this funny story. How one of *his* guys got offered a half key of coke. By some guy. Some Italian guy, but *Italian* Italian, not Italian American, you know what I mean?" Angelo glanced at Paulie and raised his eyebrows. "The funny thing was, he didn't want enough for it. What do you make of that?"

Paulie began stroking his chin now. Finally he had a glimmer of where this might be going.

"Italian guy?"

"Yeah."

"The guy on your boat. The sailboat. He was Italian, right?"

"Yup."

"Italian Italian?"

"Uh huh."

Paulie thought some more.

"They ever find the wreckage?"

Angelo shook his head. "The Coastguard wrote it down as lost at sea. Sunk."

"They didn't dive down? Make sure?"

"Too deep. We looked at that, as a way of getting the fucking coke back. Too far out."

Paulie stroked his chin some more.

"So maybe... Maybe it didn't sink?"

"That's what I'm thinking."

"So then where is it?"

"Good fricking question." Angelo grinned now. "I asked my guy to find out about this Italian guy, but no-one knows jack about him. So they dig around a little and the only thing they hear, is some other guy reckons he's living on a boat somewhere."

"A boat?"

"Oh yeah. A *sailboat*."

"Where?"

"They don't know exactly. But..."

Paulie glanced at Tommy. An understanding forming at last for what the job was.

"You ever been to Lornea Island?" Angelo asked.

"I don't do vacations."

"Well you're about to have one." He spun the computer around to show them the screen. "It's a long shot. There's a dozen places the guy could be hiding, *if* he's on the island. Marinas. Little creeks. Shit like that. Or he could have left. Or more likely he could have never been there in the first place, because he's fish food. But I need someone I can trust to go and check it out." Angelo sat back in his swivel chair and looked at the two men in front of him.

"Danny here will give you some pictures of the boat, and the guy." At the mention of his name, the guy in the suit stood and walked silently over with an envelope. Paulie pulled out the photographs of a white sailboat with a blue painted cabin. Another of a smiling young man. He stared at the photograph with a hatred and an electric thrill, hope spreading throughout him like the blossoming of a flower. When he and Tommy had been ordered to visit Jimmy the Fish, he'd been disappointed the command had been to give him a warning, and not to put a bullet between his eyes like he dreamed of doing. Paulie yearned for the ultimate chance to prove his loyalty, and his competence. And here at last was his chance.

"And if we find him? What do you want done?" He frowned as a horrible thought crossed his mind. Every time he thought he understood what Angelo was saying, he got it wrong. Might the same have happened again. Might Angelo just want another warning delivered? "Not like Jimmy the Fish?" He said.

"No, not like Jimmy the fucking Fish." Angelo angered at once. "This asshole stole my coke. I want his balls cut off and his head in a fucking box." For the first time in the meeting, it was Tommy that Angelo looked at. Paulie followed his gaze, and saw how the big man was staring calmly back, completely unmoved by the order to take another man's life. He felt a surge of jealousy. Then Angelo spoke again.

"Oh. And even more than that. I want those eighty keys *back*."

TWENTY-FIVE

THE WATER'S cold but I don't even notice. I feel – as I'm falling through the air – how the side of my kayak crashes hard into the hull of the yacht, knocking it with a thump that must reverberate throughout the entire boat. And then I'm under the water, gulping down mouthfuls of stale marina seawater before I think to close my mouth. Normally it's peaceful when you go underwater, but now I'm panicking. I've got to get to the surface, get back in my kayak and get out of sight before they get out on deck to see what's happened. I flap my arms, but it's more like a bird learning to fly than swimming. Finally my head breaks clear, and when the water drains from my eyes I look around. The kayak is right next to me, but capsized.

Moving fast I place my hands on either side, near the front, so I can lever myself back on board without capsizing it again. At the same time I glance to the cockpit of the *Mystery*. They're not there yet. I think. They're *naked*. They'll have to get some clothes on before they come out. And maybe there's other things too. I'm not exactly sure if you can just stop having sex if you're interrupted in the middle. Like with dogs. Or when you go to the toilet. No, I know that's stupid. Or just wishful thinking, because I really, really, *really* don't want Amber to see it was me who was spying on her. I don't know how I'll ever explain this if she does.

I scream at my brain to calm down. Thank God I've practiced this. Sometimes I watch tourists who come and do kayaking on their vacations, and if they fall out they usually can't get back in at all, all because they don't know the technique. You have to pull yourself up and twist onto your butt all in one smooth movement. I do it now, and slither back into the kayak. When I'm in I grab the paddle and start going as *hard* as I can. Fortunately the front of the kayak is already pointing away from the pontoon, and since going straight is quicker than turning, I just keep going, straight across the open water towards the rock breakwater on the other side. It divides this part of the harbor from the channel back to the sea, but there's a second channel too, which leads to the commercial harbor. Then I realize if I get to the second channel I can hide there, behind the rocks, so I paddle harder on my left side to swerve over to the entrance. But there's about twenty feet of open water I have to cross before I get there. So I just paddle as fast as I can, panting like crazy and expecting to hear Amber yelling out my name at any second.

But then I'm out of sight, behind the tall barrier of rocks. I stop paddling, my chest heaving up and down. I didn't really plan where to escape to, but actually it's worked out well. As well as being hidden, they can't get to me here, nor can they get over here to see who I am, at least not without walking all the way around the marina basin.

I listen, in case I can hear them shouting, but there's nothing – no sound at all. And after ten minutes of just waiting there, I loop the kayak's painter around a pointed rock, so it can't drift away, then carefully climb out. Then I scramble up the breakwater, so I can peek through a gap at the top. I'm really careful, in case they're on deck watching out, but quickly I see they're not. The *Mystery* is there, just as it was before, but the deck is empty, and so is the pontoon. They must have... Well, I don't know what they must have done. I wonder for a second if maybe they didn't hear me after all, it's hard to believe, given how hard the kayak crashed into the hull of the yacht. But then they did look pretty absorbed in what they were doing.

Yuck.

I decide not to think about that. So I focus on my situation instead. Which isn't great. I'm soaking wet. It's late in the year and I don't have any spare clothes. And the only way I can get home is on the bus. Plus, now the adrenaline from nearly being chased has worn off a bit, meaning I'm already quite cold. On top of that, I can't just paddle back to the ramp I launched from, because to do that I'd have to go past the Mystery again, and they would only have to glance out the window and they'd see me. And when I think about *that* I realize something else too. If they do suspect it was me, Amber only has to check where I store my kayak to see if it's there or not. So on top of everything else, I have to return it as soon as possible.

I'm feeling glum as I pick my way back down the rocks and into the kayak. Then I paddle all the way up the channel until I get to the commercial harbor. It's where the fishermen unload their catch, and I'm wary here, because they get super mad when tourists come in here, getting in their way. But I'm lucky, there's no one here at the moment. There's another problem though – there's no slipway here to pull the kayak out. I paddle around a bit, wondering what to do, but then figure I might be able to just pull it up the wall, since the tide's quite high. So I stop by one of the iron ladders and loop the painter around my hand. Then I climb up and when I get to the top I try to heave the kayak after me. It's made of tough plastic, so it's strong enough, but it's pretty heavy and I can't do it. For a little while I get really annoyed – I'm getting really cold now and this is just frustrating. But then I tow the kayak, back down in the water, until it's under one of the mini cranes the fishermen use to lift out the boxes of fish. You're totally not allowed to use these, but like I said, there's no boats in right now, and I know how to use them. I lower the winch, then climb down another ladder, hook it on and climb back up. Then I fire up the crane and winch it up. Then, finally, I can tie the wheels back on, and get it back in the alley where I store it.

The whole time I'm working, I keep a pretty careful watch out for Amber and Carlos, but I don't see either of them. So I'm fairly sure she doesn't see me either. It's some consolation, as I squelch around to the bus stop in the town – the one that's well away from the harbor. I almost freeze to death waiting for the bus, and I'm worried the driver won't let me on, because I must look a bit crazy. But by then I'm only kind of damp rather than dripping wet, and the driver doesn't even ask. Then I sit right by the vent for the heater, and I think without that I'd probably get hypothermia and maybe die.

I have to change buses at Newlea, but there's a waiting room, and inside I find a big radiator, which I sit on. The Littlelea bus is cold though, and it's horrible when I have to get off, because it's a bit of a walk from the stop to my house and my clothes feel heavy and damp. But fortunately the house is warm, because I left the heating on full before I left. And as soon as I'm inside I run myself a bath.

* * *

I try to decide whether Amber saw me, and if so what to do about it. On the one hand, there's no way they wouldn't have heard when the kayak hit the yacht's hull, but they probably couldn't tell what it was. Not least because they were distracted. I definitely didn't see them run onto the deck, but I didn't notice the windows. They could easily have looked out when I was getting back into the kayak, or when I was paddling away with my back turned. But on the other hand I was pretty quick, so if they did see me, it would have been the back of my head they saw. In that case, they might not have recognized me. And if Amber *did* recognize me, then she'll know that *I saw her* too, and more importantly, saw what she was doing. And I don't think she'll want to bring that up in a hurry. So even though I don't exactly feel good about how today went, I decide the best thing to do is try to forget it. And if Amber ever mentions it, to pretend I don't have any idea what she's talking about.

I still feel a bit glum, though. I reach out of the bath and pull my cellphone out of my damp coat pocket. It's a Samsung Galaxy S7. It's supposed to be waterproof to 1.5 meters, or nearly five feet, but I've never actually tested it before, on account of how cell phones are so expensive and I didn't want to risk breaking it for no reason. But actually it looks just fine. That cheers me up a bit. And now that I've shown it does work underwater, I try it again, holding it under the bath water. It's actually really cool. You can see it perfectly even when it's totally underwater, actually better than normal, because the water magnifies it a bit. You can't use the touch screen though – but I read before in the instructions how that's normal, because of how the water breaks the electrical connection. Or something, I don't remember the details.

I play with it a while, then grab a towel and dry it again. And then I think for a while.

I think about Carlos. There's something about him I don't like. Something I don't trust. His story about sailing across the Atlantic, for example. I don't believe for a minute he did that. I'm sure he's lying.

I start with Google. Carlos never told me his surname, but I remember he told me his dad comes from a place called Genoa in Italy. I check where it is on the map, and then start googling combinations of words that might find him. I try 'Carlos, *Mystery*, Genoa' – but nothing comes up. Then I remember how he said his mom is an artist in Barcelona. So I add more words to do with that. But still nothing relevant comes up, which isn't completely unexpected, but is a bit odd all the same. So then I decide to focus on the boat. If you have a boat you have to register it, and the most likely places, if Carlos is telling the truth, is that it's registered either in Genoa or Barcelona. Then I have a bit of a problem, because everything I can find about registering boats in Italy is written in Italian, and everything about registering boats in Spain is written in Spanish. And I don't speak either Spanish or Italian. But with the help of Google Translate, I mostly figure it out. But again, I don't find anything.

Then I get out of the bath. You really need a proper computer to do actual research like this, and anyway, the hot water has run out again, and the bath is getting cold.

As I dry myself off I have another idea: Amber's Instagram page. Amber is *super* into Instagram. I don't know why I didn't think of it sooner, just about the first thing she does when she meets someone – anyone – is to follow them on Instagram, and then tag them in every single photo she uploads.

It takes me a while to log on to Instagram because I don't have an actual account – I don't do any social media, and I deleted all the fake accounts I set up before to let me follow other people. But when I'm in I scroll back through Amber's timeline, expecting to see hundreds of photos of him. But there's nothing there. There's no-one called Carlos mentioned anywhere. No one tagged. No photos of him. Nothing. Confused, I go to Amber's Facebook page and check there. I figure that maybe Europeans don't do Instagram? But I can't find him on Facebook either. Or at least, if he is there, Amber hasn't friended him. Which is crazy, because I already saw they were way more than friends.

I look back over the notes I've made. I realize I've found precisely nothing about who he is, or where his boat comes from, or anything at all. It's like he doesn't exist. Or maybe like he doesn't *want to* exist.

TWENTY-SIX

I GET UP EARLY the next day and empty my backpack, ready for the day ahead. Then I pack some food – there's not much left in the house but I find an apple and make a sandwich from two crusts and some cheese. I can always stop by the store to get something nicer. Then I go upstairs and I kneel down beside my bed. I reach underneath and pull out my spy box.

Inside there's a tangle of black cables, and several Tupperware boxes from when I was organized, for a while at least. I went through this phase, a couple of years ago, when I was a bit obsessed with James Bond-style gadgets. Not the killing types – just the spy ones. It's really amazing when you think about it, when they made the films originally, the inventions that Q gave to Bond were just made up – no one thought it was possible to actually build them. But now, you can just buy them, on the internet. And they're not even that expensive either. Although as I found out, if you do buy the cheap ones, you often find the instructions are in Chinese, or if not in Chinese, then written by someone who is Chinese and doesn't speak English very well.

I empty the box onto the bed. I bought most of this stuff just after Amber and I set up our detective agency. We had to shut it down, because we found out it's illegal for people under the age of eighteen to operate as private detectives on Lornea Island. I was fourteen at the time, and Amber was sixteen, so we weren't even close. Plus you need a license which we also didn't have. But for a little while we didn't know any of that. Even so, we did get an actual case, and we did actually solve it. Sort of. We spent most of the money we earned in buying the original *Blue Lady*, but Dad wouldn't let me spend all of it, so that's when I went a bit mad buying all the spy gear.

But then the problem was I had no one to spy on. The agency was shut down, and Amber figured out pretty early on to sweep her house for bugs. Then Dad told me if I didn't stop surveilling him he'd take all my electronic devices outside and smash them with a hammer, even my laptop. So after that they just ended up here in this box under my bed.

I pick through them now, thinking what might be useful. I pick out my cell phone charger, which actually *is* a cell phone charger, but also has a secret listening device in it, my tracker, and my endoscope, which is a long cable with a camera lens built into the end. Then I stand up, and right away I notice myself in the mirror. Without thinking I've just got dressed normally, so I sort that out. I throw on a baseball cap, and get changed into some clothes I don't normally wear. Finally downstairs, I grab one of Dad's heavy overcoats. It's too big for me, but it makes me look older.

Then I go out and catch the first bus to Newlea. Forty minutes later I'm standing on the harborside looking out over the boats in Holport marina.

* * *

The *Mystery* is exactly where I last saw her, the second-to-last boat at the end of the pontoon, with only the *Blue Lady* outside of her. There's no one about. Keeping as unobtrusive as I can, I unlock the gate to access the pontoon, then make my way down towards the end. There's nothing I can do to avoid walking past *Mystery*, and I'll just have to hope Carlos doesn't see me. Or Amber. If either of them do it's not a disaster, because today I have the keys, and I can just say I'm going to do some work on *Blue Lady*. And in a way I am. Even so, I try to make my footsteps as quiet as possible as I walk past the yacht, and I'm relieved when no one comes out from the cabin. I do see the hatch is open though, and I hear music playing from inside.

Normally I love jumping onto the *Blue Lady*, feeling the way she gives a little under my feet. But today I'm focused. Very quietly I open the door to the cabin, slip inside, then close it behind me. I don't want anyone to know I'm on here. Then I finally breathe properly for the first time in five minutes.

I slip out of my backpack and Dad's overcoat, and unpack my gear. The first thing I do is set up the endoscope. I only had to pay $49.99 for it, which is a bargain, but on the other hand it is just a camera lens fitted to a long wire, with a USB plug on the other end. I run the cable up to one of the port-side windows, that looks out onto the side where the *Mystery* is moored. I open the window just enough to poke the camera outside, and gently close the window again, so that the camera lens is held in position, looking out over the yacht. Then I go back and plug the other end into my laptop, and turn it on. I have to go back up and adjust it a bit, but in the end I'm happy. I've got a nice clear view of the whole of the yacht's cockpit. No one can go in or out without me seeing them, but there's absolutely no chance that anyone can see me watching *them*.

Feeling a bit better about life now, I brew up some coffee, and open my bag of donuts.

TWENTY-SEVEN

THE THING ABOUT STAKEOUTS – and you never see this in movies or whatever – is just how incredibly boring they are. You always get things set up, and then expect that something is going to happen. But it never works like that. It's a bit like fishing in that respect.

Anyway, twenty minutes later I've brewed and drunk my coffee, and eaten three donuts, and even though I've got one left I don't want to eat it because then I'll feel sick, or sicker than I feel already. And even though I've been watching the screen the whole time, absolutely nothing has happened. So I unplug the camera from the laptop and plug it back into my phone instead. I do this so I can still see the feed from the camera, just on a smaller screen, but I can connect the laptop to the internet.

I don't actually know *why* I do this, since there's nothing I need to do on the internet, but like I said, stakeouts are boring. Then I decide to google *Steve Rose*. I suppose I want to see if anything has happened about his scientific fraud. And fairly quickly I find it has. I watch a news report which says his TV series has been canceled by the network. The report doesn't say why, or anything about how he cheated when he reported the size of the sharks, it just says it's down to unexpected and unforeseen events. I check my email next, since I haven't heard from any of the guys in Australia. That's a bit odd, because we all agreed how we should stay in touch, after the cruise finished, but then I had to leave early, and I haven't heard anything from any of them. I check my inbox and my spam folders, but I can't find anything. I wonder for a while about emailing Debbie, to ask if she knows any more. But I decide against it.

Instead I eat my last donut.

Then I have to go to the toilet. Actually it's called the head. That's what toilets on boats are called. This is actually a bit of a problem. The head on the *Blue Lady* is a marine toilet that uses seawater to pump out whatever you put in the bowl. And for reasons I don't think I need to explain, you're not supposed to use it in a marina. Normally it's not a big issue, because there's a public washroom by the end of the pontoon, but I don't want to walk past the *Mystery* again if I don't have to. So I make an exception and use the head, and then pump very quietly so that no one will hear me from the pontoon. It's OK, because it pumps out on the starboard side of the boat, which is the side not facing the *Mystery*. When I get back I'm feeling much better. And when I check the screen of my phone, I see that something's happening.

I actually almost miss it, because the image is so small. But on the screen of my cell phone I see a little image of Carlos swinging a backpack over his shoulder, and stepping over the rail of the *Mystery*. On the little screen it looks so harmless I almost go to the window to check, but I force myself not to. At least not until he goes out of sight from the camera. To be sure I count to thirty and then I peek out the window. There's no one in sight. So I quietly walk outside and jump onto the pontoon, keeping my footsteps light so it doesn't rock too much under my weight. I jog toward the stern of the *Mystery* and peer around it. And sure enough I see Carlos' back disappearing up the ramp.

I look at the yacht now. The hatch is now closed, and I'm 99% sure that means Amber isn't on board. After all, her car wasn't here when I arrived, or at least it wasn't parked in any of the normal places. Plus she's got college. Though that didn't stop her the other day.

I wait until I see Carlos open the gate at the end of the pontoon and shut it behind him. Then, when I'm sure he's gone, I climb onto the *Mystery* and try the hatch. It's locked. That's good. It means Amber definitely isn't here. But it also makes it hard to get in. Hard, but not impossible. I jump off the yacht again and fetch my backpack. I open the front compartment this time, and I pull out my lock breaking kit. I told you I had a phase when I was obsessed with spy gear. Well I also bought a lock-picking kit. It was pretty good fun. It had see-through versions of all the common lock types, and the right tools and instructions for how you could open them. For weeks I was obsessed with it. It was a bit like when Dad bought me a Rubik's cube when I was small. I just played with it week after week until I'd memorized all the different ways to solve it. I could even do it blindfolded. Well, nearly blindfold. But picking a lock is a bit like solving the Rubix cube. You just identify what stage you're at, and then perform a sequence of moves to shift it to the next stage until it opens. The lock on Carlos' yacht is a common Yale lock, so there's only three stages to solve. I do it in less than three minutes.

I slide the hatch back a little way and look inside. Seeing where he lives makes me pause a bit. I realize I'm sort of crossing a line by going down there. So before I climb down, I get off the boat again and check along the pontoon, to make sure he's not coming back already. The pontoon's empty, but I'm still a bit anxious, since I don't know where he's gone, or how long he'll be away. For a while I consider setting up the endoscope again, so that it's pointing down the pontoon, and I'll see when he returns. But the cable isn't long enough. It's annoying actually, because I could have got a much longer one for another twenty dollars. But it's too late now. I decide I'll just have to be quick, and I'm wasting time worrying about it. I abandon the idea, and climb back onto the yacht.

This time I slide the hatch right back and step down into the warm interior. I cast my eyes around. The place is a bit of a mess. There's a cereal bowl on the saloon table, along with a sailing magazine folded back against the spine. He must have been reading it while he ate. I glance at the article, about cruising in the Caribbean, but it doesn't look relevant. Then there's clothes all over the benches. I notice the carpet on the floor. I can't help but think how I saw Amber lying on it yesterday, and I have to shake my head to clear the image. Then I see his computer on a shelf – an Apple Mac, and right away I pull it out and open up the lid.

I'm annoyed when it asks for a password. I've never owned an Apple computer but I know that if you don't actually know someone's password, there's not much you can do to break in. I try a couple of obvious things – like '*Mystery*' and 'Amber' but then I give up, because I don't want it to send Carlos a password reminder – he'd figure out pretty quickly what's going on. So then I shut the lid again, and look around for what I came here for.

Of all the spy products I bought, my favorite is my phone-charger-listening-device. It's a Samsung charger – or rather it *isn't* a Samsung charger, but it looks exactly like one. You can use it like a normal cell phone charger if you want to – it works just the same – but it also has a secret listening device built into it. I can dial into it and then listen to what-ever the secret microphone on the charger picks up. Or, if I want, I can have it listen all the time, and then text me to say when it's picking something up. I think it's awesome. The only problem is, people have lots of different types of cell phone – Apple, and Samsung and Nokia and Motorola – and they all use different, branded chargers. So if you were a proper professional detective you'd need to have a whole range of different charger listening devices, because otherwise the person you were trying to spy on would see right away that someone had switched their charger for a different brand. And they might get suspicious.

However, I know that Carlos has a Samsung phone, just like mine. I noticed it the last time I was in here. The last time his phone was plugged in and charging on the little chart table, by the companionway steps. I look here now, and obviously the phone's not here – because he's taken it with him. But I don't care about that. I can't help smiling when I find the USB end of the cable, he has it taped down with a piece of gaffer tape. All I need to do is switch over his charger for mine, and I'll be able to hear every word he says when he's in the boat. I quickly follow the cable back to where it's plugged into the socket in the side of the yacht. And then I stop.

Where Carlos' real charger is plugged in doesn't look anything like my surveillance charger. I'm so annoyed with myself I hit the side of my head with my palm. Of course. Mine's made to look like a normal charger, but his is a *European* one. His has round pins, instead of the normal flat ones. The only way I can plug my charger into the boat is by using an adapter. And I don't have an adapter. Even if I did, it would look fairly suspicious. But the bigger issue is I don't have one.

I sit down on the bench. Defeated.

I think for a moment about slipping my tracker device into his jacket, or his shoes. But that's no good either. It's a non-starter. I do *have* a tracker device, but when I bought it I didn't understand how you need a monthly subscription to make them actually work. They're like cell-phones you see, they work on the same data networks. And I just used the three months free trial that came with it, but never signed up for the ongoing subscription. I suppose I could sign up again now, but I left the tracker at home on my bed. So that's out too.

I'm about to leave when I think I might as well check the drawers by the chart table, to see if there's anything interesting there. And it's lucky I do, because right away I find something.

TWENTY-EIGHT

I⊤'s the boat's registration papers. Or rather, it's *a* boat's registration papers, but it can't be this one. The papers are written in Italian, but I was looking at papers like this last night, checking to see where the *Mystery* was registered. And it is Genoa, after all. But the name of the boat isn't *Mystery*. It's *Falco*.

I stare at the papers, trying to remember what all the Italian words mean. It doesn't make any sense. The class and size of the yacht on the papers looks right for the *Mystery*. Then I notice something else. There's a little box where the description of the boat is given. This is what it says:

Scafo bianco con timoneria blu

Even with my little Italian lesson last night I wouldn't know what this means, but alongside it is a little diagram to help. It shows a side view of the yacht – and it's shown in two colors. The lower part of the hull is painted white, just as this boat is. But the upper part – the sides of the cabin – they're blue. Right away that makes me remember something. Just before I fell in, when I was coming alongside in my kayak, I noticed how the paint was loose on the side of the cabin, and underneath was another color. I wasn't paying much attention to paint back then, so I climb outside now. I quickly check around me, that there's still no sign of Carlos coming back, and then I walk around to the window that I looked through when I saw Amber and Carlos having sex. I crouch down and scratch at the paint.

Most of the places it doesn't come loose, but there's a couple of areas where the new paint hasn't bonded properly, and underneath the white, the color is a light blue. Just like in the diagram. I rock back on my heels. This boat isn't the *Mystery*. Or rather it's *a* mystery, because until very recently it was called *Falco*.

* * *

I sit there for a while trying to make sense of it. I have some ideas but nothing that really makes sense. That's when I'm disturbed by a noise. It's the clang of metal, and it's familiar to me. Almost too familiar in fact – I'm so lost in my thoughts I almost ignore it, but then I realize it's the noise the gate makes at the top of the pontoon. It sticks a bit, so you have to give it a good old pull, and when it shuts it makes this metallic clang. So suddenly I know exactly what it means. It means Carlos is coming back.

I stand up at once, and I can see a tall figure walking briskly between some of the smaller boats. I see glimpses of dark hair. It's him, already half way down the pontoon.

I feel a surge of panic. I want to get off the boat as fast as possible, but stupidly I've left my bag down in the cabin. So I sprint back down there, cursing myself for being too casual. I chuck all my gear back into my bag. I accidentally miss with my charger, and it falls on the floor under the cooker. I have to kneel down to retrieve it, losing valuable seconds. The pontoon isn't very long, and he'll be here in seconds, so I can't do anything about putting everything back the way I found it, it's too late for that. I throw my bag on my shoulder, run back up the steps and jam the hatch back hard. I feel it catch behind me and – thank God – the lock re-engages.

Then I swing over the side of the yacht and onto the pontoon between his boat and mine. I land just as Carlos comes around the corner from the main length of the pontoon. He sees me at once, and stops.

"Billy?" His voice is not unfriendly, but it's suspicious, or at least pretty curious. "What are you doing here?"

Just as I'm about to reply with my excuse from earlier, that I'm here to work on the *Blue Lady*, I notice something awkward. It's hard not to. His yacht is now rocking from side to side. It's from where I just ran to the side and jumped off. I realize I need to explain it somehow, otherwise he's going to know I was on board.

"I'm just..." I think fast. "Say did you see that RIB go past?" I try to make my voice sound annoyed, then shake my head. "They were driving way too fast. The speed limit for the harbor is four knots. And that's in the main channel." I point out vaguely at the water behind me, hoping he'll blame the rocking on the wake of the boat I just invented.

But Carlos just steps closer, giving me a strange look now. He looks behind me, at the still water. "What RIB?"

I open my mouth to repeat the lie, but I don't say anything. I've just made a stupid mistake. If a RIB had gone past the wake would be obvious, and it would make all the boats rock, not just his. I close my mouth, and shrug instead. But then maybe he does believe me, because he suddenly breaks into a smile.

"Ah Billy... Billy.... You really do love your rules, don't you?" He swings his backpack off his shoulder, and I see it's full of groceries. He shakes his head again. "You working on your boat?"

I can't quite believe my luck. I nod my head. "Yeah just some... stuff I had to do."

Carlos nods, like I don't need to say any more. And I'm about to turn away and climb back aboard *Blue Lady*, when he goes on.

"Say Billy, you weren't here the other day were you?"

I freeze. "What?"

"Yesterday. Morning, about eleven. Someone knocked on the side of the boat." Carlos smiles as he asks me, smiling openly, and looking me right in the eye. I feel guilty panic rising inside me. I force my face into a confused look, like I decided last night, but I feel my face flush deeper.

"The wrong side of the boat." Carlos goes on.

"The... what?"

"Yeah. They were in a... canoe I think. Crashed right into the side. Then whoever it was fell into the water. Amber thought it might be you."

I blink at him.

"Me?"

"Yeah."

"Amber thought that?"

"Yeah."

"She was with you?"

"Guess so."

I swallow. "No, it wasn't me."

I try to meet his gaze, because that's what someone who wasn't guilty would do. But he won't stop staring at me. It feels like my face is melting under his stare.

"The water's kinda cold for swimming huh?"

I'm about to answer, but then I figure this might be a trick. So I consider before I do. "I wouldn't know. I haven't been in for ages."

This time I manage to keep eye contact.

"Oh no?" He says. He's not smiling as much now, and I feel I'm winning whatever battle we're having. But then, just the wrong moment – I feel I need to sneeze. I will the itching to go away, but it just gets stronger and stronger, and in the end I can't help myself. I turn away and sneeze right there in front of him, and then, as I'm wiping my nose afterward he snorts a kind of laugh.

"Nasty cold you've got there Billy," he says, and suddenly his voice sounds bored. He doesn't say anything else, but he vaults elegantly over the guardrail and onto the yacht. I hear him whistling as he unlocks the hatch. And I know – he knows.

* * *

OK, he knows. Or at least he *thinks* he knows. But he can't prove anything. That's what I tell myself, when I'm back inside again, and watching the yacht through the endoscope feed. And even if he could prove it – if they took a photo of me, or something, when I saw them having sex – it's not illegal to kayak in the marina. It's not even illegal to look into people's windows. What *is* illegal is to change the name of your yacht.

Well, actually it's not. People change the names of their boats all the time, when they buy them usually, or if they just get bored of the old name. But they don't do it very often, since it's supposed to mean bad luck. But if you do change the name then you also have to change the registration documents. That's obvious.

And anyway, the *Mystery*, or *Falco*, or whatever I should call it now, isn't just a boat, not in the sense that most people have boats. Carlos actually *lives* on it. So it's more like someone changing the name of their house. No, not the name, the *address*. It's like someone changing their identity. And why would anyone do *that*?

I ponder this for a while, but my head keeps replaying the encounter I just had with him, and each time I feel more and more embarrassed. He was so casual when he asked whether I'd been looking in the window yesterday, it's like he was playing with me. I realize now that he saw through my excuse about the RIB too. He knew I was on board his yacht. And he didn't even care. He thought it was funny.

And then it's like this feeling that's been bubbling away underneath breaks up to the surface, just for a moment. I've been an idiot about this. I'm *being* an idiot. I'm seeing a problem where there isn't one, not really. OK, so Carlos and Amber were smoking dope. It's not such a big deal. I *knew* she smoked dope before I met her anyway, she told me. We stopped talking about it, but that was just because of how I didn't approve. To be honest, I'm quite unusual in my class in *not* smoking drugs these days.

I go back to watching my laptop screen again. It's showing the feed from the endoscope again. And at that moment Carlos comes out up onto the deck. He steps onto the roof of the cabin and I watch him hanging some washing out. It's a couple of t-shirts and he tosses them over the boom, arranging them carefully so they don't crease. He has his head tipped over to one side, and it takes me a while to work out why, but then I see the reason. He has his phone jammed between his shoulder and his ear, and he's speaking into it while he works. And like normal he's laughing and smiling. Then he finishes the washing and goes back down below, transferring the phone to his hand now. I feel a burst of frustration – if only my phone charger listening device had worked I could have called it up now. I could find out who he was speaking to, and what he was saying. I'd *know* if it was suspicious.

Then I have a sudden idea – but I have to be quick if it's going to work. I snatch up my own phone and dial Amber's number. As it connects I realize I have no idea what to say if she picks up – but I don't have time to worry. Because – just as I expected – she doesn't pick up. Instead the call goes to her voicemail – the line's engaged. It's *Amber* that Carlos is talking to, I'm sure of it. I hang up, not leaving a message.

And then, finally, I properly wake up to what I'm doing. It's suddenly like I'm looking down on myself from above. And I don't like what I see. I should be at school, but I'm actually here *spying on my best friend*.

And not even for any reason. I thought I was going to find out something bad about Carlos, and that maybe Amber would decide to stop seeing him. But he hasn't really done anything wrong. OK, he anchored in the marine reserve – but if I'm going to be totally honest with you, even I've done that a few times, before I discovered the ledge for the kayak. Oh yeah, and he changed his boat name. So what? Maybe he changed it and he just hasn't had a chance to tell the Italian authorities. It's hardly a big deal.

And if Amber knew what I was doing, not just trying to watch her having sex – I shudder again at that thought – but also breaking into his boat, and planting electronic listening devices. She'd go crazy. She'd be so mad. I don't think she'd ever talk to me again.

And deep down I know there is a reason why I'm doing all this. I'm jealous. Of her getting on with her life, and being happy with Carlos, when I've gone and messed mine up by doing what I did in Australia.

So then I take a last look at the yacht on the screen of my laptop, then I unplug the endoscope lead from the laptop and loop the cable up. The screen goes black, then automatically closes. So the only thing showing is the article about Steve Rose, and how he lost the TV show. How *I* lost him his TV show. I feel sicker now than when I ate all the donuts. I feel miserable as I gather my stuff together and tidy up the boat. And then I climb off, and I go to catch the bus home.

TWENTY-NINE

TOMMY AND PAULIE stood side-by-side looking out over the narrow strip of water. Where it met the land it was bordered by a wide strip of thick, gray, low tide mud. A rickety wooden jetty reached out a small way, the far end only just reaching the brown water that swirled around the seaweed-covered uprights. Somewhere around here was the open sea, but the open horizon was lost somewhere down the maze of marshy creeks that made up this section of the island's coast.

Behind them stood a different vehicle – this time a gray-brown, unmarked panel van. It was a couple of years old – neither new, nor old enough to stand out in any way – and was parked by the only building for miles around, a locked and apparently abandoned boat house.

"What'd you say this place was called?" Paulie asked.

Tommy consulted the map gripped at his side in one big hand.

"Bishop's Landing."

"*Bishop's Landing.*" Paulie repeated, deadpan. "Well if he did land here, he didn't stay long before he fucked right off again."

Tommy's hand clenched into a fist around the edge of the map, but he said nothing. They were both getting grouchy. On the boat over Paulie had been full of enthusiasm. Clearly he regarded this as his big chance to impress the new boss. But that had slowly ebbed away as they'd followed dirt track after dirt track to the hundreds of possible places you could hide a yacht.

Tommy wasn't used to working with such ups and downs. He was the sort of guy that labored at a task for as long as it took to get it done. But then that way of thinking seemed kinda old fashioned these days. He turned, ready to walk back to the van to try the next creek down.

"You coming?"

"I dunno," Paulie said. "*Fuck this.*"

Tommy's big face creased just enough to indicate he was losing patience. Unlike Paulie he no longer dreamed of achieving a position of real power in the organization – if he ever had. These days he had a different dream. Of a modest apartment, somewhere near a golf course, down in Florida. Far enough away that he wouldn't have to spend all of his days looking over his shoulder in case some kid came after him, looking for revenge, for what Tommy might have done to his father. But with the Old Man's death, and Angelo deciding he had to work with Paulie, any chance of retirement seemed a long way off. Maybe after this though. Maybe if they got a good result, recovered the coke...

"Fuck this," Paulie said again.

"Yeah you mentioned," Tommy snapped suddenly. Then he took a breath. Whatever success here meant, getting angry wasn't going to help it any time soon.

"Hey, maybe we should pack it in for the day?" He offered. "Find a motel? Grab a beer?" He didn't mention the hooker he was also thinking about, if he could find one.

"No." Suddenly there was a spark of enthusiasm in Paulie's face, which hadn't been there most of the afternoon. "No, I got an idea how we can speed this up." He turned to Tommy. "Tell me, what's the best place to hide a body?"

Tommy sighed as the beer and food slid from his mind. "Paulie, we've got to *find* the guy before we waste him..."

Paulie looked irritated.

"No, I don't mean... It's a metaphor."

"A what?"

"Come on, just humor me. What's the best place to hide a body?"

Tommy stared at him. After a while he shrugged. "A lake," he said at last.

"A *lake*? No..."

"Yeah a lake. I put more bodies in lakes than anywhere else..."

"What the fuck? What are you even talking about?"

"I'm telling you. You stick a guy in a lake, gym weights zip-tied round the thighs and shoulders, he ain't ever coming up again. Don't matter how much he puffs up."

Paulie considered this for a moment, torn between making his point and not looking like this was both news to him and unpleasantly morbid. "OK. Sure. Lakes are good. But that ain't what I mean. I'm talking about a *metaphor*. I ain't looking for the literal answer."

"A metaphor?" Tommy repeated again.

"Yeah. It's like… a saying."

"A saying?"

"Yeah."

"*What's the best place to hide a body*? That's a saying?"

"Yeah."

"Well it ain't one I've ever heard."

"Jesus fuck." Paulie looked around, as if searching for something to punch.

"How about we just get on with it?" Tommy lumbered away, shaking his head.

They walked back to the van and climbed in. Tommy into the passenger seat, Paulie behind the wheel. Then Tommy studied the map, looking to see which of the dozens of possible spots left to check was closest. After a while he glanced up, wondering why Paulie hadn't started the van yet.

"I mean it," Paulie said instead. "*Metaphorically* speaking, what's the best place to hide a body?"

Tommy studied his partner for a while, wishing he'd taken the chance to retire when the Old Man was alive. He'd have let him go, Tommy was almost sure of it.

"So you're saying you don't want an actual answer, you want to know what the answer would be *if* this was a popular saying?"

"Yeah."

"Which it ain't."

Paulie winced involuntarily.

"Yeah."

"In that case I don't know."

"Oh fuck's sake, I give up, alright? The answer is, the best place to hide a body is *in a graveyard*."

Tommy thought about this for a while. "Kinda public isn't it?"

Paulie screwed up his nose in irritation. "Yeah but…"

"And you gotta dig the grave and fill it in one hit, which could be two or three hours work depending on the ground conditions. And you get people turning up to graveyards at all hours. It's risky."

"Fuck's sake Tommy. It's a saying. It ain't real. The point is it's the last place anyone would think to look, and if they did, all they're gonna find is a load more bodies anyhow."

Tommy blew his cheeks full of air. He thought how easy it would be to carry out DNA tests on any remains, how there would be a hundred other bodies there, and how the cops would know exactly the date they went in the ground, making it easy to get a time of death by comparison. It seemed a fucking stupid place to him, saying or otherwise. But he let it go.

"If you say so. I don't necessarily agree."

Paulie exhaled slowly, counting in his head as he did so. "OK. I'm just saying we could be wasting our time driving down these shitty little dirt tracks checking out Parson's fucking creek…"

"Bishop's…"

"Whatever. We should be looking in the bigger places."

There was a pause while Tommy thought about this.

"Why?"

"Because of what I just said. If the best place to hide a body is where there's a load of other bodies, then it follows that the same goes for a yacht. The best place is to hide it with a load of other yachts. In a marina."

Tommy hesitated, but in the end he couldn't not say it. He hadn't spent three months getting wound up by Paulie without learning nothing about being a pain in the ass himself. "But the best place to hide a body is in a lake. Zip tied with gym weights…"

"Shut the fuck up Tommy. Or I'm gonna shoot you in the fucking head and zip tie you to gym weights."

Tommy shut up. But as he did so he was smiling inside.

"How many marinas are there on this fucking island?" Paulie went on. "Any marked on that map?"

Tommy looked down at the map. There were several, but they'd been checking the smaller, more tucked away places first. "Uh huh," he said.

"Well? Where are they?"

"There's two in Newlea. One in a place called Catterline. And then one in… Holport."

"OK then, let's go."

"Which one?"

"I don't know. Fucking pick one."

Tommy rolled his eyes, but stuck his finger down onto the map, then checked to see which of the towns his finger was closest to.

"Holport," he said.

"Well, let's go to fucking Holport." Paulie said, and fired the engine.

THIRTY

TWENTY FIVE MINUTES later the van cruised by the road which fronted the public harbor in Holport. A forest of masts bristled from the yacht basin, and Tommy gazed out at them, bored. Paulie swung the car into a bay facing the water.

"Now what?" Tommy asked.

"You see it?"

"See what?"

"The yacht. Do you see it?"

"I dunno. I see a lot of yachts. They all look kinda the same."

Paulie didn't answer. Instead he yanked on the parking brake and pushed open the door. Tommy waited a moment and watched where he went, down a ramp that led to the floating pontoon where the boats were moored. But he didn't get very far. A large steel gate barred his way. Tommy watched while Paulie shook it, gently at first but then harder. Then he started looking at whether it was possible to climb over, but it didn't look easy. When Paulie went back to shaking it ineffectively, Tommy sighed. He got out of the van and opened the sliding door. Inside were a number of canvas bags. He opened one and rummaged around.

Moments later he joined Paulie at the gate, carrying a large pair of bolt cutters. Wordlessly he fitted them to the lock.

"What you doing?" Paulie was incredulous.

"Opening the gate."

"*Fuck no.* You wanna just announce we're here on fucking Twitter?" Paulie roughly pushed him out of the way, and continued to stare through the mesh. There were a dozen or more yachts that could have been the one in the photograph, but they were too far away to see properly.

"Well how are we gonna take a look?" Tommy asked. The sooner they checked this marina, the sooner they could eat and finish this off tomorrow.

Paulie didn't reply.

"We get these boats checked," Tommy pushed. "Then we can get some dinner." He'd spotted a bar on the way into town, it looked like the sort of place with a chance of finding that hooker he'd thought of earlier.

"I got an idea."

"Yeah?"

"Yeah. Lose the bolt cutters."

Paulie waved away any further questions, and walked back up the ramp. After a while Tommy followed him, and shaking his head, he returned the cutters to the bag. When he looked up again, Paulie had crossed the street, and was outside the window of a yacht brokers.

"Wait here," Paulie said, when Tommy got there.

"Why?"

"Because I don't want to look like we're a pair of fags. That's why."

Paulie pushed his way inside.

Tommy felt his hands bunch up again, but he did what he was told. As he did so, he realized he usually did these days. They might have been put together as partners, but he was increasingly finding himself the junior partner. The reason for it was clear, and had fuck all to do with who had the most experience. The reason Paulie felt entitled to push him around was because he was Angelo's second cousin. And both of them knew it. Paulie had Angelo's ear.

He watched Paulie inside, unable to hear what was being said. A woman had risen from behind her desk to greet him, and now they were talking. Paulie was expressive, looking relaxed and flashing a smile. Now he touched her shoulder lightly. She was attractive too, Tommy noticed, better put together than any hooker he was likely to find.

The woman was slipping her coat on now. She picked a large bunch of keys from a hook on the wall and came to the door. Tommy turned away as the door opened, and the woman and Paulie stepped out.

"It's a lovely boat," the woman was saying. "How long have you been on the lookout?"

"Oh, you know," Paulie replied, with a leer in his voice. "I'm always on the lookout."

The woman threw her head back, showing an elegant neck. She gave a little laugh, flirting back. Tommy kicked at the wall, hating the both of them.

"Fucking Paulie," he muttered as he waited, before following them at a distance. The woman led Paulie back down to the ramp and stopped at the gate. Tommy watched as she casually unscrambled the combination lock, and led Paulie through and onto the pontoon. They stopped at the third boat along, which Tommy now noticed had a *For Sale* sign hanging from the back. When they got there she fiddled with her large bunch of keys, while Paulie slipped out his cell phone. Moments later Tommy's buzzed in his pocket. When he pulled it out there was a message with just four numbers on it.

"Fucking Paulie," Tommy said – out loud this time.

THIRTY-ONE

FROM INSIDE THE cabin of the *Mystery* came the rhythmic sound of carrots being chopped. Slowly, carefully, methodically. Carlos held the knife with an eccentric grip, his fingers curled over the sides of the blade leaving most of the handle exposed. He watched as he chopped, as if drawing some meditative power from severing each slice. And only when he was satisfied they were all a uniform size and shape did he place the knife down and tumble the carrot pieces into a pan. Then he washed and dried his hands, then stepped around into the saloon area and stood over the table.

Amber tried to ignore him, her eyes fixed on the screen of her laptop. A notebook was open beside it, her handwriting black and spidery. After a while though she had to glance up, and she saw Carlos watching her. She looked away at once, but not quick enough to miss the edges of his mouth turn up into a satisfied smile.

"What?" She tried to make her voice irritable.

"How do you mean?"

"Why are you watching me?"

"I'm wondering if you're really going to do that all evening."

"I told you," Amber replied. She kept her eyes on her work, though she'd lost the thread of what she was doing already. "I have to get this done."

"Yeah. You said."

Carlos didn't move. He didn't stop watching her either.

"And I can't exactly do it with you standing right there."

"Hey, I only have this small boat. Where would you have me stand instead?"

"You said you'd cook me dinner. Maybe you should do that?"

"Yeah." He shrugged.

"Well? Where is it?"

Carlos was silent for so long she had to glance up again. He wore the same thoughtful look he'd had while he was chopping the vegetables.

"I decided I wasn't hungry," he said, as he held her eyes on his. "Not that sort of hungry anyway."

The corners of his mouth curled up again. His teeth appeared, gleaming. Then his eyes dropped, taking in how her body was arranged on the bench seat. He took his time, then lifted his eyes back to her face.

"I gotta do this project, I'm already behind."

Carlos reached forward to stroke a strand of her hair behind her ear. He let his hand touch her face. "Do it later."

"Do *this* later."

"Let's do this now. *And* later."

"Carlos! You're insatiable."

"And you're irresistible."

Despite herself, Amber smiled. The top she was wearing was borrowed from her mom. Every time she wore it, Amber thought it was disgusting, the way it plunged at the neckline, putting her mother's boobs on display. She moved her position now, taking care to keep her chest in his view. Then she turned back to the screen. "Well you're the reason I'm behind with this project, so you're just going to have to suffer."

Carlos didn't reply. Instead he slowly began pressing the lid of the computer closed.

Amber caught his wrist and stopped him. But she didn't let it go. She uncurled her legs and let them drop to the floor, and used his weight to pull herself up. Then, facing him, she carefully placed his hand onto her breast. She watched his eyes as she did so, seeing the pupils dilate, the mouth break open. She felt his breath against her face. She let go his wrist to hold his face with both her hands, and angled his mouth down towards hers. She kissed him, feeling his hard body pressing against hers. Then, just as his other hand wrapped around her she twisted away. She had to take a moment to compose herself before she could speak.

"I really have to get this done. And I *am* hungry. So get cooking." She lifted her hand and shooed him back to the galley.

This time he gave up.   ·

"OK. But afterwards I am going to make love to you." He pointed at her with one finger, as if this were a stern warning.

"We'll see how good dinner is."

"Oh it will be good." He banged a frying pan noisily onto the galley stove, playing at being angry. "It will be more than good." He turned on the gas and it ignited with a blue whoosh.

"And not just the food will be good."

Amber laughed, then turned back to her work. The feeling surging through her body was incredible. The anticipation for what was to come so powerful. Somehow though, she felt calm too – relaxed – and she was able to absorb herself back in her work, while the little cabin filled with the sounds and smell of cooking.

"Why'd you have to do that now anyway?" His voice broke into what she was doing, and he slid into the seat next to her. Glancing up she saw a pot now bubbling on the stove. He frowned at the screen.

"I told you. My mom's going off the island for a couple of days. Some work thing, and I have to look after Gracie. So I need to get this done now, because I won't have time later."

Carlos turned away and pulled out a small plastic bag half-filled with a fine white powder. "So your Mom's away huh?" He formed the side of the bag into a funnel, and poured a small stream of the powder out onto the table top. "Meaning you have the house all to yourself?"

"To myself and my six-year-old sister." Amber's eyebrows rose mean-ingfully. "Who will totally drop me in it with Mom if I bring my *boyfriend* home."

Amber stopped. She hadn't meant to use that word, it had just come out. She glanced at him, suddenly anxious.

In return he gave her a smile she couldn't read, then reached for her college ID card, which was on the table. He used it to cut the pile of powder into four smaller piles, and began arranging them into neat lines. Amber watched him, her eyes hesitant.

"I'm actually supposed to be there tonight," she went on. She didn't mean to say it. The situation – watching him with the drugs maybe – it had suddenly made her nervous.

"Where?"

"Home. Mom wanted to talk through Gracie's routine. Like..." Suddenly she was on more comfortable ground. "Like I don't know how to look after my own sister? It's just because it's the first time Mom's gone away and Gracie is a bit special..." She stopped as he neatly rolled a bank note, and placed one end into his left nostril. He leaned forward over the first line and in a second it was gone. Then he switched to the other side and a second line disappeared. He sat back, opened his mouth, and a shudder went through his body. Amber saw those dark pupils dilate again, wider this time. He held the note out to her.

Amber hesitated. For a moment she imagined what her Mom would say if she knew what Amber was actually doing, instead of being told how to look after her sister. But at the same time she didn't need instructions. Since Mom had split up with Pete – the man whom Amber had never agreed to call her step dad – and gone back to work, Amber had played a big part in bringing up Gracie anyway. Sometimes she wondered if she ought to tell Mom what the girl liked to do. She smiled as she accepted the note. It felt delicate between her fingers. Like something precious.

She looked down at the two remaining lines. Of coke. *Cocaine.* Just saying the word made her head spin a little. She risked a glance at Carlos, who was sat back now against the seat, his eyes half-closed, his hands relaxed on the table and twitching just a little. Maybe she shouldn't do it? Maybe she should be keeping her head clear? But then cocaine didn't make you groggy the next day, not like dope did. And she'd looked after Gracie when she was high before. A few times. Moreover, *having sex* on cocaine was something else. It was incredible. Being with Carlos was strange – he was older, and so much more experienced, she felt almost like a child playing a role sometimes. But the coke stripped away all her self-consciousness. The social anxiety she hid so well – but certainly felt, the lack of confidence she disguised with attitude – it all just disappeared. The coke allowed her to feel like the experienced lover a man like Carlos would have as his *girlfriend.*

She placed the note in her nose and leaned down over the line.

There was an instant shift as the chemical hit her, like the cabin's interior rotated around her brain. She had to bite her lip not to call out. Then the colors popped around her, as if each exploded into a more vibrant version of itself, one after the other. Her hearing sharpened. The sounds of the cooking crackled and fizzed, like it hadn't been there before, but was now loud and vibrant. The smells seemed to fill every inch of her, she could pick out individual tastes, like they were laid out on a plate. When she looked up into Carlos' warm tanned face he glowed. He was impossibly handsome.

. . .

Amber reached down and pulled her mom's top over her head. She threw it on the seat opposite and leaned in to kiss him. "Come on," she said. "Let's fuck."

For a second he looked almost too comfortable where he was to oblige, but then she ran her hands over his body until she reached the hardening bulge in the front of his jeans. Then she left one hand there and wrapped the other around his head, pulling them together. They broke apart, a few moments later, only for him to smoothly move her work stuff to one side, and drop the table down to give them more room.

* * *

"Where are you getting it from?"

His eyes narrowed. "What?"

Amber blinked her eyes, suddenly aware she had asked the question out loud. She was naked now, lying under a blanket, Carlos on his back smoking a joint.

"You know. The... The coke. It's just, everyone I know says it's hard to get hold of. Here on the island."

He shrugged, relaxed again. "I met a guy in a bar."

She was quiet for a moment. But the truth was she had a load of questions. And she loved to talk after sex, it felt like an extension of the intimacy.

"But isn't it expensive? And dangerous – like you don't know what might be in it?"

"Don't worry about it."

He smiled easily, then rolled onto his side, facing her now. The joint crackled as he sucked on it, then handed it over. He began running his finger in a circle on her bare shoulder.

It was distracting, but she loved the effect her body had on him.

"I'm not *worried*. I'm just interested. I think you're interesting."

"I think you're 'interesting' too," he said, his eyes concentrating on the path his finger took. It followed the curve of her breastbone, and onto her throat.

She took a hit on the joint. Carlos had told her how the downer of the marijuana helped to balance the high of the cocaine. It made it easier the next day, when she stopped taking it. The hot smoke felt familiar, and she pulled it in deep. She closed her eyes and felt waves rolling up and down her body. She realized she ought to slow down, he rolled his joints stronger than she did.

"Well if you're worried about running out, don't be. I got a guaranteed supply."

Amber held it out for him to take again.

"I wasn't worried about that." She spoke easy at first, but then her voice tightened. *Was that what he thought? That she was just here for the drugs?* She shook the idea away, it was just the dope hitting. Sending strands of paranoia through her mind. She looked to his face, trying to read what he was thinking.

Carlos screwed up his face, like he didn't recall that he'd even said it. Then he shrugged his shoulders again and took the joint. He reached beyond her to tap the ash from the end into a saucer he used as an ashtray, then rolled over again onto his back.

"It *is* kind of expensive," he continued, his own voice easy and relaxed. "But I don't exactly have to pay for it."

Amber – still preoccupied with the flow of thoughts in her own mind – almost didn't register what he said. But then it cut through.

"Hmm? Why not?"

She glanced across, and saw him smile up at the roof of the cabin.

"When I said I got it from a guy in a bar. It wasn't an actual guy. In an actual bar."

Amber felt herself focusing now. "What do you mean?"

"OK at least, it wasn't a bar here. It was somewhere else."

Amber propped herself up, letting the blanket fall away, but unconcerned by that. "I don't understand."

"There's nothing *to* understand." Carlos seemed to have realized what he was saying too, and changed his mind about saying it. "Better you don't."

"What? But I want to." Suddenly the conversation was much more than just easy post-coital chat. She wanted to understand him. He was mysterious enough, turning up – literally – out of the blue, a European. She needed him to open up to her.

"Come on Carlos. Tell me."

Carlos contemplated for a while before replying. "You really want to know?" He turned to her, measuring, thinking. His eyes were dark, unfathomable.

"Yes. I do."

He hesitated. A long time. "OK," he said in the end. "I stole it."

"*You stole it?*"

"Yeah." He laughed carelessly. "I didn't exactly plan to. It kind of just happened."

Amber stared at him. "Who did you steal it from?"

"It's fine. They aren't ever gonna find out."

"How can you say that? Who did you steal it from?"

Carlos lifted a hand and pressed it against his temple. He looked like he wished he hadn't spoken.

"Look, I met some guys, they asked me to carry a couple of kilos from Venezuela to Florida. That's all. But on the way I got caught in a storm, and they think I sank. So that's it."

"That's it?"

"That's it."

Amber lay back down. She felt her body shaking. From what? Fear? Excitement?

"But is it safe? I mean, where is it?" Suddenly she looked around the cabin, as if she might have missed bales of cocaine amongst the general disorder.

"Not here. It's safe."

She opened her mouth to continue, but he reached forward and placed a finger on her lips.

"No more. There's nothing to worry about." Then he thought for a minute. "Actually there is one thing to worry about." He gave a careless laugh.

"What?"

"Your little friend Billy."

She frowned, "Billy?"

"Yeah. I caught him, climbing off the boat, the other day. The hatch was locked so he didn't get inside. But he was spying again. He might have an idea where it is."

Amber groaned. "Oh God. Billy." She remembered the mixture of feelings she'd felt on seeing him flailing about in the water. Laughter, but also horror at what he must have seen. Then she registered what he'd just said.

"Billy? How would *he* know where it was?"

"Oh nothing. Just the first time I met him…"

Carlos stopped speaking, and smiled instead.

"What?" Amber asked. "What is it?

But this time Carlos didn't answer.

"I'm hungry now," he said instead, jumping naked to his feet and leaving her with the blanket. He walked to the galley and stirred the pot. "For food this time." He began gathering plates from the rack on the wall and glanced back at Amber. She took the hint and got up too, though she used the distraction of his cooking to dress again before replacing the table and setting it so they could eat.

* * *

They ate in silence. Carlos seemed to enjoy it that way, and Amber forgot her concerns. No doubt she would consider what he had told her later on. But perhaps it was better this way. That there was no 'man in a bar'. Besides, she knew, from how the last few nights had gone, that Carlos wasn't yet done for the evening. She let her mind focus on that. She found it strangely exciting to listen to the sounds of the food being cut, and the careful way he moved it to his mouth. And the feel of his dark eyes on her as she ate from her own plate. When he was nearly finished he reached for a chunk of bread, and used it to mop up the sauce on his plate, but instead of eating that himself he leaned over and offered it to her, holding it close to her lips. When she parted them he placed it gently inside, and then pushed it in with his finger, his eyes never leaving her face. Still neither of them spoke. After that he took both plates and moved them into the sink, then he reached down and peeled her mother's top up and over her head for a second time.

THIRTY-TWO

"I REALLY DO HAVE TO GO," Amber said, nearly two hours later. She felt warm and comfortable, her buzz fading gradually with the help of another joint.

He watched her. "Why?"

"I told you. I have to be home tomorrow before Mom leaves. She's on the early ferry."

His eyes dropped. "Go from here."

She shook her head. "I was supposed to be there tonight, remember?" She smiled at him, trying to make it an indulgent reminder of what they had done instead.

"OK *go*." He pretended to sound put-out. Or perhaps he actually was a little. But then he softened. "You want me to take you?"

Amber's brow furrowed. "You don't have a car."

"I can take yours."

"Then how will you get back here?"

His eyes revealed him thinking about it, but then he rolled away, defeated. She took the moment to slip out from under the blanket and retrieve her underwear. But she heard him roll back again to watch her.

"Stop staring. Haven't you had enough?"

"No. I never have enough."

She leaned forward to pull her panties on, feeling awkward at how it must make her look. "Well that's all you're getting tonight." She found her bra, hanging from the corner of the chart table, and quickly strapped it on.

Then she put on the rest of her clothes. It would be OK, she thought, if he offered to walk her up the pontoon to her car. But as she dressed he showed no signs of moving. On the other hand, she kind of understood why he might be tired. She grinned inside at the thought.

"You come here after school?"

"College."

"You come here after college?"

"No I have to look after Gracie. Remember?"

He stared stone-faced, like this was an incredible hardship. And she had to laugh.

"It's only three days. You'll cope."

"Maybe you'll have to send me some photographs of yourself. To keep me sane."

"Maybe I'll do that."

Suddenly Carlos pulled himself up and sat up against the seat. The blanket that had been covering him slipped down to show his stomach, toned and tanned. Amber found her eye pulled towards it. He reached above him and grabbed the bag of coke.

"Quick one?"

"I can't. I have to drive."

"Just a quick one."

"Carlos!"

He stopped, and put it back. "OK. I'll come with you. See you to your car." He stood now, naked again, but made no move to dress.

"You going to come like that?"

He shrugged. "Why not?"

She laughed again, and made a decision. "Don't worry. I parked just across the street. And it's only Holport."

"No really, I'll come." He looked for his jeans now, but casually, as if expecting her to deny him. And she waved him away.

"No. It's fine. I have to get going. I'll see you in a few days."

She placed her hands flat on his bare chest and breathed in deeply to taste the smell of him. She kissed him, long enough to feel him becoming aroused again, but not long enough to delay her departure.

"I had fun tonight," she said.

It was cold and quiet out on the pontoon. Her footsteps echoed on the boards and the wooden walkway sank a little as each footstep pushed it down into the dark water. The low level lighting of the pontoon reflected off the surface, giving it the look of black mercury. At the end she quickly unlocked the gate and swung it shut behind her, then crossed the street and went around the corner to where her car was parked. Then an uncomfortable thought hit her. Her little car – purchased with money left to her after her dad's death, and usually pretty reliable, had recently been having trouble starting. One time last week she'd even run the battery flat trying to get it going, and only been saved because she was at college, and half a dozen of her classmates had been there to give a push start. She'd meant to get it to the garage, but instead had rushed off to see Carlos. Now, suddenly, alone on the deserted dock, and with the time past midnight, she felt exposed.

She unlocked the car, and settled into the seat, then slipped the key home. She held her breath as she turned it, hearing the motor protest as it was suddenly commanded into life. Something spun loudly, under the hood, then whined, but the motor wouldn't fire. And then, just as she was about to stop and try a second time, it caught. She pumped the gas, feeling relief flood through her just as gas flooded through the motor, and then it was revving normally, the little motor sounding eager to go. She relaxed, puffed out her cheeks, and fitted her seatbelt. Sweet little car. She looked to the sky, silently thanking her father. There was no reason to look in her rear view mirror, and even if she had, the two men inside the dark-colored van were as good as invisible. Just watching her at this point.

Amber kept the revs high as she moved out of the space, and drove out of Holport. As she climbed the hill out of town, she wound down her window, letting the cold night air flow into the car. She hoped to weaken the effects of the drugs she had taken, but it hardly mattered. Mom would be asleep by now. She glanced down at her cell phone, which she'd kept on silent. Three missed calls from Mom. Could have been worse. Then she noticed the battery was low, so she fumbled the connection to the charger she kept plugged into the cigarette lighter. She'd need it tomorrow, for college.

A few seconds later she realized her mistake.

College. She had to hand in her project for college. She'd mostly finished it, but she had to use her college ID to hand it in.

"Shit." She spoke out loud. She fought to clear her thoughts. She'd definitely put the laptop and her notes in her bag, she could see the corner of her notebook poking from the top of the bag on the passenger seat. But not her ID card. It was on the side, where Carlos had been using it to chop up the lines of coke.

She considered if she could get it later. Surely they knew who she was?

But then this wasn't school. The office where she had to hand in the project probably wouldn't know who she was, and if she didn't have the card it would mean the coursework was late. She'd get marked down. And her grades were bad enough anyway.

She clenched her fingers around the plastic of the wheel, then bunched her hand into a fist, and hit it. The impact felt weird, like it wasn't totally her own hand – the drugs were clearly still affecting her. Probably that was why she forgot.

But then what did it matter? It was late anyway. Another ten minutes wouldn't make any difference. And she would get to see Carlos again. She smiled again. There was a junction up ahead where a smaller road met this one. And with no one about this late, she slowed, and swung around in a u-turn. She almost felt relaxed now, wondering what he would be doing? Probably he would have gone to sleep. Well she'd wake him up.

She pulled into the same spot she had left only minutes before and hurried back around the corner. But before she crossed the street she stopped. Two men were leaning over the combination lock on the gate which led to the pontoon. One was large, one small, and they had a small flashlight. At once she slunk back into the shadow of the building behind her. There was no reason to feel fear exactly – there were many boats kept on the pontoon, and people could visit them at any time. But equally, there was no way she wanted them to see her. It was late. And they would probably be as startled by her sudden appearance as she was by theirs.

The gate swung open, and the two men stepped through. One was carrying a large bag. It comforted her further. They were just boat owners, probably getting ready for an early start. Maybe to catch the tide. That thought spurred her into action. Mom would definitely ask her what time she got home. And the later she did, the more of the moral-high-ground mom would claim. Amber stepped forward to get the card and get on her way.

Even so she opened and closed the gate quietly, using her palm to prevent the metal ringing out. She could still make out the silhouettes of the men half way down the pontoon. She watched, expecting them to disappear at any moment, as they climbed onto one of the boats. But they were still walking forwards. They must have one of the boats out near the end, where the *Mystery* and *Blue Lady* were kept. That was awkward, she hoped they would find their boat, and go inside their cabin before she had to walk past. But then they came to the last boat before *Mystery* and *Blue*

Lady – the last boat which could possibly be theirs – and to her surprise they walked right past that too. Suddenly her irritation hardened into something else. Confusion. Then quickly to concern.

There was no reason for anyone to be visiting either the *Mystery* or the *Blue Lady* at this time of night. No reason at *any time* really. But in the middle of the night? Her concern grew, beginning to feel a lot like fear.

She ducked left, onto one of the smaller offshoots of the pontoon, so that she was hidden if either of the men looked behind them, and she watched from behind the steep bow of a fishing skiff. And she was glad she did, as one of the men turned now and studied the pontoon behind him. She froze. Then he flicked on the flashlight, and carefully probed the semi-darkness behind him.

What the hell? Amber thought, as she ducked her head back in. She suddenly thought to call Carlos, to warn him. Of what exactly she wasn't sure. But everything about the situation suddenly felt awfully wrong. But when she went to her pocket to get her cell it wasn't there. She'd plugged it into the charger in the car.

Shit.

When she dared to look up again, the two men *had* disappeared. She looked around, straining her eyes in the gloomy light. They couldn't have. Unless they'd jumped in the water… but then she realized. They must have climbed onto a boat. But the only two boats there were *Mystery* or *Blue Lady*.

Suddenly Amber realized she was shivering, and it wasn't the cold making it happen. But it wasn't only fear that overcame her, it was confusion too. A part of her mind, which screamed out the need to stay rational, told her to question whether what she had seen was actually real. Could it not be some sort of delayed hallucination, from the dope and the coke? And the story Carlos had told her, about where the coke came from? She forced herself back onto the main branch of the pontoon, and hurried forward. And now her own footsteps began to confuse her. They didn't sound or feel real either. Like when she'd hit the wheel in her car. Everything felt like she was playing some role in a movie, or stuck in a dream. It convinced her that whatever she'd thought she saw was a hallucination. A crazy dream.

As she reached the bow of the *Mystery* she was almost relaxed again. She would surprise Carlos. She would grab her ID card, and she'd get home. And maybe another time she'd tell him of how her mind had played tricks with her.

But then she heard them.

It was shouting, or not quite. But raised, angry voices. Thuds. All muted because they came from inside the cabin of *Mystery*. But *definitely* real. Then a voice. Loud, but measured. In control.

"You move I put a bullet through your fucking head."

Amber blinked in surprise, the words were so out of context. The sound was coming from inside the boat, and it wasn't her they were speaking to, but still she felt suddenly vulnerable, standing here on the pontoon. So she retreated until she was hiding behind the concrete upright that the floating part of the walkway was anchored to, against the rise and fall of the tide.

Back here it was harder to hear. There were only fragments of voices. She considered what to do. She thought again of her cellphone, all the way back in the car. Should she get it? Who would she call? What would she tell them? And had she really heard what she thought? She figured she had to go forward again. To find out what was actually going on, before she could decide what to do.

She stepped cautiously, keeping her tread as light as she could to not cause the pontoon to sway too much. This time she went past the bow of the *Mystery*, crouching low, and feeling her legs trembling, until she reached the mid-point of the yacht. There she ducked down, so that she was below the height of the cabin windows. There was nowhere to hide on the narrow strip of wooden boards, but she could hear again, the voices coming out through the open hatchway.

"Luis. You've been very careless."

Amber dared to lift her head a little. And through the narrow cabin window she got a snapshot of what was happening inside. The two men were standing opposite Carlos, who was seated, and dressed only in his jeans. He had his hands unnaturally placed on the table in front of him.

The two men were both dressed in suits. It looked odd, in the cabin of a boat, but somehow it looked threatening too, or perhaps that was just the way they were standing. Then Amber saw the smaller of the two men move, and suddenly she could see his hands too. In one he held up Carlos' bag of cocaine. Her heart beat faster in fear. Then she gasped when she saw his other hand. In it he held a long black gun. She'd watched enough movies to know it had a silencer fitted.

The man removed a glove, and then opened the bag. He touched the tip of one finger into the powder, pulling it out with a small amount stuck to the tip. He tasted it, and looked to Carlos.

"Oh dear Luis." He shook his head, as if pretending to be disappointed. Then he turned to the bigger man, which prompted Amber to do the same, and she saw he too had a silenced pistol.

"Luis, Luis…"

Along with her horror, Amber registered that the smaller man was repeating the name *to* Carlos, as if he had his name wrong. It confused her. Another thing that made no sense. She strained her ears, desperate to understand what she was watching.

"I do believe you had an arrangement to deliver something for our employer." Still it was the smaller man speaking. He had greasy hair, slicked back, and a black earring in each ear. Should she be remembering details like this? Or trying to forget them? Amber had no idea. It felt like her brain was thinking through treacle.

"I don't know what you're talking about." Carlos replied. Her fear was intensified by just how sullen he looked. How different to how he'd been all evening.

"Oh Luis. You maybe wanna take a moment. Consider if *fucking around* is something you wanna do here?"

Why do they keep calling him Luis? Amber fought to understand. *And why doesn't he correct them?* The two possible explanations collided in her mind. They knew him by a fake name. *She* knew him by a fake name.

Then the smaller man put his gun down and lifted the bag she had seen earlier onto the table. Now she saw it was more of a sports bag than the sailing bag she had imagined she saw. He unzipped it and pulled out a small white plastic tube. He opened that and drew out a plastic spatula. Then he dipped that into the bag of cocaine and pulled out a heaped spoonful. Carefully he dropped it into the tube and screwed the lid back on. He shook it gently. He seemed to be enjoying his work. Then he turned to Carlos and smiled.

"This little test here will confirm if this is our product or not. If it turns blue, we'll know you've been a naughty boy." He began whistling as he waited. Then he held up the vial. Amber saw that the liquid inside was now a soft blue color.

"Oh dear," Earrings said.

Then there was a buzz of movement inside the cabin. It happened almost too fast for Amber to follow, but she caught how Carlos suddenly lunged forward, towards the bigger man who still had his gun. He was quick, but the big man was quicker. He moved left, out of the way, and at the same time, delivered a blow to Carlos' head. It stopped him at once, and he dropped back down to where he'd been sitting, as if he was about to lose consciousness. Then the big man snarled. His teeth were crooked and discolored. The younger man, with the earrings, looked unconcerned – almost bored – during the whole moment.

"No need for that, Luis," Earrings said. "We just want to have a little talk."

A bubble of hope filled in Amber as he said this, she was desperate to believe it, but as Carlos looked up again, she saw there was blood running down the side of his head now. He dabbed at it, looking at his finger disbelievingly. She knew then there was nothing hopeful about what was happening in front of her.

"I gotta tell you Luis," Earrings picked up the bag again and shook it thoughtfully. "You can save yourself a whole lot of pain right now, just by telling us where you stashed the rest of this. You wanna do that? It here on the boat?" his eyebrows lifted hopefully. But Carlos didn't respond at all, save to lift his eyes and glance angrily at Earrings, and touch his head wound a second time.

"No? You know I'm kinda glad about that. Give us a chance to settle a little row we had earlier, don't it Tommy?" This time Earrings turned to look at the bigger guy, who looked madder than ever.

"You see. Tommy here – they call him Tommy *the Teeth* by the way, on account of the fucked up state of his mouth – you don't want him breathing on you, believe me." He sniffed. "Now Tommy here, he don't have no style. If it was up to him, he'd be breaking your fingers by now. One by one, until you tell him where you put it. And maybe that would work, and maybe it wouldn't. Maybe you'd tell us what we want to hear, but maybe you'd give us some bullshit story and then, when we cut your fucking head off, we wouldn't have no idea where you'd stashed it." He stopped talking and picked up the bag of coke again. He opened it and dipped his finger in a second time, but this time he pulled out a little mound of powder balanced on his fingernail. He held it to his nose and sucked it up. For a second he screwed his eyes shut. Then he went on.

"And I can't have that. I came here to recover what you stole, and that's exactly what I'm gonna do. So I told Tommy he wouldn't be breaking your fingers like normal. One by one, until you squeal like a fucking pig. We'd be doing this my way." Earrings looked at Carlos's hands, both still palm-down on the table in front of him.

"So maybe you wanna say a little thank you for that," he went on.

Carlos didn't reply, and after a second, Earrings repeated himself.

"I said maybe you wanna say a little thank you, that I'm not gonna be breaking your fingers." Amber felt herself holding her breath, and even willing Carlos to do what the man asked, there was such an air of menace to him. But still Carlos was silent and still. Then in a sudden blur of movement, Amber watched as Earrings lunged forward and swung the handle of the gun down hard on Carlos' fingers. He hit him again and again, until there was blood bursting from the hand, and Carlos had it clamped to his chest. There was noise now, the sound of Carlos screaming, and swearing in Italian. Through tears of shock Amber watched as the other man – Tommy – calmly picked up a magazine from the shelf, folded it twice and jammed it into Carlos' open mouth.

THIRTY-THREE

WITH A SUDDEN JOLT Amber realized she had to do something. If she didn't she was going to watch her boyfriend tortured and murdered, she was sure of that. She dropped back down to the deck to get space to think. What the hell should she do? The police. She could call them, she *had* to call them. But she had no phone. She wept for her decision to plug it into her car, before screaming at herself to think. She could run to get it. Better still, call the cops *from* her car, where she would be safe.

But something stopped her. And she knew what. Holport was too small to have a police station, the cops would have to come from Newlea. That was a half hour by car. And how long would they take just to get ready? Before they even set off? Lornea Island wasn't the sort of place where the cops sat around expecting this kind of situation. It might be forty minutes, an hour, before anyone got here. They were torturing him – actually torturing him – now. This wasn't going to last that long. And while she fought for answers she heard the nightmare unfolding further.

"*Motherfucker*," Earrings snarled, as if he were the one who had been injured. Carlos still had the hand clamped to his chest, his eyes screwed tightly shut. Even from where she stood, Amber could tell it was badly damaged.

"So like I said," Earrings went on suddenly, as if nothing had happened. "I told Tommy we were gonna do this in a more intelligent way." Then he turned away and began rummaging in the bag they'd brought. He pulled out a small black case. He placed it on the table, and undid a zip all the way around its edge, folding the lid back. The contents were too small for Amber to see clearly, but it looked like the kind of kit vets carried about with them.

"You see Tommy's way is OK. But science has come a long way since he started out in this business." Earrings smiled now. "Tell me Luis. You ever see a movie where they use a truth drug?"

He waited for Carlos to answer this, then when he didn't he busied himself by selecting a syringe from the case, and then a small glass bottle. Eventually Carlos did reply.

"Yeah." His voice sounded awful. There was blood smeared all over his chest, from his broken hand.

"Good. And let me guess. It probably showed a guy getting injected, and afterward just spilling his guts. Am I right?"

Carlos breathed hard before replying. "Something like that."

"I thought so." Earrings ignored him for a moment, rolling the bottle thoughtfully in his fingers. After a while he went on. "It don't work like that, not in real life. I mean, just imagine for a minute if it did – you wouldn't need courts, you wouldn't need lawyers. None of that. Just stick the needle in and out comes the truth." He chuckled now. "Maybe one day."

"But what most people don't know is how they're trying to do it like the movies. You know, the CIA, Secret Service, all that bullshit. They ain't ever gonna tell us exactly what they're up to, but I heard, from a guy who's brother was in the military — special forces — that," he stopped. "Well, it don't matter *how* I know. I just know." He pressed the needle of the syringe through the lid of the bottle, then inverted it and pulled back the plunger. The syringe filled with a clear liquid.

"This is *sodium thiopental*. What it does is slow down how your brain sends messages from one part to another. It's like thinking through glue. You see, you have to consider how a lie works. You have to make up a new reality. You invent it. A lot of different parts of the brain have to work together. And that takes effort. But you pump enough of this stuff in and you lose the power to keep lying." He held the needle upwards and squirted a jet upward, clearing the air.

"But I told you, they ain't got it quite like the movies yet. Not as simple." He frowned, and looked pained. "You see, it's kinda dangerous. The dosage is real important. You need a lot before it starts working, but if you give *too* much, then the guy's heart is just gonna stop. Just like that. Second thing is this. *It don't always work.* A guy like you, who's holding onto a really big lie? Well it's *possible* you could keep it inside, even when the drug is working. If that happens we're no better than with Tommy here breaking your fingers."

Carlos didn't respond, his gaze was still on his damaged hand.

"But what no one can do is lie about *everything*. The brain just doesn't work like that. That's the real beauty of this system. If we ask you questions that don't seem to relate to that secret you're holding onto, it simply won't occur to you to lie to us. Which means we just need to take a roundabout route and we'll find the truth." He turned to the other man.

"Are you gonna hold this fucker down or what?"

Amber looked at the man called Tommy in time to see a dark look run across his face, but he stepped forward and grabbed Carlos. He spun him around, as easily as if he'd been a child, and gripped him by the throat. Amber thought he was going to strangle him there and then, and she could see Carlos, gasping in pain. But while Tommy held him, Earrings moved forward and carefully pressed the syringe into his upper arm. He pushed down the plunger, then pulled the needle out again. When Amber saw it again, the barrel of the syringe was empty. Then Tommy released his grip and sat back down opposite.

"Now we wait," Earrings said.

Outside Amber gagged and she tasted sick in her mouth. She was breathing as hard as if she were the one being tortured. She thought again about the police, wishing she'd left earlier, and almost fantasizing they were already on their way, or here. A fleet of squad cars coming to the rescue. But she knew they weren't. And if she left now to call them, Carlos would die. Her boyfriend would be dead before they could arrive. They would arrive to find his body...

The sick came out. First a mouthful, and then everything she had. It spewed onto the pontoon, and over the side into the black water. She saw fish, attracted by the movement, or the smell. She recognized what she had eaten earlier, it made everything she was watching all the more unbelievable, yet real.

Finally she stopped heaving. She stared at the mess on the decking, and blinked in horror. She *had* to do something. She couldn't just hide here, watching a murder. But what? She looked around her, searching for ideas. There was a plastic bollard at the junction of the pontoon, giving out just the barest yellow light, sufficient so that users could see enough to not walk into the water. But it was fixed down, it couldn't help her. There was a hose, for boat owners to clean the salt off. But what could she do with a hose? The two men inside were armed with guns. Huge guns, with silencers attached. The thought of that impacted her for the first time. It registered that what she was witnessing was the work of actual professional killers. The thought made her almost moan out loud.

The flare gun. On the *Blue Lady* there was a flare gun. If she got that maybe she could... The rush of hope died almost as fast as it arrived. There were two of them. They had real guns. They were professional killers. She felt tears pressing out of her eyes at the sheer frustration of it. If she couldn't think of anything then Carlos was going to die. The man she loved was going to be killed in front of her eyes.

"OK Luis," she heard Earrings start up again. "You should be about cooked now. Let's say we ask you a few questions." Amber raised herself up on her knees, just high enough to see into the cabin.

"What's your name."

"Luis," Carlos breathed in reply. "Luis Fernandez."

"That's great Luis. That's real nice. Thank you for that. And do you know why we're here?"

Amber watched, as the man she had known as Carlos leaned back now, his head lolling around on his shoulders, like it was too much of an effort to hold up. "Yeah," he said in the end.

"OK, and you wanna tell me why?"

Another pause, then Carlos replied. "I was meant to deliver... A load of cocaine. But I didn't do it."

"And why didn't you do it?"

"I dunno. I decided not to. I decided to take it back home and sell it there. I didn't think anyone would ever find me."

"That's OK Luis. We understand. A stupid fucking decision, but we understand. But tell me, where is the product now? Where have you hidden it?"

For a while it seemed Carlos hadn't heard. Or that he had heard, but the pain in his arm was blocking out everything else. But in the end he lifted his head very slightly, his eyes barely open.

"Is it on the boat?"

"No," Carlos managed in the end.

"Where is it then?"

"I buried it," Carlos said. The effort it took to speak was clear.

"Oh?" Earrings said. He turned to Tommy and his eyebrows went up in surprise.

"Where'd you bury it?"

Carlos was having trouble breathing now, it took him a while to answer.

"In the woods."

"The woods? What woods?"

Carlos took a few breaths before he was able to continue. "No not the woods, by a stream."

Earrings frowned now. "What stream?"

"Or maybe..." Carlos panted again. "Maybe it wasn't a stream. More of a lake."

Earrings' frown deepened. "A lake?"

"More of a sea really. Yeah that's it," Carlos went on, warming to it now. "The sea of tranquility I think it's called. On the *fucking moon*."

He sat back now, and stared at the mess of his hand.

"On the moon? You buried our product on the moon?"

"I might as well have, for all the chances of you *fuckers* finding it," Carlos continued, and he forced a grin before his face went slack.

But Earrings didn't look bothered. "On the moon huh? That's nice. That's a real nice hiding place. Ain't no one gonna find it there." He nodded to himself, before going on. "Say Luis, anyone else know you borrowed a little bit of coke? Huh? Or is it just you?" Earrings kept his voice casual.

Outside Amber immediately realized the danger in the question. And she stared at Carlos, willing him to see it too. But he just shrugged.

"No," Carlos shook his head, then stopped. "Yeah." He narrowed his eyes as if something had occurred to him but he wasn't sure what. "Amber. I told Amber."

The sound of her own name crashed into Amber's brain. She looked about again, she felt like she were tied to a train track, watching the locomotive charge toward her, unable to do anything to prevent what was coming.

"OK Luis," Earrings said again, keeping his voice pleasant. "Amber's that chick you were banging earlier?"

"Yeah."

"You mind if we talk about her for a while?"

Carlos didn't respond.

"She looks like a nice lay?"

Again he was silent.

"Nice, tight little ass on her anyway."

No response.

"Oh come on Luis. It must feel good, slipping one into an ass like that?"

Somehow Carlos managed another shrug.

"OK, good. You're a lucky boy. Now, does she got a surname?"

A look passed across Carlos' face, like he thought for a moment this might be something he shouldn't say, but then he forgot.

"Atherton."

"Amber Atherton. So maybe you got the coke hidden up at her place? That right?"

It took a while for Carlos to answer. It looked like a huge effort.

"I ain't telling."

"No?"

"No. No way."

"Where's she live, anyway? Just out of interest."

Amber prayed that he would refuse to tell them, but this time he hardly hesitated.

"It's in Newlea. I don't know the address."

There was a silence before Earrings continued the questioning.

"This her?"

Carlos looked confused, as something was thrust in front of his face. Amber saw what it was, her college ID card. "Hey," Carlos slurred. "Where'd you get that?"

"Why it has her address on it, right here! Thank you Luis. And you said she knows where the product is hidden? Is that right?"

"Must have left it here." Carlos was mumbling now, so that it was hard for Amber to hear him, but then he brightened, his voice clearer. "Yeah that's right. Must be right."

"OK Luis. That's great. Now, shall we ask a few more questions? Would you like that?"

Carlos was silent for a while. Then, with a big effort he lifted his head. He ignored Earrings, and stared at the bigger man.

"Hey Tommy!" he called. The big man narrowed his eyes, and tightened his grip on the gun. "You know something?" Carlos went on. Amber held her breath, unsure what was happening now.

"You're one dumb motherfucker!" Carlos broke into something of a grin, though it looked like the effort of it was nearly killing him. "You know that? Working for a fucking jerk like this?"

The atmosphere in the little cabin had changed, it was like the power had shifted, subtly but significantly. Amber watched in confusion.

"This guy's a fucking moron, so what does that make you, huh? A guy that takes orders from a fucking moron." Carlos laughed again. And he didn't stop talking.

"And I bet... I bet that's how you got those teeth, from blowing him off?"

"Is that it?" Carlos lifted his good hand and mimed the action of a blow job. "He gives you head, and you get so fuckin' excited, you knock your own teeth out?" He grinned now, manically.

And suddenly Amber knew what he was doing. He was *goading* them. He was doing everything he could to provoke them into killing him now. He knew there was no chance of getting out of this alive, and he just wanted it over with.

And finally it was enough to spur Amber into action.

THIRTY-FOUR

SHE STOOD and ran the few steps to the *Blue Lady* then leapt on board. There was a fire extinguisher mounted on the inside of the spray shield which protected the cockpit, and she ripped it off and swung it against the glass of the cabin door. It smashed at once, and she reached inside for the lock, grabbing her sleeve to protect her wrist against the glass still lodged in the window frame. From the inside she turned the lock and the door swung open.

She moved directly to the locker where the distress flares were kept. They were required by law to keep several types, and for obvious reasons they had to be accessible in the event of an emergency. Never for an emergency like this though. It took her precious seconds, but soon she found the type she was looking for – the rocket flares. She grabbed one, and ripped open the packet as she jumped back onto the pontoon.

She had no time to consider what she was doing, she simply acted. She ran the two steps across the walkway, and swung herself aboard the *Mystery*. She planted her feet on the two side benches of the cockpit, looking straight down the hatchway into the cabin. It took her a moment to make sense of the view that met her.

Carlos was still alive. But she was there just in time. The bigger man, the one called Tommy, had his gun, but the man with the earrings was now holding a huge knife, the kind explorers use to chop through jungle vines. They seemed to be arguing, horribly, about how they were going to

kill him. Then Earrings grabbed Carlos and held his head back, exposing
his neck for the knife.

"Let him go or I'll fucking fire this!" Amber yelled, holding out the
plastic tube towards them.

All three of them looked, bewildered by the interruption. The big man
was the quickest to move, he turned his gun towards her.

"Don't fucking move!" She yelled again, and it slowed the man's arm.
The flare had a pull-cord, and she already had it stretched taut, so that just
a tiny extra tug would detonate the flare. She had no idea what effect it
would have in the cabin, and there was no time to think. No time to think
anything. The big man continued to swing the weapon towards her, and
she knew he would fire. A fraction of a second seemed to stretch out
forever, but as the barrel of the weapon levelled on her she pulled the cord
as hard as she could.

The result was instantaneous. It was as if her arm itself shot out fire. It
ripped apart the air around her and a yellow-orange trail exploded down-
ward into the yacht's cabin. It didn't explode. Instead it hit the door of the
bow cabin, which was closed, but then bouncing first one way then
another, moving too fast, and too bright, for her to follow its path, but with
the effect of a pinball machine. For a second, maybe two it ricocheted
inside the small cabin, fizzing with eruptions of fire and sparks with every
surface it hit. And then it did explode. Suddenly the entire space was just a
thick red glow, so bright Amber had to shield her eyes. Then she felt a
wave of heat roll from the cabin, forcing her to drop away.

When she looked again, the cabin was still too bright to see into, and she
blinked in horror at the thought she had killed them – all three of them. But
then the flare, perhaps damaged by its fractured trajectory, started dimming,
and eventually she saw recognizable shapes emerging from the red light.
And then she saw movement. And then – with a bang – the brightness
suddenly dimmed significantly. It took her several seconds to work out
what had happened, but as her eyes adjusted further she saw the reason.
The bigger man had kicked shut the door to the forward cabin. And the flare
was now shut inside, still burning but its light hidden. Suddenly the cabin
looked almost normal, apart from the smoke now pouring up the companionway steps, and the three men inside picking themselves up from the
floor. Then the man with the earrings saw her. Their eyes locked together.

"Fucking crazy *bitch*!"

He was pushing himself up off the floor, and they both saw the gun at
the same time, right next to his hand. He had dropped the knife by now,

and grabbed for the weapon. Amber had taken just the one flare, and now had nothing to defend herself. As he turned the pistol onto her again, there was nothing else she could do but turn and run.

* * *

Amber jumped down to the pontoon, and nearly fell flat on her face. The narrow walkway that ran between the two boats was greasy and slippery from where she had emptied her stomach earlier. But some part of her brain remembered this just in time, and her arms went out to help her balance. She skidded a few feet, but somehow stayed on her feet and began running. But still, it felt like running through glue, every step took an age and with each one she expected to hear the muffled shots, to feel the bullets thudding through her exposed back.

She was nearly at the corner, where the narrow offshoot of the walkway met the main pontoon. But just as she reached it she felt something zipping through the air in front of her. Then she heard the noise, louder than she expected, but still clearly the muffled report of several shots being fired. She screamed and dropped to the decking. For a second she froze. Then something in her terror made her glance behind, as if she wanted to die facing her executioner. She saw the man preparing to leap down from the yacht. Once he was level with her on the pontoon he surely couldn't miss. She turned again, and forced her limbs to work, clambering away from him on her hands and knees but knowing it was hopeless.

Then another bang sounded behind her, and Amber froze again. But again she worked out she hadn't been hit, and when she looked back a second time she saw the man sprawled on his back on the walkway, where he had slipped in the sick. She didn't need a second invitation. She scrambled back to her feet, and fled down towards the land.

It only gave her a short head start, and seconds later Amber realized the other mistake she had made. *The gate.* She should have gone to unlock it before attacking them. Now it blocked her way, and he would catch her up as she tried to open it. Or at least, she would be an easy target, pinned against it like an animal in a trap. It was a fatal mistake, she moaned out loud at the realization.

There was nothing else she could do but keep running. She pushed her legs to run faster and faster, aware of how the muscles burned but the pain almost irrelevant. And she arrived at the gate sooner than she thought, slamming into it to slow down, and feeling the metal crack into her forehead. Her hands and fingers were shaking, almost more than she could control, as she tried to unscramble the combination lock. She was aware of herself screaming out in frustration. And she could hear him, the sound of footsteps running hard behind her as she lined up the numbers. *One. Two,* three numbers now... How would it feel when the bullet hit? Would she even feel anything? Her fingers wouldn't stop shaking again as she tried to set the fourth number. She spun the dial too far, and then had to turn round and go the other way. And all the time the footsteps were coming closer, his voice shouting now. Why wasn't he firing?

The lock opened and the latch on the gate released. She pushed through, just as she felt the man's weight arrive behind her. As she went through the gate she gripped its edge with both hands and turned and slammed it hard behind her. She felt the crunch as the metal caught on something rather than fitting into its frame, and when she looked she saw fingers were trapped between the gate and its frame. There was a scream of pain as the man tried to pull them out, but Amber put all her weight behind it now, shoving it shut. She willed the mechanism to catch, but the fingers were preventing it. She moved position, to try and increase her pressure, but he took advantage, pulling his hand out. The gate caught, shutting properly now, and she spun the combination on her side. For a second they stared at each other, close enough to touch, but with the steel of the gate between them. Then Amber turned again and fled once more, up the ramp and off the pontoon.

When she reached the land she didn't slow. She sprinted across the road and around the corner to where she had left the car. She slammed into the side, and began fumbling for her keys. But then she remembered something – her unreliable car. An image flashed through her mind, herself pinned in the driver's seat while the motor turned over, advertising where she was but leaving her powerless to escape, until he lined up his shot through the windshield.

Then she did hear a noise, the metallic ringing of the gate opening again and crashing back on its hinges. She turned again to the car, praying it would be OK, but as she tried to slip the key into the lock, her hands fumbled them, and they dropped to the street. She looked down to recover them, but it was dark. And she heard his footsteps again, ringing out as he climbed the ramp.

· · ·

She left it, and ran again. This time with no idea where she was going. In seconds he would be around the corner and see her. And really there was nowhere to run. No one lived here, at night it was just empty warehouses and closed up shops. In a panic she ducked down behind the nearest car, but it would take him only moments to see her. He would hear her frantic panting. Then a section of the wall beside her registered in her mind. It wasn't just wall, there was a narrow alleyway cut into it. It led to a space behind a small boat storage yard, and wasn't used for anything. She only knew of it because it was where Billy kept his kayak. It was hidden enough that no one vandalized it there. With no time to decide, she went for it. She sprinted into the dark alley at full speed and didn't slow down. It was another mistake. First something caught at her feet – perhaps rope, perhaps something else, but whatever it was, it sent her flailing forwards in the darkness, traveling far too fast. Then a crashing blow hit her on the front of her head. Dimly she was aware of falling, and a sharp pain on her temple. But then instead of the pain increasing, the opposite happened. All the pain, and all her feelings lessened. They drifted away. Her range of vision shrank quickly down as the blackness around her was replaced by a different shade of black that only existed in her head. Her knees crumbled underneath her.

She welcomed it. And then she felt nothing.

THIRTY-FIVE

IT WAS the cold that woke her. Creeping through the flesh of her side, deep into the bones. Her eyes opened. She didn't recognize what she saw. Her whole body hurt. Everything was cold, so cold. Her knees and hips felt stiff and her head – she went to move a hand to touch her forehead and it snagged against the rough brick of the wall that she lay against. Her eyes refocused and saw another wall just opposite, and above her a strange, green plastic roof, beyond that the sky a pale blue. The roof wasn't flat but curved and... Her brain unscrambled it to make out the hull of a kayak. Billy's kayak. Why...?

Some of it began to come back to her. She had been running, trying to escape from the man. The man with the earrings. Little black balls in each of his ears. But why...? Why had she been running? And then it all hit her, like the wake from a boat suddenly hitting a calm shore. Each one pushing a fresh flood of horror into her mind. She had left Carlos on the yacht, but then returned to collect her ID card, only to find two men torturing him. The man with earrings had been about to cut his throat. She had tried to stop them. She had fired the flare into the cabin, but... It hadn't worked. She must have escaped – she remembered running into the alley – but what about Carlos? Had they gone back to him. Was he... Was he *dead*?

Her breath caught in her throat. She felt the beginnings of a panic attack, and only just managed to get it under control. She told herself to breathe. She counted ten breaths, and only once she felt her heart rate dropping a little did she allow the question back in. Was Carlos alive or dead?

She had to find out. She struggled to her feet. She had to duck to keep out of the way of the kayak and she realized how she must have run square into it the night before. From the way her head throbbed she must have knocked herself out. She turned and looked at the small space where she had spent the night. The men must have looked for her, she reasoned, but she had been hidden. She hadn't planned it, but under the kayak jammed into the alleyway was the perfect hiding place. Yet at the same time, it was no wonder everything hurt, no wonder she felt colder than she had ever been in her life.

Then a fresh wave of fear struck. What if the men were still looking for her? What if they were still out there, with their guns ready. Perhaps even right by the entrance to the alley, if so they must have heard her already. But no – that made no sense. It must be hours later. It was dark when they chased her, not long after midnight she reckoned, though the thinking caused real pain in her temples. And now it was daylight. They wouldn't have searched for this long.

She felt for her cell phone, to check the time, only then remembering how she had left it charging in her car.

She stepped carefully to the entrance of the alley, still expecting to see the men at any moment. What she could see of the street looked normal. Even so she felt terrified as she peered cautiously around the corner. Nothing. The street looked as it always did. She could see her car, exactly where she had parked it, and a dozen yards further away, a man in blue overalls whistled as he swept the entrance to one of the small warehouses. She stared at him, longing to run over and tell him what had happened, plead for him to help her. But fear stopped her, and as she thought about it, she realized it was impossible. Her story, as she understood it, seemed too incredible. Too unbelievable. Instead she slipped out of the alley, and very cautiously made her way down the street and back over to the waterfront. She had no idea what she was expecting to see, only a deep sense of dread and certainty that somehow Carlos must be dead. She blinked back tears at the thought of that, the sheer impossibility that this had now happened.

Soon she reached the yacht basin. At first everything here looked normal too. But then looking out she saw out by the end of the pontoon, one of the yacht masts wasn't pointing straight upwards, instead it was raked at a 45 degree angle, and when she followed it to where it should meet the deck of the boat below, she saw that it was half hidden, and lying at a strange angle. The *Mystery* was still in its berth, but now it lay half-sunk. What was left of its structure above the water was blackened and twisted. Burned. Amber felt tears flowing freely down her face now. He was dead.

"You all right Miss?"

She swung her head round in alarm. A man was standing, staring at her, a small brown dog stood next to him holding an orange ball in its mouth.

"Oh." She wiped the tears away as best she could. "Yeah. Yeah I'm fine."

If anything the man looked disappointed with her answer. Like he was hoping for someone to gossip with.

"Come to see what happened?"

"Huh?"

"The yacht," the man said. "The one that sunk. I suppose you saw the flames last night? All very dramatic wasn't it? We don't often get excitement like that in Holport."

Amber stared at him, unable to reply, but shocked by the lightness of his tone. Her lover had been murdered. By professional killers, and she had only just escaped with her life. And he thought it was just some local excitement. She barely heard how the man was still speaking.

"They reckon it was gas. With that kind of explosion."

"Explosion?" Amber forced herself to concentrate.

"Oh yeah. I heard it all the way from the top of the road. And then there were all sorts here. An ambulance, the fire service... All very dramatic."

She didn't want to but Amber forced herself. "The man... The man who was on the yacht, do you know what happened to him?"

"Well yeah. They think he left the gas on and didn't notice. There's always someone doing something stupid like that..."

"Yes but, did he..." Amber couldn't make herself form the word.

"I mean..." She looked around. There was no police cordon. No police cars even, if a man had been *murdered* here the night before, surely the police would be here in force? There would be something. She turned again to the old man, this time barely daring to hope.

"I mean, did he survive?"

The words caught in her throat, and the man looked at her differently.

"Oh I'm sorry Miss," the man said now. He studied her, and Amber felt how she must look. "You didn't ... You're not *involved* in anyway?"

Everything about the situation screamed at her to be cautious. Whatever this was about, it involved drugs, professional killers.

"No... I was just... It's just so horrible." She forced herself to smile, and it seemed to work, since the man seemed content to return to his gossiping voice.

"The owner of the yacht you mean?" The man said. "They took him away in the ambulance. Seems he managed to drag himself out before the fire got too bad. They found him lying on the pontoon. He was in a pretty bad way though."

Amber blinked.

"Where is he? Now I mean?"

The man shrugged, looking confused again. "He'll be at the hospital. Had pretty nasty burns I heard..."

Amber stopped listening. She barely registered about burns, only that he was alive. Carlos was alive! She covered her face, squeezing her eyes tight shut and only then remembered the old man standing next to her, and how she must look. She tried to compose herself, but she realized her hair and clothes must be in a state, She looked at him now to see his curious expression as he watched what she was doing.

"You sure you're okay miss? Because if you know anything about this... I heard they found drugs on the boat as well."

"Drugs?" Amber dropped her hands.

"Yeah. There's a security firm looks after the marina. I spoke to the guard – I walk Elvis here every morning and night, so we know each other – and he said the guy from the yacht was a pothead. Been smoking weed out there ever since he turned up. The guard wasn't surprised this had happened. Not at all..." The old man shook his head, but he kept his eyes on Amber, clearly suspicious of her now. And this time the only urge Amber felt was the one to get away from him as quickly as possible.

She nodded her thanks, and walked back across the street, towards her car, feeling his eyes on her back the whole way. At the car she felt for her keys, then remembered how she'd dropped them the night before. She turned, and saw the man, still staring at her, and as she watched he slipped a cell phone from his pocket, but then she noticed a flash of silver from the ground by her feet. She crouched down, making a hasty attempt to look like she was tying a shoe lace, and gathered her keys gratefully into her hand. Then she stood, unlocked the door, and climbed inside.

She slipped the key into the ignition and said a silent prayer. Then she turned it. The motor turned over once, twice, three times and then the motor caught. She put her foot flat to the floor, revving it hard and sending a cloud of gray smoke from the tailpipe.

In the rear-view mirror she caught sight of the man, still staring at her but now with the phone at his ear. Then she slipped the car into drive, and pulled out of the space.

THIRTY-SIX

SHE DROVE towards the hospital in Newlea. But as she did so, her head filled with questions, and new fears. There would be police there at the hospital with him. They would want to know about the drugs. What should she tell them, to avoid getting Carlos into more trouble? What should she say to avoid incriminating herself? Worse, she was the one who had fired the flare that had put him in hospital – might the police be interested in that. Or should she just tell them everything, and hope they'd believe her? A worry surfaced in her mind. She didn't even know his name, not for sure anyway. Who should she ask for? Would they let her see him?

Then her thoughts were interrupted by the ringing of her cell phone, still plugged into the car charger.

"Oh shit."

For a second she left it, but then she grabbed the device and hit the button to accept the call.

"Mom?"

"Amber, where the hell are you? I've been calling you all morning. I have to get the morning ferry, I told you that and if you're not here, who the hell is going to look after Gracie…"

"*Mom!*" Amber tried to stop her, but it was no good.

"Don't you *Mom* me. I told you to be here last night so I can explain about Gracie's piano lessons, and you didn't come home *again*. So I texted you and said you better be here by seven at the latest and it's already 8:30 and where the hell are you?"

"Mom..." Amber's thoughts raced as she tried to compress everything that had happened into a reply to cut into her mom's anger.

"I meant to come back..."

"Where are you now?" Her mom snapped, ignoring her.

Amber looked about her. The truth was she had been driving with no awareness of the road around her. "I'm... I'm on the road into Newlea."

Her mom sighed. "Well that's something. Get a move on, and I can still catch my boat."

Then the call went dead.

Amber sat without moving for a long while, watching the tarmac flow towards her like a dream. She gripped the wheel hard, and opened the window wide, but still couldn't be sure whether she was dreaming everything or if it was real. As she came into Newlea she passed the hospital, turning her head to stare at the drab, squat building she had seen hundreds of times before but never really noticed. But rather than turning into the parking lot she kept going until, ten minutes later, she pulled up outside her house. She screwed her eyes tight shut again before pushing open the door and walking up the drive.

Her mom answered the door before she could get her key out.

"I'm so angry with you Amber."

"It's not my fault."

"Oh nothing is ever your *fault* is it Amber?" Her mom was as mad as Amber had ever seen her. She had her suitcase ready in the hallway, and she picked it up now, and carried it through the front door and out to the trunk of her car.

"I've written instructions for Gracie and left them in the kitchen. She has piano at five today, not six, and you need to be at the school by two thirty latest to pick up. Have you got that Amber?"

"Mom! I need to talk to you. Something's happened."

"Have you got that? Her piano lesson has been brought forward. Can you at least *acknowledge* me Amber? Is that too much to ask?"

"Mom, it's important."

Her mom paused, the suitcase resting on the lip of the car's trunk. "What is it?" She demanded.

Amber struggled to think how to tell her. How could she possibly put into words everything that had happened the night before?

"Well?"

Eventually she shook her head. Her mom sighed, and went back to wrestling the suitcase into the trunk.

"Was it really so much to ask? Three days? Without you making a drama of it?" With a grunt she got the case in, and slammed the trunk shut.

"It'll be just my luck if there is traffic and I'm late for the ferry." She shouted this back at the house, where Gracie was now standing in the doorway. "I'll see you in three days honey. You can call me anytime on my cell. And Amber will look after you, I promise." She smiled sweetly at the little girl, but the smile fell away when she turned back to Amber. "And you'd better. Unless you wanna be grounded for ever, 18 years old or not."

With that she stalked around to the driver's seat. Amber followed her, but before she could say anything more her mom had yanked the door shut.

Amber gave up and walked slowly back toward the house. She smiled at her sister, and put her arm around her. Together they watched their mom's car disappear down the street. Gracie waved at the disappearing vehicle.

"You should have been here earlier." Gracie told her, she didn't sound upset.

"Don't you start midget." Amber replied, but she rubbed her sister's shoulders affectionately and they went inside together.

"What happened to your head?" The little girl asked as they went into the kitchen. There was a mirror hanging by the entrance and Amber caught her reflection. Her hair was a mess, tangled and matted, and the skin on her forehead was split and bruised raw.

"I had an argument with a kayak."

"A kayak? Why did you have an argument with a kayak?"

"Because I like arguing with kayaks."

Gracie looked at her with a confused expression. "You know I don't have school today?"

"Yeah. I know that."

"Mom wrote it on the list, in case you forget."

"I didn't forget."

"She said I should do my math homework. That you'd help me. But I figured we should do something else, like ride our skateboards, and then maybe watch a movie with popcorn."

Amber smiled as much as she could. She touched a finger gently to the broken skin on her forehead. "I might pass on the skateboards, but I'll watch you while you ride yours."

"Okay," Gracie replied happily. "I'll go get it."

"Sure. But give me a moment. I'm just gonna take a shower."

THIRTY-SEVEN

THE McDONALD'S, which they had picked up from the drive-through in Newlea, was partly a prop to justify their presence on the quiet suburban street, but more a much-needed breakfast after the night which had gone so fucked up. Paulie fed fries one by one into his mouth like a drip of starch and salt, as he stared blankly through the windshield of the panel van. Tommy took huge bites out of a Big Mac and chewed the meat contemplatively.

"I'm just saying it was a fuck up. That's all," Tommy said, sucking in another bite. "And if you'd done what I said, we would have been outta here by now. Instead of sat here, wondering what to do next."

A few more fries found their way up to Paulie before he replied. "Shut the fuck up," he said.

Tommy obeyed only because he was shoving the rest of the burger in. After a few moments he opened the bag and pulled out a second burger. He unwrapped it and lifted up the top half of the bun. He began picking off the limp pieces of lettuce.

"And what was that bullshit of cutting his goddamn head off?"

Paulie ignored him.

"I mean, you figure Angelo really wants his head? Like, literally? What you think he's gonna do with it? Mount it on the wall?" He shook his head. "Plus it's gonna start rotting the moment you cut it off. I heard the brain is the first part to decompose. You'd need to pack it in ice or something. Or it's gonna start to smell like..." He stopped, and put the top back on the burger.

"Didn't I tell you to shut up?"

Tommy shrugged and took a bite, chewing more slowly this time, and watching the street through the windshield. The front door opened in one of the houses opposite, and a man stepped out. He was dressed in a suit, and carrying a briefcase. He walked to a car and zapped it unlocked, then opened the rear door to put the case inside. Then he climbed into the driver's seat. The car backed off the driveway and pulled away.

"OK. You wanna remind me why we're sitting here? And not sorting this fucking mess out?"

"This is sorting it out," Paulie replied, then he added, "and it ain't a fucking mess."

Tommy stayed silent, which served to irritate Paulie further.

"And what would you recommend? With all your years of fucking experience?"

Tommy shrugged. "We go to the hospital and take him out. We might have to leave his head in place, but least we'll know he's dead."

"Oh yeah. That's a great idea Tommy. Real good. Except that hospitals are all covered with cameras these days. They'll have you matched up on facial recognition in no time."

Tommy pondered this. The rise of surveillance had done for some of his better friends, and it wasn't an area he understood these days. Plus, it hadn't escaped his attention which one of them Paulie had expected to go in there. He changed the subject.

"Anyway. It's not whacking Luis Fernandez I'm worried about. It's going back to Angelo without the product."

"We're not gonna go back without the product," Paulie sounded frustrated. "The girl knows where it is, remember? All we have to do is find her, and she'll tell us where it is."

Tommy didn't look fully convinced by this, but he let it go.

"Maybe," he said, then shook his head. "I still don't understand how she managed to get away."

"I told you, she broke my fucking fingers." Paulie grabbed a handful of fries and stuffed them into his mouth. His fingers looked fine to Tommy.

. . .

"And I don't see why she's gonna come back here. Seems to me this is the least likely place she's gonna wind up. She'll be at the hospital. Or the cops."

Paulie said nothing.

"I mean she must've got a good look at your face, when she was breaking your…"

"Shut the fuck up man."

Tommy gave up and arranged his jacket so that it acted as a cushion against the hard plastic and glass of the van's door. Just as he was arranging his large body as best he could, Paulie spoke again, but it sounded like he was trying to convince himself.

"She ain't gonna call the cops. Her boyfriend's smuggling eighty keys of cocaine. That's the last thing she's gonna do."

Tommy shrugged again, like it wasn't really his problem, and closed his eyes.

Two tedious, empty hours later Paulie nudged him awake.

"What?"

"Open your eyes you fucking imbecile. She's here."

Outside the little Mitsubishi that they had seen Amber driving the night before pulled into the driveway. Tommy pulled himself upright, but neither man made any move to get out. Instead they watched. Amber's car pulled up on the curb, and she got out. But before she could reach the house, the front door opened and an older woman – presumably her mom – stepped outside. She was clearly angry about something from the way she was yelling and waving her arms about.

"What the fuck?" Paulie said under his breath.

Then Amber and the older woman went back inside. But the door stayed open, and moments later the woman reappeared, this time struggling with a large suitcase. Then Amber re-emerged as well, and the two of them carried on their argument all the way to the trunk of another car, this time a BMW compact that sat on the driveway.

"What they arguing about?" Tommy asked, his voice still a little sleepy.

"How the fuck should I know?" Paulie snapped back. Then a small child appeared in the doorway.

"Who's the kid?" Tommy asked.

"Again. How the *fuck* should I know?" Paulie repeated himself. But already he was beginning to form an idea.

The argument continued, but clearly the older woman was in a hurry to leave. And moments later she drove off in the BMW, leaving Amber and the child together. She was a girl, maybe five or six years old. Then they walked back into the house and shut the door.

"Well well. What's going on there?" Paulie asked, his voice different now, suddenly interested again. Tommy stared at him, frowning. He had been interrupted mid dream.

"Wait here," Paulie said five minutes later, when nothing else had happened. He pushed open the door of the van.

"Where you going?" Tommy asked.

"Just do as you're told," Paulie shot back. He slammed the door shut.

Tommy did what he was told. It was what he did. That had always been his job. But he was getting more and more pissed at doing what he was told by a fucking idiot like Paulie. With a fingernail he cleaned some of the remains of his burgers from his teeth, but he didn't leave the comfort of the van's cab.

Outside Paulie crossed the road and stopped on the sidewalk. He looked both ways but the street was empty and quiet. It looked as if most of the occupants had already left for work, or for school, and the house in front of him – the address on the girl's ID card – had no more vehicles on the drive, only Amber's Mitsubishi parked outside. He walked up the driveway. Ignoring the front door for now, he cautiously approached the window of whatever room it was that overlooked the street. He moved to the side, stole a glance, then pulled back against the wall. He saw enough to know it was a sitting room. A second glance confirmed it was empty, so Paulie stepped closer, and this time he used both hands to shield his eyes as he peered inside. It looked ordinary. A sofa, and a couple of armchairs were angled around a TV, and a collection of toys were strewn out on the floor. Through the open doorway Paulie could see into what looked like the kitchen. The light was on, but he couldn't see anyone inside. He rolled back, so that his back was against the front wall again, and thought. He *had* to get the girl, *Amber Atherton*, to take them to the cocaine. Anything else was inconceivable. Last night *had* been a fuck up, and he couldn't afford another one.

"Can I help you?"

Paulie froze, then slowly he turned around. The front door was open now, and the little girl was on the step, staring at him. He didn't answer, he had no idea what to say.

"I asked if I can help you?" The girl repeated herself. She didn't look scared, just alert. Paulie's mind raced.

"Why are you looking into my window?"

"Oh I'm just..." He pushed himself away from the wall, and forced a smile. He had no idea how to finish the sentence so he didn't. "I dunno. Say – was that your mom I just saw leaving?"

"Yeah," the girl answered.

"Oh. How about your dad? Is he about?"

"He doesn't live here anymore."

Paulie's smile became a little more real.

"Oh," he said. "So your mom, where's she gone?"

"She's gone away. For *three days*." The girl emphasized this, like it was a pretty big deal.

"Three days? Why's she done that then?"

"She had to. She didn't want to," the girl said, in a very matter-of-fact way. "It's for work."

"Oh right," Paulie thought for a moment. "So who's looking after you then?"

"My sister."

"Your sister? That's Amber right?"

The girl looked immediately suspicious. She tipped her head onto her shoulder. "How do you know that?"

Paulie considered. This was better than he could have possibly hoped for. "Oh she's a friend of mine," he said airily.

"*You're* Amber's friend?" The girl replied.

"Yeah." Paulie shrugged.

"You don't *look* like one of Amber's friends."

He laughed, beginning to enjoy himself. "Well how do Amber's friends look?"

"Better than you."

Paulie stopped laughing. He looked around the street again.

"What do you want anyway?"

"Excuse me?"

"Why are you looking in our living room window?"

Paulie ignored the question. "Where is Amber? Right now?"

"She's upstairs. In the shower."

Paulie glanced up, he realized the room above them was the bathroom. He could hear the water running.

"In the shower?"

"Yes! Like I just said."

Paulie studied the girl. From her face it was obvious she hadn't fully bought his nice-guy act. But then he didn't really give a shit about that. He allowed himself a few more seconds to consider, then made a decision. He pulled out his phone.

"Who are you calling?" The girl asked, but Paulie ignored her again. As soon as the call connected he began speaking. "Tommy, shift over and back the van up the drive. Do it right now."

"Who are you talking to?" The girl asked. "Why are you telling them that?"

"Don't ask why you..." Paulie bit his tongue into the phone. "Just... *do it.*"

Paulie slipped his phone back into his pocket, and turned back to the girl. He smiled again, trying not to make himself look creepy, which he knew he could do, from practicing in front of the mirror. Over the road, the van's motor started up. He glanced at the front door of the house, taking in which way it opened. Where he would need to stick his foot to block it.

"So what's your name then?" He asked the girl.

"*My name?* What's your name?"

"My name?" He thought. For some reason the name of his first pet came to mind, a mouse he'd been allowed to keep when he was about six. "Jason." He smiled again, thinking of the way it had scampered over his hands as a kid. "Come on. It's not going to hurt to tell me your name is it?"

The girl tipped her head over again. "No, I suppose not."

"That's right." Paulie glanced at the van. It was taking an age for Tommy to actually get moving. The guy was a fucking liability.

"OK then," he said. "So what is it?"

The girl noticed the van, moving now in front of the house, and slowing. She didn't seem to connect it to the strange man talking to her.

"It's Gracie."

"That's a lovely name," Paulie said absently. But his eyes were on the van now. It had stopped at an angle in the street. Then the reversing lights came on, and with a screech, it bumped up to the sidewalk and began backing fast onto the driveway. It stopped only a few feet away.

"What's he do...?" Gracie began, but she never got to finish her sentence, because suddenly Paulie was upon her. He threw one arm around her, picking her off the ground, and with the other he flung open the rear door on the van, then he pivoted and dumped her inside, his weight falling onto her, silencing any chance of a scream. Moments later Tommy was there.

"The fuck are you..."

"Shut up." Paulie cut him off and rolled off the girl. Now he had one hand clamped over her mouth.

"Get in here and tie her up. Make sure she doesn't make a fucking sound," Paulie commanded, then when Tommy hesitated he swore at him, until the big man was inside. He easily held the girl down with one giant arm, while with the other he searched for tape.

And when he was satisfied the situation was under control, Paulie climbed out, checked around the still-empty street, and stepped inside the house.

THIRTY-EIGHT

AMBER LET the warm water run down through her hair and eyes. At first it pooled pink at her feet, as it washed the dirt and blood from her hair, but soon it ran clear. She stood for a long time letting the warmth unlock the tension in her shoulders and back. She didn't know what she was going to do, but whatever it was would have to wait until her Mom came back and she could give Gracie back. She reached for the shampoo, and squeezed a generous handful.

Then there was a noise from downstairs.

Amber opened her eyes. She listened. But there was nothing else. It was just Gracie she decided. Slamming a cupboard door, or jumping off the table. She was that kind of kid. Amber listened for a second, but there was nothing – it was nothing – so she went back to letting the water run over her. And ten minutes later she turned off the flow and reached for a towel. She wrapped it around her and stepped out of the shower, then when she had dried herself she left the bathroom.

Right away she sensed something wasn't right. It was the quiet. Too quiet. Amber felt the hair on the back of her neck rise up. She called out downstairs, "Gracie!"

There was silence.

Amber tried again, louder this time. "*Gracie?*"

Again there was no reply.

Amber wrapped the towel tighter and looked down the stairs. The front door was open. Not wide-open, but just a little ajar.

"Gracie?" Amber called again, worried now. She stepped down the stairs, a slight sense of floating, unreality. She passed the entrance to the living room and looked inside. No Gracie. She wasn't in the kitchen either. And the house was silent. She went to the front door, feeling the slight flow of wind on her bare legs and feet. She gently pushed it wider open, then stepped onto the doorstep and looked around. Outside the street looked completely normal, but still there was no Gracie. Amber called out her name again, but quieter now, not wanting to draw too much attention while she stood there in a towel. Then she rushed back inside, up the stairs and threw some clothes on, and a minute later she was outside the house calling loudly, and checking every possible place the girl could be hiding. But she wasn't there.

Eventually Amber went back inside, reasoning that she hadn't properly checked the house – Gracie had any number of hidey-holes she liked to squirrel herself away in, dressed as a pirate or a princess, and lost in her own world of make believe... And that's when she saw the note. Scrawled on the back of a letter and pinned under a coffee cup on the kitchen work surface. Amber stared at it in disbelief, somehow realizing what it meant, even before her brain had deciphered the words:

You've got what we want. Now we have what you want. Let's make a swap.

Underneath there was a cell phone number.

Amber stared at the note in shock. They had her sister?

* * *

Her thoughts were a cocktail of confusion, hope and horror mixing what made sense with what she wanted to believe. It could be some sort of a joke. Her sister was always getting into some sort of scrape or another. So Gracie must have written the note to trick her. But of course that made no sense. It wasn't in Gracie's handwriting, hers was neater than that. It was something else then. Something separate to the crazy and bizarre turn her life had taken in the last twelve hours. But this thought only served to connect the total horror of what she had witnessed the two men doing to Carlos with *the fact they had her sister*. Her six-year-old sister.

Those men had her sister. Without thinking any further she dialled the number.

"Yeah?" It was a man's voice. Amber didn't recognize which of them it was, but then she didn't really give a fuck.

"Where's my sister? You mother*fucking* piece of shit..."

"Whoa there. Calm down lady."

"*Fuck you asshole.* Tell me where she is right now or I swear..."

"Bitch, you're gonna calm down or your sister's gonna get hurt. Which is it gonna be?"

Amber stopped talking. She could hear her own breath coming in short stabs. She wiped tears from her eyes.

"That's better, now how about we start again? You're Amber Atherton right?"

Still breathing hard, Amber confirmed it.

"It was you fired that flare into the boat last night? Damn near broke my fingers too, on that goddamn gate..."

"Fuck you. I should have fucking cut them off."

"Yeah well fuck you too. We don't have to make friends here lady. We just have to do a little business."

"Where is she? Where's Gracie?"

"All in good time. Here's how this is gonna work, it's real simple. We get the product back, you get the little girl back. How's that sound?"

Amber's mind went blank. "I don't know what you're talking about."

"I think you do. You've put plenty of it up your fucking nose."

There was a moment of silence, but inside Amber's mind it all came together. "I don't know where it is, so there's no point you holding onto Gracie..."

"Well we think you do."

What the fuck were they talking about?

"You think I do what?"

"We think you know where he hid it. No, we *know* you know..."

Amber felt like screaming in frustration. "What? How would I know?"

"He told you."

"No he fucking didn't."

"He told us he told you."

"*What*? This is insane. You're insane. Why would he say that, when he didn't? He told me he bought it from some guy in a bar."

There was a pause, and the voice – she realized it was the man she'd called Earrings now – he suddenly sounded considerably less sure of himself.

"Well you fucking better know. For the sake of your sister."

Amber caught sight of her reflection in the mirror again. Her cut forehead. This couldn't be real.

"Look this is madness. I've got nothing to do with this, and my sister has got even less. I swear to you I don't have any idea where he put it. Now please, I'm begging you, let her go."

But the man's voice was surer again now. "Don't feed me that crap. You know where it is. Or if you don't, you better fucking find it."

"But I..." Amber was interrupted this time.

"And don't even think about calling the fucking cops. If you do that we'll cut the girl up and mail her back to you in six different boxes. Then we'll hunt your mom down and kill her too."

"But..." Amber stopped talking as she realized the line was dead.

This was a dream. It had to be. There was no other possible explanation for how her life could explode into such utter chaos and horror in such a short time. But the girl in the reflection staring back at her was too real, her forehead still bleeding. It was no dream. Her next thought was to call the police. She almost didn't connect it with the final command of the man on the phone to not involve the cops. Instead she considered what she would tell them. About the drugs. About what she had seen the night before. About how they now had Gracie – these two killers – and how the police *had* to act. But all she saw were the problems. It would take so long. She would have to tell her story to one person, and then another, higher up, before they even started searching. And that was *if* they believed her. And how would they find these men? What was to stop them doing what they'd threatened long before the police caught them?

The reality of what they said suddenly made Amber's stomach turn. At first she just felt ill, but then she realized, with blank disbelief, she was actually going to throw up again. She only just got to the sink in time before the little that was in her stomach came up with a thick stench of bile.

And once she'd started, she retched over and over, her body locked into a rhythm of convulsions that made her eyes and nose water and which she feared might never end. And when it did she stared miserably at the mess in the sink for a while. This wasn't real. This couldn't be. Amber almost forced herself to call out Gracie's name again, but the note was there staring up at her. Ugly writing. She saw the machete the man had carried, heard the popping of the guns they had fired at her.

Somehow she had to come to terms with the horror of all this. And the faster she did, the better the chance for her sister. Slowly, gradually, her brain began to turn to addressing the situation in a more practical way. *Had* Carlos told her where the coke was hidden? She forced herself to revisit the conversations they had had. Carlos had introduced the cocaine into their relationship casually, and with only a little bit at the beginning. They'd smoked a joint, and then he'd pulled out a little paper slip folded into four.

"You ever tried this?" He'd said, and he'd laughed when her eyes went round with surprise. That had been three weeks ago, and they'd only done it a handful of times since, until last week, when she'd turned up to find him with a larger bag of the powder, and much keener to snort more of it.

But all he'd ever said about *where* it came from was the lie he'd told about buying it from a guy in a bar in Holport. She only knew that was a lie yesterday, when he'd finally admitted that he had stolen it. And probably – it was obvious now – he'd told the lie to protect her. The thoughts came rushed and ill-formed, and refused to stay long enough for her to properly interrogate them. A cold panicky urgency took over. Horrible imaginings about where her sister was right now, and what they might be doing to her.

He hadn't told her where it was. She was sure of it. And surely she would remember something like that? Especially now. If he'd mentioned where he'd hidden a huge load of cocaine, she wouldn't have forgotten…

Suddenly she stopped dead. He hadn't told her where it was, she was right about that. But he had said something. Something about Billy. About how *he* might know where it was.

Amber blinked at her reflection in the mirror for a long moment. The battered girl blinked back at her. Then she grabbed her keys and ran out the front door.

THIRTY-NINE

"I DON'T UNDERSTAND," I say, but Amber just keeps on shouting and waving her arms about. She's still outside the front door, where moments before she began hammering like the world was ending. Her car is parked half in our hedge, the driver's door wide open.

"Slow down Amber, you need to slow down."

"I don't have time to fucking slow down. I need you to tell me where it is, where he put the cocaine."

"What are you talking about?"

"*Arrgh!*" She pushes past me into the kitchen, where she paces up and down.

"Billy, will you just listen to me, please?"

I stare at her, not sure if I've heard right. "Did you just say cocaine?"

"Yes." She pauses, for the first time since she got here, and I take the moment to pull out a chair and sit down. Then she tells me the story again, a little bit slower this time, but it still sounds absolutely crazy. Something about Mafia hitmen and shipments of cocaine, and then the craziest bit of all. About her sister, Gracie, being kidnapped.

"And then I remembered," Amber says as she finishes the story. "Carlos – or Luis, or whatever his name is – he told me how you knew where he had stashed the cocaine."

I stare at her, still not sure if this is some kind of weird joke, or more likely, a reaction to the drugs she's been smoking. Like a bad trip. It's kinda what I feared.

"Amber... " I try to keep my voice as neutral and un-threatening as possible, which I think you're supposed to do with people on drugs. "Is this all real, or just in your head?"

In response she lets out another loud scream. When she calms down enough to speak she pulls out a letter from the pocket of her jeans.

"For fuck's sake Billy. Look at this." Then she turns it over, and there's something written on the back. The handwriting is bad so I can hardly read it.

You've got what we want. Now we have what you want. Let's make a swap.

I read it out loud, then look up at her. I'm still confused.

"Who wrote this?"

"*They did.* The Mafia guys. The guys who tortured Carlos. Who chased me. The guys who've got Gracie. And who are actually going to kill her if we don't tell them where their fucking drugs are." Suddenly Amber bursts into tears, great big sobs that make her whole body heave up and down.

I pretend to read the note again, but actually I'm just trying to get some time to think. I study the handwriting first, to see if it might actually be Amber's. She has really distinctive writing, she wants to be an artist and she's really into graphic design. So if it *is* her, she's done it with her left hand.

"So?" Amber says, pulling herself together. "Do you know where it is?"

"Where what is?"

"The drugs. The cocaine. Carlos told me you know where it is. So do you?"

I consider, just for a half second, but already she has her fists clenched again and she's making a moaning noise.

"Why would I know?"

"Because you *have to* know," Amber says, her voice suddenly sounding even more desperate. "You have to know, or they're going to hurt Gracie. Or even worse…"

I'm baffled. Honestly I didn't think Amber was really talking to me at the moment, on account of how I didn't approve of her relationship with Carlos, but then she turns up here screaming all this crazy stuff at me. It's just hard to take.

"Would you like a cup of coffee?"

"No I wouldn't like a fucking cup of coffee. I'd like some help finding my sister."

We sit in silence for a few moments. When I think it's a good moment I try again.

"Amber, I did a little bit of reading about marijuana the other day, and how it can cause symptoms of paranoia. You see people think it's not that strong, but the strains they're growing now are very powerful. And they actually cause hallucinations, where things seem really real even though they're not..."

At this, Amber sits abruptly down at the table across from me. She leans forward and takes my hands in hers. They're ice cold.

"Billy," she pulls my hands towards her, and stares, her eyes clear and earnest. "Billy we've been through a lot haven't we? Together I mean?"

She waits, and in the end I nod, because there's not much else I can do while she's holding onto me like this.

"Good. And I swear to you, I promise. This isn't a hallucination. It's totally real, and I am *desperate* for your help."

Looking at her now I see there's a cut and a bruise on her forehead. I frown at it now.

"What happened there?"

She doesn't hesitate. "I told you. The kayak."

She doesn't take her eyes off me as she speaks, pleading with me. Her chest heaving up and down.

"Where you ran into it?" I check. "When they were chasing you?"

She nods. It looks nasty actually. It's certainly not part of a hallucination, unless I'm having one.

"What did you say happened to Carlos? While they were chasing you?"

"I don't know. The yacht caught fire. It sank. I spoke to a guy who says he got out. But I don't know. I don't even know if he's alive. I don't even know if that's his *name.*"

She hesitates for a minute. Then, still staring right at me she goes on.

"Which means you were right by the way. About not trusting him."

Again I consider, this time for a little bit longer, while Amber continues to stare earnestly at me. I did always think there was something not quite right about Carlos.

"And you actually saw them? You saw the guns they had, and... this machete?"

"Yeah. I saw it. I saw it all."

I feel myself blinking quite a lot.

"Well you have to go to the police," I say in the end. I can't think of anything else *to* say.

But Amber lets out her frustrated scream once again and looks away.

"I *can't*. I told you. If I go to the police they're going to hurt Gracie. That's what they said..." It looks like she's going to continue, but instead fat tears appear again in each of her eyes. This time she wipes them away.

"But don't they always say that?" I ask. "Kidnappers? They always say not to go to the police, but actually it makes sense to ignore them and go anyway. And we have quite good contacts with the Lornea Island police force, I'm sure they'd listen to us, what with all the murderers we've caught already."

Amber gives an animal-sounding howl at the word murderer.

"I'm sorry," I say. "I'm sure they're not going to... do anything to hurt Gracie. Why would they? She doesn't know anything about this. She is only six years old."

"Because Billy, they think I know where their cocaine is. And they're professionals. Actual hitmen. They've probably killed dozens of times before."

"Then call the police," I say again. "That's why you have to call them. They're the experts. They'll know what to do."

Amber screams again, but this time, when she's finished, she pulls out her phone and slides it on. But then she stares at it, as if she's forgotten how it works.

"What do I call?" She asks.

"Nine one one."

She breathes heavily, staring at me. "You're right. The police will have people for this. They'll know what to do."

I get up, relieved to have my hands back, and that this madness is starting to come under control. I start making coffee. Even if Amber doesn't want any I need some. "Yeah. They'll know."

"Okay," she says as she takes a deep breath. "If you think it's the best thing to do, I'll call them. I just want Gracie back. I don't care what happens to me, or even to Carlos. I just want her back safe."

I listen to this as I pack the grounds into the machine.

"Sure. Did they have island accents?" I ask, a little offhandedly.

"What?"

"The mafia guys. Did they have island accents?"

"Why do you ask that?"

"I don't know. I was just wondering."

Amber thinks for a moment, her fingers poised to press the digits. "No. I don't think so, at least. They sounded from the mainland."

"Oh," I say.

"Why? What are you thinking?"

"I'm not thinking anything." I say, and I'm really not.

"Are you saying the island police won't be able to handle it?"

"No…"

"Well you're saying something. And you might be right. I mean they were totally fucking useless with the Principal Sharpe thing, back when we were running the detective agency."

"No, I really didn't mean that. I was just…"

"And if we do get the police involved, they'll never let them get their drugs back. They might hurt Gracie out of spite. They might kill her… Oh my God Billy."

"No, I wasn't saying that. I really wasn't." I look at her. "Call them. If this is real you have to call them."

Amber looks like she's barely heard me. But then she nods, and this time she dials. She keeps talking as she does so.

"You're right Billy. I'm glad I came here. I just want Gracie back as soon as possible. Unharmed. And I thought you really might know where the cocaine was being hidden, because Carlos said something about it. About the first time you met, and then I thought we could just give it to them in exchange for Gracie, and that might be the safest thing."

As Amber speaks I suddenly get the strangest feeling. It's like a really bad thought. Or really important. But I don't know what. I don't know what it is, just that there's something.

"911, what's your emergency?" I hear through the phone.

"Oh hi," Amber begins. She pauses, screwing her eyes tight shut.

"Hello ma'am please state which service you require…"

Amber opens her eyes, ready to speak, but then I suppose she sees my face. And I must look wrong, because then she doesn't speak after all, least, not into the phone.

"What is it?" She says instead, talking to me.

I don't reply. I try to figure out what it is I just thought of. But I can't get it.

"Billy? What is it? What are you thinking? Have you remembered something?" Amber says, as the voice on her phone repeats their call.

"Ma'am, are you OK? Which service do you require?"

I still don't really know what it is I'm thinking, but a shape has come into my mind. Or rather a series of shapes. Landscape. Or more accurately, a seascape. It's like my brain is playing me a video. The way water is cut in half by the sharp bow of my kayak, and the rhythmic splashes either side of paddle strokes.

"Billy? Talk to me. What have you remembered."

"Ma'am? Are you in danger? Are you unable to speak?"

"Billy..." Amber begins. But I hold up a finger to keep her quiet.

"What? Did he tell you? Did Carlos tell you where it is?"

I think some more. And now I know where this is going. It's like I'm retracing the trip I took out to the nature reserve, when I went to photograph the octopus. The *Octopus Burryi.* The time I first saw the *Mystery,* and the man who turned out to be Carlos – or Luis – spear fishing in the reserve. Only, because it's a nature reserve, there's loads more fish there than anywhere else on the island. And if Carlos really was an experienced spear fisherman, there's no way he would have been that far away from the yacht without any fish.

"I think I know where the dope might be," I say, my voice hushed.

"Ma'am..."

"I'm fine. Wrong number," Amber stabs her finger down to kill the call. "Where?"

I tell her. I explain about the time how I saw Carlos spear fishing. Only he had an empty bag, and how seeing me made him jump. Jump so much he actually dropped his spear. Like he'd been caught doing something he didn't want anyone to see.

Before I've even finished she jumps up to her feet. "Well where are they? These caves? Let's go. Let's get it." So then I have to explain because Amber hasn't been to the caves. Not many people have, on account of how they're actually very hard to get to, because you're not allowed to anchor nearby, and because that side of the island is very exposed to swells. Plus you need a spring low tide to actually access the caves, unless you've got proper diving equipment.

Then I stop and think because that might be relevant. And yes, it *was* calm the day I saw Carlos, because I wouldn't have gone otherwise, but it was definitely low tide too. It wasn't an issue for me, but I noticed how low it was when I pulled the kayak up on my ledge.

"But how would Carlos have known all that?" Amber says now. "How would he even know about the caves?"

I shrug. "They're marked on charts. But, I don't know..." Understanding why people hide drugs where they do is not really a specialty of mine. "Maybe he was desperate to find somewhere, and he just got lucky?

He probably didn't want to come into the harbor with all the drugs on board."

She nods at this. "So when can we get it?"

I walk to the window and look out at the beach below. The swell isn't huge, but it's still way too big to get access to the caves. "The tides are good," I say. "We're on springs. But the waves are too big. We'd need to wait for the swell to drop."

"Well when will that happen?"

So then I pull up the lid of my laptop, and open up the site I use for the weather. There's an icon that switches the display from showing the weather for the next few days to showing the expected swell. It's actually more accurate than the weather forecast, since it's not really a forecast at all, it just shows what swell is actually already there, and which will just keep rolling until it hits the coastline.

"Hmmm." I say.

The site shows the east coast of the island, and the sea around it is colored in various different shades of yellow and red and even purple. When it does that, the waves here get huge. I wouldn't even think of going to the nature reserve unless the waves showed as green for a couple of days, just to be on the safe side.

"Oh shit," Amber says. I didn't notice her leaning over my shoulder. "Is that another storm?"

"Yeah," I say. "Looks like it."

She runs her hands over her hair.

"Well we don't have to get it *for* them," she says now. "We just need to tell them where it is."

I don't answer her. Instead I click to see the higher resolution models. Then I type in my password. You have to subscribe to the site to get the most detailed information, and even though I'm not a member, the surf lifesaving club is. And they let me use their password, as long as I log out once I've used it, otherwise they can't log in. And looking at it now, I see there is a narrow window of time when the wave height shows as green, or less than half a meter of swell. It's tonight, and it's only for a few hours, before the wind kicks in and the wave height builds. But it's there. Then I let my mind imagine being out there at night, with a storm coming in. It wouldn't be nice.

"I'm gonna phone them." Amber's words bring me back to the present. "I need to get Gracie."

FORTY

"AND DON'T EVEN THINK about calling the fucking cops," Paulie spat into the phone. "Or we'll cut the girl up and mail her back to you piece by piece." He quit the call, and when the connection was dead he slammed his hand on the dashboard.

"*Motherfucker!*" He shouted.

Tommy, driving the van a little too fast on the road out of Newlea, glanced across. He waited for Paulie to go on, but he didn't.

"Well? She say where it is?"

Paulie didn't reply.

"The coke? She tell you where it is?"

"Not yet."

"*Not yet*? The fuck's she waiting for?"

Paulie ignored him again, so Tommy asked him a second time, but Paulie snapped back.

"Will you shut the fuck up? I gotta think." He noticed their speed. "And slow down, we don't want to attract any attention."

Tommy did what he was told, easing off the gas a token amount. He glanced in the rear view mirror at the girl, her hands and legs bound with tape, half her face covered with the silver material. She was staring back at them, he could see her eyes.

"Sure. Because kidnapping a kid ain't gonna do that," he said in the end. Then when Paulie didn't react, he went on. "Attract attention I mean..."

"Fuck you Tommy. She's the broad's sister. With her we've got *leverage.*"

Paulie went back to thinking.

"You call it leverage? I'd call it a big fucking problem."

"Yeah well what would you know about it?"

"What would I know? I been working with the old man since you were in short pants, you think I don't know how to…"

"And the old man's *dead.* In the fucking ground. And your new boss, who happens to be my cousin, put me in charge since he knows you ain't smart enough to take a shit unsupervised. So watch your fucking mouth."

Tommy considered correcting Paulie, that he was Angelo's *second* cousin. But he settled for saying it in his head. First *or* second, the asshole had a point.

Paulie checked the speed again. "So slow the fuck down, or I'll be telling Angelo you have a loyalty problem."

It looked like Tommy wasn't going to reply, but then he changed his mind. "Yeah. You're in charge alright. And you're doing a great job too. With your CIA bullshit interrogation methods. And now kidnapping a random little kid? It's a great fucking operation you're running here. First class."

"She ain't random."

"And you know what? I'm gonna be sure to report back all the details of the amazing job you're doing…"

"She *ain't* random," Paulie insisted. "The broad knows where the coke is, that dumb fuck told us so last night. And he did so precisely *because* of my methods. We tried your way, remember? Breaking his hands up. He told you to go look on the fucking moon. Let's tell that to Angelo shall we?"

Tommy had no answer to this, so Paulie went on, laughing now. "What you gonna do, go back to Angelo and suggest building a space rocket?" He mimed being weightless for a moment, floating in space, but he did it badly.

"What about the cops?" Tommy said in the end. "They're gonna be looking for this kid everywhere. Probably already are."

Paulie shook his head. "No. The bitch is dumb, but she won't go to the cops. Not if she wants the kid back in one piece. Besides, she's up to her neck in it."

Tommy glanced across. He didn't feel the same confidence.

"Even so, what we gonna do with…" He jerked his thumb towards the back of the van. "We can't leave her in the van. She's gonna need food. To go to the bathroom. She might bang on the sides, attract attention..."

Paulie interrupted at this.

"Well she might now, you dumb fucker. You've given her the idea."

"Jesus Paulie. I'm just *asking*. What's the plan? I assume you have got one?"

"Course I got one."

"Well? What is it?"

For a long time Paulie didn't answer. But just as Tommy opened his mouth to speak again, Paulie cut him off.

"We go somewhere quiet and wait till she calls us back. Tells us where the coke is."

"OK. And if she don't?"

"She will."

Tommy might have pursued his line of questioning further, but at that moment they drove past a junction where a police cruiser was waiting to join their road. They both fell silent, trying not to look as they swept past. Then they both studied the mirrors, to see the cruiser pull out behind them, two uniformed officers visible.

"Watch your speed," Paulie said.

"I *am* watching my speed," Tommy replied. The police cruiser didn't have its blue lights on, and it hung back, not obviously watching, nor interested in them.

"OK *boss*," Tommy asked, "So where exactly does this plan of yours say we hole up and wait?"

Paulie kept his eyes on the cruiser for a long while. Then glanced at the dashboard to check their speed. Then he grabbed the map they'd been using earlier. Suddenly he smiled.

"I know just the fucking place."

FORTY-ONE

THE VAN BUMPED down the track, until eventually they arrived back at Bishop's Landing. Just as before it was totally empty, the only signs that anybody ever came here were the jetty reaching out into the creek – the tide higher this time – and the old wooden boathouse. Climbing out the van, Paulie crouched down to inspect the tire marks on the ground. The only ones he could see were theirs from the other day. He stood up, nodding with satisfaction, and pulled open the sliding door of the van. He ignored the frightened grunts and squeaks from the kid, and instead pulled a large crowbar from a canvas tool bag.

"Wait here. Watch that," he told Tommy, gesturing to Gracie with the crowbar. Then he stalked over to the boathouse.

The double doors were secured with a padlock. Paulie studied it for a moment, noting how it looked rusty all over. Then he inserted the end of the crowbar under the clasp, and leaned on it hard, until the screws began releasing their grip on the weather-softened wood. He felt Tommy watching him, critical of his technique, and he ended up frustrated that even with the clasp half off, he still couldn't wrangle the door open with his bad fingers. He nearly reached for his gun, but finally, and with a lot of grunting, the clasp was on the ground. He resisted the urge to give it a kick, thinking, rightly, that all he would do is add a couple of broken toes to his tally. He nudged it aside instead, then yanked open the door.

Inside was dark and musty. A small open fishing boat that had seen better days took up half of the room downstairs. Next to it, a tractor stood with its motor partly stripped down. Above them a small mezzanine floor was visible, reached by dusty wooden steps. Paulie climbed them carefully into a small workshop area. Everything looked old, and every surface was covered with cobwebs. He pulled a finger across the worktop, and inspected it in the half light. His fingertip came back black. Paulie smiled. He looked around again, then jogged lightly back down the steps and outside.

"No one's been here for years," Paulie said, as he got back to the van. "We'll stash her here and wait for the broad to tell us where the coke is."

Tommy looked around, trying to find fault with the location. But he stayed silent.

"Come on, give me a hand."

Together they carried the bound Gracie into the boathouse and up the stairs, where they lashed her to a beam with more carpet tape. Paulie began to feel very pleased with his morning's work. Until Tommy opened his mouth again.

"How do you know the broad is gonna phone?"

There was no time for an exasperated Paulie to reply, because at that very moment his cellphone rang.

* * *

With a grin, Paulie answered the call, then put it on speaker. At once Amber's voice rang out from the speaker.

"Is this the motherfucker who's got my sister?"

Paulie felt himself smiling, feeling very happy.

"Yeah, it is," he replied. "And is this the dumb broad who thinks she can just steal eighty keys of coke and get away with it?" He glanced at Tommy, his eyes dancing. Tommy stared blankly back.

A pause.

"Where is she?"

"Somewhere safe," Paulie turned back to the phone. "Where's our product?"

"Let me speak to her. I need to know she's OK."

Paulie looked at the girl, her mouth covered and her whole body wrapped with carpet tape, holding her against the post.

"She can't talk right now. She's kinda tied up." He chuckled out loud at the joke, glancing again at Tommy to see if he appreciated it too, but still his face was blank. Humorless fucker.

"I'm not saying anything until I speak to her," Amber said.

Suddenly Paulie's mood burst.

"Well then you clearly don't feel too strongly about seeing her again, because I'm making the rules here, and she's fucking tied up. Literally." He frowned. It was unbelievable he had to explain his joke to these idiots.

"Well you piece of shit," Amber spoke carefully, after a moment. "I don't know what eighty kilos of coke is worth but I bet it's millions. And I sure as hell ain't telling you where it is unless I speak to Gracie. So unless you want to be down several million dollars, you better untie her. *Asshole.*"

There was a moment of silence, during which Paulie regretted putting the phone on speaker. He felt Tommy watching him, and he tried to consider. In the end he sighed.

"For fuck's sake. What the hell?" He indicated to Tommy to pull the tape from the girl's mouth. "No loss to me bitch," he spat at the phone, while Tommy unwrapped the tape. He noticed how he did it carefully, not just yanking it away. But then the kid did look in a pretty bad way. She had grime all over her face, with little lines running from her eyes where she'd been crying. And judging from the stench she'd already pissed herself. When the tape was released she said nothing. Stupid little chin quivering.

"Well?" Paulie said, a moment later. "Ain't you gonna say nothing?"

"Gracie?" Amber asked. Are you there? Are you OK?"

The little girl began crying again, but she managed to get out a single word. *Amber.*

"Oh my God. Don't worry," Amber said down the line. "We're gonna get you. I promise you…"

"Alright that's enough," Paulie cut in. "Tape her back up, and let's stop fucking around." He snatched up the phone and switched off the speaker.

"First of all, you better not have gone to the cops, because if you have, the girl dies. Do you understand that?"

There was a pause, then Amber's voice came through again.

"Yeah."

"Have you gone to the cops?"

Another pause. Then a strangled reply.

"No."

Paulie thought for a second. He wanted to ask how he could know she hadn't gone to the cops, but there was no way she could prove it. He tensed a little, as if sensing how this had slipped out of control. But he suppressed the thought. Then he realized the girl on the end of the line was crying. For some reason this settled him a bit.

"OK. So where is our product?"

"It's hidden."

"Hidden where."

"Where you won't ever find it."

"What?" Paulie sighed.

"I'm not telling you until I get my sister back."

"Well you ain't getting her back until you tell me."

"I'm still not telling you."

There was another pause. Paulie felt the tension returning. How the fuck was he supposed to break this stupid deadlock?

"Why not?" He asked in the end.

"Because if I just tell you, how do I know you'll give Gracie back?"

Paulie considered. He gave the best answer he could think of.

"You'll just have to trust me."

"*What?* Why would I trust you? You're a fucking *hitman.* You've *kidnapped* my sister!"

The beginnings of a smile crept onto Paulie's lips as he heard the word. He'd never thought of himself as a hitman exactly.

"And anyway, it's not that simple," Amber went on.

"It sounds pretty simple to me." Paulie said, meaning to ask again where the coke was so they could get on with this. But then a second thought broke in too. Wasn't this what police negotiators taught? To make things *complicated*? To slow things down, to give them time to track down the location of the perpetrators. He tensed. The thought crossed his mind to consult with Tommy. If only the guy wasn't such an asshole.

Then there was another pause, and this time Paulie heard a second voice in the background, barely audible.

Tell them they're gonna need a boat.

"You're going to need a boat." Amber repeated.

"Who the hell is that?" Paulie snapped back at once. "I just heard a voice. Have you called the fucking cops?"

"No!" Amber replied.

"You better fucking not… Your sister's as good as dead."

"No, please," Amber cut in. "I swear I haven't. It's… Oh fuck, Billy can you speak to them?"

"*What?*" Paulie asked, but he didn't get any further as there was the muffled sound of the phone being manhandled, then the second voice came on the phone more clearly.

"It's just it's a bit complicated," the new voice said. Unbelievably it sounded like another kid. A boy this time.

"Who the hell is this?" Paulie demanded. "What the fuck is going on?"

"I'm a friend of Amber's," the boy replied quickly. "And it's compli-cated because of where it is. The cocaine I mean. Or where we think it is. Where we think he must have hidden it."

"Where?"

"Well we can't say that. But even if we could it's very hard to actually get to."

"*What?* Why?"

"Well if there's eighty kilos, then it's going to be quite big, and obvi-ously quite heavy – well eighty kilos – which is quite heavy unless it's packed into smaller parcels, which it usually is on the TV. But there'll still be a lot of them. And there's a lot of swell on the way, and wind, and that's going to make it very hard. You'll need quite a lot of time to get it out..."

"Get it out of where? The fuck are you talking about?"

Another pause. Paulie felt Tommy watching him. Even the fucking girl.

"I can't tell you where it is. I already said that."

"Why... *Fuck that.*" Paulie frowned, and turned away so Tommy couldn't see his face. "How old are you anyway?"

There was another pause, then the boy's voice continued, sounding confused.

"I'm sixteen. Well nearly. But I don't see why that's relevant."

"Sixteen? What the...?"

The dumb bitch has gone to another kid for help... Paulie felt his stress levels rise. How in the world was everyone so fucking *dumb*. He told himself to calm down. This was nuts, but it was *good* nuts. There was no way the cops would put him on the line with a sixteen-year-old kid. Not in a million years. So all he had to do was figure out a way to make the exchange. But now the damn kid was talking again.

"So we're thinking, if we give you the instructions for how to get it, in exchange for Gracie, then you can get it when the weather is right..."

"Shut up," Paulie said. "Just shut the fuck up." The voice went quiet. Paulie tried to think. But the more he tried, the less he had any idea about what to do next. The more he felt Tommy's eyes on him. The more his fears about the police grew, listening in behind the voices on the phone.

There are no cops. It's just a couple of goddamn kids.

Stop messing around and get this done.

"This ain't happening on the phone," he said suddenly. "There's a restaurant, on the road out of the ferry port. It's got a big fuck-off anchor on the sign, you know it?"

A pause, then: "Do you mean *The Schooner*?"

"I don't know. Does it have a fuck-off great anchor on its sign?"

Another pause. "Yes."

"Then I mean *The Schooner*. We're gonna meet you there in *one hour*. Just the two of you. We see a single sign of the cops, the kid dies. You make sure you bring whatever you need to get this fucking coke back. If not, the kid dies. Is that fucking clear enough?"

There was another pause, a long one this time. Finally the kid broke it. "One hour is a bit tight from here. Could we make it ninety minutes?"

"*Fuck sake*." Paulie looked at his watch. "Let's do 3pm. Does that work?"

"Erm." The line went quiet, and Paulie could hear them conferring. "OK," the boy said.

"Fucking wonderful." Paulie hung up, and turned back to Tommy, his chin jutting out in a challenge.

"What'd you say that for?" Tommy asked.

"Because it's all part of my fucking master plan. And I'm hungry. So let's just get the hell out of here."

FORTY-TWO

NEITHER OF US say much as we drive towards Goldhaven. We both know the restaurant they mean, it does well with tourists who come off the boat because it's kind of the first big place you come to, with parking and a big anchor on the sign that kind of tells you what they serve. In my bag I've got a map, and a chart, which shows the location of the caves, plus a print out of the weather that I just made, and a set of time tables. I don't know how I'm going to explain it all though, we haven't discussed a plan. Amber just wanted to get here as soon as possible. She's driving really carefully too, given how she hasn't actually stopped crying. I realize after a while that she's checking the mirrors all the time, not because she's driving carefully, she's seeing if anyone is following us.

As we pull into the parking lot I check too. There's a dozen or so cars here, a couple of trucks and small vans, but nothing that looks especially suspicious. At least, I don't really know what would look suspicious. Amber finds a space and stops the motor. She looks at me.

"You need to clean your face," I say. She nods at me, and pulls open the glove box. She finds some tissues, and then what I suppose is a make-up purse, and I go back to scanning the parking lot while she sorts herself out.

"OK," she says a moment later, even though she looks like she's going to burst into tears again. "Let's go."

It's a weird feeling crossing the parking lot. It's like we can really feel how we're being watched. But I've got no idea where we're being watched from. I've never been to *the Schooner* before, but it's obviously not the type of place where you get shown to a seat. So when we get inside we look around the restaurant, which is nearly empty, seeing where we ought to go. And when Amber shakes her head, that she doesn't recognize anyone, we go and sit down in a window booth so we can keep an eye outside. Then we wait. No one comes to the table to serve us. I've got the maps in my bag under my table, and I can feel my hands sweating, fiddling with the straps. Neither of us says anything.

Then the door chimes, and two guys walk in.

I know it's them from the way Amber stiffens. One of them is quite small, and kind of looks normal, in a sort of gangster way with a shiny blue suit on. But the other one is massive, a great big lumbering giant of a man, and when I look at his face I see his teeth are all messed up. It's obvious they see us right away, but they look around anyway, as if pretending they don't. And then I realize they're checking out the restaurant. The big, ugly guy goes over to the restroom, but it's not because he needs it, because he opens both doors, then comes right back out again, and shakes his head at the smaller guy. Then they both come over to where we're sitting. They don't ask or anything. They just sit down.

"Well ain't this nice?" The smaller one says. He's got a round black earring in each of his ears, and I remember now how Amber told me about this. How she never got this one's name, but called him Earrings. Neither me nor Amber reply.

"What's your name?" Earrings asks, looking me up and down.

"Billy."

"Nice to meet you Billy." He gives a kind of snort of laughter. "You really are sixteen."

I don't correct him.

He drums his fingers on the table top.

"Where's my sister?" Amber asks suddenly.

"Don't start with that already," Earrings replies. He drums his fingers a little more. Then he suddenly smiles. "Let's start afresh shall we?" With this he picks up the menu, pretends to study it, but I see his eyes flicking up and glancing at Amber and me. He looks kinda nervous.

"So how is this gonna work?" Amber tries instead, but he ignores her.

"Pancakes. That's what I'm gonna have." He raises a hand and clicks his fingers, grinning at me now. The waitress, who's ignored us so far, comes over. She's got a bored look on her face, like she really hates tourists, but this is the only job she can find. A lot of the restaurants on Lornea Island have staff like that.

"Yeah? What can I get you?"

Earrings orders the Schooner All Day Breakfast Special, which is a big pile of pancakes with blueberries and maple syrup. The other guy, the really scary looking one, asks for a burger. Then Earrings turns to us.

"How about you guys? You want anything?"

"I'm not hungry." Amber says. She looks like she wants to say something else, but can't since the waitress is still here.

"You sure? It's on me. My treat." Earrings looks at me. "You like pancakes?"

I've not actually eaten much today, on account of how I've kind of run out of food at home again.

"I'll have some fries," I say. "And a coffee. Actually and a burger too."

I feel Amber staring at me, then Earrings looks at her again.

"I told you, I ain't hungry."

The waitress gives us all a look, like we're the weirdest bunch of tourists she's seen all season, but she isn't going to worry about it. Instead she scribbles the order down and goes away. There's a moment of silence. Until Earrings launches into a speech.

"OK. I accept we none of us got off on the right foot. And that's kinda my fault. I accept that," he says.

"But none of this is difficult. You got what we want. We got what you want. It couldn't be more simpler. Amber – you mind if I call you that?"

He waits, until she gives a shrug. "OK. We don't wanna hurt your kid sister. There ain't nothing in it for us, going down that route. And as of right now she's fine. She's somewhere safe. And just as soon as we get our product back, you'll get her back. OK?"

I look to Amber to see if she's going to answer, and when she doesn't, I figure it's up to me.

"OK," I say.

"Now, let's just deal with the cops issue. Have you contacted them?"

"No."

"You sure about that?"

"Yeah."

"Good. Because if anything happens to us, then little Gracie ain't gonna be found. Not before she runs out of food, or water, or whatever else she needs."

"You piece of shit asshole motherfucker." Amber interjects.

"Jesus!" Earrings says. "I'm trying to be nice here."

I decide to keep things on track. "So how is this going to work?"

But he doesn't answer, because at that moment the waitress comes back with our drinks. We're all silent while she works out who ordered what, and she's a bit useless, but eventually we figure it out. Then she goes away, only he still doesn't reply, and I'm beginning to think he doesn't actually know how to do this. But then he surprises me.

"You said we needed a boat. I'm guessing he's hid it underwater somewhere?"

"Not really..." I say, before Amber's elbow jabs into my side and shuts me up.

"Or an island?"

Amber stares at me, and I don't say anything.

"OK – but we need a boat to recover it?"

I look to Amber – we already told them this. After a few moments she relents, and nods her head.

"Yeah," I say, turning back to Earrings. "But we've got one."

"Good. Thank you." I'm pretty sure he doesn't hear my last comment. He dumps sugar into his drink, and stirs it thoughtfully. Then he turns back to Amber.

"Amber. Honey. I can see you ain't so comfortable telling us exactly where it is while we've got your sister. I understand that. But you should understand how we're not going to release her until we have the product back in our possession. So the way I see it, that only leaves one option. We're gonna have to recover the product together. Then you get what you want, we get what we want. And we all go off into the sunset together. Only not together." He smiles sarcastically. "Anyone disagree with that?"

Amber doesn't answer, but I don't think it means she agrees exactly.

"You wanna maybe discuss for a minute?" He waves a hand at the two of us.

Amber looks at me now. But only for a second. She turns back to the man.

"OK."

"Good. *Great.*" Earrings looks kinda relieved.

"So. Either of you know anything about boat hire services?"

"I've got a boat," I say again.

"Not a fucking row-boat kid. I'm talking a proper boat. Like with a motor."

"It is a real boat," Amber interrupts. "It's a thirty-two foot fishing boat. The one next to the yacht you sank last night."

Earrings looks at the guy with the teeth, who looks blank. So then he shrugs.

"OK. So you've got a boat. Where do we need to take it?"

I glance at Amber. I've still got all the charts, the tide tables, and the weather readings in my bag. She gives the smallest of nods, and I'm about to pull them out.

But I don't get the chance, because as mad as all this is, right then things go *completely* nuts.

FORTY-THREE

"*Billy!*" A voice calls out from across the restaurant. "Billy! What a coincidence! Mate!"

Even though I know him so well, it's so out of context it takes me a few moments to register who the voice belongs to, and he's already walking quickly over to our table before I get it. It's Steve. Steve Rose. You know, from *Shark Bites*.

"Jesus, this is... this must be *meant to be* or something." He's grinning and shaking his head in disbelief. As soon as he reaches us he holds out his arms like he wants to hug me, but then pulls one back so it's just a handshake he expects. I don't really mean to hold out mine, but I do anyway. Then the next thing is he grips my hand so hard it pulls me out of the booth, and onto my feet, and then he won't let go, pumping my whole arm up and down.

"What an amazing coincidence. You know I just got off the ferry... and I was hungry because the food is..." He screws up his face. "Well I bet you've been on it often enough to know." He stops shaking my hand now, but doesn't let me go.

"Hey, Billy. What are we doing here? How about a hug huh?" And then without waiting for me to reply he wraps his arms around me and squeezes.

"Steve?" I manage to say when he lets me go, but he interrupts me at once.

"No. No, no. Let *me* speak Billy." Only then he doesn't say anything.

He holds up a finger, and I can see in his eyes how he's working out what to say.

"Hey! Buddy!" Earrings says from behind me. Not in a nice way either. But Steve doesn't notice. He's ready to speak now.

"Billy... *Jeez!*" He stops, and gives a goofy grin. "Look I wanted a little time to work out exactly *how* to say this, and now you're here already, and I don't have it straight in my head, but..." I take a glance behind me, and see that both Earrings and the big guy are now looking totally freaked out. Then I see a flash of black metal, as Earrings pulls out a pistol from his jacket. I blink in disbelief as he holds it on the table, covered by the menu.

"Steve!" I interrupt him, as loud as I dare, because I really think Earrings is going to shoot him if I don't.

"Hey sorry, my manners, huh?!" Steve gives another grin. But then instead of leaving he turns to the others. He sees Amber then reaches out his hand again. She shakes it, but her mouth is hanging wide open while she does so.

"Hi. I'm Steve. Steve Rose. Nice to meet you."

There's a second, and then she doesn't answer, so I have to.

"Err, this is Amber?"

"*Amber!* Billy's told me all about *you*." He flashes a different smile at her, I remember it from the research trip - he used the same smile on the girls there too.

"Don't worry, it's all good." He winks at her now. Then he turns to the others, to the two kidnappers.

"How ya doing guys? You must be friends of Billy's? Any friends of Billy are friends of mine." He turns back to me. "I mean that Billy. I really mean that. I know I was kinda mad when you left, but I'm past that now. I swear to you."

He turns back to Earrings. "Sorry buddy. What'd you say your name was?"

Earrings has his mouth open pretty wide now too, and suddenly everyone is looking at him, waiting for an answer.

"Jaso... Justin." He says in the end. He doesn't accept Steve's hand, I guess because he's still holding the pistol, so Steve leans over and kind of hugs him, like this is the beginning of a beautiful friendship.

"I'm Steve. *Great* to meet you Justin. Really great." He nods, like he really means it, then turns to the big guy. The one who Amber told me was called Tommy. He's kinda squinting at Steve, like he recognizes him, but the person he thinks he is, doesn't make any sense. Which it doesn't.

"Hey big fella, I'm Steve. Steve Rose." He holds out his arm again, rock-solid muscles holding it still and firm.

The big man stares at it but can't ignore it. He lifts his own hand and shakes. There's a moment when the big man gives a weak half-smile, and I think Steve gets to see his teeth, but he pretends not to notice. Then there's a weird silence.

"*The* Steve Rose?" The big man says in the end.

Steve grins. He glances back at me, like the both of us were expecting this reaction.

"Uh huh..." He nods.

"The shark guy? From the TV show?"

"That's right buddy. Well, except I don't actually *have* the TV show at the moment, since it was canned, mostly on account of your friend Billy here." He turns back to me, and quickly holds up both his hands. "Though I'm totally not holding that against you Billy. What you did was right. I was the one who was out of order." He hesitates for a minute. "Actually that's kind of why I came." He stops now, screwing up his face like this is causing him pain.

Then he turns to the others again. "Look fellas, I don't want to interrupt your little..." he hesitates for a second. "What is this, a late lunch or an early supper?" He gives a little laugh. "Whatever it is, I do need to speak to Billy. I've come a long way to find him. Actually, all the way from Australia." He glances at the kidnappers again and smiles. The contrast between his Hollywood white teeth, and the big guy's oversized yellow ones is kinda horrible.

"Yeah, that's where we were filming, ain't that right Billy? But I didn't treat him so well, and things kinda blew up, so I had to come here to apologize. In person. You know what I mean?"

There's another stunned silence. Earrings – or possibly Jason – breaks it.

"What the fuck is this?" He says.

Steve raises his eyebrows, like he's doesn't think the profanity is really appropriate.

"Hey buddy, I'll just be a minute OK? No need for that kind of language." He tries to laugh the moment away, but he looks pained now. Justin/Earrings doesn't seem to care about his language.

"Who the fuck are you?" He asks now, loudly. "And what *the fuck* do you want?"

Steve doesn't answer. I think he finally understands that something isn't quite right here, but the moment doesn't last long.

"It's the shark guy," the bigger kidnapper says now. "From the TV. You know, he does diving with killer sharks? Don't even use the cage half the time. Guy's a legend."

Steve laughs again, and it's like he's happy to be back on familiar ground. "Hey, when you understand these creatures as well as I do," he says to the big guy now. "Well, you kinda know when you're putting yourself in a dangerous situation and when you're not."

"I don't give a fuck who it is," Earrings snaps back, trying to take over again. "I wanna know what the fuck he's doing here?"

"Hey, so not everyone's a fan," Steve says. He stays talking to the big man. "Listen buddy, you want an autograph or a selfie or anything you just say. Right after I speak with Billy here."

"He don't want a fucking selfie. And he don't give a rat's ass who you are. Just get the fuck outta here."

"Whoa," Steve says. He looks around us all, then finally settles his gaze on me.

"Billy, is everything OK here?"

I swallow. Then I notice how Earrings is looking at me. Threatening. Like he's warning me how things are gonna get bad if I don't get rid of Steve right away.

"Yeah," I say cautiously. "Sure Steve. Everything's OK. We're just having lunch."

Earrings nods and turns to Steve. He's still got the gun hidden under the menu, I can see by the way the paper doesn't lie flat.

"It's all fine," I go on. "Maybe we could meet up later, and you can tell me what you want to say?"

Steve pauses, but then he nods his head. "Sure OK. I mean I've mostly said it already. It's just..." He winces. "It's just I had to come tell you how I was wrong. And you were right. About how the science mustn't be compromised. No matter what. And how it may feel I've lost everything right now, but I haven't. What you did was give me a gift. You've put me on the right path."

There's a weird silence again.

"OK." I say, in the end. And then I realize that Steve's about to go. And suddenly I don't want him to. I mean, I feel like I need to get him to see what's going on here. So he can call the police, or do something to help us.

"OK," I say again. I've got no idea how I'm going to tell him.

"OK," Steve repeats. "Well I've got your number – I didn't want to call you in advance, I thought you maybe wouldn't wanna speak to me... But maybe I'll call later. We can speak then?"

"OK."

"OK." Steve gives me a smile. Then he looks at the others. "Alright. Great to meet you…" He glances up at Earrings, and I can tell he's searching for the name he gave him. "Justin."

Earrings doesn't move, and Steve turns to the big man. He looks blankly, like he can't remember the guy's name, even though he never gave it in the first place. But now he gives a sort of half smile, like he's a bit star struck. He shows his crooked teeth again.

And suddenly I know what to do.

"*Carcharodon carcharias,*" I say.

"What?" Earrings says at once. I see the tendons in his arm tense, as he grips the pistol tighter. And Steve gives me a weird look. I glance over at the big guy and repeat what I said.

"*Carcharodon carcharias.*"

"What's that Billy…" Steve starts, his face scrunched up in a frown. I know he understands what I'm saying, but I need him to make the connection. I slide my eyes across to the bigger guy's mouth, full of its horrible crooked teeth.

"*Carcharodon carcharias.*"

Then I see Steve silently following my gaze, and moments later I know he's made the connection. It's the Latin name, for great white shark. *Crooked tooth.* Steve doesn't know what it means, but he knows we're in danger.

Then suddenly he smiles again. "OK. Well look, I'm real sorry to interrupt you guys…" He starts to back away, but he glances at me with a look that tells me he understands. I don't know what he's gonna do. I don't know what he *can* do. But at least someone out there knows something bad is going on.

Steve raises his hand, to wave goodbye. But then he doesn't get a chance.

"Don't you fucking move," Earrings snarls.

FORTY-FOUR

THE NEXT THING, Earrings jumps out of the booth. He moves incredibly quickly, and before I know what's happened I see he's got the gun pressed into Steve's stomach. He's shielding it from the rest of the restaurant with his own body, but I see him twist it, digging it in hard.

"I don't know what the fuck just happened there, but you better take a seat."

Steve is obviously shocked because he does nothing to resist, and Earrings is able to walk him back to the table and shove him down next to me. Then Earrings takes his seat opposite, using the menu again to cover the pistol. I see the big guy has also got a gun out now and he's doing the same.

"And whatever it was, you just joined our little party."

We all sit there in silence, while Earrings takes it in turns to point his gun at each of us, making sure we see it. Actually though, I think he's working out what to say next.

"OK. Here's what's gonna happen. You're gonna tell me *right now* where my product is, or this gets very messy, very fucking quickly. Are we clear?"

I glance at Steve. His eyes are wide and he's white-faced, blinking in amazement. Then I look at Amber. Her eyes are red and raw from all the crying she's been doing. She looks back at me, and after a few seconds she nods her head. So then I tell them.

"It's in a sea cave down the east coast of the island. At least, that's where we think it is."

"Where? *Specifically*?"

"It's hard to explain. You can only get there by sea. I can show you though. I brought a chart."

Earrings is cautious. "OK. Bring it out. Slowly."

I do what he says, moving really carefully in case he thinks I'm tricking him and going to bring out a weapon. I pull out the chart, unfold it, and point to the area of the national park where the caves are located.

"Just there."

Earrings looks at it, then turns the chart round for a better look.

"That a road? Why can't we drive there?"

"No, it's a footpath." Because it's a chart, there's not much detail about the land, so it's hard to see. "We could walk there, and I suppose you could get down the cliff with ropes, but even then, the entrance to the cave is underwater, so it's easier by boat."

"Why'd he put it here?" Earrings asks.

I don't know the answer to this, but I guess it's fairly obvious. "Because no one ever goes there?"

He thinks for a while."Are you fucking with me kid?"

"No."

Then he glances at Steve, then back at me. "How's he fit into this?"

"He doesn't. Not really."

"Then what the fuck is he doing here?"

I hesitate. "It's a bit of a long story…" I stop, expecting he won't want me to tell him, but he waggles the gun under the menu, so I figure he does.

"Well… We were doing a population study of sharks. Off the coast of Victoria. In Australia," I begin. He doesn't stop me, so I keep going. "Basically counting the number of individual animals from each species and estimating their size. Because if you know the size of a shark you can make an accurate estimate of its age, which are the two variables you need for a population study. Only then I discovered how he'd been overstating the size of the sharks we were counting. Not just on the trip I was on, but earlier trips, meaning the data was unreliable. And… well it was just really bad science…" I look at Steve, in case he wants to add anything.

"I came to apologize," he says. "I was unprofessional, and I behaved badly and I came to see Billy to apologi…" But Earring's cuts him off, speaking to me.

"Does any of this have anything to do with our current problem?"

"No," I say. "I don't think so."

Earrings stares at us both.

"Then spare me." He looks back at the chart. "My product. You reckon it's in a sea cave? How do we get there? How easy is it to get at?"

"That's the problem," I say. Actually I'm relieved to get back onto the point. "We need the right combination of low tide and calm weather. And although it's calm now, the forecast is for strong winds to come in from tonight, so if we don't go now, more or less now, we might not get another chance for a week. And even then it's going to be quite difficult, and we'll need diving equipment, because we can't actually go into the cave with the boat. We'll have to swim in and take it out that way."

He thinks. "Swim?"

"Yeah. The entrance to the cave is underwater, even at low water."

Earrings stares at me, like he still isn't sure whether to trust what I'm saying.

"Swim," he repeats, after a while. Then he looks at his friend. "You said this asshole was some TV shark expert?"

"Yeah," the bigger guy replies.

"Goes in the water without the cage. Free diving expert?"

"Yeah. I think so."

Then Earrings turns to Steve. He just waits.

"I'm the Australian Speed-Endurance Apnea National Champion." Steve shrugs. "Three years running."

"The fuck does that mean?"

Steve doesn't answer for a moment, but eventually he has no choice. "It's a distance event. Basically it's how far you can swim underwater, on one breath."

"Well? How far can you go?"

"Two hundred fifty meters."

Earrings shrugs. "How far's that?"

"It's five lengths of an Olympic swimming pool."

"Whoa. On one breath.?"

"Yeah."

Earrings weighs this up, impressed. Then he looks at me. "How big is the cave?"

"What?"

"The cave, how fucking big is it? How far do you have to swim underwater to get in it?"

"Oh, nowhere near that far. *I* can do it."

"Perfect. Looks like the two of you are going for a swim then. Let's fucking move."

FORTY-FIVE

EARRINGS MAKES us all stand up, keeping us covered with his pistol. There's an awkward moment when the waitress comes hurrying over, because she thinks we're walking out before our food has even arrived, but then Earrings pulls out a hundred dollar bill and throws it on the table. I think she's going to say something but instead she just gives him a look, like she hates mainlanders. Then she turns away to the kitchen to cancel our order. And we leave the restaurant.

They march us over to a gray panel van. The big guy opens the rear doors and we're forced inside. We're made to kneel, facing the front, with our hands behind our backs, and while we're like that something is wrapped round our wrists, it feels like a plastic zip tie, and they do it tight too, so that it cuts into my skin. Then they do our ankles too, so we're stuck, kneeling there on the cold floor.

"Roll over onto your butts," Earrings says. And when we do he inspects us.

"Cell phones," he says next. "Where are your cell phones? I know you've all got them. Hand them over."

Then we all look at him, since obviously we can't move at all. I think I kind of look down at my pocket though, and the next thing Earrings is patting my jeans, which feels weird, until he finds it, and then he puts his hand into my pocket.

"You'll get it back," he says, like he's irritated by the way I try to squirm away from him. He does the same to the others, then switches all the phones off. Then he slams the doors shut, and we're left there in silence.

But it's not for long, because then they both climb into the front, and turn round to look at us.

"So. Tell me more about this cave," Earrings says to me.

"What about my sister?" Amber replies, before I get a chance to do so. "You can't have this all your own way. If you don't tell us where she is, we're only going to lead you to the wrong place." She looks at me while she's speaking, a warning.

There's a pause, and Earrings tries ignoring her. "The boat's in Holport right? Next door to the other one, the one she blew up."

"I mean it." Amber says. "You can have your fucking cocaine. I swear it. But I want my sister back first."

I think he's going to ignore her again, or tell her to shut up, but there's something about her voice, she sounds serious.

"OK." Earrings lets out a long sigh. "A deal's a deal." He smiles now. "We'll pick her up on the way. She can come out on the boat with us. Does that satisfy you?"

Amber doesn't reply, but she nods, and I get the sense that just maybe things aren't as bad as I think, because maybe these people are reasonable.

"But if you don't get me back my product, I'm gonna make you watch as I drown her, right in front of your face." Earrings stares right at Amber. "You get me?"

Amber's face goes a little whiter, then she nods, and with that Earrings turns to the front and starts the motor.

The big man keeps his gun trained on us from the passenger seat as we set off, bumping our way out of the parking lot. I can keep track of where we are for the first ten minutes or so, just because we're on the main road south. But after that we take a turning and I lose track. Then we take another turning, onto what must be a dirt track, because the three of us are thrown about in the back.

We can't use our arms properly to protect ourselves, so we get banged around, and I start to worry that with the bumps the big man might accidentally pull the trigger on his pistol and shoot us. But there's nothing we can do except try to stay as wedged as possible until the van finally comes to a halt.

"Stay there," Earrings says. I think for a moment he's talking to us, but then I realize he means the big guy, who stays where he is, keeping the gun fixed on us still.

Then nothing happens for a few minutes, until the back door is suddenly thrown open, and there's Earrings again, but he's carrying something this time. It takes all of us a few seconds to work out it's Gracie – bound and gagged. Amber lets out a scream, and Gracie starts kicking on Earrings' shoulders.

"Move up," he orders, gripping her tighter. "And stop fucking wriggling."

We do our best to budge along, and he leans forward and puts Gracie down into the van. He doesn't do it gently.

"Asshole," Amber snaps, but she doesn't really even look at him, instead she shuffles herself over and manages to get Gracie up and sitting next to her, and then she's cooing over her sister, talking to her in a soft voice. Then the back doors of the van slam shut again, and I realize I didn't even get to see where we were.

"So. About this cave then?" Earrings asks again when he's back in the front. "Where do we go?"

I tell him, and answer all his other questions, about whether the boat is fueled and ready, and whether we have all the equipment we need on board. I explain how we keep spare wetsuits and snorkeling gear on board, for the tourists to use when the weather's warmer. Then he takes my bag, and makes me show him on the chart the exact location of the caves, and how to read the coordinates. And after he's studied everything, he steps out the van and makes a phone call that I can't hear. And then he climbs back in, and we're off again, back down the incredibly bumpy track.

When we're finally back on the main road again, the big guy finally turns back to the front. He glances back every few moments, but it looks like his neck hurts or something, twisting around all the time. And the noise in the van gets louder too, back here we can hear the tires on the road pretty loud, and Steve uses the distraction to turn to me and ask very quietly what's going on. I don't want to say anything at first, since I think it will attract the attention of the big man, and he'll watch us again, but he doesn't. So keeping my voice as low as possible I do my best to explain to Steve what this is all about, and where we're going. Right away Steve narrows in on the practicalities, like where we are going to anchor the boat, and how easy it will be to find the stuff in the cave. Obviously I don't know many of the answers to this, and I start to worry – what might happen if we get there and can't find the cocaine? Because, until this point, it hasn't even occurred to me that it might not even be there. Or that we might find it, but not be able to get it out. Or that it'll already be too rough to get in there. But Steve stays calm and almost sounds relaxed.

"It'll be a breeze," he says.

"But what if the weather gets bad, or swell comes in earlier than the forecast?"

"It won't. And even if it does, we got this. Piece of cake."

I don't really understand his optimism, but I do know he's done some pretty crazy things in his life. So maybe this is just quite tame by comparison. I hope so. Then he changes the subject, and starts talking about why he came to see me. He tells me how his whole life has fallen apart since I emailed the journal. First the editor contacted him to say they were going to retract all his papers. Then the TV network canceled his show, and then he was fired by the university where he does teaching. Basically his whole academic and scientific life is ruined as a result of what I did. I watch him as he explains it all.

"Only it wasn't what *you* did, Billy," he insists, quietly, but firmly. "The fault was mine. It was all mine." He's not laughing now, his face is grim. "It just started off as a little exaggeration which wasn't supposed to impact the data. And by the time it did, I didn't feel like I could stop it. I should have stopped though. A long time ago."

I don't know what to think about it really. I mean, I don't think I'd know what to think about it even in normal circumstances, but with everything else that's going on, it's just a bit much.

"But why did you come here?" I ask.

"I told you," he replies, and he grins now. "I had to tell you face-to-face. That you were right. Not just right, but brave. Incredible really. You stood up for the science, while all I cared about was my career. Whether I got another series of *Shark Bites*." I guess I must look confused because he shakes his head.

"What I'm trying to say is, this whole business has made me realize something. I thought everything was going good, but it wasn't. I was on the wrong path. The cheating path. That's not who I am. Not who I want to be anyway. So I had to do the right thing. And that began with coming here and apologizing to you. Mano-a-mano."

"Why didn't you just email me?" I ask. Steve doesn't answer that, so I don't push it. Instead he sits there, bound up next to me, and looking a bit sorry for himself. Still I don't know what to say.

"How's Rosie?" I ask in the end.

"Oh yeah, she's good. Real good," Steve replies, smiling again. Then, a moment later he adds. "Actually she's left me. But again, it's only what I deserve."

"Oh," I say.

It's not really possible to talk with Amber, she's got her whole attention on Gracie. Amber's somehow gotten her hands in front of her, and now she's got Gracie on her lap and she won't stop holding her. She's peeled off Gracie's gag too, with her teeth, and she just keeps talking to her in a very quiet voice. Gracie says she's thirsty, but when Amber asks Earrings for some water, he tells her no. Well that's not exactly what he says.

And then, just from the glimpses of the world outside that I can see from where I'm sitting on the floor, I realize we're coming down the hill into Holport. And soon Earrings is backing the van into a parking space, then he kills the motor. There's silence for a moment.

"OK boys and girls. You get the drill by now. We're gonna cut off those ties, then we're all gonna walk out to this boat nice and quiet. And if anyone tries anything then we're gonna start shooting. So let's remember to be good. Huh?"

FORTY-SIX

THEY GET OUT, and a few seconds later the back of the van opens. They've parked right next to the ramp that leads down to the pontoon, so it's not far to go. The big guy leans in, and uses a box cutter to free our hands. He does it carelessly, even though he could easily cut our wrists with it, and I get the sense he's done it before. I don't know if that makes me feel more or less anxious, but it's nice to have my hands and feet free again.

Then they make us all get out too, and they walk us down the ramp towards where the *Blue Lady* is moored. I risk a look around, hoping that someone will see us and think it's odd, the way we're walking, but it's late in the day already and there's no one about.

We get to the gate. I think maybe I can trick them by not saying the combination, but they don't even ask, and put it right in.

As we walk past the other boats, I check each one, in case anyone's aboard. I know most of the other owners, at least the ones who use their boats regularly, but I don't see anyone, and then I feel the muzzle of the gun in the small of my back again, and Earrings growls at me to speed up. Then I see the *Mystery*. She's still in her berth, only she's mostly underwater with just a bit of her cabin showing. As we get closer you can see the deck and the rest of her a couple of feet down.

"Keys," Earrings says. I don't realize he's talking to me, because I'm still looking at the sunken *Mystery*.

"Gimme the keys. Now." He digs the muzzle of the gun harder into my back, and I dig in my pockets and hand them over.

Earrings gives them to Tommy, who climbs onto *Blue Lady* and glances up and down the deck. I don't know what he's looking for, but after a few seconds he unlocks the cabin and disappears inside. A couple of minutes later he reappears and calls us aboard.

I always feel good when I step onto my boat. Even now, with a gun being pressed into my back. I feel at home suddenly, and a bit more confident. I ask right away if Gracie can drink something now.

Earrings looks annoyed at the question, and ignores me. Instead he tells Tommy to go and lock Gracie up somewhere. But then Amber won't let her go, and tells him there's no way she's leaving her again. So then Earrings tells him to lock them up together, and I see him taking them to the fore cabin downstairs. And I see as well that he sees a bottle of water and takes it with him. That just leaves me and Steve and Earrings. I look around the boat. I notice the broken window where Amber broke in to get the rocket flare.

"Come on. Get this fucking thing moving," Earrings says, irritated.

I brace myself, then try something that I thought about as we were coming down the hill.

"I have to radio the harbor masters office," I say. "We're not allowed to go to sea without letting them know."

"Sorry Billy," Earrings says. "But I don't think that's going to be possible." He steps into the cabin, and I see at once why not. The radio is fixed to the wall above the chart table, or it used to be. I see now that it's been smashed off, and it's only just hanging in place. I suppose Tommy must have broken it when he came on board first.

"Just get us out of here."

So we do. I start the motor, and a couple of minutes later Steve releases the mooring lines, while I climb up to the bridge. I slip the motor into reverse, and back the *Blue Lady* out of her berth, swinging her around, and taking care not to get too close to the sunken *Mystery*. Then when we're clear, I push the gear lever forwards, the prop bites, and a gentle trickle of bubbles pushes out our stern.

Tommy is back now. He's sitting in the saloon, and he doesn't stop watching us the whole time. Earrings is watching me too while I steer the boat. I keep the speed to six knots as we leave the harbor, so I don't draw any attention to ourselves, but still there's nobody about anyway. Nobody really uses their boats at this time of year. And even the fishing boats won't be going out with the bad weather forecast.

When we are out past the breakwater I push the throttle forward and take the *Blue Lady* up onto the plane. She's quite a heavy old boat, and doesn't do it easily. After a while I notice Earrings is gone, and when I look for him, I see him at the stern, making another phone call.

"How long till we get there?" He shouts up at me suddenly.

I look at the electronic chart display. At least Tommy didn't smash that.

"We're seven nautical miles away," I call back, over the noise of the motor. "We'll be there in about half an hour."

He repeats this into the phone, then calls up again.

"What's our coordinates? Now?"

I consider giving him a fake position. But I still think our best chance is to do what they say, so I read out the numbers and watch as he repeats them into his cell. When he's done that he hangs up. He climbs the ladder back up the bridge, and then he pats me on the back, with the side of the gun.

"OK. Good. This old tub go any faster?" He almost sounds like he's enjoying himself. I shake my head, but he ignores me, and pushes the throttle forward with the side of his gun. We surge forward a tiny bit faster to *Blue Lady*'s top speed. I never go this fast as we use a lot more fuel, but I'm not stupid enough to tell him though.

Earrings makes me keep *Blue Lady* at full tilt as we race around the coast. The sea is mostly flat, but there's a growing breeze, pressing dark gusts of wind onto the cliffs, and the further round we go, the more they're pushing a light chop onto the surface of the water. That, combined with the sun having already dropped below the island on our starboard side, gives an ominous feel to the trip, like it's not just darkness that's approaching, and a storm, but some malevolent force. Finally we get close to the cliffs where the sea caves are, and I'm pleased to be able to slow the boat down. I bank over into a turn so we roll back off the plane without our own wake catching up and flooding the cockpit. Earrings who was sitting examining his gun, looks up sharply.

"We here?" He asks. I nod.

He looks around. "Where's the cave?"

I point. There's just a tiny bit of the roof of the entrance visible. The water looks dark and uninviting.

"Good. You better get on it."

"We've got to anchor first," I tell him. "It's not like parking a car."

He says something else, but I ignore him. This is actually one of the most difficult parts. It's not just that you're not allowed to drop an anchor here, the bottom is so rocky that it would be easy to get it stuck. I motor slowly around, going as close to the cave entrance as I dare, and keeping a check on the depth gauge. All the while Earrings is moaning, but in the end Steve comes up to help me, and even tells him to be quiet.

Then Steve kind of takes over, checking the depth. I remember the sandy area where I watched the octopus. It all seems a very long time ago.

"There's a clear area," I tell him. "Somewhere around here. If you go forwards you should be able to see the sand beneath us."

So Steve goes forward, still covered by Tommy with his pistol, and through a combination of shouts and arm signals, we position the boat as close as we can to the mouth of the cave. Now we're nearer it's clearly visible above the water as a black arc. Then Steve releases the anchor and there's the familiar hammering of metal on metal as the chain slides out. I put the boat in reverse to help the anchor hold, and when everything seems okay I slip it into neutral. We're about thirty feet from the base of the cliff, which is now deep in shadow. And we seem to be holding. Earrings keeps asking what we're doing, but more quietly after Steve asks him if he wants to be on a shipwreck. When we're happy the anchor is secure, I kill the motor. Everything goes eerily quiet after that, especially with the whistle of the building wind, and the slapping of the choppy swell against the side.

We're way closer to the rocks than I'd ever be comfortable coming in any normal situation, and the anchor could still drag. But now my concern shifts to going into the water. The light has properly gone now, and the water looks black. I can't help but think about the big boulders down there, and what might be lurking amongst them. I know we don't have any really dangerous animals come here, but snorkeling at night somewhere so exposed is still scary. Earrings doesn't seem worried about this though. He almost seems to be enjoying it.

"Well?" He says. "Hadn't you better get in the water?"

So I take Steve to the locker where the wetsuits are kept and we each of us get kitted up in a suit and diving mask and snorkel. I manage to find a couple of waterproof flashlights too, with rechargeable batteries, and I'm relieved that Dad's always hot on keeping them topped up. The whole time we are watched over by Tommy and Earrings, who are impatient and keep telling us to hurry up. Finally we're ready though, and we go over to the stern, where the diving platform is just above the water level. The sea isn't smooth now at all, and the gusts are stronger now, and cold.

I'm about to lower myself into the water anyway, when Earrings takes hold of my shoulder.

"Hey kid. You're not planning anything stupid are you? Remember we've still got your friend Amber and her kid sister. If you do anything other than recover our product and bring it back to us, you're gonna get them shot. You understand that don't you?"

I look out at the black cliff face, with the ink black water slapping up against it.

"Sure. I get it."

"Good." He lets go of my shoulder. "Clever kid."

I look at him, and then slip down into the water.

FORTY-SEVEN

THE FIRST THING that hits me is the cold. I'm not in my proper wetsuit, just one we use for the tourists. They're fine for the summer, but not much good this late in the year. I expect a trickle of water down my back, but it's more like a flood. I suppose it's good in a way, since it clears my head. It makes me super aware of what we're trying to do.

The second thing I register is the light levels. I've done a lot of snorkeling, here and in other places. But I've only ever been in the daytime. Now the light is low even on the surface, and when I put my head down and look below me, I can hardly make out the bottom. The rocks and caves I'm floating over are filled with shadows. It seems deeper. It seems scarier too.

I click on my flashlight. It casts a yellow glow a few yards ahead of me, lighting up the water, and the particles suspended in it, but it doesn't penetrate. Then I see Steve's flipper slipping into the water beside me, and suddenly the whole of him crashes downwards, and then all I can see are a billion bubbles, blue, black or gold where they hit the light. I pull my head up, and wait until he surfaces. He spends a few moments adjusting his mask, then turns to me.

"OK Billy, lead the way," he says. He doesn't sound scared, more a kind of grim calm.

We swim on the surface, away from the boat. I try to talk at first. I want to ask him if he's got any ideas for what we should do, now we're able to talk without them listening, but it's too choppy, and I keep getting mouthfuls of water. So instead we just fall into line, me leading the way and Steve on my shoulder. It's comforting having him there, and I think he knows it. After a while I duck my head under the surface and use the snorkel, because I'm worried about swimming right onto the rocks where they get shallow, and Steve does the same, so I can look across and see him right there.

Suddenly I feel Steve's hand on my back. I stop, surface, and look up. We're close to the cliff face now. Thankfully the waves are still quite small – it's just chop really, not real swell, and it's slapping against the rocks, rather than crashing as real waves would do. Or will do in a few hours time. I point at the entrance to the cave. It's visible even in this light as a darker semi circle set into the bottom of the dark cliff face. It doesn't look like the sort of thing you'd want to swim into, but I know that just under the surface of the water is a large tunnel, several meters across. Most of the time the entire entrance is well under the water and you'd need proper diving gear to get through, but because it's coming up to low water, we'll be able to swim through.

"How long do we swim underwater for?" Steve asks. He has to shout over the noise of the waves hitting the cliff.

"It's not too long," I reply, reminding myself how I've done this a half-dozen times in the daylight and it's easy. The first time I was really worried, but it's not that far.

"It's only about ten feet."

"Okay," Steve calls back. "Piece of cake. You take the lead and I'll follow."

I take a couple of good deep breaths, then roll forwards into the water and swim towards the darkness. As I get up to the cliff face I dive down, seeing how the light illuminates the face of the cliff, and then how it disappears as I move inside the underwater tunnel. I force myself to stay calm, and kick with my legs, letting my flippers propel me forward. All I can see is the yellow puddle of light from the flashlight, and it's hard to know if I'm going too deep, or too shallow, and I'm going to crash into the tunnel's roof. Then suddenly the light changes, I see something reflecting from above me again, and I know I must be inside. I give a couple more kicks, then push up to the surface.

Right away everything has changed. The noise of the chop slapping against the cliff face has gone. Instead there's different sounds. The noise of water droplets falling from high above me, and ringing out as they hit the surface of the pool. I shine my light around. The ceiling is mostly low, but in a few places it stretches high above me. Where the walls meet the water mostly they just drop straight down, but in a few places around the cave there are ledges, some quite large, and at the back the water shallows and even forms a little beach of round pebbles. Then beneath me I see the yellow glow of Steve's flashlight, which gets brighter and brighter, until he surfaces beside me. He exhales calmly, and joins me shining his light around.

"Wow," he says. "This place is cool." His light has a second bank of LEDs that give out a wider source of light, and he switches to this now, so that the whole cave is dimly illuminated. I know how the walls here are actually amazing colors, from the mineral deposits from water running down the inside of the cliffs above us, but mostly now it looks different shades of black.

"So where do you think he'll have stashed it?" Steve asks.

I don't answer. Instead I push the beam of my flashlight around the ledges, hoping to see something that will tell me I haven't made a horrible mistake. But there's nothing. At least nothing obvious.

"Maybe it's over by the beach?" I give a couple of kicks, and send myself gliding smoothly through the calm stillness of the pool. Soon my hands feel the pebbles below me, and I pull myself forward and out of the water. Steve does the same, until we're both clear of the water.

There's only beach here because the tide is low right now. And even so it's pretty tiny, just a strip of stones that meets the cave's back wall, and where it does, the headroom dips right down so that you can't stand. It's about the only place I can think of where the drugs might be hidden, and I crawl towards it hopefully.

My flashlight works better here, picking out the detail in the rock, and I explore the many little folds and crevices, all the time expecting to see packages of drugs. It *has* to be here. But after ten minutes Steve and I have each explored the whole length and found nothing. So then we re-enter the water, and between us we search the whole perimeter of the cave, hauling ourselves out onto each of the ledges and checking wherever we can with our flashlights. All the time I call out to Steve to ask if he's found anything, and my voice echoes back at me. But every time he shouts back that there's nothing, and I can hear how his voice gets more and more grim.

After another twenty minutes, we meet back at the little beach.

"So..." Steve begins. "Are there any other chambers in here? Maybe somewhere else he could have stashed it?"

I shake my head, then remember how it's dark, and he won't see me. "I don't think so. At least, I've never heard of any," I say. I've got it wrong, there's nothing here. That means we've got to go back to the boat empty handed. I don't know how the two men are going to take it. But it's not going to be well.

I fall silent and try to think. Steve shines the flashlight around again.

"So, if it's not here..." he begins, and I can hear how he's trying to keep his voice positive, but it's beginning to sound anxious. "How far is it to swim outta here? Where's the nearest we can get out the water and call the cops?"

"We can't," I say. "Amber's on the boat. And Gracie."

Steve doesn't answer at first. "Look, maybe one of us swims for help. The other goes back, try to convince them to let us all go?"

"No. And it's miles anyway. It's cliffs all the way to Hunts Beach, and Holport to the north."

"How far?" Steve insists.

It's barely worth answering him, with the incoming weather it would be suicide.

"Ten miles?" I guess. "You saw how long it took to get here. That's basically the closest place to get out."

He doesn't answer, and I figure he's given up the idea. I'm sure he could swim that far in good weather, but at night, along the foot of a cliff with a storm pushing him against it? There's no way...

"I can do that," he says, his voice doesn't sound anywhere near as confident as before. "It'll take me a couple of hours, but I can do it. And come back with the police."

"But what do *I* do?" I hear how petulant I sound in my own echo. I don't mean to. It's just I'm not sure what he expects me to do. Steve falls silent again. And as he does so I get the glimmer of an idea. Then Steve goes on.

"You could tell them you're still searching. Make them believe it's gonna take two or three hours, and they just have to sit tight..."

"Underwater!" I interrupt him suddenly. "We haven't looked underwater."

"What?"

"He must have known – Carlos I mean – that people sometimes come into these caves, because they're marked on the charts. So he wouldn't have just left it on the beach or on the ledges. He'd have hidden it properly. So maybe he anchored it under the water."

Steve doesn't say anything at first. But then he refits his mask.

"You take the left side, I'll take the right."

So then we push back into the water, and this time do our best to search the bottom with our flashlights. Inside the cave it's not as deep as outside, and the bottom is more regular than the seafloor outside. And this time it doesn't take me long to find it.

The drugs are in small packages, each about the size of a loaf of bread, and held down by what looks like a piece of old fishing net. The corners and edges are weighed down by rocks. Steve must see it about the same time I do because he comes swimming over, and together we dive down. We both tug at the rocks, but he's able to stay down much longer, and I have to resurface to grab a breath. By the time I sink down again, Steve has shifted enough rocks so the corner of the netting is loose. He pulls out one of the parcels and points upwards with his flashlight sending me to the surface again.

This time we surface together, and Steve hands me the parcel. It's quite large, and surprisingly heavy. It's wrapped in a combination of clear plastic and parcel tape.

"This what you were looking for?" I can hear the grin in Steve's voice. "Go get the bag. I'll go and grab a few more."

It takes no time to fill the net bag that we brought, though it's obvious we can't get it all in.

"I can hold the flashlight in my mouth," I say, "Then I can take a package in each hand." But Steve shakes his head. "We'll have to do two runs anyway. And it could be hard to swim against the wind." He shines his light on the package, inspecting it. In the half light I see him shaking his head. "We might as well get this first batch back. They'll be wondering where we are."

So then we pull the neck of the bag tight and take a few deep breaths, ready to swim back through the entrance and into the open sea.

Straight away I'm struck by how the weather has worsened outside the shelter of the cave. The waves hitting against the side of the cliff are bigger now, perhaps two or three feet high and I can see the *Blue Lady* is not riding well on her anchor. She is lying stern towards us and the lights are on, making it obvious how much she's rolling around. It must be pretty uncomfortable to be sitting waiting.

Talking is impossible again, even swimming is hard, and I just follow Steve, aiming for the boat. I'm glad it's him towing the bag.

Then there's a new light. The big flashlight, the one we keep clipped to the wall above the chart table. It's shining from the stern of the boat, its light playing over the sea. I guess it must be Earrings looking for us, then I hear him shouting too, his voice almost lost to the strength of the wind. There's no point trying to shout back, we're better off just swimming, and Steve obviously thinks the same, because he stretches out ahead of me, even with the extra weight he's carrying. By the time I get to the ladder he's already on board, and then he reaches an arm down to help me. I climb up just in time to see Earrings, holding his pistol with two hands, and looking angry.

"Hey!" He shouts. "I asked you a question." Steve ignores him and keeps helping me on board, physically pulling me up the ladder until I'm kneeling on the deck. But then suddenly Earrings steps forward and whacks his gun across the side of Steve's head. It makes a noise like a loud crack.

"I asked what took you so long."

I don't think the blow was as hard as it sounded. The boat's moving so much, it took the power out of it. But even so Steve touches his fingers to the side of his head, like he's feeling for blood.

"That was just a warning," Earrings says, regaining his balance. "Now answer me, or you're gonna get something a lot worse."

"You wanna calm down a little?" Steve tells him. He goes back to the ladder and pulls the bag up from where he'd clipped it on. "It was well hidden. The kid did good to find it at all."

Earrings stares at Steve, like he still wants an answer to his question. But eventually the sight of the bag wins out. He kicks at it suspiciously, then bends down to shake it open. But it's tied shut, and he can't open it without lowering his gun.

"Open it," he tells Steve, who doesn't move.

"I said open it."

Slowly Steve does what he's told. He picks at the knots around the neck. It takes him a few moments.

"Where's Amber?" I ask, but no one answers me.

"Where's Amber and Gracie," I go on. "You've got your drugs…"

"Keep it shut kid," Earrings snaps, then turns back to Steve. "Is that it? Where's the rest?"

"Still inside."

"What? Why the fuck didn't you bring it all..?"

"We brought as much as we could. I told you to calm down. We're doing exactly what you asked, in very difficult circumstances."

This seems to silence Earrings for a moment. He picks up one of the packages, and inspects it one-handed. I glance at Steve. I can tell he's judging whether Earrings is distracted enough for him to launch an attack at him. I'm terrified by the prospect, but at the same time I try to make myself ready to help if I can. But then the other man, Tommy, steps out of the shadows of the cabin.

"Hands where I can see them," he says. He's got his pistol trained on us as well.

Earrings glances up, and sees he can use both hands safely. He shoves the pistol into his waistband and inspects the package properly. I don't know what he's looking for, but he seems satisfied. At least for a moment. Then he shakes the other parcels free and kicks the empty bag towards Steve. Then he pulls out the gun again.

"Well? What the fuck are you waiting for? Go back and get the rest."

There's a moment of silence, and I look back at the water. I suddenly realize I'm tired. The last thing I want to do is go back in there. But I don't have any choice.

"Hold on," Steve says.

"What for?" Earrings replies.

"I want to know the plan," Steve says. "You've got what you wanted. I want to know how you're planning on letting us go."

"What the fuck are you talking about?" Earrings says.

"Exactly what I said. We've given you this," he points at the drugs. "I'm no expert but I know it's worth a ton of money. And all we want is for you to let us go. But how do we know we can trust you?"

I glance at Earrings face, and I see it's twisted into an angry sneer. "I don't care if you trust me or not. We've got the girl and the little kid locked up in the front. So you better do what the fuck you're told."

But Steve doesn't move. "Not until you tell me the plan. How are you gonna get out of here, and how are you gonna release us?"

There's a standoff that lasts a long time. I get the sense that me and the other guy, Tommy, are just waiting on the rocking and rolling deck to see what happens. I think for a second that Earrings is simply going to shoot Steve, and my next thought is super selfish – how I'd have to go into the cave on my own if he did that. But Earrings doesn't. I guess he figures he might not get the rest of the drugs that way.

"OK." He says in the end, "this is the *plan*." He shrugs like it's no big deal to tell us. "You get the rest of it, then we'll take you back to the marina." He stops and I sense he's making it up as he goes. "We'll lock you in the boat, that'll give us enough time to get away and out of town. After that you're on your own. That good enough for you?"

I look to Steve. I've got a host of questions, but Steve just stares at him a long time. In the end he nods his head.

"OK, now get back in that goddamn water and get me the rest of my packages."

Slowly Steve gets up. He ties the bag around his waist, then turns to me. "Billy, you ready?"

FORTY-EIGHT

I'M ALREADY COLD, but I know better than to say anything. Instead I nod, and try not to look at the water as I step carefully back to the ladder. I've still got my flippers on, so the easiest way is to jump back in. I don't want to, but there's no choice, and I step off, and plunge into blackness. Another bucket full of water flushes through my suit, and I come to the surface gasping for air, then fit my snorkel and mask.

Steve takes the lead this time, now he knows the way, and he makes me swim fast, which helps to warm me up. I try to talk to him as we go, but he shakes his head, and swims away, not even hesitating at the entrance to the cave, but ducking straight under the water. That makes it easier to get through the tunnel too, as all I have to do is follow the yellow glow in the water ahead of me.

Once we're back inside the cave, I expect him to stop and talk to me. He must have some kind of plan, at least, I hope he does. But straight away he dives down, and this time I watch from the surface, as he works underwater, moving the rocks and un-snagging the remaining packets of cocaine. It's amazing how long he can stay down. I thought Dad was good – he used to practice staying underwater to help with when he surfed big waves – but Steve is like a seal or something. He only needs the one breath before he's recovered it all, and then he ferries it to me on the surface, and I pack it into the bag. Five minutes later and we're done. But then, instead of heading back through the entrance and swimming back to the boat, he points at the little beach at the back of the cave, and swims that way instead. And there he pulls off his mask and snorkel.

"We need to do something," he says as I get there too.

"What?"

"I don't know. But something. Or this isn't going to end well."

"Why do you say that?" I ask, but I know the answer really, it's just I don't want to think about it.

"Did you hear him?" Steve asks.

Then I don't answer, and the next thing, he's shining the light right into my face. "Jesus! Billy! Are you OK? You're white." Suddenly he grabs me, and starts rubbing up and down on my arms and chest, using friction to warm me a bit. I think he's going to stop, but he keeps going, for what must be four or five minutes, and actually I almost get hot.

"There," he says, he's out of breath now. "That better?"

I nod.

"Good. Now I need you to concentrate. Did you hear what he said, when I asked what the plan was?"

I nod again, though this time I remember how he can't see me. "To lock us in the boat while they escape."

"Yeah, but did you notice how he had to make it up on the spot? There was no plan. Or if there was, it wasn't that."

I'm feeling a little bit better now I'm warmed up. My head is starting to function again. "So what do you think they'll do? When they get the drugs back?"

Steve clicks his light to the lamp mode again, casting a dull yellow glow that illuminates the cave better. He shakes his head. "Billy, we've seen their faces. Not just a glimpse either. There's only one thing they were ever planning to do."

I don't need to ask what he means. I already know. It's obvious. But then I have to check, because all this feels impossible, sitting here in a cave with Steve, a bag packed full of cocaine at our feet.

"What?"

It takes him a while to answer. But then he doesn't hide it.

"They're going to murder us, Billy. If we give them this cocaine, they're going to take it, and they're going to shoot us. And if we don't go back, they're going to execute your friend and the little girl."

There's a moment of silence. I know he's right, but it's surreal to hear him say it out loud.

"So what do we do?" I ask, in the end.

"We need a plan."

I feel a faint flickering of hope. Not strong. "OK... What?"

He's a long time in answering, and the glimmer fades.

"Billy I'm sorry but I got nothing."

The hope is snuffed out completely. I feel the gloom around us pressing down.

"We've got to stay positive," Steve says. "There's more of us than them. They're outnumbered. That *has* to work in our favor. We have to find a way to make it work in our favor."

I try to do what he says, to be positive. But I can't help but want to protest. We might outnumber them technically, but Amber and Gracie are locked in the bow compartment. And Gracie is only six. And two grown men. Armed men. Then it's like he's been reading my mind.

"Your friend, Amber. Can we get a message to her? Is there a window in the bow compartment?"

I think, to answer him, but he's already moved on.

"Maybe we can tap out a message to her, through the hull? Would she know Morse code?"

"I don't think so," I say. "I do though."

His head jerks around to look at me.

"What? I'm a bit rusty, but I taught myself when I was a kid. I thought it might come in handy."

Suddenly he gives a snort of laughter. "Shit Billy, why doesn't that surprise me?"

I don't know what he's talking about. And I'm still wondering when he stops laughing. Again his voice is hard, bitter.

"If only we had a *weapon*." He starts hunting around him, looking for stones, but here it's just pebbles. "We can take rocks from the bottom. If I can get close enough, maybe I can knock the cocky one out with it. The fucker with the earrings."

He's talking to himself mostly, and it gives me the time to imagine how it might go. The bigger guy, Tommy, he watches all the time. He's always holding his gun, and he's got a kind of competence about him that terrifies me. If Steve tries to attack Earrings with a rock, even if he manages to get one blow on him, the other man will just shoot him.

I watch now. He's crawled down to the water's edge, where there's some larger rocks. He selects a couple now, feeling the weight, and then he puts them in the bag.

"Come on kid," he says.

I feel like asking if that's it? That's the plan. I thought we were going to come up with something for how to get us out of here. And now it just seems I'm going to get to watch Steve get shot and killed when he tries to beat two big guns with a rock.

"It won't work!" I say out loud, and Steve stops.

"It's dark, the boat is rocking. There might be an opportunity."

"But what if there isn't?"

"Listen Billy," finally his voice snaps, and he sounds angry. "If you've got a better idea I'd love to hear it."

I don't, so I stay silent.

"Come on. When we get there, you need to look for a chance to distract them. I don't know how, just anything. Wait until I've got the rock and I'm close enough to…"

Suddenly I remember.

"I've got it!" I cry.

He turns to stare at me.

"I know where there's a weapon!"

FORTY-NINE

"Where?" Steve asks. He doesn't move at all.

"When Carlos – or whatever his name is – when I saw him here it must have been after he hid the cocaine, because I didn't see it at all. All I saw was he was spear fishing, and this whole area is a nature reserve."

Steve stays silent.

"He hadn't shot anything by then, he probably wasn't even trying to, he just had the gun for protection, but I didn't know that, so I swam up to him, to tell him about the nature reserve, and how he wasn't allowed to fish here, and he was so surprised that he dropped the spear gun. It was in deep water and he didn't even try to get it. I know, because I waited so I could watch him actually leave. It's still there. I know where it is."

Suddenly I'm in such a hurry to leave I find myself tugging at Steve's shoulder. But still he hesitates.

"How do you know where it is?"

"I saw it below me. After he left. It fell into one of the holes, and I was annoyed because it was too deep for me to get, and I thought it was littering. But I know exactly where it is."

He hesitates again.

"One of the holes? How deep?"

I stop. The truth is I don't really know. I've just assumed that Steve will be able to get it, even in the dark, because he's a free diving champion. I hadn't thought that I'd have to go down there.

"Maybe fifteen feet?" I say. But really I'm already working it out. It's got to be more than that, because the tide is higher today. "Could be twenty."

There's a short pause before he answers. But he nods his head. "Twenty feet is OK." I don't tell him I didn't measure it, It could be more than that.

"Show me where it is."

So we take the bag, and once again we descend under the surface for the quick swim through the underwater passage that connects the cave to the sea, but this time, once we're outside we don't swim directly back to the boat, but instead I try to work out where Carlos dropped the gun. I know what I need to look for, in order to find it, but it's so dark beneath me that I can hardly see the seabed, let alone recognize the features. And it's so choppy and rough on the surface now that just swimming in the same place is difficult. I sense Steve alongside me – we're both careful to keep our lights shining down, so that no one on the boat can see what we're doing – but the light only helps illuminate the tops of the shallower sections of rock.

I stop, pull my head out of the water and think. The octopus was on a shallow piece of sand near to the cave's entrance. I'm able to locate that quite easily. Then I take myself back. The *Mystery* was anchored further out than *Blue Lady* is, and further to the north too. I try to make the same swim now, and all the time I'm pushing my head down into the water and straining to see as much as I can.

Eventually we're treading water over roughly where I think the gun must be. But it's hopeless. Even shining the flashlights down just reveals water, the light doesn't reach the bottom.

"It's somewhere around here. Down there somewhere." I say to Steve, but I shake my head as I speak. I don't even know if he's going to bother trying. It's obvious now that this is impossible. Yet he hands me the bag with the drugs in, and then he floats on his back for a minute or so, saying nothing. I don't know how he's even managing to do that, with the way the swell is buffeting us both around. And something makes me not interrupt him, just wait for what happens next. Then he rolls over and I see his eyes through the mask, fixed and staring. He gives me a thumbs up. And then he rolls forward, and disappears under the water.

Right away I use my snorkel and mask to watch him descend. He's got his flashlight on, and I see it sinking down. Slowly down, further and further. And I wonder if I really am in the right place, or if I've just sent him towards the empty bottom. Or worse, a section of the reef where it's way too deep for anyone to reach. Still the light is dropping away below me. Then finally I see how it lights up the rock around him, he must have got to the sea bed.

A wave overtops my snorkel, and I get a mouthful of salty water. I nearly panic, and come to the surface choking and coughing to clear my airways. Then I blow hard through the tube to empty it, and look down again. The light is moving now, slowly crabbing along the seafloor. It's hard to see but it looks like he's making his way along a crevice in the rock. That worries me. I don't think there were any crevices where the gun was dropped. It was more like a round hole in the reef. Then I worry about something else. I'm breathing normally, or as normally as I can through the snorkel in such choppy water. But Steve's just got one breath. I decide to hold my own breath, as a way of measuring how long he's been down there. So I push the snorkel from my mouth, and instead pinch my nose closed.

I keep watching as the light, far below me, crabs further to the right. Then it stops. I wait, still counting in my head. I get to twenty before I can feel the pinch on my chest, the need to get more air in. I try to ignore it, to will it away, but it just grows stronger and stronger. On forty I know I have to release my grip, and breathe again, but I also know what it means for Steve. He's been down there far longer than I've been holding my breath, and now the light isn't moving. I realize it hasn't moved for thirty seconds or more. I begin to panic at what that means. Maybe he's unconscious? Maybe he's already drowned.

I splutter and resurface, gasping at the air, but disgusted at myself that I couldn't even count to a minute. I fight to calm myself and look down again. But this time there's nothing. I don't mean there's no movement. I mean there's no light at all. I turn my own flashlight off, so it's not blinding me. But still I can't see anything. It's just an ocean of blackness.

The feeling in my stomach is sheer, cold terror. I look up and around me, but it's just empty sea. There's a rare break in the clouds, and the moon is visible, the sloppy swell breaking its reflection into shards of light on the water. A little way away the *Blue Lady* is still riding her anchor, her deck lights still rolling in lumpy arcs. Behind me the cliffs hang dark and threatening. But there's no sign of Steve, no head above the water. I look underwater again, unable to breathe myself now. But nothing has changed. It's still just darkness.

There's literally nothing I can do. Something must have happened down there. Free diving is dangerous, even in normal times, all sorts of things can go wrong, and I'm powerless to help. Even if I could get that deep I'm too late. Fear spasms through me. He's probably already dead. He's ahead of me. By what? Fifteen minutes?

What do I do now? Should I go back to the boat anyway? Give them their drugs, and let them shoot me? At least I might get to see Amber again. Or is it better to try and swim away. I'll drown before I reach anywhere, no question about that. Or should I try and go after Steve. Perhaps Steve found it, before he ran out of air. Perhaps I can swim down. I fight to take a breath, ready to duck forward and dive down. But even as I do, I know I'll never make it. I couldn't get the spear gun in daylight, in good weather, when I was calm, and when the tide was lower. It's impossible now.

Ooooffff.

Suddenly something punches me in the stomach. I get another mouthful of seawater, and then something surfaces right in my face, gasping for air, just like I am. For a second I don't realize what it is, then with an explosion of joy I see it's Steve. Neither of us can speak, but then I see the gleam of his teeth in the dull light, and then he holds up a long metal spear gun in his hand.

"I got lucky," he says, panting through the wind and the waves. "Flash light failed, but only after I saw the gun."

I don't answer. I feel sick, from thinking he was dead. "It's a good one too," he says, a minute later, after he's done breathing hard. "Christ alone knows how you found the spot where it was."

Dimly I appreciate the compliment. I must have put us right above it.

"Come on. They won't be expecting this," Steve says. And without stopping to tell me the plan he starts swimming again, back to the *Blue Lady.*

FIFTY

AGAIN WE'RE PICKED out from the rear platform of the boat by the spot light, but we get closer this time before they see us. I can't see which of them is operating it, but I'm worried they'll see the spear gun. It's quite big. Steve stopped on the swim to load it, pulling the thick elastic band back and clipping it onto the spear. It only has one shot, but the force is deadly. I've seen them go right through fish, even large ones, and I've watched videos online of people shooting other things, trees and TVs and they go through anything.

When we reach the ladder, Steve pushes me to go first, so I climb aboard, and see if there's anything I can do right away to distract them. Earrings is right there, clamoring for the bag with the drugs, while Tommy is hanging back, his feet spread wide to compensate for the roll of the boat. I feel how he watches me, the pistol loosely aimed in my direction. His attention focused completely on watching me.

"Where's the other one? The shark guy?" Earrings asks. I don't know the answer.

"He's right behind me. Or he was."

"And where's the coke? Where the fuck is my coke?"

Steve had the bag, so I don't know the answer to this either, but then his voice suddenly sounds out, from the water. "It's here."

For some reason he's appeared on the port side of the boat. Then he swims back to the ladder at the stern, and we all watch him climb up onto the platform, using both his hands. Then I see the bag is tied around his

THE APPEARANCE OF MYSTERY 269

waist this time, and he slowly hauls it up behind him. But I can't see where he's got the spear gun. Has he dropped it? After all the effort it took to get it. But then he gives me a look, and I notice there's a thin line tied round his foot. With spear guns you have a line that connects the spear to the gun, else you'd lose the spear every time you fired it. It's this line he had round his ankle. He must have cut it with the propeller blade. The gun must be suspended in the water below him.

Earrings doesn't notice anything, least I don't think so. He's only interested in the drugs.

"Is that all there is?" He snaps when he gets the bag open again. Steve nods, gradually moving his foot. Once he gets into the cockpit he might be able to hide the gun behind one of the bench seats.

"It looks light."

"It's all there was," Steve replies. "You're welcome to go take a look yourself. But right now we're cold and the boy needs to get out of his suit and warm up."

Earrings glares at him, but then turns away and opens the bag further. I keep my eyes on Steve, and see how he's watching both of them. But Tommy is keeping his eyes fixed on Steve. Then Earrings kneels by the bag, pulling out the packages and tossing them inside the cabin where the first batch are piled up.

"How many's that?" he asks Tommy. I glance up, and see the flicker of irritation on the bigger man's face. He still doesn't take his eyes off Steve and me. But he counts the packages anyway. Using his feet.

"Fifteen."

Earrings seems happy with this, and Steve tries again.

"Come on buddy. We've done our part. Let the kid get dried off. He's freezing cold."

Earrings doesn't make any sign he hears. Instead he pulls out his cell phone and clicks the screen on. He stares at it for a moment, then clicks it off again. He looks disgusted.

"No fucking signal," he shouts, more at himself than anyone else.

"Come on man. This kid's gonna get hypothermia if he doesn't get warm now." I don't know what Steve's plan actually is, but I try to go along with it. I make myself start shivering, which isn't hard, because I really am cold. My teeth start to chatter. That makes Earrings look up.

"Like I give a fucking shit." Earrings replies. Then he turns away, and looks out towards the open sea for a moment. I don't know what he's looking at, but then he suddenly yells out.

"Over there!"

Suddenly I realize we're not alone. Because not far away I see the navigation lights of another boat. Not far away at all. I feel a rush of relief. Maybe Amber's somehow managed to get out, and used the radio – but no, didn't Tommy smash it up?

"At fucking last," Earrings says.

"What's going on?" Steve demands, but Earrings ignores him again. Then Tommy steps over to Earrings' side of the boat too, and for a moment all three of us are staring out into the darkness. The other boat has deck lights and the windows of the cabins are illuminated too. It looks like another private fishing boat, but newer and bigger than *Blue Lady*. My dad calls them gin palaces. It's coming close. Then I look back at Steve, just in time to see him swing the spear gun over the gunwale, and gently place it on the deck. Then he slides the loop of cord off his foot.

"Who's that?" He asks again, when he's done.

"None of your fucking business." Earrings replies.

"You said we were going back to the port. You'd leave us there."

"Yeah well I fucking lied didn't I?" Earrings turns again to watch the other boat. A spotlight plays on us, picking us out one by one. Then, when the boat is within hailing distance a voice calls out, across the water.

"Why aren't you answering the radio?"

Earrings looks at Tommy, annoyed, then he shouts back. "Tommy smashed it up."

Then there's laughs, rolling over the water. "Tell Tommy he's a fucking idiot."

I can make out figures on the other boat now. At least four men, and there's enough light to see that two of them are standing on the top of the cabin, holding on with one hand and with proper automatic assault rifles slung around their necks.

"Are they with you?" Steve persists.

"Course they're with us," Earrings snaps, then looks annoyed at himself for bothering. He shouts again.

"Tell Angelo we got fifteen packets back. He better be fucking grateful!"

There's a pause, while the other boat's motor roars as it struggles to hold position. Then the voice comes back.

"Tell him yourself! You think he'd let anyone else skipper his new boat?"

Suddenly Earrings seems incredibly happy. He almost seems to forget we're here. "Tommy, you hear that? Angelo's here himself. We're done here. We fucking done it."

Then the voice comes again. "Who's the civilians?"

Earrings stops smiling at once. He glances at Steve and me, then yells back. "No one. No one important."

There's a long pause, while the other boat's motor roars again. In the reflected light I can make out the name *Mea Culpa*, painted across the stern. I see the men scurrying across the deck. Then the voice rings out again.

"Then get rid of them. Angelo wants this sorted fast. Bad weather coming."

The light gets brighter as the other boat comes closer still, but they're pointing the other way from us.

"We'll turn around, come alongside." The voice says now, and the spot-light abruptly breaks away, like they want to give some privacy, and we're back to just the low-level deck lighting on the *Blue Lady*. We all heard what the man said, and we all know what it means. Earrings turns to Tommy.

"Well, you heard him. Get it done."

No one moves. No one speaks. Until Tommy does so. The longest sentence I've heard him speak.

"I thought we were gonna let them go," he says in the end.

Earrings turns to look at him. When he speaks, his voice is a snarl.

"Yeah well, we ain't."

"We made a deal."

"Angelo didn't. So stop fucking around. Shoot them."

There's another silence.

"What about the two in the cabin?" Tommy asks. "The girl, and the kid?"

"What about them? Shoot these two, then shoot them as well. It ain't fucking hard."

Earrings stares at Tommy, who's relaxing and tightening his grip on the gun.

"Yeah but the little girl... She's nothing to do with this."

"The fuck are you saying Tommy? You just got a *direct order* and you don't wanna do it?" Earrings stares at Tommy. They're both holding their guns, and I could almost believe they're more likely to shoot each other.

Then Earrings snaps. "You don't want to shoot a six year old kid? Fine. I'll fucking do it. But shoot these fuckers now while I get this sorted." Earrings bends down, and sets his gun on the deck so he can use both hands to move the drugs into one pile. He snorts angrily while he works. Terrified, I look up at Tommy. He's looking right back at me. He raises his gun.

"Shit," he says. "Sorry kid. I wish there was another way."

My mouth opens to speak. To tell him there is another way, that there must be. But no sound comes out. With his other hand Tommy pulls back the slider on the top of the gun, pulling a bullet into the chamber. He shakes his head slowly.

"Fenders!" I say, the word garbled in my mouth.

"What?" Tommy lowers the gun a fraction.

"You'll need fenders. If you're going to have that other boat come alongside. You'll need fenders, or we'll smash holes in each other. I know where they are."

I can hear my breathing, desperate, fast, in-and-out as I watch Tommy's reaction. The gun tips sideways as he gives a little half-shrug. "OK…" He turns to Earrings.

"Paulie," he says. "These guys, they're not soldiers. They're not involved. This isn't the way the Old Man did things."

But Earrings has finished what he was doing now. He picks up his gun again, and this time he holds it out. His arm straight, pointing directly at me. "Yeah, and how many times I gotta tell *you*, the Old Man's gone. New times. New rules."

Then there's a strange sound, or two strange sounds. The first is the release of pent up pressure on the elastic of the spear gun, the second is the sound of the metal harpoon piercing first the flesh of Earring's shoulder, then the wood of the wheelhouse structure behind him, pinning him in place. Then there's a clatter as the gun he was holding falls to the deck. The noise distracts Tommy, who turns to look, confused by what's just happened. It gives Steve the time to react. He dives at Tommy, tackling his legs and in a second they're both on the deck together, Steve's voice screaming out.

"Get the gun Billy!"

I'm a bit slower to react, and Earrings goes to pick up the gun before I can. But suddenly he can't move. He's stuck in place by the spear, and I'm able to crawl across near to him and pick up the gun. I hold it, shaking in my hands and aim it at him for a second, then I spin around and point it at the moving tangle of limbs and bodies that is Steve and Tommy. In the dim light it's impossible to make out who's who, or which of them is winning.

"Freeze!" I shout, as loud as I can. It works, and then Steve rolls away. I can't see where Tommy's gun has gone, but he's looking right at me. In a flash Steve is by my side. He carefully takes the gun from my hands, then holds it out towards Tommy.

"On your knees."

The big man doesn't respond.

"I'm telling you. Get down right now. Or I'll shoot your legs out from under you."

"You can't win this." Tommy replies. Still not doing what Steve says. "Don't you see they're armed on that boat? Fully automatic assault rifles. They'll cut you to pieces."

"Last chance motherfucker," Steve ignores him. "Get on your knees or I'll shoot your legs out."

This time Tommy does what he's told. I don't know if I just started hearing it, but now there's the sound of Earrings moaning. He's trying to move, but he can't.

"Now lie down. Hands behind you. Billy, come here."

Steve holds the gun pushed up against the back of Tommy's head, while he makes me tie his hands together. I'm pretty good at knots, but even so Steve checks it. Then he rolls Tommy over again, and I tie a second rope, securing him to the chest where we keep the drinks, so there's no chance he can move. It's all happened so quick, the other boat is still finishing its maneuver to turn around and come alongside. It's coming back now, the searchlight clicks back on, and wobbles around, trying to pick us out.

"Billy, get the motor started. We've got to get out of here," Steve shouts now. And when I hesitate he yells it again. "Now! I'll dump the anchor."

Then the searchlight rests upon us. And I feel the glare as it must pick out Earrings, still pinned to the side of the cabin, calling out now. I don't hesitate any more.

The motor on the *Blue Lady* fires first go, and straight away I see Steve has released the anchor. He doesn't bother trying to pull it in, it would take too long to get all the chain back on board. Instead he frees the end of the rope and casts it overboard.

"Go!" He shouts at me, and I don't hesitate. I ram the gear lever forward and the boat rears up as the power pushes the bow high. The *Blue Lady* is heavy though, and she takes a while to coax onto the plane. And in this weather I have to work hard to keep her straight through the chop and swell.

"Lights," Steve yells, "lose the lights." I do what he says, hitting the switch, then grab a look behind me, and see the search light flailing around, trying to locate us. I guess they maybe take a few moments to figure out what's happening, because they don't move at once. It gives us a head start – not much, maybe a hundred yards before I see the bow of their boat lift up too, white against the black of the cliffs. And then we're both flying along, charging out into the deeper water and the approaching storm.

"They're onto us!" Steve shouts into my ear from beside me. I stare at him. I don' t have anything to say. "Here, let me steer. Go release Amber."

I do what he says, dropping down the ladder from the bridge to the cockpit. I see how Tommy is being bounced around, tied to the floor, and then I see the other man, Earrings, and how he's still pinned to the side of the cabin, and how each time the boat lands from a wave he's screaming out in agony. But I don't have time for him, instead I make my way inside and up to the bow cabin, where Amber is screaming too. I work as fast as I can to unpick the knots that Tommy tied to keep the door closed, but it's hard with how much the boat is moving. We'd never normally go full tilt in swell like this, and I've never seen the inside of the boat crashing around this much. Finally the rope is out the way, and the door falls open.

"Billy! What's happening?" Amber looks desperate. She's still holding Gracie, trying to calm her down, but not really getting anywhere.

"We're getting away." I breathe. "We've escaped." There's a huge crash, as the boat lands in a trough between waves. We slow then accelerate again. It's horrible this far forward. "Sort of escaped. They're chasing us."

"Who is?" Amber asks, but already I'm heading back to help Steve.

When I get back out of the cabin I see the other boat has already halved the distance between us. Its search light keeps picking us out, and then losing us as both boats crash up and down. And then, every time the light is on us I hear the rat tat tat of their weapons, firing at us.

"Get down," Steve shouts, from up on the bridge. Too late I drop to the deck, pulling Amber and Gracie with me. But it doesn't matter as we must be impossible to hit in this water state.

"They're closing fast. Bigger boat. It rides the swell better," Steve yells down. "Hold on. I'm gonna try to out corner them."

Without any more warning he suddenly sends the boat into a hard turn to starboard. Their light loses us at once, and we stretch out our lead by a boat length or two. But it doesn't take much for them to pick up our wake, white against the dark water, and find us again. Steve tries again, but this time whoever is steering the *Mea Culpa* is quicker, and turns harder, cutting the distance again. Another rain of bullets flies across our stern.

"Shoot them!" Steve yells. "Shoot back." I don't know where the gun is, until I remember I left it on the floor by the bow cabin. I stagger back to get it, and then see Amber already has it. She's white faced in the doorway of the cabin, before I pull her to the floor. Then there's a series of loud cracks, and I realize we've been hit by a volley of bullets. They don't hit anything vital – at least I don't think they do – but it's impossible to know if they've hit us below the waterline.

She shrugs me off, and aims at the boat behind us. She's quite good with guns, but it's obviously hopeless. The men on the following boat are protected by its bow, high up out of the water, and by the fact that both boats are leaping and crashing through the seas. What's also obvious is there's no chance of us escaping. The other boat is faster and more maneuvrable, and we're hopelessly outgunned. Then Steve makes a shallow turn, and for a moment the side of the chasing boat is revealed. Amber aims again, and empties the rest of the magazine behind us. Obviously she does enough to worry them, and for a moment they turn away from the chase. But only enough to put them on a parallel path. It looks like they're going to come level and then rake us with fire. It means we're in a straight race. And the *Blue Lady* is being overhauled at a frightening rate.

"You got a life raft on this tub?" Steve shouts down.

"Yeah!" I scream back at him.

"Then go get it. Get ready to throw it over." He takes his hands off the wheel for second. At once the boat rears wildly, and he has to grab it again, hard.

"What do you mean, throw it over?"

"It's dark enough that we can get it in the water without them seeing, if we put it over the other side. Then jump in after it. They'll keep chasing the boat."

I try to make sense of this.

"Just do it Billy. Now!"

His words jerk me into action. We have two life rafts on board – we have to, because of the passengers we carry – they're stored in explosive canisters on each side of the boat. The idea is they're super easy to get ready, and they self-inflate when they hit the water. And we have to do drills with them, so we know exactly how to operate them, just in case an emergency happens. I clamber around the side deck now to reach the port side canister. The other boat is now creeping alongside us on our starboard side, so I'm hidden from view. I rip open the buckles, my fingers are shaking. Then Steve makes a sudden swerve to port, widening the gap between the two boats. The other one is slower to respond again, allowing us to pull ahead.

"Don't pull it yet. I'll tell you when," Steve yells. "Put a life jacket on the kid." He turns around and shouts to Amber. I don't hear what, but I see her go off to the stern locker and pull it open.

"What about you?" I shout up.

"Can't leave the wheel. She won't stay straight."

"So what are you gonna do?" But he doesn't hear me. I turn and look at the water flashing past beside me. Whenever we've practiced deploying the life rafts we've been stopped, in calm water. I don't even know if it will work properly at this speed.

I check the other boat. It's about a hundred yards away now and closing again. We're going along the lines of swell, so the boats are crashing up and down less. Their superior speed is working against them now.

Then I see what Amber is doing. She's holding a small green plastic gas container. We keep it there to run the little outboard for the inflatable tender. Only she's got the top off, and she's sloshing it around, over the cockpit, and then inside the cabin. The smell of gasoline is suddenly everywhere.

"What are you doing?" I scream, over the noise.

"Distraction." Steve yells.

"You're going to set the boat on fire?!"

"Not just this one Billy. Are you ready there?"

I glance again at the flashing water. I check I've got all the buckles free. I just have to pull the quick release handle, and the canister will roll overboard. In theory it will self-inflate.

"I asked if you're ready Billy?"

"Yeah."

"OK Amber. Light her up. I'll make a hard turn to port. Release the raft and jump all together."

There's no time to argue. I crouch over my task, my whole hands shaking with fear and adrenalin. Then I see an orange glow appear behind Steve. He waits a couple of seconds – long enough for the glow to brighten, and then he leans the *Blue Lady* into a hard port turn.

"*Goooo!*" Steve screams. And I don't hesitate. I yank my handle as hard as I can, and I watch as the final catch holding the canister in place tears away, and the whole barrel rolls over the side, splitting open as it does so.

"Go Billy. Jump now!" Steve yells. The other boat anticipated our turn, because they're closer than ever, and shooting at us again.

"What about you?" I call again, as behind me I see Amber and Gracie on the side of the boat. And then they're gone, into the water, and immediately lost in the darkness.

"Don't worry about me. Just jump." Steve screams back to me. Still I don't do it. The whole of the cockpit of the *Blue Lady* is now alight, smoke flooding out the cabin and flowing out behind us.

"*Jump Billy.*"

I push myself up, and leap sideways off the boat.

FIFTY-ONE

I HIT THE WATER HARD. It's like being smashed by a wave, and then tumbled underwater. It's so dark I'm totally disorientated. I don't know where up is. And I didn't even think to take a breath. I don't so much panic as feel incredulous, am I just too far underwater? Is this how I'm going to drown? But then one of my hands breaks the surface, and a reflex kicks in – I struggle to get my head up. And at once it's quieter. Then I spin around, just in time to see an incredible sight.

The *Blue Lady* is a fireball. Already it's fifty feet away, and flame and smoke billowing out the back. I can still see Steve on the bridge, at the wheel, his body silhouetted against the flames. The other boat is still alongside, still both at full speed. But just as I look, the *Blue Lady* cuts hard to starboard, away from the chasing boat, like Steve's making one final desperate effort to escape. At once the driver on the second boat follows, like he's used to it now. But then Steve must throw the wheel as hard as he can around the other way, because just as the second boat begins turning, the *Blue Lady* suddenly cuts back and turns the other way. But now there's no room for her to do so. The two boats are going almost directly towards each other. A second later they collide, the *Blue Lady* riding right up and on top of the other boat. They both slow, and finally stop, and I see they're locked together. I can hear shouts, screaming. There's people jumping into the water. And then there's a massive explosion.

I have to shield my eyes, as the night sky is lit up. Bits of boat shoot up, high in the air, then fall like solid pieces of rain. Both boats are stopped now, dead in the water. And both are on fire. It's mesmerizing, almost beautiful. But horrible because I know Steve is on there somewhere. I get a mouthful of salty water, and I realize I'm screaming, shouting out his name. Not because he might hear me. Not because he might still even be alive. Because I know there's no chance. He was right in the middle of the two boats. And now there's nothing left. I fall silent. I know I'm crying, my tears mixing with the salt of the ocean. And I know there's nothing I can do. Then I remember Gracie and Amber. I turn around.

I can't see anything behind me, not even the land, let alone her and Amber swimming somewhere out in the dark. But then there's a flash of red in the darkness. The life-raft has a built-in light that operates automatically. I lose it for a second, then catch it again, rocking from side to side about a few hundred yards away. I don't know what else to do, so I begin to swim towards it.

My shoulder muscles are sore and stiff from my swimming earlier, and it takes me a long while. I try to keep my eyes open, watching for Amber or Gracie floating somewhere in the water around me, but it's pitch black now. The still burning boats are so bright they make it hard to stay focused on the beacon on the raft. But finally I get there, and I feel for the fabric ladders that hang underneath. And when I pull myself inside, I see Amber staring back at me, sitting on the bottom of the life raft, with little Gracie resting on her knees. She doesn't say anything. She just gives me a weak smile, and I know she's crying just like I am.

EPILOGUE

I'M STANDING on the edge of the cliff. It's the one outside my house, only it looks funny because there's fog rolling in off the sea and rising up all around me. I can feel the breeze it's riding on, cold and wet. It's pushing my hair back from my forehead. I don't know why, I hold out my arms. I can feel my jacket flapping where the wind catches it. I step forward. Close to the edge now, so as to really feel the wind. Then I take one more step, right out into the nothing ahead of me. And then I'm falling, my arms still stretched out beside me, my jacket flapping harder as I accelerate down.

But then something weird happens. Instead of just falling down, I start to fall outwards, away from the cliff face, and over the rocks and beach below. I don't flap my arms, I just hold them outstretched, and they work as wings, like I'm a bird, soaring on the air currents. Like my pet herring gull I used to have, Steven.

I get the hang of it. I dip one arm, and I turn that way, gaining speed. The sand and water race towards me as I swoop down to it. So I dip the other hand, and I'm level again, flying effortlessly above the Littlelea sands. I breathe. Pulling the fresh, cool, damp air deep inside me, and feeling its invigorating touch.

I breathe more. I rise up, high above the beach now. Above the dunes, higher than the cliffs even. I look down on our little house. My bike dumped in the drive, where I should have put it in the shed. Dad's truck forced to park at an awkward angle — no, still moving, like he's just arriving. But he shouldn't be here... I float in the air, hanging above the truck as the door opens and then Dad gets out, staring up at the sky, squinting against the sun. He's animated, calling my name up to me so that gently I float back down to earth, calling out his name, while he calls out mine. *Billy, Billy, Dad..!*

"Dad?" I open my eyes.

"Billy," my Dad actually replies. His face is lined with dirt, and his hair looks long and streaked with oil. He takes my hand. "Billy! Are you OK? Jesus you gave me a scare." He shouts, away from me. "Hey, he's awake! A little help here…" Then he turns back, squeezing my hand, and smiling.

"Where am I?" I ask, but I already know the answer. The white-painted walls and tubes running into my body give it away.

"You're in hospital."

"In Newlea?"

"That's right."

"What happened?"

"That's what I've been wondering. What we've all been trying to piece together. You've been out of it for three days. You nearly died."

I stare at Dad in wonder. "What of?"

"Hypothermia. Amber said you lost consciousness in the life raft."

"Amber," I repeat. "Is she alright?"

"She's fine. Pretty cut up, but fine."

"Cut up? Why?" A thought hits me. "Is… Is Gracie… Did she not…"

"Don't stress, Gracie's more than fine. Thinks it was all a grand adventure. No, it's Amber's boyfriend who didn't make it. The guy that started all this mess." Dad takes a breath. "He passed away."

"Oh." I say.

"Yeah. He was pretty badly burned by all accounts, so maybe…" He doesn't finish, but I know he means it's maybe better that way. I don't know about that, so I don't reply.

"Listen, what the hell did you get up to anyway? I leave you counting sharks in Australia, I come back, you're chasing drug smugglers down the back of the island? The cops say they've made the biggest drugs bust here in ten years because of what you did."

It's too long a story to answer this, so I stay silent again.

"Not just the cocaine either, but you've given them the whole gang behind it. They fished most of them out the water. There's one guy — they found him tied to an ice-box — according to the cops, he's been telling them everything. Details on the whole lot of 'em. Enough to put them away for years."

I almost go to smile, but then how it happened. How Steve drove the

Blue Lady into the other boat. How he must have burned to death too. And then I don't think I'll ever smile again.

But I have to ask. I need to know for sure. "Steve Rose," I blurt out. "Did he…" I begin. But I guess I must be weak still, since I can't finish the sentence.

"Did I what mate?" A voice cuts in. A voice I know.

"Steve?" I don't know if I'm still dreaming, but I can't be. I'm not flying.

"Hey Billy." He's got one of his arms wrapped in white bandages, but lifts it up and waggles the fingers in a greeting. There's more bandaging on his face and chest.

"What mate? You look like you seen a ghost!"

I don't reply. It kind of looks like I have."

"This is nothing. There was a good few seconds after the boats hit before the fire kicked off. Wetsuit got a bit melted but figured it would be OK for a little swim." He laughs. "What? You didn't think you'd get rid of me that easy, did you?"

* * *

A while later Amber comes in. She's quiet and withdrawn, but she leans over the bed and gives me a big hug. I can see she's been crying a lot. Then her mom arrives with Gracie, who's clearly loving all the attention. It looks like Amber and her mom need to put in a bit of work before they're going to trust each other again, but at the same time, I can see her mom is trying hard. I guess I'm going to have to help though too, making sure Amber's OK after everything that's happened. But I know she'll come through. She's tough, is Amber.

Then they all leave, and two detectives come in. I don't know them, since they're from the mainland, but they set up a recorder and say they need to take a statement from me about everything that happened. It takes ages, because so much *has* happened, and they want to know every detail, and they've got a million questions about everything I tell them. At first I try to ask them questions too, but they won't tell me anything because it could influence what I say, apparently. But then I realize I don't care anyway, because they're just a bunch of criminals, and I'm not interested in criminals. So then I just lie here and do my best to remember it all, but I get more and more tired, and slowly the voices of the detectives just drift away until they go completely quiet. And then later on, I know I must have fallen asleep, because the detectives are gone, and everything's dark.

The next time I wake up it's daylight.

"How are you doing, Billy?" Dad asks me, when he sees I'm awake.

I smile back at him, just enjoying the quiet for a moment, the way the sunlight is hitting my bed covers.

"What time is it?" I ask after a while.

"I dunno. Morning, sometime. But don't worry about it. You just rest as long as you need."

"No it's not that. It's just I'm starving hungry."

Dad smiles at this. "OK. I'll go get you some breakfast."

But then I notice that Dad's not alone in the room. Steve's here too, and from the way they have their chairs arranged, they must have been talking. He gets up now, and ambles over, holding out a bag of grapes.

"Here. I keep getting given things. Trials of being a celebrity huh?" Then he glances at Dad. "Well, you know, a minor one."

I take the bag and try a couple of grapes. They're nice and sweet.

"I'll go get you some breakfast," Dad says again, but this time I stop him. There's something I feel bad about.

"Hey Dad, I'm sorry about all this. And about you having to stop working on *Blue Lady II*. Just because of me."

Dad shakes his head. "I didn't."

I'm confused by that. "Why not?"

Dad shrugs. "I didn't have to stop because she's finished. She's all fitted out. All ready." Then he glances at Steve, a little bit strangely. "Actually we've been... talking about that, Steve and I, about whether we could maybe do something. I don't know exactly what, but if you didn't want to just go back to running the whale watching trips. We could..." He stops.

"What?"

Dad shrugs again. "I dunno. I really don't know. But we were just... it's just an idea. Something to kick around over the next few weeks."

I want to ask more, but then Steve speaks again.

"Hey listen Sam, you stay here, I'll go grab some food for the both of you. You look like you haven't eaten in days too." He goes to the door and I think he's going to walk out, but then he stops again.

"Hey Sam, I didn't say this before but..."

Dad's quiet. He does look tired.

"I just wanted to say, that's one helluva kid you've got there." Then Steve taps on the door twice before pulling it open and stepping through. When he's gone I look back at Dad, but he won't meet my eye, but then he does and I can see he's welling up with tears. He doesn't say anything but picks up my hand and gives it a squeeze.

And then I squeeze him back.

THANK YOU!

If you're reading this you've probably made it through all three of the *Rockpools* books, so I want to say a big thank you for taking the time and sticking with me, and with Billy. It's really something to sit here at my desk and know that these stories have been enjoyed all around the world.

It's just over two years ago that the idea - for a slightly annoying, but kind of clever; independent, but also clearly lonely - eleven-year-old boy wandered into my mind. I remember the first time I thought about him, he was strolling along a beach, wearing a backpack stuffed with techy gadgets, and carrying his shoes and socks to let the waves wash over his feet. I wanted him to live by a beach that he felt he owned, and for it to be the kind of place that combined the small coastal-town atmosphere I knew from my own childhood on England's east coast, but mixed in with wild empty spaces of Scotland and Cornwall where we took most of our holidays, and that I loved. I don't remember at what point Billy moved himself across the Atlantic to the US, and holidays became vacations, although I think it was something to do with bigger geography than the UK offered (perhaps Cornwall and Scotland have got busier than when I was a kid).

The first *Rockpools* book has sold well over a hundred thousand copies, and it's now being translated into German, Czech and Spanish. It's also attracted interest from Hollywood (no more than a signed option agreement at this mind, but it *might* happen). Billy is also far-and-away my favourite character to write — it's really fun to think like Billy. So though the last couple of years have been kind of crazy, it's also been really, really nice.

I am going to take a break from Billy now for at least one book – I've already started a new story that is set in the new reality of our post Covid world – but I suspect I'll be back writing more stories about Lornea Island before too long. I deliberately left a few loose ends in the book which are going to need tidying up, and a few possible new beginnings.

If you'd like to know when there's more to Billy's story, or to find out about my other books, the best way to stay in touch is by signing up to my email list. It's free, and I'll give you a free copy of my novella Killing Kind (see over for a preview). I also try to make it fun too, with the odd insight about life as an author. You can sign up from this link, but if it doesn't work, type the following into wherever you access the internet:

greggdunnett.co.uk/nextbook

Next some thanks. I'm hugely helped by the team of Beta Readers who go through the books before they're released, and catch all the errors that evade my attempts to weed them out. I always do a terrible job of noting down every name, because I'm very unorganised (and that was made worse this time around as I'm launching the book in 'lockdown'. But I think I've managed to add the name of everyone who worked their way through this book, if you did and I missed you, I'm sorry, but you know who you are. It goes without saying that any errors that remain are mine.

Finally, if you're able, it would be greatly appreciated if you could leave a review on Amazon, Goodreads, or wherever else you like to review books.

Gregg
May 2020

Huge Beta-Reader-Thanks to:

Ali Frith, Wendy Tulloch, Teresa Perrie, Andy Pearce, Angela West, Ashley Gillies, Paul Coulson, Margaret Grant, Pam Wolak, Christine Ryder, Paul Sweeby, Tina Mickeborough, Susan Porter, Diane Lockland, Sheila Kent, Monty Reid, Tracey Smith, Wendy Tulloch, Jim Small, Brian Moore, Tiziana, Stephen Sasse, Michelle Myers, Melanie Burton, Julie Brinker, Marilyn Naylor, Tracey Miller, Julie Robson, Rob Campbell, Lisa Singleton, Karen Sawyer, Dawn Sloan, Lyn Savage, Sonia Einerson, Patricia Dubious, Mary Johnson, Leo Lee, Carole Grey, Daniel Simpson, Catherine Brown, Karen Turton.

READ KILLING KIND FREE

Killing Kind: A novella

by Gregg Dunnett ⌄ (Author)

Customer reviews

⭐⭐⭐⭐⭐ 4.8 out of 5 ⌄

63 customer ratings

5 star		81%
4 star		15%
3 star		3%
2 star		0%
1 star		0%

A killer is leaving notes on London's park benches, confessing to their lifetime of crimes.

A detective has the chance to solve cases that have baffled her colleagues for decades.

But only if she can work out who he is, before he gets to her.

Because - in a story where not everything is what it seems - not even murder is black and white.

Killing Kind is a tense novella with a twist that will stay with you.

Read free by visiting this webpage:

greggdunnett.co.uk/nextbook

KILLING KIND SAMPLE CHAPTER

Emilia Smithson was a good reader for her age. Which was - at the time she found the first note - just seven and a half years old. She'd recently gone through a heavy Roald Dahl phase, and was now embarking upon the first of the Harry Potter series, so in some ways she was well prepared for the horror of what it would say. But she quickly realised the difference between a story and - whatever this was.

She found it in the park near her home, left on a bench. It was placed in a white envelope, and weighed down by a small porcelain frog with one eye missing. It was that which first attracted her. It just looked so funny sitting there. Like it was guarding the envelope. And when she picked up the frog for a closer look, five words were revealed, printed on the envelope.

Do Not Read
Call Police

Emilia read the words twice, making sure she'd understood. Then she put down the frog. She looked around for her mother, who was sitting on a blanket spread out on the grass, chatting with her friend. They'd been like that for ages, and Emilia thought she could probably turn into a frog, and hop twenty laps of the park, before her mother would notice her. Then Emilia spotted that whoever had left the envelope hadn't licked the sticky strip - she could easily pull the pages out, without having to tear it. So she could always put them back without anyone seeing. She checked her mother again. Still chatting. What was the point of reading anyway, if you didn't actually read things? Emilia carefully opened the envelope.

There were four pages inside. The text was printed quite a bit smaller than what she was used to. But it didn't look too bad. She sat down on the bench and began to read.

There were quite a number of 'difficult' words, but mostly she was able to understand, until she got to the third page, where she did get stuck. There was one word - *dismembering* - which finally defeated her. She looked over at her mother again, and hesitated. It was a risk, asking Mum. Emilia never knew when her mother was going to snap at her, just for asking a simple question. And the note *had* said do not read. Emilia wavered for a while. But then she was nearly finished anyway...

"Mum!" Emilia made her decision.

Her mother's name was Jane. She was talking with another mother about yet more mothers and how they behaved as they queued at the school gates - the ones who were friendly to your face, but who, Jane and her friend somehow knew, were bitching about them behind their backs. Jane completely ignored her daughter's interruption, but since the little girl was used to this, she went on as if they had each other's full attention.

"What does *dis-remembering* mean?"

Her mother went on talking.

"*Mum?*"

Now Jane did glance up at her daughter, to see her holding what looked like a letter.

"Dis-*remembering*? I don't know. Forgetting?" She turned back to her conversation.

"You've forgotten?"

"No. *I* didn't forget." Jane sighed. It was so tiring the way Emilia constantly interrupted her with ridiculous questions. "It doesn't mean anything. Unless someone wrote it to mean they forgot something."

Emilia pulled her confused face at this, but Jane ignored the look. She turned away again. The conversation had turned to how Sarah (Olivia's mother in 3R) wasn't with her husband any more. This was quite a scandal.

"How could you forget *a body*?"

Irritated, Jane looked back. "What?"

"And it's not dis*remembering*. I read it wrong. It's dismembering. '*I thought about dismembering the girl's body.*'"

A strange feeling came over Jane as those words settled on her mind.

"What's that you've got there?" She held out her hand for the papers, but Emilia sensed trouble. She began to move them behind her back.

"Give that here Emilia."

It wasn't just Mum's serious voice - which would have been enough on its own for Emilia to hand over the pages. There was a clear element of fear in her voice too, which instantly bridged the gap between the generations. Emilia gave her mother the pages.

Jane Smithson noticed the envelope first, then with a deep frown she began reading.

And her stomach filled with horror.

The first time I killed another person I was fifteen years old. It was in the summer of 1954. I barely knew what I was doing back then, and I was extremely fortunate not to get caught. The whole experience of it, and the aftermath, shaped how I would go on to kill for many years, perhaps for the whole of the rest of my life. You could say she taught me *how* to kill. That's how I like to think of it anyway. It means she didn't die for nothing.

I didn't plan to do it. I want to make that clear. But at the same time, I could certainly feel it coming. It started as strange thoughts. Fantasies. Urges. I was like a vessel being filled with some invisible power, growing stronger and stronger. I could feel it building up within me. And eventually it would have to come out. And when it did there would be a mess to clean up.

She was a year or two older than me, and though I didn't know her, I often saw her on the walk to school. White socks, blue skirt. Pretty, in a superior kind of way. That's what I remember most about the time before I killed her. The dismissive look that would appear on her face if our eyes ever happened to meet. Before her nose went up in the air and she looked away.

It was a lovely morning. I think it was the summer, or maybe the late spring, I remember that the banks of the little stream were dry. It was a shortcut we children sometimes used. You could climb down from the main road where it met the stream, which then passed underneath the road in what I understand is called a 'culvert'. We called it a tunnel. I think even the newspapers did too. But call it what you want, it was big enough to walk through without getting your feet wet, and from the other side you could continue along the banks of the stream to the back entrance of the grammar school, which was a shorter and more pleasant route than walking along the main road.

It was good fortune, on my part, and perhaps poor judgement on hers, that I was just a dozen or so yards behind her when she cut off the road and began to step carefully down the slope, meaning to use the tunnel and then take the short cut by the stream. As she disappeared from view, something prompted me to break into a run. At that point I didn't know what exactly. But I arrived at the top of the slope just in time to catch sight of her again, before she disappeared a second time, inside the tunnel.

I was lucky too that there was no traffic (although there just was less traffic in those days). I was able to dart quickly across the road and look down from the other side onto the stream and the little path beside it. I got there before her, so that I had to wait for the girl to reappear - rather like a game of pooh sticks. And it was in those moments of waiting that I noticed how the stonework of the bridge was decayed and old. So much so that one of the stones - about twice the size of a house brick - was actually loose.

I can still remember how strange I felt for those few seconds, waiting for her to come out into the light beneath me. I felt the most electric tingling in my fingers, so that they seemed to have little minds of their own - but all working together, on some devious task that I wasn't entirely in control of. It's a sensation I'm now used to, but back then it was most curious. My hands began pushing and prodding at the stone, working quickly as I only had moments before she came back into view. A few pieces of mortar fell and splashed into the water, and the girl may have wondered what caused this - for when she did finally appear - she had her head tilted back, squinting a little from her sudden re-emergence into the light.

I pushed the stone out into the air. There was a glorious half second as she saw me, and saw the stone, spinning down towards her. She even tried to move out of the way.

It hit her on the forehead, but just a glancing blow, since she was already moving. Even so she crumpled like a sack of potatoes. I wondered if she were dead, but then, on the ground she began moaning and writhing, so it was immediately clear that this wasn't the case. I feel sure I hadn't intended to do any more on that occasion than I had already done. But now I knew I couldn't just leave her there. She had seen who I was. I felt gripped by a new feeling. A kind of panic.

There was no way down to the stream from that side of the road, so I had to wait for a bus to go past before I could cross back over, scramble down the slope and pass through the tunnel myself. I could see her as I stepped through the darkness. Still on the ground, now with a flower of blood spreading out across her forehead and down onto her blouse. She was recovering somewhat, and her moaning had got louder. She saw me coming, and it turned into screaming.

Ignoring that I was in my school shoes I stepped into the stream itself and picked up a good sized rock from the bed. Then I hurried through the tunnel and I adjusted the rock in my hand so that it would be comfortable. She was scrambling to her feet now, trying to run, but then she stumbled, and fell into the stream. I was already wet, so I simply knelt over her, using my body to hold her still, and feeling her writhe underneath me. Then I bashed her head with my rock. Many times, until her head was all but gone, and she stopped writhing.

Do you see what I might mean now? About learning from her death? Goodness gracious - I was covered in mess. In blood and bits of her brain. And my fingers were bleeding too, from where I'd scraped them on the exposed parts of her skull. And I had to be in school in less than twenty minutes!

I was in a most precarious situation. Anyone could have seen us from the road above, or another child could have walked through the tunnel at any point. I almost gave up, I expected to hear shouts, the whistle of a policeman (they still had them in those days). But when I looked around we were still alone. And a third sensation overcame me. A kind of analytical calmness. I considered my options - poor as they were - and chose the best one. I pulled her upstream, back through the tunnel where she was at least partially hidden, and then further upstream where there was an abandoned area of overgrown bushes that overhung the water.

It was pure luck that no one was walking over the bridge during the time it took me to get her there. They would have had a clear view of what I was doing and I would surely have been captured. But luck was on my side - or was it some higher power? Whichever, it allowed me to drag the poor girl's body through the water until I could get her out of sight. I wedged her as best I could, under some branches, then I splashed back to the scene of the crime, as it were, which was still covered in blood (as was I). I knew that another school child might pass that way at any moment, so I was desperate. I splashed water against my bloodied body, and then pulled off my shoes and used them like buckets, trying as best I could to wash the blood from the rocks.

Again, I can only put it down to luck. Some days there would have been somebody passing either over the bridge, or through the tunnel itself, every few minutes. But that day I had ten clear minutes to work uninterrupted. And that little stream carried away the worst of it. Had she fallen onto the path itself, I would never have been able to remove the blood in time. But a few moments later I looked around, and you couldn't tell anything had happened there. I quickly returned upstream to where I'd hidden her, disappearing out of sight just as two boys climbed carelessly down the slope. I knew them from school. I watched them. Petrified that they would see something I had missed. But they didn't even pause in the area where I'd killed the girl. They walked straight past.

I thought about dismembering the girl's body, but I had no knife. And in the end I just left it there, wedged under a bush, and I concentrated on working out what to do with the mess I was in...

Emilia's mother - you'll remember she was called Jane - stopped reading at this point. The recurrence of the word 'dismembering' reminding her that her seven year old daughter had got this far too.

"Tell me where you found this," she said, her voice cold. Emilia pointed guiltily to a bench not a hundred yards away, Jane pulled out her phone and called the police.

* * *

It took some time before the note ended up in the hands of Detective Inspector Beth Jordan. This was in no small part because no one quite knew how to explain what had been found, not least Jane Smithson to the 999 operator.

"You're phoning to confess a murder madam?"

"No. I think I've found a *confession* to a murder. Or I think my daughter has. She's seven. Oh my God. *It's horrible.*"

A confused pause.

"Is anyone there injured or in need of medical assistance?"

"*No.* Well I don't think so. He says it was in the nineteen fifties. But there might be."

"Who says?"

"The murderer!"

Another pause, shorter this time.

"Is there someone with you now madam?"

"No. Oh God! *He might be.* It was left on a bench. Oh God."

"What was left on a bench?"

"The confession!"

"It was left under this frog." (This was Emilia, who had been closely following the conversation.) She held it up for her mother to inspect.

"It's only got one eye."

"Oh my God," Jane Smithson said again. "Can you just send someone here as soon as possible?"

Jane Smithson didn't read any more of the neatly typed text. And Emilia certainly didn't. The uniformed officer, who arrived ten minutes later in a police car with the blue lights flashing, didn't either. In fact he didn't even read as far as Emilia and her mother had before working out he needed help. The way he saw it there were two possibilities. Either this was some kind of elaborate hoax, in which case he'd probably never live this down whatever he did next, or it was real, in which case there was a psychopathic killer watching him right now from the nearby bushes, probably waiting to jump out and beat him to death.

He allowed Emilia and Jane Smithson, and their white-faced friend, to wait inside the police car, and feeling bloody nervous about it, he ventured over to inspect the perfectly ordinary bench. And there, keeping a close eye on the nearest bushes, he called his Sergeant.

The Sergeant passed it to his Inspector, who consulted the Chief Inspector, who finally took a degree of control of the situation. He ordered the park closed and searched, and demanded a photocopy of the text be brought to him right away, while the original was examined by forensics. Thus it was actually the forensics team who were the first to read to the very end of the first note:

I didn't try to dismember her in the end. I'm glad in hindsight. I do have some experience of dismembering these days - we'll come to that - but even then I sensed it would be very difficult without the correct equipment, and I had nothing. It's actually a time consuming and difficult job even with bone saws and a stable gurney to work from - but as I say, we'll come to that later.

When I was sure she was hidden as best she could be, I looked to my appearance. I'd been carrying a bag, which I'd quite forgotten about, but it had my overcoat in, and that somehow had stayed dry. This was fortunate, since my shoes and trousers were soaking wet and dark with blood. I left those on but removed my blazer and shirt. I washed the worst of the blood out of them, squeezed them out then put them in my bag. Then I zipped up my coat over my top and thought about getting home.

The world was different then. Less busy. Less built up. I could get nearly all the way home down back alleys and using derelict strips of land. But even so, other people used the same short cuts I knew. But I was lucky again. No one saw me, at least, not close enough to notice my strange appearance. I was able to get all the way home. There, I expected to have to sneak into my room to get changed. But I found my mother was out - probably to do the grocery shopping. I suppose I was lucky too that we had just acquired an electric washing machine (as we called it then). I had no idea how to use it, but I filled it with powder and hoped for the best. And while I waited I concocted a story about how some older boys had pushed me into the river, but I never needed to tell it. The machine finished its cycle and my mother still hadn't reappeared. I stuffed my clothes into the airing cupboard, then ran to school before my mother returned.

Obviously the list of mistakes I'd made was longer than my arm, even when you consider that forensic science was a lot more primitive in those days. But there were a number of external factors that demonstrated how, once again, luck was on my side. The girl's school assumed she was ill that day, and didn't report her absence to the parents, even though they hadn't telephoned to say so. Even more remarkably fortunate, they had previously agreed, with the parents of one of her school friends, that she would spend that night with them. When she didn't turn up the friend's parents assumed the arrangement had been cancelled - again, without telephoning to confirm - while the girl's parents believed it to have gone ahead as planned. So it was only the following afternoon when the alarm was raised that she was missing. And by then it had rained heavily for a number of hours, further washing away any evidence from the murder site that I had failed to adequately deal with. It then took a further four days for her body to be discovered, which meant any physical evidence had more time to degrade.

I followed the case as best I could, getting information through the newspapers and the local rumour mill.

The police were able to ascertain (to my surprise) that the girl wasn't a virgin, and from this they made a number of incorrect assumptions. One, even though there was no sexual element to the murder (this was not reported, but I obviously had privileged information on the matter), they concluded there must have been a sexual motivation to the crime. Two, because of the force of the blow to her head - presumably the stone I dropped from high up on the bridge - the killer had to have been exceptionally strong. A manual labourer perhaps (I believe that's who they blamed it on, in the end) - certainly a *fully grown man*. Either way, there was never any indication that they were searching for a soaking wet school boy.

But don't misunderstand me. As lucky as I was that day I drew my own, very clear conclusions from the episode. If and when I struck again, I had to be a *lot* more careful.

And by then, it was clear enough I was thinking about when. Not if.

Killing Kind: A novella
by Gregg Dunnett ~ (Author)

Customer reviews
⭐⭐⭐⭐⭐ 4.8 out of 5 ~
63 customer ratings

5 star		81%
4 star		15%
3 star		3%
2 star		0%
1 star		0%

Read the rest free by by visiting this webpage:
greggdunnett.co.uk/nextbook